C000193709

# THINGS WE CHOOSE TO HIDE

JANE RIDDELL

Published in 2014 by Jane Riddell

Cover Art: Lisa Firth

Copyright © 2023 by Jane Riddell

All rights reserved.

No part of this book may be reproduced in any form or by any electronic or mechanical means, including information storage and retrieval systems, without written permission from the author, except for the use of brief quotations in a book review.

*To my partner Peter, for everything and more.*

# CONTENTS

**1**

---

What role does honesty play in a relationship? Of course I like your dress.... I don't fancy your friend.... How about: I love you but there are things about me I'm scared to tell you?

I'd never thought much about this.

The day my life changed direction began with a letter telling me the company organising my trip to India had gone bust.

So, no India. Sinking onto the sofa, I thought of the cotton skirts and loose tops lying on the guest room bed. My new zoom lens that I'd use to photograph sunsets, wildlife and vegetated mountains, while sailing along the Brahmaputra River. The canvas bag containing Imodium, mosquito repellent and host of other remedies. Just in case.

If Steve and I had been in a better place, we'd have gone to the local Greek restaurant that evening, where I'd console myself, temporarily at least, with lamb stifado and creamy tzatziki.

But now a sickening feeling gripped me – the realisation

he was the last person I wanted to talk with about such a huge disappointment.

After work, instead of going straight home, I called at my aunt and uncle's.

'Such short notice,' Marion said, when I told her about my cancelled trip. 'Will you find something else in India?'

My aunt, in jeans and cotton sweater, looked younger than her sixty-five years. Young but motherly. Few people knew better than her how keen I was to return to the country of my early childhood. To meet with my parents' closest friends from there. Learn more about their years in north India.

'Or go somewhere with Steve?' Geoffrey suggested, peering over his newspaper, tugging at the hole in his cardigan.

'I'll organise something,' I said. Now wasn't a good time to discuss my crumbling relationship. My aunt and uncle worried about me enough already.

As always, I studied their sitting room for signs of change. The bay window had been painted cream since my last visit. Otherwise, the room remained the same: spacious, welcoming. The grand piano gleaming in June sunshine, the photos on it reflecting milestones in our lives. Two portraits of me always drew my attention: the first – taken on my sixteenth birthday – a smiling teenager, now thankfully free of the metal brace on my upper teeth; the second, a year later, conveying a similar young woman, but thinner. My mouth smiling, my eyes sad. A before and after my parents' fatal car accident.

And here was a new sepia photo of my mother and father, taken in Kashmir. They were standing beside a willow tree, distant mountain peaks in the background. As I caught Marion's eye, our faces doubtless conveyed a myriad emotions. Regret mainly.

Noticing my expression, she enveloped me in a prolonged hug. 'They would have been proud of you.'

When I turned eighteen, I bought a flat with my inheritance. Only once I'd signed the contract, did I realise the emotional implications of living on my own. The first Sunday after I moved in, Marion invited me for lunch. Anna, their younger daughter, was there, and I welcomed being with family again.

As I was leaving, Marion said, 'You'll have lunch with us every Sunday – unless you get a better offer.'

And I often did go there for lunch, occasionally staying the night, enjoying being back in my old bedroom. Sundays therefore became my anchor. Eighteen is young to be an orphan – especially if you don't have siblings – and though I was now studying nursing and making new friends, the continuity of my aunt and uncle in my life provided immeasurable comfort.

'Had a feeling this would happen,' Steve said when I told him about my cancelled holiday. He was sprawled on the sofa, browsing on Spotify. From the doorway, I could smell his feet. And the empty mugs of Ristretto coffee littering the coffee table. 'You could still come to the bothy. The female dorm has spaces.'

'You really think I'd enjoy that?' I muttered.

He shrugged and returned to Spotify.

Lying in bed two days later, from some deep part that frequently surprised me, I said, 'This isn't working, Steve. *We're* not working. I'm sorry.'

In the silence, my heart beat faster. I was due on the ward at seven the following morning. Just now was a bad time to risk an argument.

'Is this somehow connected to your holiday falling through?'

I thought for a moment. It wasn't, of course, but since hearing about it, I'd felt there was nothing to look forward to. Certainly not with him. This wasn't a healthy way to feel about a relationship. We coexisted like flatmates. Or brother and sister.

'I do love you, you know,' he said. 'I should probably tell you more often.'

'I had my hair cut today.'

'Did you?'

'You never notice.'

'Not noticing your hair cut isn't a valid reason for splitting up.'

'You never really see me.'

He propped himself up on one elbow. 'What are you talking about?'

'What was I wearing this evening?'

A defensive note crept into his voice. 'Jeez, I don't know. What you always wear. Jeans, some kind of top.... How is this relevant?'

'What sort of top?'

'For God's sake. What does it matter? I don't get uptight if you don't notice my haircut, or what I'm wearing.'

Of course he didn't. And part of me could understand why my clothes didn't register with him. As long as we watched television together in the evenings and had the occasional beach walk – the perfect antidote to a harrowing shift for me or a stressful day for him at school – things were okay. From his point of view.

It was hard to communicate what the problem was. Complaining that he didn't notice my hair or clothes sounded petty but this was easier to explain than the fact that I didn't feel properly seen by him. Only superficially. The person with a smiley face or streaming nose. The one who produced tasty meals (sometimes) and vacuumed (occasionally).

Part of me knew I was being unfair. The hours he put into teaching were crazy, rendering him zombie-like when he got home, falling asleep in front of police procedurals on the evenings when he didn't have marking to do. A bigger part knew we weren't suited. The initial attraction of his lightness, the ease of being with him, the consistency of his feelings for me – so lacking in the stream of commitment phobes who'd previously plagued my life – was no longer enough. I'd been avoiding admitting this, even to myself, for too long.

'I need more,' I said.

'You're tired. You'll feel better tomorrow.'

The usual rationalisation. Reducing my feelings to something physical.

I said nothing and the atmosphere changed. As if something had clicked. His arm collapsed, he lay down on the pillow and turned his back on me.

'Do you realise how superficial you sound when you talk about me not noticing your clothes and your hair? Jeez, it's not as if I treat you badly, is it?'

He didn't get it. And I'd run out of words to explain in language he'd understand.

'Steve–'

'Fine, I'll move out this weekend. I'm fed up with your moods.'

And that was it. When I returned from shopping on the

Saturday afternoon, his stuff had disappeared. Everything. His state-of-the-art music system. His schoolbooks and teaching notes. His climbing gear. Already the atmosphere felt different. The smells of school – floor polish, sweaty trainers – which inexplicably he managed to bring home – gone. So had the signs of what I considered embedded masculinity: splayed toothbrushes, crumpled notes and used tissues. Yet I felt sad. At the same time, excited at the new world beckoning me.

'Of *course* you can stay with us,' Diana said when I phoned her. 'For as long as you like. Anyway, Doug works such mad hours at the hospital, it would be great to have company. But can you wait until next week? His parents are here at the moment and they're using up most of my energy.'

When my plane touched down at Peretola Airport, Diana was waiting to drive me into Florence, holding a large sign in purple letters: "RACHEL GROSVENOR", surrounded by red balloons.

First came the sound of screeching tyres, then a crashing noise. From my high vantage point on the Piazzale Michelangelo, I attached my telephoto lens and zoomed in and down to the other side of the Arno at the place where two cars had collided. People were gathering. A fire engine had appeared. As I rushed down to the street below, I could hear sirens, see a police car with flashing lights. An ambulance. More people were gathering and the police were cordoning off the area.

Two cars with smashed bumpers and windscreens lay like something out of a cops and gangster movie. The paramedics were working on the victims, an elderly woman and man. One shook his head, glanced at the other who also shook his head.

Carefully, they lifted the bodies onto stretchers, covered them with sheets and loaded them into the ambulances. I heard crunching as the vehicle moved off, continuing at a solemn speed. The crowd now drifted off, and before I could rush to somewhere private, I retched.

'*Stai bene*?' a man asked, and when I didn't reply, added, 'Are you okay?'

He handed me a bottle of water and I drank thirstily.

'Would you like to go for coffee, or a drink?' he asked after a few moments.

I nodded, extending my hand, then withdrawing it, feeling too British. 'I'm Rachel Grosvenor.'

'Tommaso Vitale.'

We found a café where my good Samaritan ordered a latte for himself and an orange juice for me. The interior, virtually empty, smelled of real coffee and fresh paint, not helping my queasiness. I shouldn't have agreed to this. I wanted to be on my own, but it would be rude to leave, reject his kindness.

At first, we didn't talk. While he sipped his coffee, I studied him: dark-haired, olive skinned and wearing spectacles with a red and brown frame. His green shirt sported the Gucci logo and his watch looked expensive. My eyes focused on his hands, medium-sized and beautifully shaped. The kind sculptors would yearn to create. Had Diana sculpted many hands? Outside traffic noises were muted. I heard a woman shout, a child cry.

Tommaso summoned his energy. 'The accident, it has shocked you?'

'My parents died in a car accident and it took me right back. Even though I wasn't with them at the time.'

I stopped, transported back to my family home when the police rang the doorbell. To this day, I remembered the whiff of polo mints and cigarette smoke on the police-woman's breath. She'd broken the news to me about my parents' car accident. then tried unsuccessfully to contact my aunt and uncle, then Diana's family. Finally arranging for me to spend the night with a neighbour.

'I am sorry,' Tommaso said.

'It was a long time ago.'

He removed his spectacles and I noticed how attractive he was.

'Are you on holiday in Florence?' he asked.

'I'm staying with some friends. Diana's a sculptress.'

'Diana King?'

'You know her?'

He finished his latte and replaced the cup on the table. 'I read an article about her work.'

'She's giving an exhibition soon.'

Tommaso was fiddling with a pepper sachet. 'She is talented.'

Underneath the table, his long leg grazed mine

'Sorry,' he said, removing his leg.

The contact had been accidental, of this I was certain. Otherwise, I'd have left. Nevertheless, now I felt embar-rassed. At the same time, noticing more details about him: the copper bangle on his right wrist; the almost closed hole in his left ear where an earring had been.

I wondered if he was assessing me, and what he thought.

He'd replaced the torn sachet of pepper.

'Do you live in Florence?' I asked.

'Near Napoli. But my business takes me to Florence often. I design and sell leather products.'

'What sort of things?'

'Jackets and bags mainly.... Where's your accent from?'

'Guess.'

He thought for a moment. 'Scotland – because of your hair.'

'Many Irish people have red hair.'

He smiled and leaned forward. 'Shur, I know an Irish accent when I hear one.'

Reluctantly I stood. 'I must go. We're entertaining this evening. I said I'd help.'

'Shall I order a taxi for you?'

'I'll be fine.... You should come to Diana's preview – if you're in Florence. Here's her card.'

Even as I handed over the card, I wanted to prolong our time together, but I'd promised Diana I wouldn't be back late.

While walking away, I hoped I hadn't been too pushy about the exhibition. But I wanted to see Tommaso again. He wasn't classically good-looking, his eyes fractionally too far apart, his forehead on the large side. Nevertheless, there was something about the way he searched my face, as if truly interested in what I had to say. A sense he'd be the kind of man who'd need to know the detail and texture of his partner's life. Who'd put loads of energy into a relation-ship. And be like a rocket in bed.

But such thinking was crazy. Less than ten days since ending a long-term relationship, here I was, attracted to another man. My life was about more than being with someone. However, while walking on the dusty streets, alongside the mud-coloured fast flowing Arno river,

Tommaso's eyes kept flashing into my mind. Had he been attracted to me?

The traffic was now heavy, tempers – frayed by the heat – resulting in excessive honking, prompting expressions such as, "*cretino*, idiot" and gesticulating hands. The air was thick with dust and several cyclists wore masks. With relief, I eventually reached a side street where the traffic noise and smog faded, replaced by birdsong and the fragrance of flowers. The atmosphere felt semi-rural, the businesses and apartment blocks yielding to tree-lined streets and houses.

I wished Tommaso and I had arranged to meet again.

## 2

——————

At home, I found Diana at the kitchen table, slicing tomatoes and surrounded by a medley of vegetables. For a moment I lingered by the door, appreciating the late afternoon light flooding past shuttered windows, intensifying the ochre walls, gleaming on the aubergines and green peppers. Scented roses from an open window sweetened the air. Radio 4 played at low volume, the familiar Scottish voice of Eddie Mair hosting *PM*.

'How was your sightseeing?' she asked, glancing up before returning to the tomatoes.

'Interesting.... God, it's hot. At least you have AC.'

She laughed. 'It would have been *hotter* in India. The travel agents really should have arranged something else for you.'

I found some kitchen roll and mopped my brow. 'I explained. They tried to but it wasn't the places I wanted to visit. Besides, I'll get to India sometime.'

'How long have you been saying this? Finish chopping these tomatoes, would you?'

I ran my hands under the cold tap and lifted a heart-shaped tomato.

Diana shook her head. 'We haven't enough basil.... I could shred Doug. This was meant to be a simple meal for Allegra and Giovanni. Then he invited some Australian colleagues. Asked me to do something *Tuscan*.' She grabbed the knife from me. 'Thinner slices. Like this.... Allegra and I need to discuss the exhibition. How can I do this *and* play dutiful hostess? And he won't be back before seven.'

I checked the floral Tuscan wall clock. Five minutes to six.

'Di, get the basil. Shall I fry the tomatoes?'

'We need more ice cubes. Bottom shelf of the freezer. And maybe you could set the table. Stuff's on the sideboard.' She grabbed her purse and car keys. 'Back in a moment. Finish the tomatoes. *Thin* slices.'

At eight o'clock, while Diana was mixing Campari and sodas, the doorbell rang.

Greetings of *buona sera,* good evening, rang out in the hallway and I hovered while the prolonged business of exchanging kisses took place. Allegra was small, dark and lively, and smelt divine.

'Diana talks of you often,' she said. 'I am so pleased to meet you. How do you like Florence?'

'As wonderful as everyone says.'

By nine o'clock, we were onto our third Campari (apart from Diana who was sticking to fruit juice) and neither Doug nor his colleagues had arrived. Two empty bowls of olives and plates of crackers with homemade paté sat on the table. Giovanni was making patterns with olive stones, Allegra studying the kilim on the terrazo floor. Seated by the window, Diana chewed her lip and fidgeted with her bracelet, turning frequently to peer out. Every time I heard a car, I hoped for her sake it was Doug's. When she went into the kitchen, I followed her.

She opened the oven door and prodded the pasta. 'I need to talk to Allegra about the exhibition. While my brain's still functioning.'

'Do it now. While we're waiting.'

She shook her head. 'Bad form here, leaving company, to discuss work before we've eaten. We should mix the salad. There's cress and artichokes in the fridge, and rocket. I'll do the vinaigrette.'

The front door opened as we were finishing the salad, and Diana muttered 'at last', rushing into the hall. I heard her greet her guests and direct them into the sitting room. Then her tone changed.

'What were you *doing* Doug? Allegra and Giovanni have been here since eight. You promised to be home on time.'

'Sorry, darling,' he said cheerfully, popping his head round the kitchen door. 'Hi Rachel, I trust you're being helpful.'

Shoulders tense, face flushed with anger, Diana reheated the *pappa al pomodoro* and added more basil leaves. When Doug joined her, I returned to the sitting room and our guests.

Wine flowed freely while we ate. For a while, Diana spoke animatedly about her forthcoming exhibition and her garden, more relaxed, her earlier irritation with Doug seemingly forgotten. When the sky darkened, he lit candles around the dining room, and lanterns outside the house came on, casting light on the wrought iron bench and the barbecue stand in the corner, shining on silvery shrubs. The wine was kicking in, relaxing me. In the kitchen, as she arranged biscuits and I loaded the dishwasher, the doorbell rang once more.

She looked up from the plate of biscuits, eyes flashing. 'Not more *colleagues*. I hate this about Italy, people turning up for dessert and coffee.'

Doug returned from answering the door, raising his hand to reassure her. 'Nothing to worry about, love. Just Nico returning my saw.'

In the sitting room, Allegra caught Diana's eye and the two of them left the room.

An hour passed and conversation continued, Doug's male Australian colleagues in full flow, Giovanni contributing the occasional comment. Adjusting to the summer heat, drowsy from the wine and food, however, I now craved sleep. When Allegra and Diana returned, Allegra was smiling but Diana looked strained, and her mouth tightened as Doug offered limoncello.

Shortly after, Allegra and Giovanni made their farewells, leaving Doug and his colleagues. Face impassive, Diana cleared away the biscotti as he launched into a passionate conversation about the football match in Rome that weekend. Scents of candle wax and alcohol filled the air.

In the kitchen, Diana's hands trembled as she emptied and restacked the dishwasher.

'Did you get things sorted?' I asked.

'Fine, it was fine. We'll visit the gallery again tomorrow.'

She lifted a plate from the worktop and dropped it. I retrieved the pieces – cursing as a pointed edge grazed my hand – and disposed of them. She stood by the sink, her expression haunted.

'Di, what's wrong? It's not just the exhibition, is it?'

She sank heavily onto a chair by the table, put her head in her hands. A moment passed before she spoke. 'We've been trying for a baby. Nothing's happening and it's getting harder and harder.' She clasped her hands, resting her chin on them, staring at the table. Then, sighing, she stood, loaded more plates into the dishwasher, added soap liquid and shut the door, turning to face me. 'I've read all this *stuff* about infertility – these writers, they're really onto something here, such a loaded topic for so many people. I'm taking nutritional supplements, I've cut out alcohol, I've lost weight. What does *Doug* do? Doug drinks wine like water, and he's hardly touched his vitamins. You'd think he'd know that I notice.... We argue about it the whole time.'

'How long have you been trying?'

'Three years.'

I gasped. Since she'd got married, in fact. Since Steve and I became an item. Why hadn't she told me about this before?

'I wanted to tell you,' she said, reading my mind. 'But doing so would have made things real, if you know what I mean.... Of course, three years isn't that long. I mean, some people have to try for ten. Anyway....' and she drummed her fingers on the table.

She needed things to happen now. Not some distant time in the future.

'Di, I'm so sorry you're going through all this.'

My heart bled for her. Of all the women I knew, she was the one keenest to be a mother. Even at school, I'd suggest a bike ride but she'd want to make doll's clothes. Further on, when the rest of us did community work, she opted for a placement in a children's hospital. She'd consumed books on child development, analysed the research on the pros and cons of the MMR vaccine and could discuss the theories behind Rudolph Steiner and Montessori education.

I yearned to reassure her, without resorting to platitudes and clichés. Who else knew? I wondered. Her parents? Other friends?

'I'll be back in a moment,' I said, heading for the loo. There I pondered what I *could* say to Diana. The nurse in me knew that twenty-eight was still young in fertility terms. It also knew that staying calm was important. The friend in me realised that the situation would become increasingly stressful for her and perhaps make it less likely for her to conceive. Like many women hoping for children, she was trapped in a vicious circle. All I could do was encourage her to chill out, and be there for her when she needed to talk. If only we lived closer together – Skyping and all those real time apps were no replacement for face-to-face contact.

When I returned from the loo, ready to talk again, she had abandoned the tidying up and was slouched over the table, flicking through a copy of *Sculpture*. From the hall I could hear Doug saying goodbye to his colleagues. Shortly after he came into the kitchen with a tray of clinking glasses.

'All right, love?' he asked, bending to kiss her head. 'I'm off to bed, have an early meeting. Great meal, by the way. Brad and Dale were most impressed.'

'You reek of limoncello,' she said.

He sighed but said nothing.

After he left, in a choked voice Diana said, 'He has no idea. No idea how important this is to me. That's the problem. It feels like it's only *me* who's involved.'

Before I could respond, she stood and muttered something about going to bed herself. Next chance I had, I'd talk to her.

Later in bed, mulling over my conversation with her, my mind turned to Tommaso, wondering if he'd come to the exhibition preview.

## 3

'Wake up, Rachel, someone's sent you gorgeous flowers.'

I surfaced from a dream, glanced at my alarm clock, then at my friend. At eight-fifteen, smudges of clay already patterned Diana's pottery apron and her long dark hair strayed from its combs. As she opened the shutters, I could smell the vinegar she used to conceal the odour of clay.

'Get a move on, the flowers will have died at this pace.'

'I don't know anyone here.'

Then I remembered Tommaso. That he'd know my address from Diana's business card.

Minutes after I'd showered and dressed, my face beaded with sweat. In the kitchen, coral roses and white calla lilies rested in a bucket by the kitchen door, filling the room with fragrance. The card read: *I wish to invite you to dinner on Friday, 7.30 pm at Enoteca Pitti Gola e Cantina. Tommaso.*

I rushed out to the patio where Doug and Diana were sipping orange juice.

Diana studied my face. 'So? You've been here, what, three days?'

'I met him yesterday.... It was an unusual situation,' I said, explaining what happened.

Doug poured me coffee, glanced at his watch and jumped up. 'Ward round.'

He bent to kiss his wife. 'Bye, love.'

Diana whisked off her apron, leaned forward. 'So, is he hot? Do you *want* to see him again? Isn't it a bit soon after Steve?'

'He's...yes, I suppose he is. Tommaso. Hot, I mean. He's asked me out for dinner to the Enoteca Pitti Gola e Cantina.'

She gasped. 'One of the top restaurants in Florence! Have you anything smart to wear? I'm talking tailored, not your bohemian maxis.'

'I haven't accepted his invitation yet.' Of course I would and Diana knew that.

'Go shopping, splash out. He'll appreciate it, Italian men always do.'

The day before my date, I received an apologetic text from Tommaso announcing he had to stay in Napoli and would contact me when he returned to Florence. But he wouldn't. He was probably cursing his impulsive invitation to dinner and I shouldn't have attached so much importance to seeing him again. Being Italian, he'd chat up women all the time. And yet he'd sent flowers....

'Now Rachel, I'm sure he'll rearrange something when he's back,' Diana said, like an older sister called upon to rally round.

'I'm only here for two more weeks.'

'So, stay longer,' she said, inspecting her nails. 'I must get a manicure before the exhibition.'

'If I'm not encroaching.'

Her expression resembled a mournful mongrel. 'You won't be. Doug's going to a conference in London after the exhibition. You'll be company. It's bound to be an anticlimax after all the build up.'

For several days, I wandered the dusty streets of Florence. Hearing the rich chimes of the campanile, the clatter of shutters closing. Taking refuge under sun umbrellas when I stopped for lunch, eyes watering from the odour of Marlboro cigarettes at neighbouring tables, and the acrid smells of traffic. Half-heartedly, I gazed at famous paintings in the Uffizi and Palatina galleries, dismayed at myself for letting this cancelled dinner affect me so much. I took photos, of course, but with less enthusiasm, and I didn't rush to import them to my laptop.

I heard nothing from Tommaso, and packed up my special dress, ready to return it.

Diana came into the hall before I left.

'You're not taking the dress back?'

'Why keep it?'

'You can't not keep it. It suits you so well. Anyway, it's a change to see you in something you haven't bought in a charity shop. Do you never get sick of secondhand clothes?'

'Shopping in Oxfam is one of my favourite Saturday activities.'

'Wear the dress to the exhibition. It'll be a smart affair, you know. Anyway, I'm sure Tommaso will be in touch.'

I dumped the boutique bag on a chair and left the house, determined to pull myself together, use my time properly. Perhaps I'd visit the Alinari National Museum of Photography.

Instead, I found myself strolling by the Arno. This morning the water was brown and fast flowing. A pack of gulls swooped down on the river before flying off again. The stench of sewage reached my nostrils. Nobody else was around the area where the accident had happened. No evidence testifying to the event. But somewhere, siblings, children too, perhaps even elderly parents, had had their lives ripped apart. And here I was, ruminating over a cancelled date.

I visualised the bodies, which would have been examined on a laboratory slab. Cut open and photographed. Pathologists determining cause of death. Had this happened to my parents? A distressing thought.... How did ambulance staff cope? And how long did it take them to recover from the awful events they'd witnessed? I'd read that paramedics often don't live long after retirement. Too much trauma seen. Too much stress experienced.

On the road above, a steady hum of traffic tugged me back to the present, some distance away, the unrelenting chug of a digger. Nearby the dome of a church gleamed in afternoon sunshine as its bells struck three o'clock.

The next few days, I took buses into the hill towns of the Tuscan countryside, launching myself into my photography, refusing to dwell on Tommaso.

When I returned to Diana and Doug's house one afternoon, Diana rushed to greet me. 'Guess who called round? Guess who wants you to have dinner with him tomorrow? If you're free. Anyway, I told him you were.'

'Tommaso was here? Why didn't he text me?'

'Bet you're glad you didn't return the dress.'

$\sim$

Tommaso met me outside the restaurant, presenting me with a raspberry smelling purple lapel orchid, which contrasted well with my dress. The saffron yellow tailored one Diana had urged me not to return.

Inside the restaurant, the waiter led us to a secluded corner table, described the special dishes on offer and proffered the wine list. I glanced around me at the well-spaced tables, the racks of wine. My mouth watering at the smell of freshly baked bread and roasted garlic.

I studied Tommaso while he bantered with the waiter. This evening he wasn't wearing his spectacles and his dark brown eyes were brighter than before, his thick brown wavy hair swept back. His silver Rolex watch gleamed against his skin, as did the copper bangle he wore on his other hand. Despite my expensive dress, I felt inadequate.

As if guessing my thoughts, he smiled at me.

During the meal, Tommaso pummelled me with questions: my upbringing, my world-views, what I wanted out of life. Each response encouraged another question.

'I'm an only child and my parents were killed...I think I mentioned that when we met. It was twelve years ago,' I told him.

'You must have been very young then.'

'Sixteen.'

He reached for my hand and held it, his grip firm but not cloying. 'This is too young to lose your parents. I would be very unhappy to lose either my mother or my father.'

I let my hand rest in his, not for the sympathy, but because it felt good, enclosed in his. 'My aunt and uncle took me in. They had a large house just outside Edinburgh.'

Tommaso released my hand. 'You were born in Edinburgh?'

'India.'

His eyes lit up. 'India! What was this like, to live in India?'

'I was only there until I was seven. We lived in the mountains. In Shimla. The heat wasn't so bad, being high up.'

Even as I spoke, I felt myself transported back to the Ridge, a large open space in the heart of Shimla. My favourite place. A place for crowds to gather at dusk to walk or talk. I could see the magical misty light, smell the freshly cooked paneer pakoras and nan breads, remember my mother refusing to buy me anything, saying it would spoil my appetite for dinner. I recalled the clip clop of horses carrying excited but timorous children. Having a tantrum when my parents wouldn't let me ride one. Despite its throngs, the Ridge had never felt noisy or intimidating.

'But when we visited Delhi or Mumbai, where my parents had friends – this was awful. Such heat and dust and cars everywhere. Honking. And the smell from piles of rubbish, great piles of rubbish.'

'I imagine,' Tommaso said. 'And also to see such poverty every day. Why did your parents live in India?'

'My father lectured at the university in Shimla.... That's enough about me. Where are you from?'

'Sicily. My parents own two restaurants near Catania. What work do you do?'

'I'm a nurse. But I'm about to study photography. Then I'll set up a photography business.'

'A nurse.... You do not wish to be a nurse now?'

I hesitated. 'Burn out...exhaustion. Not enough time to give the care that patients need...I don't want to talk politics.'

He leant forward, 'I can see the photos on your camera?'

Taken aback, I passed him my camera, expecting him to whizz through a few shots, make some vague comments, then return the camera to me. To my surprise, he scrolled slowly through the photos, nodding at some, murmuring "*bella*" at others, returning to earlier ones. Such attention pleased me enormously. So unlike Steve, who'd never asked to see what I'd taken, but at my suggestion, would skim through my latest batch. Finishing off with, 'These are good, Rach.' His mind already on something else.

'You have talent,' Tommaso said. 'You know what is a good picture. You understand the light.'

Suddenly his interest felt overwhelming. 'Tell me about your job,' I said.

'I work for a leather company in Napoli. In design, mainly. But I sell products also.' He then described how his company only sourced hides from cattle raised on a nutritional diet. Those protected from the ravages of insect bites and other conditions.

We stared at each other often. Me furtively, Tommaso more openly.

'*Il quanto per favore*, can I have the bill, please,' he requested of the waiter when we finished our coffee.

Having attended to the bill, he gave a hefty tip, spoke briefly to the maître d', promising to return soon.

'You will take a walk?' he asked, once we were outside.

As we strolled around the city, shadows gradually crept up columns and arches and my camera worked hard. Perhaps this was the best time of day to appreciate the wonderful architecture, the streets quieter but the light strong enough, evocative enough, to stir my emotions.

Once darkness had fallen, Tommaso took my hand, saying, 'There is one view which you must see.' From the lamplight, I noticed his intense expression.

After walking several blocks, we turned a corner and I found myself facing the Duomo, perhaps 100 yards away. I'd seen it before, of course. But not from this direction. Despite

being unable to detect its pink, white and green marble
façade in the dark, the massive cathedral was even more
impressive at night.

'This is one of my favourite views in Italy,' he said,
watching for my reaction.

I switched off my camera. 'It's stunning, in daylight, too.'

Now it seemed natural for Tommaso to slip his arm
round my shoulder.

Shortly after, he flagged a taxi for me. 'I will leave early
tomorrow to fly back to Napoli. I return next weekend. Can
we meet again?'

I nodded, he opened the passenger door, gave the driver
my address and the car shot off. The scent of Tommaso's
aftershave lingered on my neck from the brief embrace we'd
exchanged.

Tommaso returned to Florence the following three
weekends. On the Fridays, he worked, but for the remainder
of the weekend, he devoted his time to me. One minute we'd
be picnicking in Tuscan fields of bellflowers and glorious
hazy light, the next, racing back to Florence in the green
vintage Fiat borrowed from his friend, to attend a concert.
Or rushing from snorkeling off the sandy beach in Elba to
catch the ferry to Piombivo where he'd made a dinner
reservation.

"I want to show you this" and "You must see this" were
two of his most frequent remarks. I loved being swept along
with everything, thrilling to his enthusiasm for life.

There was always one more thing he wanted me to
experience: an opera I'd love; a restaurant serving
wonderful truffles; a bell tower to climb, a location noted

for spectacular sunsets. If I'd put together a character description for the opposite of Steve, it would have included the qualities Tommaso possessed. During the week, he dominated my thoughts. I kept seeing those dark eyes, remembering the way he stared at me until I had to look away.

One memorable date was when he took me to the Palazzo Gaddi Arrighetti to hear Wagner's *Tristan und Isolde*.

'Lucky, lucky you,' Diana said when I told her. 'The building is amazing. So, let's see what I have that you can wear. And before you ask, you must look smart and I don't think you should wear your yellow dress again so soon, not that it isn't beautiful.'

'I'm not a diva.'

'What about this?' she suggested, producing a black velvet dress.

'Not my colour.'

One by one, she offered me dresses, silk blouses with wide-leg trousers, kimono tops with matching long skirts.

'That's all I have,' she said eventually, gazing at her bed, now strewn with rejects.

Finally, we agreed on a sage green chiffon knee-length dress.

On the evening, Tommaso collected me. His flight had been late and everything was rushed, but when I got into the taxi, he stared at me, murmuring '*Bella, bella*'. Through the mirror, the driver nodded in agreement. Tommaso was wearing a dark grey suit with a white shirt and pale blue tie, and seated next to me, his thigh rested against mine. I was glad to be sitting so that my knees didn't shake. Glad that he couldn't be aware of my racing heart.

The building itself was a mass of marble, arches and mature plants which would have been wonderful to walk around, but we only had time to deposit my jacket in the cloakroom.

To my delight, Tommaso had managed to purchase seats near the front of the small concert hall, and when we took our places, I felt like royalty. As for the music, my mind floated away from my body. At the same time, only too conscious of him seated next to me, his expression rapturous throughout the performance.

Occasionally he turned to stare at me, and I had to look away, only to glance at him seconds later and find him still staring. The finale of Act 3, the frenzied climax of Wagner's famous *Liebestod*, the strings giving it everything they had, rendered me weak with emotion. And longing for something I couldn't put into words.

After the concert, I wanted to go home. Unwilling to risk anything spoiling the evening. I certainly didn't want to talk about the music, for words would have reduced the feeling experience. Strangely, Tommaso understood. Perhaps he felt the same.

We were walking around the Museo di Palazzo Vecchio late on a wet Saturday and Tommaso was describing a painting. It was our fourth weekend together. Over lunch, he'd been quiet which I'd attributed to tiredness, due to his early flight from Napoli. Now, however, his descriptions lacked his usual enthusiasm and expansive arms movements. Furthermore, he hadn't taken my hand once, let alone embraced me, apart from when we met at the restaurant.

Gradually I was becoming more worried. Frantically thinking of reasons for this change in behaviour. Tiredness couldn't account for it all. Perhaps he was bored with my company, disappointed at my lack of knowledge of classical art. Or perhaps I'd misread his signals: he regarded me as a friend, someone he'd sensed wanted company while in Italy. Meanwhile, my feelings for him were far from platonic. Nevertheless, I wouldn't make things difficult.

Turning to face him, I was on the verge of pleading a headache and saying I wanted to go home.

He spoke first. 'Let's go for a drink.'

Of course, he wouldn't break things off in an art gallery.

We took a taxi to the Fiaschetteria Nuvoli wine bar. Again, we didn't talk much as we drank our wine, and now I was convinced he was plucking up courage to end the relationship.

'Tommaso–'

He grabbed my hand. 'You will come with me to the hotel?'

I nodded, swallowing hard. It felt like being at the edge of something exhilarating. Something I was powerless to resist. Something fearful.

At the hotel, Tommaso took my hand and we proceeded to the elevator, where the wooden lift door closed silently, discreetly, behind us. When we reached the fourth floor, we walked along the marble corridor to his room, our feet sounding disproportionately loud in the surrounding silence.

Outside his room he fumbled with the key card, then the door was open and we were tugging at each other's clothes.

Later, we stood on the balcony, gazing over night-time Florence: its illuminated church domes; the blackness of the Arno patterned with silvery pools of light; the welcoming interiors of restaurants on the opposite side of the street.

Tommaso then kissed me and we stepped inside again.

**4**

During her pre-exhibition week, Diana was drowning in so many last-minute tasks that I took over on the domestic front. Now missing Tommaso, I welcomed being delegated simple chores: shopping for fruit, fresh fish and locally produced cheese at the Sant'Ambrogio market; doing the laundry; watering plants. In the evenings, I usually cooked for the three of us.

'Where did you learn to cook such good Indian nosh?' Doug asked one night.

'My mother taught me.'

'Of course. I forgot you grew up in India.'

'Only for a while. But Mum continued making Indian meals for us back in the UK. She was a great cook.'

The air was heavy and humid, unbearable for sightseeing, so I went to the Pavoniere outdoor swimming pool after lunch every day, mobbed as it was. All the time hoping for a thunderstorm, for the air to clear, for the much-needed water to restore yellowing grass to green again. Doug had set the sprinklers to work at dusk when the temperatures dropped slightly, but it never seemed to be enough. One evening Diana sat on the lawn, waiting for the sprinklers to reach her.

Now the streets reeked of overflowing rubbish bins, often making me queasy. Car horns were more intrusive. As were sirens from fire engines and ambulances. Arguments erupted due to the physical discomfort people was experiencing.

At the railway station, staff dispensed bottled water to passengers awaiting delayed trains. Passengers lingered in the ticket office because of the air conditioning. In the piazzas, children, dogs and cats cooled down in fountain jets, and at home, the air conditioning was on full blast. Everyone prayed for rain before a water ban was imposed. At dinner we discussed the raging fires in Portugal and Spain, thankful Italy was being spared similar problems.

I woke one morning to the sound of Diana shouting at Doug, 'They've got to come today or I'll go crazy.'

'That's what everyone is telling them,' he said.

'Lie, then. Tell them I have a rare condition.'

'Hardly original, darling.'

Tentatively, I went downstairs.

'The air conditioning's knackered,' Diana told me, hands clasped, biting her thumb. 'At times like this, I wish we were renting. Then the landlord would be duty-bound to sort things out pronto.'

Already I could feel a marked difference in temperature, water trickling down my back. Cooking smells from last night's dinner dampened my appetite. All I wanted was ice cold water. Gallons of it.

Diana was now berating Doug for not having closed the shutters. 'It's okay for you, you'll be back at the hospital soon. I have to work here.'

'Calm down, Di,' he said.

'You must keep cool, especially your goollies,' she told him. 'To keep the sperm in good condition. You know this...'

He glared at her. 'For the love of God, could you just lighten up?'

'Could *you* try harder?'

I noticed his cheek pulse throbbing. This was so unlike him, as was his sarcastic retort, 'Well, as you've pointed out, I'll be back in my nice air-conditioned hospital soon.'

'Perhaps it's more important for Doug to feel relaxed,' I ventured.

Diana was scrunching her fingers through her hair, teeth gritted. 'Whose side are you on, Rachel?'

'Di, it's not about sides. Besides, you both want the same thing. Have a shower in lukewarm water.'

Fortunately, before returning to work, Doug managed to get an appointment for an engineer to fit a new air conditioning unit the following day. Diana thought a bribe might have been involved but was sensible enough not to ask.

Two evenings before the preview, she and I relaxed on the patio, enjoying a slight breeze and the scent of the crimson china rosebush she fussed over even more than her glasshouse plants.

'How are things with Tommaso?' she asked, while sipping my homemade lemonade. 'Heavens, you didn't half go crazy with the sugar.'

'Come on, surely a little in lemonade won't harm you?'

Her eyes were sombre. 'You know why I bother.'

We were silent. The exhibition had been so preoccupying that I'd temporarily forgotten what gnawed at her.

'No developments, then?'

She shook her head and sighed heavily. 'And Doug wants to visit his family in York after the conference. It'll be my fertile time... I'd hoped he'd be back in time for it. Sorry,

is this really hard for you to listen to? After...you know....
Anyway, you didn't tell me how things are with Tommaso.'

'I think I'm in love. Correction, I *am* in love.' I wanted to
dance from the thrill of it all. It had been years since I'd felt
this way about a man. Heightened reactions to the scent of
flowers or perfume, noticing beauty in odd places, like the
browns and pinks of cracked paint on an old door. I was
waking at six o'clock each morning, longing for the day to
begin. Even the unusually hot spell hadn't worn me down as
it might have done at other times. In the shower, I warbled
tunelessly. I shimmied across my bedroom while brushing
my hair. Most significantly, I talked to Tommaso all the time
in my head. Wondering what he'd think of my outfit, if he
thought I should straighten my hair, wear it shorter.

Diana clasped her hands and rested her chin on them.
'And does he feel the same?'

'He hasn't actually said.'

She leaned forward. 'Now, Rachel, be careful. Italian
men can blow hot and cold.'

The desire to dance evaporated and irritation flared.
About to go inside, I paused on feeling a drop of rain, then
more drops and a crack of thunder. Laughingly we sat as our
clothes got soaked and the thunder drew closer and sheet
lightning lit the sky.

'At last,' Diana said.

The evening before the opening, Doug arrived home early.
'I've booked a table at Dolce Vita. You've got half an hour to
make yourselves glitzy.'

Diana spun round from hosing the palms in her green-
house, in her excitement, spraying him with water. 'Angel –

exactly what I need. Not that your cooking isn't good, Rachel.'

All tables were occupied and a queue of hopefuls waited patiently when we arrived at the restaurant. I glanced at Diana. There were shadows under her eyes and she was chewing her lip. Maybe somewhere less noisy would suit her better. Before I could mention this to Doug, however, the waiter led us upstairs to a roof garden with a metal trellis supporting various vines. Here, he showed us to our reserved table. A welcome breeze cooled us and the traffic below sounded muted.

When the wine waiter arrived, Doug raised his eyebrows at Diana.

'Why not?' she said, and Doug relaxed.

As a woman wearing a beret walked into the roof garden, we laughed.

'I was flummoxed the moment I first saw the two of you,' he said, a smile creasing his face. 'Even if you'd worn different colours of beret, it wouldn't have been so funny. And those questions you asked, as if it was an interview.'

Diana laughed. 'We wanted to bring humour into it. Remember, lonely heart ads were more stigmatised in those days. Anyway, it worked, didn't it? And we were so impressed you were the only candidate to offer references? *Very* risky. How many ex-partners would give a positive testimonial?'

Doug lifted his wife's hand and kissed it. 'Cynic.... How long have you girls known each other? Twenty years?'

'We became friends on our first day of secondary school,' I said. 'We were both waiting for the loo at the same time. And we're twenty-eight, so...sixteen years.'

Diana tilted her head and smiled at me. 'And to think I nearly went to another school.'

I produced my camera. 'Doug, move closer to the missus...closer.' I took several shots of them.

'Now I'll take one of you and Diana,' Doug offered.

'You have to push the button halfway down to make sure we're in focus,' I pointed out, but he'd already taken the photo, which was lovely of Diana and had me with my mouth open.

Unexpectedly hungry, I watched the waiter approach our table with a starter of white cannellini beans.

Diana reached for the balsamic vinegar. 'If the exhibition's a success, I might get more commissions than I can manage. Wouldn't it be lovely to choose what I want to do?'

'I'm sure it will be successful, darling,' Doug said. 'You put in more hours than I do at the hospital.'

Briefly, her eyes flashed with anger, then she moved her mouth in the direction of a smile. 'Impossible.'

He refilled my wine glass. 'Told you this year would be successful.'

Diana pinched a bit of his mozzarella cheese. 'You said the same about last year.'

'People will love your work, darling. Are you enjoying your beans, Rachel?'

'They're very...beany.'

'Cannellini beans are big in Tuscany,' Diana said. 'You can't not like them.'

The air was fragrant with perfume as we discussed and tasted each other's dishes, agreeing that balsamic glaze worked so much better than the bog standard vinegar.

Doug eyed his wife fleetingly then ordered another bottle of *Vernaccia di San Gimignano*. 'A new resident started on the ward today,' he said. 'So young. So innocent. Naturally, we had to tease him with the customary practice.'

'Which is?' I asked.

Doug sipped his wine and waited, determined to achieve maximum appreciation of his anecdote. 'We sent him to find a fallopian tube. He walked at least six steps before turning round and glaring at us.'

Doug doubled up with laughter. 'It never fails.'

Beside me, I sensed Diana stiffen. Then she rose from the table and headed for the ladies'.

'Shit! I wasn't thinking,' he said.

'You certainly weren't, you wally.'

When my friend returned, she looked composed but strained. The earlier lightness didn't return.

Diana took two hours transforming herself from be-smocked working sculptress to glamorous new name in sculpting. She'd chosen loose fitting tailored black trousers and a fuschia pink silk blouse, which contrasted with her dark hair. For the first time since my arrival, she wore her engagement ring, a rectangular emerald (ethically sourced, of course) set in an unadorned matt silver band. Doug smiled appreciatively at her as he emerged from the shower, relaxed in his checked dressing gown.

Poutingly, she asked him, 'Will I do?'

Before he could reply, I butted in, 'You look amazing.'

And she did, although I knew her complexion well enough to realise she'd spent considerable time with her make-up in order to conceal the dark rings under her eyes, that she'd added a lot of blusher to give her cheeks more colour. Despite it being summer, she was spending little time out of doors. Even on the occasional cooler day.

'I'd better make an effort, too,' Doug said, winking at me.

After slipping into my saffron dress and studying myself

in the mirror, I wished I had another option. The colour suited my red hair but tonight it didn't bring out the blue of my eyes. Worse still, the dress was more clingy round the stomach than when I purchased it. This was the problem with being in the heat: less exercise but the same amount of food and drink.

I wondered if Tommaso would turn up at the exhibition.

Decorated in cream, with Tuscan columns at each corner, the gallery defined understated elegance and I experienced a frisson of excitement at being there. Circulating the room were women in tailored dresses or long skirts, sleek and exotic. Not to be outshone, men in smart suits and hand-stitched shoes engaged in lively conversation, orchestrated by expansive arm movements. Unobtrusive waiters dispensed glasses of *Brunello di Montalcino*.

As time went on, the noise of conversation escalated.

'Rachel! How lovely to see you again,' Allegra said.

Diana's friend looked stunning in a pearly grey and powder blue beaded dress`. Catching my reflection in one of the gilt framed mirrors, I cringed inwardly at my comparative paleness. My hair looked more brown than red, my saffron dress as well as being clingy, crushed beneath the waist, despite having been subjected to extensive ironing.

Allegra and I discussed the exhibition, then she noticed an old friend.

'I will phone you to arrange dinner,' she said, before moving away.

Diana's exhibits inspired much admiration. Formed from clay, marble, wood or stone, contemporary styles blending with more traditional ones. A series of foot high mother and child figures made from her favourite material, the pure, white marble of the Carrara quarries above Pisa, prompted animated debate.

I studied one sculpture of a mother cradling her baby, marvelling at my friend's attention to detail: the wrinkles on the mother's apron, the dimples on the baby's hands, where knuckles would in time develop; the outline of the safety pin on the nappy. No disposable nappies for this cherished one.

While gazing at another of these sculptures – a woman pressing a child against her chest, its arms round her neck, its expression conveying security and contentment – it seemed no coincidence that Diana applied so much effort and craftsmanship to a subject pivotal to her life. How had she felt working on these figures, day after day, as she and her husband tried to conceive a baby? Did she have a lump in her throat while shaping and forming? Or had she harnessed her emotions into thinking positively, as if by working the marble to produce such a result, at the same time, her body would do its own creating?

While searching for someone to talk to, my heart raced: at the other side of the gallery, I spotted Tommaso, talking to a man. When I joined them, he smiled, kissed me but didn't put his arm round me. Despite the air conditioning, sweat glistened at his temples, and a pulse throbbed in his cheek.

'Rachel, this is Maurizio,' he said, his voice strained.

Maurizio had one of those unfortunate faces where the nose gave the impression of sneering, regardless of any expression in his eyes. Independently of that, however, his smile was mocking: '*Piacere di conoscerti*, pleased to meet you.'

'Rachel is a friend of Diana's,' Tommaso said, his tone casual.

I clasped his arm. 'Why didn't you let me know you were coming to the preview?'

Silence.

I waited for him to slip an affectionate arm round me, to

make it obvious we were an item. He didn't. Furthermore, whenever I spoke, both men responded briefly and several times Maurizio checked his watch. I could have been an irritating colleague. After five minutes or so, I said, 'I'd better leave you to your important conversation,' and strode off, humiliated by their obvious relief. Managing to avoid the few people I knew here, I slipped outside to give myself time to recover.

A horrified thought occurred. What if Tommaso was one of those men who was phobic about being a couple? I'd served my time with such boyfriends. Their hallmark behaviour was avoiding any communication indicating we were a couple, when out with friends. On our own again, expecting to become romantic.

I didn't talk to Tommaso again that evening. Several times, I noticed him approaching me, but did a body-swerve.

Later, while Doug and Diana discussed the preview, I struggled to contribute, mulling over Tommaso's strange and hurtful behaviour. Later still, as I lay in bed, too strung up to sleep, it was difficult not to dwell on what had happened. Even though he might have had a plausible explanation.

The following day, still pondering the situation with Tommaso, I took the nine o'clock train to Siena, my phone switched off, reluctant to speak to him. At the same time, not wanting to know he hadn't phoned. On arrival, I headed straight to the famous Piazza del Campo, but while reading my guidebook, I regretted not being with him. He would have described the historic famous bullfights hosted in this square, more vividly than any tourist information source. Nevertheless, determined to enjoy my day, I strolled around the city, losing myself in its red brick lanes; discovering back streets lined with colourful flags; peering into picturesque courtyards.

At lunchtime, I found an Indian restaurant. However, the chicken dish was too mild despite being described as spicy, and the rice, too, was bland. I should have predicted this.

After I paid and wandered off, I heard shouting, and moments later a procession came into view, waving flags and chanting, "*No all'aborto*" and "*L'aborto non è la soluzione*". An anti-abortion march. My pulse raced, my breathing became shallow. As I pushed through the crowds, now wishing only to reach the station, sweat trickled down my face, stinging my eyes. For the half hour journey, my heart hammered. Unable to forget the bloody images displayed on flags.

When the train pulled into Florence, I noticed Tommaso pacing the platform – Diana must have told him I'd gone to Siena. How many trains had arrived and departed while he waited for my return?

He strode up to me, arms fanned out in greeting.

'*Amore*, I planned a lovely day for us.'

'Why didn't you tell Maurizio we are seeing each other?'

He looked puzzled then understanding dawned. 'You are annoyed because I didn't give you much attention at the exhibition. Perhaps you have reason but let me explain you. Maurizio told me his wife is ill. It was difficult to introduce you as my...my *amore*.'

'Hardly a reason for not telling him about us.' I waited for a more plausible explanation but none was forthcoming.

'Tommaso, if you have a problem being part of a couple, be straight with me. We don't owe each other anything.'

He wrestled with himself, mouth twitching, expression perplexed. I waited, unexpectedly detached.

'I love you,' he said, taking me in his arms.

As he held me, I nestled into the softness of his shirt, inhaled the familiar scent of his aftershave. It should have been a wonderful moment.

'Invite him to dinner,' Diana said that evening when I relayed what had happened.

Already I anticipated disaster.

## 5

----

The weeks Doug was away passed slowly. While wandering the backstreets of Florence and venturing further afield, I tried to understand what bothered me about Tommaso. Kind and attentive, he put a lot of effort into planning things he knew I'd enjoy. He listened to me. Took me seriously. The opposite to Steve, who laughingly had tolerated my whims, brushing away my concerns like cat hairs. But despite loving Tommaso's air of mystery, what I hadn't admitted to Diana was the niggle I had about him.

'Does he know?' she asked one evening at dinner.

'Does who know what?'

'Does Tommaso know about what happened to you?'

Diana was one of the few people in whom I'd confided about my termination. Who understood the awful circumstances, those being that on the day my parents died, I'd braced myself to tell them of my pregnancy, hoping they could help me decide what to do. Who knew that a post-abortion infection prevented me from having children.

'I haven't told him, no,' I said, hearing my defensive tone.

'You've never changed your mind...about wanting kids?' she asked.

I shook my head. When discovering I couldn't have children, I'd been grieving for my mother and father, disconnected from any latent maternal feelings. Even after accepting the loss of my parents, being unable to have children wasn't an issue I'd needed to work through. Having grown up with two people who adored each other so much, despite knowing they loved me, I'd acquired the belief that a couple could be self-sufficient. Consequently, unlike other women who'd received such news, who'd have given much to have children, I wasn't noticing buggies everywhere, or posters on public transport showing cute baby faces. I didn't have to avert my eyes when television advertised breast pumps or the latest in pull-up nappies.

'You never really explained why you and Steve split up,' Diana said.

I didn't want to become embroiled in a conversation about my ex this evening, but my friend was in "I need to understand" mode and it would be easier to give some explanation than continue to fend her off.

'There was no energy in the relationship. It felt like a battery running flat.'

'But he didn't treat you badly, and–'

'No, he didn't. I just needed more than that.... I never felt like I was special to him.... It was as if anyone would do.'

Diana still looked baffled. 'Don't you miss him at all?'

'Sometimes. He was kind to me in his low-key way.'

I took our plates through to the kitchen, calling back, 'You'll like Tommaso when you meet him properly.'

But now, every time I mentioned him to her, my right eyelid twitched. And the dinner, the occasion after which she would present me with her definitive opinion of him, was rapidly approaching.

Tommaso arrived at Doug and Diana's, arms filled with yellow roses and chocolate truffles. He'd been unable to fly to Florence until the afternoon, so I hadn't seen him before now.

Diana reached the front door, seconds after I did. 'Oh, chocolate truffles, I adore these,' she squealed. 'I suppose I can have an evening off my low sugar diet.'

I could sense Doug's relief from the dining room where he was de-corking wine.

During the meal, I listened to Diana question Tommaso, aware of my strained smile, my shoulder ache from hunching. I knew most of the information. New to me was his dislike of football and poncy cars, endearing him to me even more, at the same time increasing my desire to protect him from Diana's grilling.

'Are you from a large family?' she asked while serving *panforte*, a traditional Sienese flat cake with nuts and candied fruit.

'I have two older sisters.'

She handed me a slice of cake. 'Are they married?'

'Yes, and they both have children.'

Tommaso sounded relaxed enough in his responses but a pulse throbbed on his cheek. He would know he was being assessed for partner suitability and his pride would be hurt.

Diana opened her mouth to pose her next question, but before she could, he added, voice admirably level, 'They live in Sicily, in Catania, near my parents' home. My parents own two restaurants. Sometimes my sisters help them, too.'

With remarkable speed, Diana composed herself, asking, 'You've never been married, yourself?'

'For God's sake, Di, you should have been a barrister,' I said.

She gave a hollow laugh.

A few blessed moments of silence followed. Then Tommaso asked Doug about his job and his opinion on health care provision in Italy compared with the NHS. A conversation followed about private versus public medicine. My shoulders relaxed, the tension in my neck lessened. Leaning back on the sofa, legs crossed, Doug seemed comfortable, chilled out by the wine and the meal, but articulate, switching to Italian when Tommaso struggled. For a moment, I loved my friend's husband for his laid-back manner. For giving my guy a chance. Diana, conversely, sat upright, lips pursed, a permanent frown on her face. I itched to tell her to ease up, to have some wine. To be more open-minded.

For distraction, I opened the truffles, passed them round, expecting Diana to grab a couple. But she waved them away, expression preoccupied, as if considering what else she could ask Tommaso that would ferret out of him what she needed to know. In my irritation, I forgot that if I had a niggle about him, it wasn't unreasonable for her, too, to have reservations.

It seemed as if her mission was to unearth flaws in him, so uncharacteristic of her that I attributed it to sadness about her childless state. Tarnishing her normal willingness and ability to see the best in people.

'Tommaso has to go now, he has an early meeting

tomorrow,' I said after our second coffee, bundling him out of the dining room.

'Sorry about the interrogation,' I said when we reached the front door.

Tommaso stroked my hair. 'It's okay, they wish to protect you. Come back to the hotel with me.' His breath was hot against my face.

'Not this evening,' I said. 'Sorry.'

If the dinner had been more successful, I would have asked him to stay over.

He didn't linger and I wondered if deep down he'd been hurt by Diana's scrutiny.

When he left, I trudged back to the sitting room. Diana was gazing out of the window but Doug flashed me a sympathetic look, amid a mouthful of chocolate.

'Jesus Christ, Di, did you have to interrogate him? Poor guy. He was a guest. If I'd known you were going to behave like this I wouldn't have invited him.'

She raised her eyebrows. 'What's wrong with wanting to find out more?'

'We're not engaged.'

She spun round. 'I should *hope not*. You've known him for...five weeks?'

'You were a bit over the top, love,' Doug said, reaching for another truffle. 'Rachel's right. Why didn't you go into law? You're wasted as a sculptress.'

He was joking, of course, and if she hadn't been so wound up, Diana would have realised. Instead she glared at him and when he went to comfort her, pulled away, eyes welling.

'I didn't mean it, darling,' he said, enfolding her, stroking her back, in the way my father had done with me when I was a child. 'But you can overdo it.'

Again she extricated herself. 'Have you ever believed I had talent? Will you ever regard sculpting as a proper job?'

'I'll make more coffee,' Doug said, knocking back the glass of wine in one gulp before making his way to the kitchen.

'Christ, you're impossible,' Diana called to his retreating back. 'Can't you enjoy yourself without alcohol?'

Doug twisted round. 'Can't you be more fun?'

I left them to it. Tomorrow I'd elicit their verdict on Tommaso.

Sleep arrived slowly that night. Did Diana have a hunch about Tommaso? An omen? I imagined her remarking in five years' time that it was a blessing he and I hadn't stayed together. Admitting her worries about him from the outset. Before descending further into gloom, I heard an owl hoot, then a whistling sound. Finally my eyelids grew heavy.

'I didn't get a chance to ask what you think of Tommaso,' I said next evening at dinner. My friends had both been out by the time I surfaced that morning, which was partly a relief, wanting to postpone hearing their opinion. Already expecting something less than positive.

Diana halted in the middle of helping herself to rice, clutched her chin, making a show of considering my question. 'He's pleasant enough. Attentive.'

'But?'

'I don't know exactly.... There's something – do you trust him?'

My face flushed. 'What sort of question is that? Of course I do.'

I turned to Doug. 'What do *you* think?'

'I agree with Di.' Registering my expression, his tone softened. 'But who are we to judge? It's what *you* think.'

'Now Rachel, don't rush into anything,' Diana said briskly. 'Let Tommaso make the effort. He can visit you in Edinburgh.... More pork, Doug?'

My laugh sounded derisive.

'You're welcome to stay as long as you like,' Doug's voice broke into my thoughts when we were clearing away the meal.

'If I'm not in the way....'

Diana appeared at the kitchen door. 'Of *course* you're not. Be *care*ful. That's all I'm saying.'

When Doug had gone to bed, Diana and I sat in the garden. 'So, why Tommaso and not Steve? I still don't understand. You got on so well together.'

'I've explained all this. Steve's a lovely guy, I know, but he was too...there were no ups and downs with him and–'

'Ah,' she said triumphantly, as if having discovered an earth-shattering fact. 'So you need an edge, and Tommaso has that edge. Hmm.'

'I wouldn't put it like that' I said, wondering if she was right.

'There's an air of mystery about him and that's got you hooked.'

I adjusted the cushion on the lounger, lay back. 'Di, spare me your psychobabble. Tommaso's got energy, physical and mental energy. He wants to get out. Do things. You know, travel and stuff. If Steve and I had to cancel a holiday, for example, that wouldn't be a problem. He'd go to work the next day and not bother, whereas I'd be sick with disappointment. Tommaso's always got ideas of things to do. He's spontaneous. He has *en*ergy. Steve settled for so little.'

'He was reliable,' she said primly.

'I know, but he didn't.... Tommaso notices everything, how I look, my mood. He's interested in my photography. He gets it, how important it is for me.'

'And Steve didn't?'

I rearranged the cushion under my head. 'Oh, he went through the motions but he was only really interested in a photo if it had a crane in it...or a digger. Or an animal. He said I never took photos of people.... Tommaso comments on lighting and composition and atmosphere.... The biggest excitement for Steve was finding back copies of *Earthmovers*.' I paused, feeling guilty about slating my ex so much, yet needing Diana to understand. 'If I came home with a leg missing or my head had fallen off, he might have noticed. But not a haircut or new shoes. I didn't feel seen. Not properly. That's all. And his idea of a good Saturday was watching football and going to the pub. Tommaso would rather eat out and go to a concert.'

Diana stared at me for a moment, then reached out to pat my arm. 'Oh Rachel....'

Tommaso returned to Florence in the middle of August. I expected him to take me out for dinner on Friday evening. At eight o'clock, however, he phoned to say his flight had been delayed and he wouldn't arrive until after eleven o'clock, but wanted to take me away overnight the next day. 'Pack a bag with smart clothes.'

Assuming we'd be going into the Tuscan countryside, perhaps to Prato or Fiesole, I was surprised the following day when we headed for the motorway leading north east.

'Where are we going?' I asked for the third time, when the traffic snarled us up again.

'Venezzia, Venice to you,' he said, reaching over to kiss me.

He was wearing a new shirt and his chinos had been well ironed. His hair was brushed back and his snazzy sunspecs gave him a film star appearance.

My heart pounded. He was going to propose.

'I must do business there,' he added.

He wasn't going to propose.

'It won't take long,' he said, noticing my crestfallen expression.

When we arrived in Venice midafternoon, Tommaso left me in the Campo dei Mori, in the north of the city, promising to be back within two hours. I wandered by the canal, glad of the relative quiet, that he hadn't dropped me off by the Piazza san Marco, bound to be heaving on this hot August afternoon.

The sunny sky changed to a murky grey and a memory surfaced. As a ten-year- old, I'd holidayed in Venice with my parents, and much of the time sensed from their covert glances at each other, their frequent caresses, that they'd rather have been there on their own. During gondola rides, the visit to a glass factory in Murano, in coffee shops.

A similar experience occurred in Paris. Aged twelve, I was too old for a babysitter, yet not quite mature enough to safely be left on my own, in order for them to enjoy a romantic dinner cruise on the Seine. Finally, they'd compromised: dinner on a moored boat for the three of us. I remembered my father, seated beside me, reaching for my hand under the table, feeling the smooth gold wedding ring my mother insisted he wore. My parents had often described their relationship as a "great love", telling me they hoped I'd be equally lucky.

Tommaso returned beaming after a successful meeting.

'I am sorry to be away for so long, but I wanted to go to the mass afterwards.'

It was past five o'clock and I was starving. 'Let's find a place for cake.'

At the café, he took my hand, saying conspiratorially, 'I have a surprise for you. This evening we are dining in a special place.'

'Where?'

He waited a moment before saying, 'I booked a table at a restaurant in Burano. We must take the vaporetta there.'

Again my hopes soared: a romantic restaurant, the obvious place to propose. But he hadn't suggested we change at our hotel. Perhaps I was off target.

The water boat to Burano took ten minutes. A wind had now whipped up, messing with my hair, waves splashing my dress. I didn't mind. When Tommaso gripped my hand, I could feel his pulse, sense his excitement. By the time we reached Burano, it was pouring, and we ran to the restaurant, entering the building as thunder cracked through the air.

'Where is the waiter?' he muttered several times, after we'd chosen from the menu. Outside, waves slapped against the concrete bank.

By the time we finished eating and waited thirty minutes to pay, the rain had eased off. It was nine o'clock and the sun had recently set.

Tommaso grabbed my hand. 'If we walk quickly, I can show you the most beautiful canal here.'

For ten minutes, we rushed along canal paths and crossed quaint bridges. Then we stopped.

'Isn't this wonderful?' he said in satisfaction, as if he were the architect of such perfection.

I gazed at the buildings lining the canal, their grey,

cream and pink façades, their dark green shutters and hori-
zontally hanging metal streets lamps. I stared at the small
boats with bright blue or red tarpaulin covers, wondering if
they were used or simply there for show. It was pretty, and of
course I had to capture it with my camera. Tommaso waited
patiently while I experimented with different lenses. I
sensed he was proud of my passion for photography.
Perhaps because I didn't just point my camera and click but
put care into selecting shutter speeds, f-stops and filters.

'I'm glad you brought me here,' I said.

He grimaced. 'I am sorry about the restaurant. I think
the management has changed since I eat there before.'

He pressed his face against my hair and kissed it. The
rain started again, so we scampered to the pier to wait for
the next vaporetto, after which we picked up the car.

Our hotel was in the Cannareggio area. The wooden
bedroom floor creaked and the small window overlooked a
dingy courtyard – the opposite of the marble floors and
balcony with canal view I'd anticipated, but this became
irrelevant. After we made love, Tommaso held me for ages. I
moved away only after hearing his soft, rhythmic breathing.

The next day we took a gondola trip on the Grand
Canal. Followed by an overpriced lunch in Piazzo san
Marco, served by an indifferent waiter. The square was
predictably mobbed, with too many English voices in
earshot, which didn't appear to bother Tommaso as he
pointed out buildings and described exhibitions he'd seen
here. Enthusiasm bubbling over. We must have seemed
quite the couple. While adjusting my camera to photograph
him, several bystanders offered to take a shot of us together.

My niggle about not having told him I was unable to
have children was gaining momentum. The timing of such a
revelation had always been difficult with boyfriends.

Announcing it at the start of a relationship might suggest I was already planning a dreamy future for us and freak the guy out. Leaving it too long made me vulnerable to accusations of concealing important information.... And Italian men loved children.

'There's something I haven't told you about me,' I said as we reached the car.

Tommaso stroked my cheek. 'You are not ill, *amore*?'

'I can't have children...there was a problem, a long time ago. I didn't know when to tell you.'

He searched my face. 'Do you mind this?'

Without hesitation, I replied, 'No', then fearing I sounded too harsh, added, 'Not really.'

'If it is not a problem for you, then it is not a problem for me, either,' he said, starting the car engine.

On the return drive to Florence, we didn't speak much. Tommaso seemed preoccupied, responding briefly to my conversation. I was convinced he was pondering the children situation. And yet, his response hadn't been a kneejerk one. Should I reintroduce the subject? After all, we hadn't discussed a future together.

When we arrived at Diana and Doug's house, I debated whether or not to invite him in. Give him another chance to impress my friends. Instinct warned against.

As I clutched the door handle, he reached for me. 'Don't go yet, please.'

Despite his inscrutable expression, I sensed he'd detected my worry. Wanted to make things right, with no idea how to do so.

'I hope you enjoyed Venice,' he said.

'I did,' I replied, managing a smile, aware now of how much I'd expected a declaration of eternal love. A proposal. Despite the short time we'd known each other.

'Perhaps I will visit again next weekend.'

I reached for his hand. 'If you don't have meetings here, why don't I come to Napoli, give you a rest from travelling?'

Silence.

'I'd love to see where you live,' I tried again.

Silence, then, 'There will be another time.... I must go now. My flight will leave early tomorrow.'

To my relief, the house was quiet, only the hall light on, so I went straight to my room, hoping not to bump into either Diana or Doug on the landing. In bed, I pondered what had gone on between Tommaso and me in Venice. If mood swings were the norm for Italian men or if something troubled him. The children issue. If he hadn't been honest about this.

What bothered me most was the realisation I was smitten. Too smitten, when considering the barriers to a long-term relationship: an Italian Catholic man settled in his job, an agnostic woman returning to Edinburgh to study. Perhaps I should break things off.

As I switched on my kindle, my phone went.

'It is Tommaso. Please marry me?'

It was what I'd been longing for, waiting for, and yet I heard myself say, 'I don't know,' and the line went dead.

Ten minutes later I phoned him back and said, 'Yes, I will marry you.'

## 6

Doug and Diana were gardening and looked up expectantly when I emerged the following morning.

'How was your weekend?' Diana asked, flicking soil from her gardening apron. 'Where did you go? What did you do?'

'Venice.'

'Romantic,' Doug said, winking at her.

'And I have news.... Tommaso and I are getting married.'

Doug dropped the weeds he was holding. 'Well, lass. Amazing!'

Diana gasped. 'You hardly know him, Rachel.'

'Do we ever really know anyone?'

Silence.

'I know enough. I'm in love.'

'Infatuated, more like,' she said, putting down the secateurs. 'You're infatuated by him, Rachel. You're in love with *Italy*.'

Doug chucked a clump of weeds into a bin bag. 'Calm down, darling.'

I tried again. 'I'm in love with *Italy*, with life, and most of all, with him. HIM!'

When Diana announced she and Doug were engaged, before I could congratulate her, a spat had broken out on the bus between two women over the space reserved for buggies. We'd laughed at the timing. I was delighted for Doug and her, but even if I'd had reservations, I wouldn't have spoiled her happiness. Now I resented her spoiling mine.

Diana lifted the secateurs again, released the safety catch. Then she frowned. 'It takes time to commit like this. Doug and I were together for two years before–'

'Well done you.'

'Sarcasm doesn't suit you, Rachel.'

'My parents got engaged after a few months. And they were extremely happy.'

'You've known Tommaso for what...six weeks?'

Our ping pong conversation continued.

'How can you possibly know he's right for you? You should give it longer.' With renewed vigour, she snapped away again at the flowers.

'Don't you like him?'

'As a dinner guest, not your husband,' she said, dropping the secateurs, turning to me. 'Can't you see it's too quick? Even if it had been six months, you could make a more informed decision.'

'Informed decision? Come on, this isn't a business venture.'

'Cool it, girls,' Doug said, enjoying his self-appointed role of peacemaker.

'What do you have in common, anyway?' Diana asked.

I thought for a moment. 'Walking...travel. Classical music.'

'And since when were you interested in classical music?'

'You now I've loved the concerts he's taken me to. And he's keen for me to do well in my photography. And–'

'Where did he propose?'

'Diana, for God's sake, this feels like an interview.'

'Where did he pro*pose*?'

It was so tempting to say we were on a midnight gondola ride. 'Actually, I was here. He–'

'Here?'

From Diana's expression, anyone would think Tommaso had proposed at a sewage works.

She resumed her deadheading, the snapping of the secateurs even louder.

'He phoned last night, shortly after I got back. He asked me then.'

She rolled her eyes. 'Bizarre. You spend the weekend together but he doesn't ask you until you get back. Don't you think it's weird?' She whipped off her gardening apron. 'Anyway, I need to get back to work.'

When she left the garden, Doug and I exchanged glances.

'She's such a worrier, there's nothing too small for her to bother about,' he said.

'She thinks I should have stuck with Steve.'

'Yeah, she told me. She feels protective of you, that Steve would have–'

'Been a safe choice. I know. But I want more than a safe choice. Surely you can understand that?'

Doug nodded but all he said was, 'Give it half an hour then talk to her.... I must get to the hospital. Tell her I might be home at lunchtime.'

I went to my room and uploaded my weekend batch of photos, selecting which to keep, which to enlarge. Then I went through photos I'd taken in Florence, editing them. Knowing I'd have to face Diana, reluctant to embroil myself in another unpleasant conversation, yet unable to leave things as they were.

It was noon before I hovered at the door of my friend's studio, observing her at the table ticking things from a list. As soon as she noticed me, she came over and hugged me. 'Oh Rachel, I'm sorry. But you've been through so much already that I can't bear to think of you not being happy. You do under*stand*, don't you?'

'What *you* have to understand is that Tommaso does make me happy. I know it's quick...but....'

She wiped her hands on her pottery apron and swigged from a bottle of water. 'Doug and I knew each other inside out before we considered even living together.'

'But are you happy? You've hardly smiled since I arrived. I know you were anxious about the exhibition and upset about...about not getting pregnant, I get that, I do, but...'

She slapped a piece of clay, the worktop moving under the pressure. 'It dominates everything: when we should make love, dreading another period. We won't be complete until we have a family.'

I studied the room: the slabs of white and blue-grey marble on the floor; the shelf of flat and claw chisels, wooden mallets and iron hammers. Even in her sculpting, Diana used traditional tools. No pneumatic hammers for her. On a table lay a large drawing pad, beside it, a bundle of glossy books on sculpting. In one corner of the room stood a metal kiln. In another, a large dusty cheese plant. The room smelled of vinegar and herbal teas. A lovely, creative space.

For a while I watched as she checked through other lists, then as I dusted the cheese plant, about to ask her why she didn't move it to her glasshouse, Doug came into the studio.

'Didn't expect you back so soon,' Diana said.

'It's one o'clock. Coffee, Rachel? Do you want one, love?'

Diana raised her eyebrows. 'Didn't we agree to the coffee substitute?'

In exasperation, he tapped the side of his head and left the studio.

'See what I mean? Another example of his attitude. Coffee isn't advised for conception, but will he stop drinking it?'

'Maybe he thinks he's having to sacrifice too much.'

She lifted another piece of clay. 'What about my sacrifices? I assume you'll get married in Edinburgh.'

'I'd like it to be here, actually.'

I shifted a bundle of magazines from a chair, plonked myself at the table and studied Diana's concerned face. 'Knowing everything doesn't guarantee happiness. Besides, I know enough about Tommaso to believe he's right for me.'

'I don't even know what work he does.'

'He told you. He works for a leather company in Napoli.'

'But why haven't you met his people? You know how close Italian families are.'

Perhaps focusing on me distracted her from her own worries, her own unhappiness.

'Sicily's far away. The wedding will be soon enough to meet them,' I said, more confidently than I felt. 'Can't you be happy for me? Please?'

'Why don't you wait for another few months. I really think you're making a mistake. Look Rachel, if *I* can't tell you this, who can? I mean, your *own* family haven't even met him.'

I was so hurt that I left the room. If Tommaso had still been in Florence, I would have contacted him.

Instead, I wandered around the city, choked up, feeling

more isolated than I'd done for years. My friend was right, though. She was the only person who'd be so direct with me. But part of me hated her for her pessimism.

It was an afternoon of drizzly rain, robbing the streets of any vibrance. No pavement life, sun canopies closed, the red and yellow begonias subdued. In my favourite ice cream shop, I bought a carton of raspberry and pistachio, but only ate half of it.

Reluctantly, I returned home around six, wanting to spend the evening in my room but not to appear like a spoilt child who hasn't been given her own way.

Diana was peering out of their sitting room window when I walked along the path. She opened the door and flung her arms around me.

'I'm *so* glad you're back. I missed you.'

She took my hand, led me through to the kitchen, and sat me down at the oak table. Then she sat down, reached for my hand, her strained expression conveying the effort she was making.

'There's a room at the gallery which would be great for a reception,' she told me. 'I can get a special rate for it, if you fancy it. Our treat.'

Tears pricked my eyelids. 'Thank you, thank you.'

We sat for an hour or so, discussing the reception, and when Doug got home, we were eating last night's leftovers.

'Glad to see you smiling at each other. You're friends again,' he said.

Diana and I raised our eyebrows.

'Men,' she said. 'Such simple specimens.'

Doug winked at me. 'That's why you love us. We're easy to understand.'

Diana's tone changed to one of gravitas. 'Now, Rachel,

remember you can change your mind about this wedding at any time. Doug and I will support you.'

I scraped back the kitchen chair as I stood. 'I'm off to download some photos.'

Diana called after me, but I ignored her.

Weeks passed while I sorted out the necessary administrative stuff. Tommaso and I had agreed on a civil ceremony due to our religious differences and we hoped for Saturday, September 1. Subject to the paperwork being completed.

Meanwhile, in my temporary home, all was far from calm. In my room at night, I often opened the window to let the crickets' chirping drown out conversations from the sitting room. Although I couldn't hear what they were saying, it felt uncomfortable, wondering if my friends were bemoaning my situation or theirs. I wondered why Doug continued to drink coffee and so much alcohol, when this distressed Diana. Why he didn't take his nutritional supplements, which she'd spent hours researching. If they'd consulted a fertility specialist. Considered adoption.

'What do you think?' I asked Doug, flaunting my left hand in his face. Finding an engagement ring Tommaso and I both liked had been unexpectedly easy, in fact. Afterwards, we'd celebrated with champagne in a snazzy bar. Then he'd had to leave for a meeting, and I'd rushed home, dying to show off my ring.

Doug studied the orange sapphire and gold band. 'It's beautiful, Rachel, unusual.'

'I liked the double twist in the band. Makes it different. I hope Diana approves.'

'Go and show her. She's in the glasshouse, resuscitating a palm.'

Two days later, Diana and I shopped for a wedding outfit. I'd been eagerly anticipating our trip, but on the bus journey I noticed how rough she looked.

'Stomach cramps,' she told me, conscious of my concern. 'Period, of course.'

I touched her arm. 'Maybe next month. Perhaps you need to chill out a bit?'

'I told Doug this morning, but it wasn't the right time. He was presenting a case study to the new professor and was nervous. The thing is, I can never find a suitable moment.'

Inhaling deeply, I asked, 'Are you sure...absolutely sure he wants children?'

'We could give a child everything.'

We lunched in an old restaurant near the Ponte Vecchio, seated by the window, overlooking the slate grey fast-flowing waters of the Arno. Surrounding us were animated conversations, the undulating tones musical. When the wine waiter arrived, I declined the wine, so that Diana didn't have to, opting instead for *gingerinos*, hoping the bitter taste from the herbs would make her forget these fruit drinks contained sugar.

Afterwards, when walking away from the restaurant, I noticed a window display featuring an ivory satin midi dress with a short lacy jacket. Burnished copper coloured high heeled satin shoes and a spray of silk flowers in autumn colours completed the outfit. I wanted all of it.

The shop assistant found the dress and jacket in my size and showed me to a changing room. My hands trembled while I slipped on the clothes.

'What do you think?' I asked Diana who was flicking through a bridal magazine, commenting on weird choices of flowers and ridiculously expensive shoes.

'Perfect from the front. Let's see the back.'

Ten minutes later we were finished.

After we left, I expected Diana would want to head home and return to work.

'Fancy going to a pavement café to people watch?' she suggested. 'I get inspiration for my sculpting from doing this: how they move, facial expressions.'

We did just that, enjoying the sunny afternoon underneath the shade of a sun umbrella. Guessing who were tourists and where they were from, commenting on both gorgeous and hideous outfits, laughing uncontrollably at times, despite being sober. In our festive mood, the busy streets and traffic noise seemed muted, the way alien languages can sound when you don't understand the words. And Diana, for the moment, returned to the person I used to know.

'See that woman?' she said. 'By the statue. Her bloke's just left her and she's telling herself she doesn't care. That she doesn't need a man to define her. She's put on a stone since they split up and she's relieved she no longer needs to wear make-up each day or high heels when she goes out.'

'Very good,' I said. 'What about that man over there?'

Diana thought for a moment. 'He's just been offered a three-book deal but been told to kill off one of his favourite characters so he's wondering whether to approach another publisher.'

I noticed a child tugging at a yapping dog's lead and

said, 'That girl has stolen the dog while it was chained up outside a shop. She's wanted a dog for ages but her mother only agreed to a hamster. The child wants a dog because things at home are grim and at least she can escape to walk the dog. When she gets home – if she gets that far before someone realises what she's done – her father will make rude comments about the dog looking like an overgrown rat.'

'And that man sitting behind us has been sacked for always being late,' Diana remarked. 'He doesn't give a jot because he hated the job which, with a Masters in Physics, he was vastly overqualified to do and he's thinking about starting out again as a horticulturalist, except he's allergic to plants.'

It was such a relief to see Diana's spark again. I took several photos of her.

Tommaso phoned later. 'I am counting days until our wedding. I am making plans for our honeymoon but it is a surprise. You will love the place.'

'No clues?'

He laughed.

An indefinable anxiety kicked in.

Three days before the wedding, Tommaso took me to Siena for an early dinner. He arrived at Diana's late and flustered and drove quickly along the autostradale, honking at cars in the wrong lane. Too twitchy to talk, I remained silent. Ignoring his puzzled glances. Wishing we'd taken the train, or better still, the bus which terminated in the city centre. Tommaso, however, was a snob about public transport and I'd given up trying to change his views. We arrived in Siena with enough time to walk around the town before eating.

At the Piazza della Signoria Campo, he said, 'Do you know about the bull fights?'

I had more immediate things on my mind. 'How's your mother? Has she–?'

'You aren't interested in the history of my country?'

'For God's sake, Tommaso, I want to know how she is. Also, I need to discuss the wedding.'

'Later, *amore*. At restaurant,' he said wearily, as if being asked to discuss tax returns.

I smothered my concerns while we walked to a view-point above the town. While we gazed over pantile roofs and towers, and beyond to green and yellow fields, inhaling the fragrant air. As I retrieved my camera, Tommaso reached into his shoulder bag.

'I have a surprise for you,' he said, handing me a slim brown box. 'Please.'

With feverish eyes, he watched me untie the ribbon, open the box and lift out the gold necklace.

'It is made in Sicily,' he said.

The twisted horn charm attached to the chain flashed in the sunlight.

'It protects from the evil eye,' he told me, slipping the necklace round my neck.

'Thank you,' I said, shivering despite the warmth of evening sunshine. 'Come on, let's eat.'

He put his arms round me. 'I am longing to have you for myself all day and all night.'

I managed a smile, wishing I could rid myself of anxiety.

Our restaurant was located at the edge of town, our table facing a field and row of poplar trees. After a small glass of wine, Tommaso relaxed even more and his eyes sparkled, his good mood infectious. My worries retreated as we discussed the reception. The catering, what sort of speech his best man Salvatore would make.

'I'm so looking forward to travelling together. Where do you want to visit most?' I asked.

'There are many beautiful places to see in Italy,' he said.

'But what about other countries? I'm keen to return to India.'

'It would be too hot for me.'

'Tell me about the honeymoon,' I said as we drank our coffee.

'I told you it is a surprise. No questions.'

'Come on, Tommaso, I need to know about clothes.'

He replaced his coffee cup. 'I give you a small piece of information. But afterwards, no more questions. It will be in Italy, and it is beside the sea.'

'I love being by the sea,' I said, sighing. 'This is partly why I did my nursing training in Edinburgh. There are so many coastal walks nearby. I can't wait to show you.'

He gazed out of the window.

'Tommaso, I have another question.'

His attention now focused on a neighbouring table.

I reached for his hand. 'Tommaso?'

Eventually he turned his head, his eyes meeting mine. 'No more business talking this evening.... Take a photo of us together. The last one before we are married.'

'Wedding plans aren't business.... One question. Diana needs to confirm numbers for the catering. How many of your family are coming, apart from your parents?'

His expression was half defiant, half apologetic. 'No one is coming from my family. It is not possible.'

## 7

'No one? Not even your parents?'

'I explain you already. The doctors make an operation for my mother's hip.'

'It's because I'm not Catholic, isn't it?'

Tommaso's jaw jutted forward but he said nothing, and in doing so, confirmed my suspicions.

'I've already explained, Tommaso. I can't convert to Catholicism. Even if I were religious, which I'm not, I wouldn't consider this. I'm sorry. But I don't want your parents to disapprove of me because of this.'

After a moment, he said, '*Amore*, they will like you. But they will need some time to accept the situation.'

Diana's warning came to mind. Instinctively I knew the pointlessness of saying anything more. Tommaso was staring out of the window.

Now I felt both foolish and emotional. As tears stung my eyes, I rose to leave, the strap of my bag catching on the table corner.

In the loo, a torrent of emotion poured out and hard as I

tried, I couldn't suppress my tears. Outside the cubicle, I heard worried Italian voices, the volume mounting as more people came in.

'I'm okay,' I called.

'Ah, *straniero*,' came a voice. Foreigner. This reassured them.

When I sensed everyone had left, I emerged from the cubicle, splashed water on my blotchy face and returned to our table.

Tommaso stood when he saw me. '*Amore*, are you ill?'

'I hardly know you. I haven't met your family.... Diana was right.'

'We love each other,' he said, stroking my hand. 'After the wedding, I take you to Sicily to visit my family.'

But I still wouldn't be Catholic.

On the return drive to Florence, I fell asleep, not waking until we reached Doug and Diana's house. I didn't invite him in.

Unbidden, envy of my friends' settled relationship consumed me as I prepared for bed. Their evening routine. After dinner, Doug would be on his laptop or watching football on television, unwinding from the hospital. Diana would check her clay, maybe practise new techniques on marble. Later still, if they weren't deep in conversation – no longer did I need to open the window to let the cricket sounds dominate – they'd listen to music or watch the late news, before going to bed. There, presumably, they'd make love, safe and comfortable with each other. Except, of course, that their longing for a baby would bring its own tensions.

While struggling to fall asleep, I suppressed the thought that only days from my wedding, it was odd to covet what my friends had.

Tommaso and I were married on Saturday, September 1. The prospect of a hot day had worried me but luckily the maestrale winds decreased the temperature to the late twenties. Nevertheless, as I stepped into my ivory satin dress, a chilling low mood seeped through me, which I sensed had nothing to do with pre-wedding nerves. I knew what to expect from the civil ceremony and the Italian wedding reception. While attaching a satin bow to my hair, I tried to comfort myself with the knowledge that after the honeymoon we'd return to Edinburgh and familiar territory.

Diana hovered while I applied eyeliner, then wiped it off.

'What's wrong, Rachel?' she asked.

A vision of waiting at the Registry Office on my own appeared. Wondering where Tommaso was. But I couldn't tell Diana this. Not with the reservations I sensed still existed within her.

Standing behind me, she bent down and kissed my hair, saying gently, 'It'll be okay. Let me do your make-up.'

Skilfully she applied eyeliner, eye cream and mascara. Then she outlined my lips and finally applied lipstick. As I inserted an earring, she grabbed my hand. 'No gold jewellery until after the ceremony. It's bad luck here.'

'How much I have to learn.'

She hugged me. 'Taxi's arrived.'

I studied her, the mulberry knee-length skirt, jacket and fascinator, and what she described as her "grown-up" shoes, black with a slim three-inch heel. Today she sported the demeanour of settled wife and emerging sculptress. Not the sad and desperate would-be mother.

As soon as we arrived at the medieval town hall, I saw

Tommaso standing there, upright and so poised that I wondered why I'd harboured such doubts. He presented me with a bouquet of cream lilies, orange and yellow roses and gypsophila, and the scent of them brought tears to my eyes.

'You look wonderful!' I said, taking in his charcoal suit and silver tie, the brushed back hair and sparkling dark eyes. His tantalisingly subtle aftershave reminded me of the first time we made love.

He took my arm. 'You are beautiful. We will be happy, *amore.*'

As the mayor conducted the short ceremony in businesslike but pleasant style, I felt dazed. Several times I caught my uncle's eye, saw him smile, before I returned my attention to the proceedings. Afterwards, I realised guiltily that I'd hardly heard a word the interpreter spoke, as he translated the traditional wedding vows and the Italian law relating to marital status. My aunt and uncle, my cousins Debs and Anna, and Doug and Diana, and Salvatore, the best man, whom I'd met two days ago and liked, witnessed the service.

Outside the town hall, children showered confetti on us. Marion was wiping away tears, Geoffrey awkwardly rubbing her shoulder, and to my relief, emotion surfaced. Anything was better than feeling disconnected.

'I am proud of you, my wife,' Tommaso whispered while we posed for the photographs.

The photographer directed us here and there, flinging his arms around, shouting, "*Si, si, bella, bella*", "*la sposa, per favore*". The wind had now dropped, and a few tendrils of my hair escaped from their satin bow, clinging damply to my face. My make-up was probably smudged but I didn't care. When we left the town hall, more children ran up to us, throwing rose petals.

Around thirty people attended the reception in Diana's gallery, today festooned with gladioli and roses and garlands of ribbon. Once again, I felt uncomfortable because despite being the *straniero*, more guests were from my side than Tommaso's. To my delight, more than a dozen of my Edinburgh friends had flown over, compared with the few friends and colleagues of his from Florence and Napoli. Most of whom I hadn't met. From time to time, I caught myself glancing at the door, as if willing more of his friends to arrive. By now, however, I was becoming accomplished at dismissing disconcerting issues. Besides, it was my wedding day.

Embracing his role of *in loco parentis*, Geoffrey gave a short speech, which Salvatore translated into Italian. Then Salvatore spoke, saying what a great friend Tommaso had been to him, recounting a few stories from their university days, and wishing us a long and happy marriage.

The feeling of strangeness – mixed with love for my husband – lingered throughout the reception: while Salvatore dispensed sweet liqueurs for the women, stiff drinks for the men; during the elaborate meal; as Tommaso and I danced and he kissed my hair and murmured endearments. During the established customs, such as dropping a wine glass, the number of broken pieces predicting how many years of happiness we'd have together, and the constant "*evviva gli sposi*", "hurray for the newlyweds". I felt more and more detached as if intruding on someone else's wedding. I didn't understand any of the short speeches given intermittently by the Italian guests, and although the atmosphere was warm and enthusiastic and my family and friends were participating in the customs, it wasn't enough to make me feel part of it.

'I've hardly spoken to you today,' I told Geoffrey and Marion.

'You look lovely,' Marion said. 'Your parents would have been so proud.'

'I wish–'

Her eyes were dark. 'I know, dear. I wish they could have been here.'

I remembered she'd lost her adored sister, in addition to a brother-in-law she'd regarded as a brother.

Geoffrey squeezed my shoulder and turned away. 'We miss you.'

'I'll visit as soon as possible after we're back in Scotland.'

'Bring Tommaso, too,' he said.

Conversation with friends was snatched and often unsatisfactory, concluded by promises to get in touch when we returned to Edinburgh.

Tommaso rushed up to me. 'It is time to change. You must be quick. Soon the taxi will arrive.'

Now I actually wanted to be on our honeymoon. To be on our own. To make love and feel truly united.

'I forgot to pack perfume,' I told Debs.

She produced a bottle from her bag. 'Have this... It's okay, I have so many perfumes I can never use them all up before they go off.'

'Andy's been offered a job in Australia,' she said while retrieving my going away dress from the wardrobe in the small changing room off the gallery. 'I haven't told Mum and Dad yet. They do so love having the baby around.'

'Which part?'

'Queensland, the Australasian Golf Academy, his dream job. Can you believe it? Before we got engaged, he told me if a job became vacant in Australia he'd want to go. But I never said anything to Mum and Dad.'

She described his job and their plans for buying a house.

'You look fantastic, Rachel. Rust really suits you,' she said as I studied myself in the mirror.

'Debs, if Andy had never mentioned Australia, and out of the blue told you he'd accepted a job there, how would you have reacted?'

She handed me my gold earrings. 'It's hard to imagine him doing anything like that. He's always been so open about it, about everything.'

'But if he hadn't?'

She scrutinised me. 'Is Tommaso secretive?'

A knock on the door spared me from replying. It was Anna. 'Tommaso's getting agitated, Rach. Are you ready?'

I glanced at my watch. 'Heavens...'

The setting sun cast a warm glow over Florence when we left our reception to drive to the airport. Guests were now throwing mesh bags containing sugar-coated almonds.

'*Bomboniera*, wedding favours,' Tommaso told me. 'It is a tradition to avoid childlessness,' and as I stiffened, he added, 'It is okay. I told you I do not mind if we don't have children.'

During our drive, Diana's fears about us rushing things came to mind, and momentarily my entire body trembled. I forced myself to breathe deeply. Tommaso loved me. He would be a fine husband. Within a year, I'd feel I'd known him all my life and wonder why I'd been anxious. Nevertheless, I continued to hear Debs' words: "Andy's always been open about everything" during our flight to Napoli.

Our honeymoon began in a tranquil old hotel on the outskirts of Napoli, the bedroom facing Mount Vesuvius. On our first night, we sat on the balcony, accompanied by the sound of crickets, scent from lemon trees pervading the air. When we'd finished the wine, Tommaso reached for my hand and wordlessly we stepped into our room. Finally, while making love, I experienced what I'd been waiting to feel all day: joy.

We spent several days strolling round galleries and gothic churches, Tommaso regaling me with enthusiastic descriptions of their history. Late afternoons, however, were my favourite times, away from dusty streets and chaotic traffic and the endless blasting of horns. We sat under a canopied table in the hotel gardens, looking over to palm and lemon trees, or swam in the open-air pool. The waft of fragrance was heady, and as the sun moved west, the immediate landscape changed, throwing a palm tree into relief, highlighting a pink bougainvillea or hibiscus. Between gaps in the trees, we could view the sea, its changing colours.

Then I found myself thinking ahead to our life in Scotland. Studying would absorb much of my time, so it was important for Tommaso to integrate quickly. He could find work at a leather business in Edinburgh. Or perhaps at the Italian Cultural Institute. Or he might decide to start his own business.

A happy future stretched ahead.

∼

Morning mist clung to the rocky headland as I stepped onto the balcony. Behind me, jagged limestone peaks of the Lattari mountains soared into an unblemished blue sky. Every day I loved waking to such glorious views, such lovely weather, and couldn't imagine ever taking it for granted.

Below, several scrawny cats stretched lazily on a flat cement roof. My husband of eight days slumbered on our wrought iron bed, a sheet half covering him.

After showering and dressing quietly, I slipped out of the apartment. The stone alley leading to the main road round Positano was still in shadow, but from open windows, already I could hear and smell signs of lunch preparations: the musical babble of female voices; chopping of vegetables; the smell of garlic and sizzling oil.

At the grocer's on Via Rosa, I ordered a tomato and mozzarella sandwich. Giuseppe nodded and smiled, as he'd done the day before and the one before that, starting the ritual: slicing a crusty roll; cutting through oval tomatoes, yielding slices of scallop-edged succulent red flesh; sprinkling salt on the tomato before adding glistening slices of mozzarella; trickling olive oil onto the bare side of the roll and lastly, pièce de résistance, laying on dark green basil leaves.

Every morning, I indulged in one of these delights. Savouring each mouthful. Tommaso usually slept longer than I did and I relished this time on my own. At first, I'd considered asking for the sandwich without salt and oil, but refrained, reluctant to diminish an Italian experience. To portray myself as simply another holidaymaker unwilling to embrace local eating habits.

From our stocked fridge, I could have made something similar myself. Having it prepared by Giuseppe, however, allowed me to exchange greetings with him. To deliver a few faltering statements about the weather or a newspaper headline.

'*Buona giornata*, have a nice day, signora,' Giuseppe said, when I left with my sandwich.

'*Grazie.*'

'*Prego,* you're welcome.'

I then wandered down the road to one of the myriad staircases around the old town. Sitting on its worn, shiny steps, I ate my breakfast, while watching the boat skimming the sea to Amalfi, a neighbouring town.

As soon as we arrived at our accommodation in the old cliffside town of Positano, I'd known it was Tommaso's home. The rooms felt lived in. Masculine, certainly, with an absence of fabrics and plants, but ones regularly inhabited. An atmosphere hard to create in an apartment used infrequently, regardless of how much effort had been put into achieving homeliness. He'd grinned sheepishly when I asked him. Then pointed to a parcel on the table.

It was another leather jacket, this time a beautiful cream one with a Mandarin collar and angled pockets.

'You're spoiling me,' I said.

'Spoiling? This means that I damage you?'

'I mean you are giving me too many gifts.'

'*Capisco*, I understand. Okay, I love to spoil you. Put it on. Please.'

It fitted beautifully, of course. All the leather goods Tommaso had given me so far were perfect: the tan jacket, a black shoulder bag, olive-green sandals.

From our first day here, we slipped into a leisurely lifestyle: eating lunch on the balcony, before catching the boat to Sorrento or Amalfi, sometimes further afield to the delightful islands of Ischia and Procida. Early evening meanderings around Positano, stopping to admire ceramics or paintings on display, to buy ice cream, to study a restaurant menu. We made love with heightened feeling as thunder blasted the air around us and waves crashed to the shore. Apart from his going to Mass, we did practically everything together.

On this perfect morning, sitting on the staircase, camera poised for action, I remembered the transience of my time here. It was the second week of September. Time to organise flights and Tommaso's surplus luggage. To switch into studying mode. Decisions to make about his apartment here: renting it out? Selling it? I'd raised these issues at the start of our honeymoon but always the conversation deviated to another topic.

As for our future home, I'd made a list of work to do: replacing the bedroom and sitting room carpets with sanded floors; repainting the intricate cornice of the sitting room; making the bay window more of a feature. From the Architectural Salvage Yard, I would find a moulded front door in keeping with the others in the tenement. Finally being able to dump the cheap veneer one installed before my time. Other potential improvements crowded my head, the prospect of sharing my home with Tommaso an incentive to achieve its potential. In a year's time, my flat – our flat – would be amazing.

A year after Steve moved in, he'd offered to lift the sitting room carpet and clean the floorboards. It would take time, he'd warned me, launching into an explanation about cleaning and sanding, scraping and sealing. And all before he could varnish or stain the wood. Initially I'd agreed, then panicked about the amount of work. The subtext, a knowing friend pointed out, was that I didn't want him living with me.

Church bells ringing out returned me to the present. Back at the apartment, Tommaso was on the phone, speaking in rapid Italian. He ended the call when he saw me.

'*Buongiorno, amore,*' he said, kissing my hair. 'Did you enjoy your breakfast?'

'An extra basil leaf today. I'm getting used to fresh herbs. I'll use these at home now – no more dried stuff. And I love balsamic glaze, no more balsamic vinegar for me.... Was that your mother you were speaking to? How is she? Has she had her surgery yet?'

In all the busyness of the previous weeks, I hadn't often asked about my mother-in-law and now felt ashamed of such self-centredness.

'*Si, si,* the doctors have repaired her hip.'

'Is she having physiotherapy? I can–'

'I don't know. I did not ask.'

'If she hasn't, I can send her some exercises to do. But when am I going to meet her? I'm so keen to meet your whole family.'

'When it is a good time. Today we will visit Ravello.'

'You're on holiday now and we don't have much time here. Why don't we go down this weekend? It's only an hour's flight. And it is so much easier to go from here than Edinburgh.' I rubbed his arm persuasively.

Frowningly, he pulled away. 'I will speak to my father soon. Today we go to Ravello.'

'I feel like having a lazy day. Can't we go tomorrow?'

He poured me a glass of grape juice. 'We must go today. I will drive.'

'I'd rather take the boat.'

'*Si, si.* But I have a reason to drive. I have a surprise for you. I'll explain you later.' He scrutinised my clothes. 'You must change.'

I sipped my juice. 'I'm comfortable like this.'

His tone harboured an edge and his jaw became more

prominent. 'Ravello is a smart place. Where do you buy your strange clothes?'

I hesitated. 'Charity shops.'

'What are charity shops?'

I grabbed a dictionary and found the right page. *'Negozi solidali.* Perhaps you don't have them here. They sell second-hand clothes.' Again I reached for the dictionary. *'Vestiti di secondamano.* And other things: books, ornaments.'

'You buy clothes which someone else wears before?'

'The money goes to good causes. Everyone benefits.'

Tommaso screwed up his nose.

'I wash them after I've bought them, several times, if necessary,' I added, annoyed to be defending myself. 'But I'll wear something smart today.'

I suppressed a sigh. It constantly amazed me how much importance Italian men, and especially my husband, attached to appearance. Tommaso noticed if I conditioned my hair, if my jewellery complimented my outfits, whether or not my collars sat neatly. He could discuss skin care more knowledgeably than any of my women friends. On balance, I liked it as it made me feel truly seen, feminine. But I missed being able to leap out of bed and throw on yester-day's jeans and sweatshirt, shove a scrunchy round my hair.

When I emerged from the bedroom in a green linen dress, my hair tied back with a matching scarf, he nodded approvingly. *'Si, si,* this is better.'

'What's the surprise?'

'You are so beautiful. Now even more men will look at you. It makes me jealous.'

'If they stare, it's because of my red hair,' I said. But I was aware of looking better. Of the red-haired people I knew, I was the only one who could take a tan, and I knew it suited me. And with Tommaso's encouragement, I was choosing more flattering colours to wear.

We'd never driven to Amalfi before and now I understood why. Tommaso had to swap his cavalier style of driving to one of care while navigating one hairpin bend after another, passing villas that clung to the hillside. From the open window I could smell the salty tang of the sea.

In Amalfi, I got carried away with my camera. Tommaso, as always, infinitely patient as I adjusted shutter speeds and pondered over whether or not to use a filter.

Remembering the night before – it must have been after three when we finally got to sleep – I smiled at him. He didn't return my smile. Maybe he, too, was conscious of our honeymoon flying past so quickly.

'We don't have to go on to Ravello,' I said at lunch. Perhaps it would be more sensible to return to Positano after we'd finished eating. Make plans for Edinburgh, discuss my thoughts for the flat and my business ideas. Woo him with descriptions of gastronomic indulgences to be found in Valvona and Crolla.

Tommaso smiled, eyes sparkling. 'Remember that I have a surprise for you.'

The drive up to Ravello took twenty minutes. Having parked the car outside the ancient portals, he took my hand, strolling along the road, humming an opera, as if longing to burst into song. At thirty-one he was only three years older than me, but often seemed younger.

As I paused to gaze at the white and terracotta villas with their red pantile roofs and the dramatic backdrop of mountains, my husband's voice broke into my thoughts.

'Famous people have stayed here: Tennessee Williams and Greta Garbo. This evening we will eat dinner at the restaurant where Jackie Kennedy ate. Then you will know the surprise.'

'Come on, tell me now.'

Beaming, he slipped his arm round my shoulder. 'A concert. It is Brahms' *A German Requiem.* We will listen to the music in the gardens of Villa Rufolo. Are you happy?'

'It's years since I've been to an outdoor concert.'

Nevertheless, something unidentifiable bothered me.

After dinner, we walked to the Villa Rufolo where we took our seats on the terrace. The sky was starry, and sitting so far above the sea seemed an appropriately dramatic setting for the concert.

The soprano, in fact the whole choir, was amazing, but each time I turned to look at Tommaso, his expression was disturbingly unfathomable.

From deep within my subconscious, I heard myself say: 'We'll miss all this in Edinburgh.'

When he didn't respond, my niggle took shape.

On the drive back to Positano, we stopped for a nightcap in Priano. I sipped my wine, hoping to draw courage from it. Tommaso drank a double espresso. Two flies wouldn't leave us alone, however, and exasperation from this combined with my anxiety, caused my mood to plummet.

'We need to plan for Edinburgh,' I said, more abruptly than I'd intended.

'*Si, si*, we talk about this,' he said, waving his arm dismissively.

Perhaps he'd been thinking the same thing. My heart rate slowed. Besides, we didn't have to sort out everything now. Just agree first steps.

Had he informed his company? Might they expect him to work several months' notice? Being so engrossed in our romance and wedding, I'd never asked him many practical questions.

'I presume you've resigned from your job.'

Silence. His head shot up, chin jutting forward. Not positive signs.

I forced myself to stay calm. '*Have* you handed in your notice?'

He leant over and took my hand. '*Amore*, I want us to live in Italy.'

## 8

I t was a moment before I could speak. 'We agreed to live in Edinburgh.'

Avoiding eye contact, Tommaso said, 'There are many reasons for staying here. I have a job. My family is in this country.'

'But I have my photography degree.... We agreed.'

It was hard to be coherent. My new husband felt like a stranger. It was obvious now he'd had no intention of relocating to the UK. Hence spending most of our honeymoon in Positano. His deviousness upset me as much as the prospect of living in Italy. I felt sick and so, so cheated.

'This is a pleasant life. You see for yourself how beautiful Italy is, how friendly are the people.'

'Why didn't you tell me before?'

He reached for my hand. 'I wanted to give you time to love my country. Your life is with me. I am your husband.'

I withdrew my hand. 'What's this – the eighteenth century?'

He straightened in his chair, eyes narrowing. 'These are Italian customs.'

'But *I'm* not Italian.'

He flinched and reached again for my hand. '*Amore*, please,' as if I were the unreasonable one.

Lashing rain hit us when we left the bar, and below the coastal road, waves thundered onto the shore. We said nothing for the remainder of the drive. Back in the apartment, I plonked myself down on the sofa, ready to list my reasons why we should live in Edinburgh. To my dismay, however, Tommaso emerged from the bathroom, announcing he was going to bed. I could see he was tired and that further talking this evening would be pointless, so I sat in the kitchen, drinking coffee, risking insomnia. In bed, I put my hand on my husband's arm. He didn't respond.

'I don't speak Italian.'

'You can learn,' he said sleepily.

The following day Tommaso went to an important meeting in Napoli, having already apologised about this happening during our honeymoon. That morning, on the balcony, I imagined living here, determined his behaviour wouldn't affect my decision. Never before had I appreciated how much my life in Edinburgh meant. My family and friends. My flat. Not to mention the photography degree I was about to start. Tommaso didn't understand its importance to me. Besides, how did he imagine I'd spend my time in Italy? Lunching with friends? Once I'd made any. Hosting elegant dinner parties? He'd no right to expect this of me.

And yet it was beautiful here – different to the beauty of my home city, but a place where many would love to live.

'I'll give it a year,' I told him the following evening. 'If it doesn't work out, we move to the UK. And I won't change my mind about that. Really, I won't.'

His eyes shone. 'You won't regret it.'

Once my Italian improved, perhaps I could study a basic

photography course here. And I'd have to find work. Even if I did make friends quickly, I wouldn't become one of those "ladies who lunch".

My flight to London was delayed and I caught the last day train to Edinburgh with minutes to spare. The buffet car was closed, and a signal failure south of York resulted in further delay. When I eventually let myself into my flat, it was a strange feeling, knowing I'd only be there for several weeks.

I recalled my delight when my offer for it was accepted. The flat had whispered to me as I walked round it on my first of two visits: its spacious sitting room with bay windows and intricate cornice; the roomy kitchen. Even the tiny internal bathroom didn't detract from my enthusiasm, as immediately I pictured its green walls softened by candle-light. It had been mid-autumn and across the playground of the community school, a row of orange and yellow oak trees glowed in the sunlight.

Back in it again, ten years after buying it, I appreciated it as much as ever, perhaps more so, due to my changed situation. During the first week, aided by a neighbouring DIY aficionado between jobs, I removed the sitting room carpet, cleaned between the boards and sanded the floor. Not as thoroughly as Steve would have done, but adequate enough for the moment. Lastly, I retrieved a Turkish rug from the hall cupboard and laid it. It fitted perfectly. Which only increased my sadness. I wanted to live here with Tommaso. I wanted to study photography. To spend time with my friends and family.

On a corkboard in the kitchen, I studied the tickets for a

jazz concert at the Usher Hall in November, with a note beside them saying: *Liz and Charlotte at Dishoom after.*' A reminder to renew my subscription to the Film Guild. A photo I'd taken of a group of children at the refugee organisation where I volunteered.

In the evenings when Tommaso and I Skyped, I felt tugged between two worlds, the one with him in Positano, and the familiar one, less vibrant but full of emotional anchors, continuity and purpose. If he detected my turmoil, he didn't question it. And the fact he hadn't asked when I would return to Italy suggested he understood what was going on. Would be wondering if I'd return. Each time I planned to reassure him, his deception triggered my residual anger. Yet I was deeply in love with him.

Conversations with friends about my move to Italy had provoked a range of opinions, depending on their life views. Most of them thought I should give it a go but insist on coming back to the UK if it didn't work out.

A week later, I'd found tenants; secured my possessions in the box room; put financial arrangements in place. Rental income would provide a degree of financial independence. A huge relief. While home, I'd thought a lot about what I'd do in Italy. Then, having apologised to the university for cancelling my place so late on, the course administrator had suggested I sign up for a distance learning degree in photography. I had. With a goal, I now felt better about returning to Italy.

That evening I had dinner with Marion and Geoffrey. Debs had finally told them about Australia, and I knew my aunt, in particular, was struggling. Obviously, my news wouldn't help, but they deserved to hear it face to face. The one thing that made it easier was my longing for Tommaso.

With the passing days, I missed him increasingly, our regular Skypes only heightening my yearning.

I waited until we were eating before telling my aunt and uncle about Italy. Unseasonably warm for September, we were eating in their back garden, fragrant with late flowering honeysuckle. Reluctant to paint Tommaso negatively, I presented my news as a joint decision.

Geoffrey was first to react.

'Italy's close compared to Brisbane,' he said jovially. 'We can visit easily enough, even for a long weekend.'

'You'll always be welcome. You were so kind, taking me in when Mum and Dad died.'

Marion was staring over at the rose bed, giving herself time, then her expression became stoical as she helped herself to more salad. 'We've never regretted it.'

Love for them overwhelmed me and all I could do was hug them both.

That night I wept while lying in bed in my old room. Triggered, I suspected, by the Mornay French Fern soap on the corner basin, a scent strongly associated with childhood. I wept for my parents, for the baby whose life I'd ended. For the country I'd chosen to leave. The depth of my emotion shook me.

Tommaso's body was obscured by fragrant pink lilies when he met me at Napoli airport. As we drove along the Salerno peninsula, the sea calm, the moon low, I felt excitement. Before reaching Positano, he stopped the car in a lay-by, rushed round to the passenger seat and pulled me out. For a while we stared over the town, its cluster of houses straddling the gorge, the mountains – invisible in the darkness bar the occasional twinkling light– almost palpable.

'I am so happy that you returned to me,' he said.

'Me, too. But you must be honest with me from now on. Otherwise, our relationship won't work.'

He hesitated before saying, '*Amore*, of course.'

After dinner, we snuggled up on the sofa, the smell of candle wax mingling with that of wine and coffee. Later, we made love as if we'd been apart for longer than several weeks.

## 9

The woman in the apartment block at the end of Via Sorrento took so long to answer the buzzer that I turned to leave. Then the main door opened.

'We've been having problems with the entryphone,' she said. 'I'm Omera de Lucco.'

'Rachel Grosvenor.'

Omera, in her late fifties, I reckoned, had dark eyes and greying hair twisted into a French roll. She was dressed in an ankle-length striped cotton skirt, a loose top, accessorised with chunky beads and bangles. Having hastily closed the door of another room, she showed me into an eggshell blue sitting room with a wrought iron balcony overlooking the sea. In one corner stood an easel and a blank canvas, palettes of oil colours, cleaning rags and bottles of chemicals littering the floor.

In another corner, a large cage contained two African Grey parrots. As I stared at them, one of them squawked '*Gelato*', and the other hopped on the perch, screeching

'*Tiramisu*'. I laughed, and to my enormous surprise and pleasure, heard them imitate my laugh so accurately it could have been mine.

Omera indicated I sit. 'Okay, Rachel, convince me why I should teach you Italian. I don't like timewasters. I believe in teaching grammar, so if you're only interested in learning how to ask for a coffee or directions to the nearest beach, I'm not the teacher for you.'

I returned her steely gaze. 'If this was all I wanted, I'd use the section in my guidebook. Fortunately, for you, I'm Scottish and accustomed to direct communication or I'd be out of your apartment by now.'

Omera's eyes widened then she laughed. 'We'll be a perfect match. Tell me about yourself.'

'Okay... so, to summarise, I married an Italian about six weeks ago, we got together quickly. I don't know how long we'll be here but I want to integrate.'

'Where are you from?'

'The UK, Edinburgh. I came over to visit friends in Florence and–'

'And fell in love.... What chance does a young woman have of escaping love when she visits Italy? It happened to me, too, but we divorced many years ago.' Omera was gathering up scraps of paper and empty paint tubes. She gave a half-smile, eyes glinting. 'The locals regard me as eccentric. I don't fling my arms about or have histrionics over the smallest thing. I'm a painter but I also teach Italian.'

I studied the room again, this time noticing the Indian throws and a painting of the Golden Temple in Amritsar.

She noticed. 'I'm Indian as you will have observed. I return there when I can to see my family – they live in Kashmir.'

Kashmir! A connection. I sat forward in the comfy

armchair. 'My parents met in Kashmir and they lived in Shimla after they married – I was born there. I'd love to go back to Shimla, and to see Kashmir.'

'You should. All the hill towns are lovely, but Shimla is my favourite.'

Omera discussed the options for teaching, we agreed on two lessons a week and to begin in two days' time.

While she retrieved her teaching materials, a photo on the small table near the window caught my attention. It featured a priest, in a black cassock, standing by a lake with a backdrop of snowy mountains. I lifted the photo. The man had brown hair cut short and striking green eyes. He resembled Omera but his skin was lighter. About forty, I reckoned.

'That's Pasha, my half-brother.'

'It's a powerful photo,' I said, eyes lingering on this priest, my hands stroking the amber frame.

'We share our mother. Pasha's father is British.'

At home again, I clicked on Tommaso's work number, then switched off my phone. My news could wait until he returned from Napoli this evening. Too excited to settle to anything cerebral, instead I blitzed our apartment, thinking ahead to the time when my Italian would be reasonable enough to immerse myself here. The last place to tackle was his study. I'd only been in it twice, on both occasions with him, his manner territorial.

This afternoon I welcomed the opportunity to study the room in more depth. What interested me most, apart from its tidiness, was his music system which included a record player, and the cabinet of records – most of them classical, many opera, everything alphabetically arranged. Two index boxes of cards sat on the cabinet, each one containing information about the record: composer, principal singer, pianist etc. The saying came to me: *external order, internal disorder*. I dismissed it.

The room was dust-free, the tiled floor shining. Nothing to be cleaned here. His sanctuary. His man cave.

That evening, Tommaso listened silently while I babbled away about Omera and her parrots.

'She's blunt, feisty,' I added. 'But I like that.'

'How much will these lessons cost?'

'Fifty euros.'

He frowned. 'That is 400 euros each month.'

'You insisted we live in Italy. Aren't you pleased I've organised something?'

'There is also your photography course.'

'I'll pay for the course myself.... The lessons will last ninety minutes so it's more than reasonable. Besides, she has to plan lessons, and mark my homework... Are we short of money?'

Tommaso had questioned my spending before, despite his frequent extravagances.

But today he wouldn't be drawn into a conversation about money, and after a while I dropped the subject.

My days were developing a routine. The online photography degree had begun and I now devoted three hours each morning to it. Initially the topics covered things I already knew, but it was useful revision to read again about the basics of cameras and lenses, photoshopping and other topics. At times, though, when I realised I was missing out on the social aspects of studying, resentment towards Tommaso surfaced. When this happened, I'd go onto the year Facebook page and talk to other students, which helped me feel less isolated. And once I'd begun my Italian classes, my afternoons would be busier.

'Omera says I have a good accent,' I mentioned one night at dinner. 'And I'm quick to learn. She thinks I'll be comfortable in Italian by summer.'

Tommaso nodded.

'But I need more practice in speaking and listening in Italian. Perhaps we could have two days a week of speaking Italian together. What do you think? And we could watch DVDs in English with Italian subtitles. Or vice versa. Omera thinks–'

He pointed to my plate. 'Why are you not eating?'

'You do want me to become fluent?'

He whipped back his head. 'Of course I do. Now, please eat. We are meeting friends at Peppe's for grappas and ice cream.'

I took several more mouthfuls of food before replying. 'I'm tired... One drink only. Okay, let's go.'

He studied my clothes. 'You don't want to change?'

'No.'

At Peppe's, Tommaso introduced me to Natalie and her French husband, Louis, and immediately I warmed to them. Natalie, tall, slim and glowing with health, was a physiotherapist working part-time at an organisation which offered support to refugee children. It was named *Sorgente*, which means "source", she explained. Louis was the lawyer for Tommaso's firm. They hadn't attended our wedding due to being overseas.

'Do you miss nursing?' Natalie asked.

'Sometimes. But I was burnt-out.'

Natalie's sympathetic expression encouraged me to elaborate. 'We were always short staffed.... Always bringing in agency nurses who obviously didn't know the patients. There was so little time to give emotional support. Now it's a relief not to be under such pressure.'

'What sort of photography are you interested in?' Louis asked.

'Until now, mainly celebrations: graduations, weddings, a few bar mitzvahs.' I broke off, conscious of embellishing my situation. I'd done no more than six commissions, and mainly for friends. 'But I want to branch out into landscape photography, urban and country. I've gone a bit crazy with my camera since arriving here.'

'Did you study photography?' Louis asked.

'I'm doing an online degree. My Italian isn't adequate enough to study here.'

Tommaso must have detected something in my tone because he said, 'Rachel was going to study photography in Edinburgh, but now she is here in Italy....'

I struggled to contain my irritation. Now Natalie and Louis would think I was the type of woman who cancelled her plans to fit in with her man. Which, of course, I had done.

'You should enrol yourself at the Photography Institute of Napoli,' Louis suggested. 'You will meet other people studying photography. Some of them will speak English.'

'This is a good idea,' Tommaso said. 'Rachel is learning Italian, but it will take time.'

'Are you happy to have commissions?' Natalie asked.

'If it's for a good cause.'

'Something that has gravitas,' Louis said.

'Exactly. But perhaps not at the moment. I'm trying to

keep a structure to my day, for the course and my Italian lessons. But thanks for thinking about it.'

'I distract Rachel,' Tommaso said.

It was true. Sometimes he worked from home, and on a particularly beautiful day, might suggest we drive into the mountains, or to one of the other coastal towns for lunch and a walk. He'd then work in the evening. For me this was more difficult, thriving as I did on routine. Which to date, I'd had – school, nursing college and then nursing itself. Yet those day trips with Tommaso were so enjoyable that I couldn't turn them down. "Carpe diem," my father had often quoted, and since my parents' sudden deaths, I'd realised nothing in life is guaranteed. It was impossible to be certain that what we had today we'd have tomorrow.

Consequently, when I heard Tommaso's footsteps on the marble tiles, my heart leaped with a child's excitement. My husband didn't walk. He strode. And the sight of him striding towards me always triggered a frisson. It wasn't a soldierly walk. Yet it conveyed so much purpose, so much energy, that it was almost sexual. And ten minutes after he'd appeared in the spare room that I'd appropriated as my study, we'd be off somewhere, like pupils released early from school. He never decided the night before that this was what he wanted to do. Not for a weekday trip.

Before parting company that evening, Natalie invited me to have lunch with her the following week. For the first time, I felt more integrated as we walked back to the apartment. Strange how one invitation could make such a difference.

'I was thinking we could spend Christmas in Paris,' I said to Tommaso one evening after we'd watched a French film. 'Or

Vienna, or Zurich. Somewhere snowy and romantic.... But you'll want to be with your parents and sisters. That would be fun, too.'

'Don't you want to see your family in Edinburgh?'

'Would you like that?'

He nodded. 'Yes, and because it's a popular time to travel, you should book flights soon.'

His lack of concern about being with his family at Christmas surprised me. Nevertheless, the following day I spoke to Marion to check we'd be welcome, then booked flights.

Several times over the next few weeks, Tommaso arrived home from work with parcels that he wouldn't let me open.

'He's so charming and attentive,' Marion said, the day after we arrived in Edinburgh. 'And generous.'

I laughed. Tommaso had peppered them with gifts – candied fruits, bottles of Marsala, a Venetian glass decanter, Sicilian lace. He had remarked on the elegance of my aunt's silver necklace and matching bracelet. Asked my uncle where he bought his shirts – taken aback when a startled Geoffrey replied that Marion bought most of his clothes and he believed she shopped at Marks and Spencer.

On Christmas Day, Tommaso ate his plate of traditional fare in record time. 'What a delicious dinner, Marion.'

The warm dining room smelled of lilies, sausages and used Christmas crackers, reminding me of Christmases past when our families got together, either at ours or Marion and Geoffrey's.

She beamed with pleasure. 'A bit different to what you eat at Christmas in Sicily, I expect.'

'Equally good,' he said, lifting the last cracker and indicating I pull the other end.

Later, he helped Marion and Anna clear away while I played chess with Geoffrey. Not knowing whether to be pleased or exasperated by his willingness to assist, given his laziness on the domestic front at home.

On Boxing Day, Tommaso insisted on making a traditional Sicilian meal. While he was cooking, Geoffrey, Marion, Anna and I drove to Perthshire for a long walk. There, I produced my camera, delighted to be photographing my family again.

'You'll warn us if we're featuring on your website, won't you, dear?' Marion asked, laughingly.

Anna slipped an arm round my shoulders. 'We should charge.'

When we returned, an appetising aroma of cooked cheese and garlic filled the house. Shortly after, Tommaso served us baked aubergine with parmesan, followed by *Polpettone alla siciliana,* a form of meatloaf. For dessert he had made pastries filled with almonds.

'It's lovely to see a man cook,' Marion said, smiling at him. 'I've suggested Geoffrey learn but he won't consider it. You can imagine how twitchy he got when two of his friends told him they were going to classes. He was terrified they'd be successful.'

'Brian gave up after learning to make a cheese sauce,' Geoffrey intervened. 'He's still got bits of sauce on his shoes.'

Later, while Tommaso and Geoffrey talked, Marion, Anna and I played Scrabble, the King's College *Festival of Nine Lessons and Carols* on quietly in the background.

Hearing this never failed to transport me back to childhood Christmas Eves: Mum peeling chestnuts for the turkey stuffing; me cutting apples and bananas for fruit salad; the

smell of brandy added to the Christmas pudding and those
of the lemongrass, lime zest and ginger she'd put in the fruit
salad. The kitchen warm from oven heat.

Dad appearing with yet another bottle of wine,
consulting with Mum over choice. Becoming merrier each
time he popped his head round the door. Sometimes he'd
wear antlers, other times, a Santa beard. Once he wrapped a
plastic snake round his neck, causing Mum to drop the pan
of cranberry sauce, leaving sticky patches on the kitchen
floor for weeks afterwards. Another time, my mother threatened to leave him if he didn't stop playing his Swanee
whistle to accompany *Once in Royal David's City.*

'I want to take you to a concert,' Tommaso said, two days
before we left. 'And there are many famous places I haven't
seen in Edinburgh.'

'You'll wear yourself out,' my uncle muttered.

Geoffrey had a point. Apart from Christmas Day and
Boxing Day, Tommaso had insisted we sightsee as much as
possible, and I was exhausted. We'd visited three exhibitions, looked round the Royal Yacht Britannia that I found
boring but he loved. We'd been on a guided tour of the
Castle and the Old Town, visited Holyrood Palace and spent
two hours in Jenners where, to my surprise, he purchased
only an overpriced wallet.

To my delight, our stay had been an unqualified success.
Tommaso had fitted in well, chatting often to Geoffrey,
showing Anna how to make the almond pastries she'd raved
about, and impressing Marion with his compliments and
willingness to help with the dishes.

On the return flight to Italy, one thought occupied my
mind. 'When will I meet *your* family, Tommaso?'

He waved away my question like an irritating fly. 'Why is
this so important?'

'Why wouldn't it be?'

'Soon. I will take you there soon.'

'Actually, you've been saying that for months. I want to come next time you go to Sicily.'

Perhaps he simply didn't get on with his family. And for a proud Italian man, this would be difficult to admit. Sooner or later, though, he'd have to explain the problem. As his wife, I had the right to know.

Amalfi heaved with weekend visitors as I got off the boat. From the outset, it had been one of my favourite places. Regardless of the rows of sun loungers and umbrellas on its Marina Grande, and the inevitable tourist traps, I preferred the atmosphere here to that of Sorrento. I loved the square of whitewashed buildings, the backdrop of bare rock, the dominating Roman Catholic Cathedral, imagining it before the days of tourism.

Now I found a pavement café and waited impatiently as cooking smells taunted my hunger. The other customers were mainly older, but one couple of similar age to me, caught my attention. I was struck by the energy their conversation conveyed: his expansive hand movements; her rapid head nodding as she listened to him; his rapt attention when she spoke.

My thoughts turned to Tommaso and our relationship. Things had changed. We didn't argue, and our lovemaking felt as urgent as ever, but he took little interest in how I spent my time. On the three or four days he commuted to Napoli, I always asked him how work had gone. But he seldom reciprocated. We didn't talk now in the way we had done initially.

Furthermore, he often napped on Saturday and Sunday afternoons, emerging later from the bedroom in irritable mood. When I urged him to accompany me on a walk at those times, he found a reason to refuse. If I questioned him about all this sleep, he pointed out abrasively that work took a lot out of him. That I should be more understanding.

Occasionally I wondered how much Tommaso was even conscious of my presence at dinner. He would praise my cooking, especially the Indian dishes, then fall silent, a preoccupied expression tenanting his face. After our meal, he'd often wander onto the balcony, but instead of calling for me to join him as he originally had, I sensed he now preferred to be on his own. On the odd evening when I took the initiative and sat beside him, he'd frown. Once he edged his chair away from mine.

Equally disturbing, he didn't attend Mass so regularly these days.

At least I had my degree to anchor me. The less attention Tommaso paid to me, the harder I worked. And now my daily structure was more embedded. Each morning I studied for three hours. After lunch I practised my Italian or had a lesson with Omera and then wandered round different parts of Positano or further afield, taking photographs which I later sorted into what I could use for assignments and what I might include on my website. Twice a week I went over to the Photography Institute in Napoli to attend a class, use the library or meet up with some students I'd got to know. Occasionally, I accompanied them when they had photography assignments, participating myself, discussing our results later over a glass of wine. I thrived on the company.

Domestic chores were fitted in around everything else.

'You don't clean our home so much now,' Tommaso had remarked one evening.

'How much time do *you* spend doing that?'

As far as I could see, apart from his study, he did very little housework – and for once he was wise enough not to comment that such activity was an Italian wife's duty. I mopped the tiled floors when the notion took me. And usually prepared a decent home-cooked meal. But my energy was reserved for more creative activities, and for studying.

During the return boat journey this afternoon, I thought about how to raise with him the issue of our changed relationship. Already bracing myself for accusations of being intrusive or worrying too much. Walking back to the apartment, seeing the magnolia trees in flower, however, restored me to peace. Things would be okay.

That night I cooked a special dinner. When we eventually ate, though, instead of displaying his usual enthusiasm, Tommaso picked at his *insalata caprese*, shoving aside the basil leaves.

'Aren't you hungry?' I asked. 'That's the buffalo milk mozzarella, by the way.'

'We shouldn't spend so much money to buy food.'

His comment hit me like a slap. 'Then why did you insist on drinking champagne last week for no obvious reason?'

He shrugged, managed a mouthful of mozzarella.

'Tommaso, I wish you'd tell me if we have money problems. Don't you think I should know about our financial situation?'

'There is nothing to worry about.'

Our following conversation was sporadic and flat, like passengers stuck in a waiting room, conversing through boredom.

When we finished eating, Tommaso retreated to his study. After doing the dishes, I knocked on his door but he didn't reply. Perhaps he'd fallen asleep. I opened the door to find him standing by the window, peering out.

I approached him and slid my arms round his waist. 'You seem different. Is something wrong?'

He pulled away. 'No.'

'Why are you so quiet these days?'

He waved his arm dismissively. 'I explain you. Everything is okay.'

'Come on, Tommaso. We don't talk the way we used to. What's changed?'

Now he was gripping his hands. 'Why do you worry?'

Abruptly he moved to his desk and shoved several folders into a drawer.

'You never ask me what I do during the day,' I said, trying to keep my tone light. 'Why don't you ask about my studying or my Italian lessons?'

'You tell me about these things.'

'But you never take the initiative. When we first met, you always wanted to know what I'd been doing. Every last detail. You were interested in my photographs. I've taken an interest in your designs – when you've let me.'

And I had, often commenting on bags I liked, or shoes. Hoping he'd discuss his ideas with me. Value my opinion.

He returned to the window, opened it and leaned out. I waited. He came back in, closed the window.

'You are like a...' he began. 'I don't know the word. A thing that sticks.... You stick to me. You ask me questions. You want me to ask you questions, what you do, what you feel, what I think. It is too much.'

Anger surged. 'Do we have money problems? One

minute you're buying me expensive jewellery, the next you're implying I spend too much on food.'

He blocked his ears. 'You are my wife. You must not ask questions about what I do.'

'For God's sake, spare me that medieval crap.'

'Stop, stop. This is too much. Go, please go. Please.'

Stunned, I moved towards the door. Then I turned round. He was rummaging in a drawer.

'Go,' he reiterated.

## 10

I t still felt strange being in Tommaso's inner sanctum and my heart beat faster as I scanned the office. As if I might be discovered snooping. Impossible, as he'd left that morning for Sicily.

On previous occasions, the room had been immaculate. This afternoon, envelope files, leather swatches and artists' pads with half-completed designs swamped his desk, his computer shoved to one side. The wastepaper basket overflowed with discarded paper, and at the bottom, to my concern, lay several wine bottles. I hated to think of him drinking on his own.

Something in one of the open desk drawers caught the light – a man's watch. Gold dial, Roman numerals and a brown leather strap, "Elisa" inscribed on the underside of the dial.

I sank onto the sofa, scrutinising the watch. It was modern, so obviously not a family heirloom. My heart raced. Who was Elisa? For a while I sat unmoving, willing myself to stop panicking. Then I returned the watch, leaving the drawer open, as I'd found it.

Half an hour later, worry drove me back to the study where I rummaged through another drawer, unsure of what I dreaded finding. Letters, cards from Elisa? Other evidence Tommaso was having an affair? About to stop, I noticed a brown envelope, lightly sealed, stuck to a piece of plasticine.

Having carefully opened the envelope, I found myself clutching a bank passbook in his name. Dating back several years, it showed up-to-date, regular payments of €600 credited and soon afterwards, debited. I couldn't find any indication of either the source or destination of the money. Could this explain why he gave such mixed messages about our financial situation? His reluctance to discuss it?

As the apartment walls closed in, I grabbed my jacket and left, yearning for my home in Edinburgh, my own space, things within my control. The predictability of my life – occasionally previously bemoaned – now seemed blissfully reassuring: no scary brown envelopes in the post; no secrets awaiting discovery. No one and nothing to hurt me.

The beach was unusually quiet. As I hesitated about where to go for coffee, I noticed Omera waving to me from Da Ferdinando's. She was with a man. The waving became more insistent so reluctantly I went over.

'This is my brother Pasha,' she said, when I reached her. 'And this is Rachel, one of my Italian students. A hardworking one.'

Pasha was wearing a pale green shirt and khaki trousers. A different creature to the cassock-clad figure of the photo in Omera's sitting room. When he stood to shake my hand, I could smell rose cream. His arms were tanned and muscly, and some brown chest hair showed at the top of his shirt where one button remained undone. He seemed so physical, so vibrant, that my first thought – shamefully quick – was how he coped with celibacy.

After a moment, Omera despatched him to order more drinks. Once he'd left, she removed her oversized sunglasses and leaned over the table. 'What's wrong?'

I feigned surprise at the question.

'Rachel, I haven't been teaching you Italian for four months without getting to know you.'

I told her about the watch but didn't mention the bank account.

She tutted. 'You have a right to know. You British...you are so...restrained. If you were Italian, you'd already have shouted at each other.'

'Actually, Tommaso's away at the moment. And I don't want to have such a conversation on the phone.'

'Insist he tell you,' she said with characteristic brusqueness. 'It's probably a woman in his past but you have a right to know.... Where is he?'

'Sicily,' I said wearily, remembering the row we'd had when I challenged him about why he wouldn't take me, an ideal opportunity to meet his family.

When Pasha returned, my thoughts were partly still focused on the watch while we discussed his work in Srinagar: teaching geography in the mission school; supporting refugees; visiting patients in hospital. Omera had told me he studied geography before entering the Church.

'What brought you to Italy?' he asked.

I explained about meeting Tommaso, our speedy romance.

'And are you planning to work here?'

When I told him about my course and described my ideas for a photography business, he asked if I had a studio, at which point Omera chipped in, saying she knew of several for rent in Positano, if I was interested. Having my own space appealed. It would be somewhere to study as well as a creative place. At the moment, I was using the spare room to study in. The more I thought about renting somewhere, the more advantages I came up with.

'Rachel?' Omera reined in my attention. 'We're going to Capri tomorrow. Do you want to join us? We'll take the boat, have lunch, and a walk. Avoiding the ghastly tourist shops, of course.'

I nodded, aware of needing company. Already anxiety about the watch and the bank account was receding. Besides, perhaps Tommaso would reassure me about both these things. As the four o'clock church bells rang out, I felt uplifted, hopeful.

Having made my way up the winding road in record time, I bought the local newspaper before returning to our apartment. There, I sipped my homemade lemonade on the balcony while studying the property ads. Sure enough, I spotted two studios for rent. Both available in three months' time. Perhaps Omera would visit them with me, assist with any negotiations. More than ever, I appreciated my financial independence.

Buoyed by the prospect of a studio, I returned to the essay I'd been working on. It was entitled: *Photography and Narrative*, and I'd been struggling over an introduction. Enthused, I rewrote the lacklustre text.

'We must cancel our boat trip,' Omera told me the following morning. 'Pasha has a sore back.'

I made some sympathetic comments before saying, 'I've seen the ads for the studios. Would you phone and see if you can arrange a time for me to visit? And come with me?'

Half an hour later, she got in touch to say that we could visit both studios that day.

The first one was small with little natural light, a fusty smell, and situated opposite a garage.

'The second one will be better,' she whispered as we left. 'I have a good feeling about it.'

'I hope you're right. Actually, the more I think about it, the more appealing it is to have a studio. 'Something about valuing myself, I suppose.' And having a separate space unconnected to Tommaso, I thought, but didn't say.

Omera's hunch proved correct. The second studio, above the main town, was an old building, like most of Positano. Its interior white roughcast walls provided an attractive backdrop to the work of the current tenant, a weaver, and with effort, I tore my eyes away from her abstract designs in rich reds, creams and blues littering these walls. One glance at the view of the coastline and I turned to the landlord, saying, 'I'll take it.'

'It won't be vacant for several months,' Costanzo reminded me.

'When can I sign the contract?'

Omera tugged my arm. 'Don't you want to think about this?'

'No need.'

Costanzo smiled. 'I will speak to my lawyer about a contract. Can you return next week? I work in the building next door.'

I couldn't wait to tell Tommaso when he returned from Sicily.

Later that day, I stopped to watch a wedding party in Amalfi. It was led by the bride and groom who were being filmed in dramatic poses – the bridegroom on bended knee handing a rose to his bride; a passionate clinch at the end of the pier. All progressed smoothly as the groom clutched his new wife's hand to lead her into a waltz. Then the crowd gasped as the photographer doubled over in pain. Fortunately, a doctor emerged from the gathering and attended to him. Meanwhile, the bride – who looked about eighteen – was in tears. What would happen to the video recording?

'Can I help?' I asked, showing the newlyweds my camera.

The woman spoke to her husband, who nodded, and I switched my camera to video mode, signalling to them to continue their dance. All smiles again, they slipped into a waltz, tentatively at first, then with more confidence. Several minutes later, I noticed the darkening sky, conferred with them and agreed to go to the reception.

At the hotel, five minutes' walk away, I recorded the meal and the speeches. Soon after the dancing started, a small rotund middle-aged man entered the room, scanned it, agitated fingers running through his thinning dark hair. When he saw me filming, he darted over.

'I am Domenico, the manager of Amalfitana Nozze Magia Videocassetta.'

In faltering Italian, I explained, 'I'm a photographer. I can finish filming the wedding.'

'*Si, si.* There is no one else. I must go home. It is my daughter's birthday party.'

To my relief, the band paused and I offered to show him what I'd already filmed.

Having switched the camera to edit mode, I replayed the last few minutes of footage.

'*Si, si,* is good,' he said.

At the end of the reception, after the couple had driven off, Domenico reappeared. 'The photographer will be in the hospital for several days. It is food poisoning. Can you work again tomorrow, please? There is a wedding in Cetera.'

We discussed money and other practical issues. We also arranged that he'd use me on an ad hoc basis, which suited me perfectly. It would help offset my studio rent.

Tommaso arrived back from his trip to find me asleep on the balcony. A tap on the arm woke me. He was kneeling by the lounger.

'*Amore*,' he said, stroking my hair.

I reached up to hug him. 'You look exhausted.'

'You are tired, too, to fall asleep. The trip was successful. We made important decisions about the restaurants.'

That evening we went to La Roseceno where we sat at an outside table. In the balmy night, the air filled with the scent of jasmine and wine, I forgot my concerns over my husband. And when he asked what I'd been doing during his absence, I was so delighted by his interest that I launched into a description of my studio.

He stared at me for a moment. 'You are not happy with our home?'

'You'll like it when you see it. The light is lovely and it has–'

His eyes narrowed. 'It is so important to be independent?'

Determined to avoid arguing on his first day back, I replied calmly, 'It would be easier to study in a place of my own. And once I build my business, I'll need more space. Don't worry, I'll pay for it.'

'You arranged this yourself? You did not speak to me.'

I took another mouthful of crab, wondering whether or not to mention Omera's role in this. 'Omera helped me.'

'Omera! I wish that you never meet this woman.'

For a while Tommaso sat scowling at his food, then he said, 'It is my responsibility to take care of you.'

'Part of taking care of me is to respect my needs. And I want to have a studio.'

He lapsed into silence again.

Rather than besiege him with questions, I observed him. Minutes later, I heard myself asking about women in his life.

His head whipped back. 'There has never been anyone particularly important. Why do you ask me this question?'

'Come on, no one special that you wanted to marry?'

He shook his head and his face closed down. I refrained from further questioning, relieved to have avoided two potential rows.

After dinner, we strolled along the harbour to our favourite spot at the end of the Spiaggia Grande. There, we sat in silence on the rocks, gazing over to the twinkling lights of the huddled houses. The night chatter of starlings and the slapping of water onto the shore was so peaceful I felt I could remain here forever, my head on Tommaso's shoulder.

And then my inner devil intervened, goading me into dangerous play and I said, 'I found something in your study.'

His expression was horrified. 'My study, my possessions are private.'

Ignoring his barely concealed anger, I continued, 'But you want me to be a domestic goddess, don't you? Someone who keeps our home clean and tidy.... Who is Elisa?'

In the nearby streetlight, his cheek pulse twitched. 'Elisa?'

'I found a watch with her name engraved on it.'

His eyes narrowed and his voice contained an edge. 'I don't want a wife who interferes.'

'As your wife, am I not entitled to know?'

He stood and glared at me. 'Don't search my room. Don't interfere, Rachel.'

I reached out to clutch his arm, to my dismay, mine shaking. 'Tommaso, are you having an affair? Is this why you go away so much?'

'I am not having an affair. This is ridiculous.'

He stormed off, feet displacing mounds of sand. Eventually I followed, my steps heavy, the rushing and sucking noises of the sea no longer calming me.

For the first time in our married life, I slept in the spare room, waking several times from nightmares about thundering horses and colliding planets. When finally I surfaced, my tongue felt dry and cracked, my shoulders sore. It was past nine o'clock. I slipped through to our bedroom, hoping it would be one of Tommaso's home days, that he'd be asleep or showering. The bedroom was empty. As were the other rooms. In the kitchen, I searched for an apologetic note, pleading that he loved me, that he'd be home early and we'd have a pleasant evening. Nothing. On the worktop, his half-empty cappuccino cup, and the crumbs from a pastry.

I packed a bag and left the apartment.

# 11

I trudged up the stone stairway to the main road. Past small, pastel coloured houses and gardens with red bougainvillea. Past wisteria clad walls and vine covered pergolas. Charming scenes that, in my distressed state of mind, increased my sadness. Twice, I stumbled over a sleeping cat. I heard a baby cry, then adult voices tending to it.

The bus journey to Sorrento gave me motion sickness, the combination of winding roads and fatigue, deadly. During the train journey to Rome, I dozed, frequently disturbed by announcements or passengers bumping me as they navigated corridors. Fortunately, the train to Florence was quiet and I slept for much of the three and a half hour journey.

Neither Doug nor Diana answered when I rang from the station. Nevertheless, I took a taxi to their house and pressed the buzzer. No response. I rang again and waited. Doug would be at the hospital but Diana usually worked in her studio into the early evening. Perhaps they were away. On the verge of leaving, I heard the slow shuffle of footsteps on the terrazzo floor. A moment later, Diana opened the door, clad in her lilac kimono, her dark hair dishevelled, her eyes dull.

'Rachel!'

'I tried to phone.... Are you okay? You–'

'I was in bed,' she said, staring at my grip bag.

I followed her into the kitchen where she sat down at the table.

Breaking off a piece of pizza from its cardboard container, she half-heartedly chewed it. Diana never ate pizza.

'Di, what's happened? Are you ill?'

She said nothing. As the silence continued, I joined her at the table and helped myself to a slab of cold soggy tomato and cheese and hard crust.

'Doug had a vasectomy,' she said eventually. 'In California. Before we met.'

I stared at her. 'Oh God, I'm so, so sorry.'

'All these years, we've been...I've been trying for a baby, and he knew it wouldn't happen. All the things I've been *doing* to make it more likely...the herbs, the supplements.'

She was tearing at a kitchen cloth, knuckles white with the effort. I took her hand and gently removed the torn cotton.

We sat in silence for a moment, then I asked, 'How did you find out? Did he just, well...come out with it?'

She stared past me to the window. 'It was last week. I was despairing because I had another period, so I confronted him.... I knew what stuff I'd ordered – you know, how many multivitamins, all the other things – and I knew he *couldn't* be taking them. He'd been up early that day, and two patients had died unexpectedly and he was tired and emotional.... We shouted at each other.... I should have been more sympathetic, I should have... but I couldn't, I didn't...I just didn't have the patience, the energy.'

She broke off and buried her head in her hands. Then she continued, her voice so low I had to lean forward to catch her words. 'Anyway, he just blurted out it wasn't going to happen. That he'd had a vasectomy when he was younger.'

She stopped, bit her thumb, deliberating over what to say next. When she continued, she spoke slowly, clearly, like a teacher conveying important information to a class. 'He was afraid of getting a girlfriend pregnant and he was pretty sure he *didn't* want children.' Once more she stopped. Her desperate expression freaked me out so much that I moved nearer and put my arm round her.

'He said when we got together he could never find the right moment to tell me. He wanted to. He said...can you believe it...? He said that during five years he just couldn't tell me.' She pulled away from me. 'So, he let me think it might just happen because that was easier. Easier than coming clean.'

I now noticed the dirty dishes on the worktop, the grease stains on the floor tiles. The general stuffiness.

'He's staying at the hospital – I can't bear to see him. It's the deceit.... The fact he let me go on *hoping*.'

I could think of nothing helpful to say, so again I put my arms round her and held her for a long time.

That evening we talked and talked as shadows crept over the garden and darkness eventually fell. Diana's pain absorbed her so much that she didn't ask why I'd descended on her. I didn't mind. It felt like visiting a prisoner in her cell of grief. I could get close but not close enough.

∾

'I need to get out of the house,' Diana said. 'Fancy a trip into the countryside?'

During our drive to Chianti, we didn't talk much. Tired from another poor night's sleep, my energy stretched no further than enjoying the scenery. Despite the circumstances, the hazy light and muted colours lifted my mood.

'You seem better today,' I remarked as we picnicked near a vineyard.

Nearby, a large hare with black-tipped ears hovered before running for cover. Overhead a crow cawed.

Diana handed me more bread and cheese. 'I need to get on with my life, decide whether to stay in Italy or go home.'

'You and Doug are definitely finished then?'

'It'd be hard to stay here. So much is associated with him...but there's my work. If I went back to the UK, I'd have to start over. Lose everything I've built here.'

She described the commissions received since her exhibition. Then her expression changed, her eyes darkening. 'A woman contacted me and asked to meet in her home. I don't normally work like this but I agreed. There was something in her voice – a heaviness, a weariness, as if she'd run out of energy but had one more thing she must do.' Diana paused, eyes filling with tears.

'When I arrived, the woman had a distended abdomen as if she'd just had a baby. Anyway, I was about to congratulate her, then I noticed there was nothing to indicate a baby's presence. No cards or flowers. No baby things. No vibe of a baby being around. And no joy on the woman's face. Just a haunted expression which was more than tiredness. She'd had a stillborn child, a girl. She'd taken photographs of her and wanted me to make a sculpture.'

'Oh my God, poor woman.'

'I didn't know what to say,' Diana continued. 'On the one

hand, I was overwhelmed by emotion and sympathy for her. On the other, I didn't know if I could create such a thing. Not that I don't like a challenge in my work. But to do it badly could make things worse for her. She'd had a horrible birth, she hadn't found the midwives supportive – she was a single mum and she sensed they disapproved, and one of the doctors was rude to her – and she had a struggle to persuade them to let her spend time with the baby before they took it away.... She showed me the photos.... So, I agreed. Eventually. But on the condition she'd only pay me if she believed it truly resembled her child.

'I did the sculpture and took it to her. She loved it and wanted to pay me double what we'd agreed. In the end, I wouldn't take any money. It seemed like...I don't know... profiting from her grief. The following day, my period came and I found out about Doug's vasectomy.'

Tears were slipping down my face. Such terrible timing for my friend. Cruel. Desperately cruel.

We were silent for a while.

'I should have visited before,' I said.

'Ironically, the week before I found out, we'd been talking about paying *you* a surprise visit.'

Diana's phone went. She listened for a moment before saying, 'Somewhere neutral... Six-thirty. For coffee, nothing more.'

She clicked off.

'Actually, it must be difficult for Doug, too,' I said. 'Concealing this from you for so long.'

'Whose side are you on?'

'If he comes back with you this evening, I'll move into a hotel.'

She packed away the food. 'There's no need.... I never asked why you came here, Rachel. Is Tommaso away?'

I explained what had happened, but apart from shaking her head several times, she didn't comment. I was grateful she didn't remind me of her warning. We then stretched out under the shade of a poplar tree and drifted off to sleep in the warm, soporific air.

While Diana was out that evening, I continued working on my essay. Having found a helpful book at the Institute of Photography and assembled some thoughts in addition to the course notes, I managed to complete a first draft.

After that, I drifted into the garden and lay on the lounger. Watching lizards scuttling along the stone wall separating Diana's house from its neighbour. Drowning in the fragrance of honeysuckle and rose. On my own now, each thought not embroiled in her situation, I longed for Tommaso. For some communication with him.

Diana returned shortly before eleven while I was clearing away my meal.

'How did it go?'

She bit her thumb. 'I don't know. I don't know *how* I feel.'

She poured herself a large glass of wine, and this mundane act illustrated how much her life – her dreams – had changed. She caught my eye, shrugging as if to say, "No reason not to drink now."

'He wants to come back,' she continued, 'but how can I live with him after what's happened? I don't know.... I'm so tired.'

'Get some sleep.'

She emptied the remains of her wine into the sink and flung her arms round me. 'I'm glad you're here.'

Not until my fourth day in Florence did I realise how much Diana had recently changed over a short period of time. In addition to the most obvious difference – her thinner face with its more prominent cheekbones – she now usually wore her hair up. And although she'd retained her studio uniform of leggings and tunic top, after work she opted for a tailored dress or smart trousers. As if bidding farewell to the phase in her life where she'd wear something comfy and practical for raising a young child.

Her clothes suggested she'd moved on. Not so her manner. Although her smile was as sweet, her face at rest displayed a disconcerting mixture of grief and hardness in her eyes, a furrowing of her brows.

That morning, I mentioned the situation with Tommaso again.

'So, you need to talk to him,' she told me when I'd finished. 'And if he won't tell you, keep asking. You have the *right* to know.'

'Actually, he resents me asking anything. That isn't normal...is it?'

'Where's the spirited person who challenged the chemistry teacher, what was his name? Adams? About not encouraging girls to study science? Or told the deputy head there was no reason not to have a girls' cricket team?'

Where was she indeed?

Diana's landline rang as we were leaving to go out for lunch. 'Get that, would you?' she said. 'If it's Doug, I'm not here.'

It was Allegra. They chatted briefly and Diana's "everything's normal" tone suggested her friend didn't know what had happened.

The phone rang again. 'Let it ring,' Diana said, before lifting the receiver.

From her raised shoulders, I surmised the caller was Doug, so I went into the garden. Several minutes later she came to find me, shaking her head.

'I've agreed he can come round tomorrow – after work.' She gave a hollow laugh. 'How could I be so stupid? Not that it will make any difference. He wanted to make it today.'

'I'll find a hotel.'

She sighed. 'No need.... Do you mind if we skip going out for lunch?'

I followed her through to the studio, watched her don an apron and knead a fresh clump of clay, her expression distant.

Then, without a word, she pushed back the chair and left. I heard the kitchen door open and saw her stumble past the window to the swinging chair. Carefully, she eased her way onto it and rocked backwards and forwards, gazing at the sullen sky, wiping her face.

While debating whether or not to check on her, my eye was drawn to the glass fronted cabinet and the tiny sculptures of people on the lower shelf.

I knelt by the cabinet and peered in. The blue-grey marble figures all depicted pregnant women, from the first breast swelling to the slightly protruding abdomen to the stage shortly before birth. About sixty of them, I reckoned.

What struck me most was the way she'd captured the radiance on each figurine's face.

Diana returned to find me holding one. Her expression was anguished. 'When I found out about Doug, I came in here and that's all I could do. For three days I hardly left the room.'

'Has he seen them?'

She shook her head. 'The awful thing is, I'd hoped it would be cathartic.'

'And it's too late for it to be reversed – the vasectomy?' Even as I asked, I knew the answer. If there'd been any hope of reversal, she would have told me. Wouldn't now be feeling so wretched.

She fiddled with a piece of clay. 'He's tried to, twice. When he went to London recently, you know...for the conference.'

'Have you considered adopting?' Other options?' Again, I knew the answer.

I reflected on my friend's purism: avoiding convenience foods – not even a stock cube, let alone a bottled sauce, ever appeared in her kitchen; often making her own clothes with organically grown materials.

She blew out her cheeks. 'You mean *sperm* donation? No.'

'Di, it would still be part of you.'

She swallowed hard. 'The dream's gone. I'm twenty-nine and this is my life.'

I hated hearing this, but platitudes, however well-intentioned, would have undermined her grief. This cut to the core of her existence. And more than most of the people who tenanted her life, I understood the enormity of her loss.

The sound of crashing woke me and when I crept downstairs, I found a wild-eyed Diana hurling the figurines around her studio. When the last sculpture smashed against the table, she slid down the wall to the ground, so I knelt down and put my arms round her. Once her trembling subsided, she fetched a brush to shovel up the broken marble. Miraculously, one sculpture remained intact, having rolled under the cabinet. A positive sign, perhaps. Furtively, I slipped the figurine into my pocket.

Late that afternoon, I went for a long walk – regardless of what Diana had said, she and Doug needed space. Besides, I needed a change of scene. Confronting my vertigo once more, I climbed the Arnolfo tower in the Palazzo Vecchio and gazed down over the city and the brown waters of the Arno. Today many people were out on stand-up paddle boats, and I watched them cross under the Ponte Vecchio.

Later, while waiting in a park for restaurants to open for dinner, I thought about Tommaso. I'd been away for five days now, and with each passing one, I missed him more. Time to resolve things. Diana was right: he had to talk to me. Even if this resulted in more rows.

After prolonging my dinner with another drink and a second coffee, I returned to find the house in darkness. I could detect no cooking odours or other signs of a recent meal. No cushions in disarray on the sofa. Nothing to indicate Doug had been here, in fact. Now I wished I *had* booked into a hotel. If a reconciliation was underway, I'd rather not be around. Later, as I tried to sleep, I heard the door next to mine open, the loo flushing, then the door closing again. He was in the other spare bedroom.

The next day I woke early, went onto my laptop and booked a train ticket to Napoli. Decision taken, I fell asleep again. When I surfaced for the second time, Diana was in her studio, pale and bleary-eyed, but less tense. As if she'd cried out so much of her pain that nature had intervened to give her a modicum of peace.

'Is Doug still here?'

Expression inscrutable, she said, 'He's desperate for us to get back together.'

'And you're sure you don't want to?'

'He insisted on coming back this evening to talk again. Even though I've told him there's no point. The thing is, I'd forgotten I'm meeting Allegra. So, it'll be you and him for perhaps an hour – he's arriving at eight. Is that okay? I could tell him not to come.'

'It's okay. By the way, I've booked my ticket home. For tomorrow.'

'Great,' she said. 'Not that it isn't nice having you here. Don't take any crap. *Make* Tommaso tell you what's going on. You have the right to know. Ironic, me telling you this,' and she gave a glimmer of a smile.

That evening Doug arrived punctually at eight. From my bedroom window, I watched him linger at the front door, scratching his head, wondering perhaps whether to ring or let himself in. I rushed downstairs and opened the door while he was inserting his key in the lock. We stared at each other, then I invited him in as if he was a normal visitor.

'Where's Diana?' he asked.

I explained she'd be back around nine.

'If I could do anything, I would.... I love that woman so much,' he said. 'Can't bear the idea of not being with her.'

His expression was so anguished I wanted to hug him.

'You should have told her the truth,' I said. I hadn't planned to mention this, but it spilt out.

'Too much of a coward.'

'But Doug, what did you think would happen? That her dream would simply disappear?'

To his credit, he made no attempt to justify his behaviour. Nor did he criticise Diana in any way. As we sat on the patio listening to the crickets, the intermittent noise of traffic, the occasional church bell, we didn't talk much, in fact. When it grew darker, we moved inside again and I sank onto the living room sofa, knackered. Absorbing another person's sadness is draining, even if you're in a good place yourself. And I wasn't.

He sat down beside me, put his arm round my shoulder and pulled me towards him. 'I'm not trying it on.'

I hesitated. He was misguided but not bad.

'One dodgy move....' I warned, leaning back against him.

I remained like that, aware of receiving comfort in addition to providing it.

The door opened and Diana came in, flung off her shoes and adjusted the air conditioning. 'Christ, it's hot for April. I'll get some iced tea. Do you want any, Rachel?'

Doug, having pulled away the moment she entered the room, sat upright, aghast.

I followed her into the kitchen. 'Di, you do know nothing happened, nothing would have happened, don't you?'

She reached into the fridge for a bottle of iced tea. 'If I can't trust *you,* Rachel, who *can* I trust?'

Her comment struck me with tidal force. They *were* washed up.

In the sitting room we sipped the iced tea. Diana was chewing her lip. My back ached, a sign of stress.

'How did your meeting go?' Doug asked Diana.

'Fine.'

Flinching at her brief reply, he persisted. 'Allegra like your ideas?'

'Most of them,' she said, standing. 'I'm off to bed.'

'We were going to talk,' he reminded her.

'Too tired. Anyway, there's nothing left to say.'

Doug's face crumpled as she left the room. Moments later, I heard the bath running.

I patted his shoulder. 'Goodnight.'

'Don't go, please.... Would you talk to her?'

'And say what?' I couldn't look him in the eye. His despair equalled Diana's.

'Has she told you she's leaving me?'

'Doug, she wouldn't tell me before she'd told you.'

But I did feel sorry for him, too. It couldn't have been easy, living with such a lie. I wanted to tell him this but it felt like being disloyal to Diana.

'She won't adopt or use donated sperm. Only chance we've got is if she accepts we won't have sprogs.'

Perhaps Diana was being too uncompromising. By accepting only "homemade" as she described it, she'd ruled out a future for them. But who was I to judge? I hadn't inherited a single maternal gene.

Back in Positano, I found Tommaso on the balcony watching the sun set. In an orange shirt, he looked so handsome that my heart lurched. All I wanted was for our relationship to return to how it had been early on in our marriage.

'I am sorry about our argument, *amore*,' he said, standing to embrace me. 'I worried about you. I didn't know where you were.'

'You could have phoned me or texted.... I'm sorry I left.'

'Please explain me why you left.'

'Not this evening.'

I then updated him about Diana and Doug, without overly dwelling on their sadness. Anxious, perhaps, about triggering an admission on Tommaso's part about wanting to be a father. Despite him having reassured me about this on several occasions.

We agreed to go to a concert the following evening, and when he suggested I buy something smart to wear, for once I didn't protest.

Next day, I caught the eight o'clock bus to Sorrento and the hydrofoil to Napoli. The sunny sky and choppy waves exhilarated me and I arrived in high spirits, determined to find a dress Tommaso would admire. Buying it in the second shop I tried was a positive omen, I told myself.

That evening, Tommaso gazed at me often during the music. My coral dress – stretch jersey with a cowl neckline and side ruche – looked even better in evening light, making me feel young and sassy. After the concert, we walked to our favourite place at the far end of the beach. The sea yielded an earthy aroma, predicting a storm. Still we sat, his arm round me, my head on his shoulder, saying little. I felt the thrill of being with him that I'd experienced during our earlier days.

Several months passed. Happy ones. My studying was going well and my Italian continued to improve with Omera's teaching. She worked me hard, but was quick to praise, especially if she sensed my dejection from slow progress.

Ours was an easy relationship, prompting me to drop in to say "hallo", which often continued with a salad lunch with her friends on her cluttered balcony. An opportunity for me to meet more people. Natalie and I met for coffee regularly, a friendship I valued.

One afternoon, while I was working on an assignment for university, the apartment buzzer went.

'*Si*?'

'*Sono Fabrizio Vitale, sono il padre di Tommaso*, I am Fabrizio Vitale, Tommaso's father.'

Mind racing, I pressed the entryphone to let him into the building. Finally, I would meet one of my in-laws, but I hadn't imagined it happening like this.

Like his son, Fabrizio Vitale was tall and slim, but his hair was greying and cut short. He wore a navy suit and pale orange silk tie.

He extended his hand to shake mine, his dark eyes alert but kindly. '*Sono Fabrizio Vitale. Sono il padre di Tommaso*, I am Fabrizio Vitale, I am Tommaso's father,' he repeated.

'*Sono* Rachel.'

He studied me.

'Tommaso is at his office in Napoli today,' I said.

'You are his cleaner?'

'His wife,' I replied, the strange question failing to register immediately.

'His wife!'

'We were so sorry you couldn't come to the wedding.'

'My son is married?'

'You didn't know....'

## 12

We stared at each other for a moment.

'He...he told me his mother was having a hip operation. And this was why you couldn't come to the wedding.'

'This is true. My wife had surgery last summer.... This marriage, when did it happen?'

'Last year. September 1<sup>st</sup>. How is your wife?'

Signor Vitale shook his head. 'Why did he tell us nothing of this?'

'Please, come in.'

He hesitated, then silently followed me into the apartment.

'This is a shock for me, too,' I said. 'Would you like coffee?'

'When did you marry?' he asked again.

'Last September. In Florence – Firenze.'

Tommaso's father produced a worn photograph from his wallet. It featured a younger, more relaxed Tommaso.

'This is the person you are married to?'

I could have been in a police interview room, defending

myself, but with effort managed to reply pleasantly, 'My husband, Tommaso.'

'Excuse me,' he said. 'I must call my wife.'

I showed him into the sitting room, retreated to the kitchen and shut the door. While waiting for the kettle to boil, I tried not to hear his rapid Italian. Tempted to phone Tommaso. Insist he return home immediately.

The kitchen door opened and Signor Vitale stood there. Now I could see even more of a resemblance between father and son: the hunching shoulders, a slight raising of his right eyebrow, the square jaw. He seemed to have aged over the last ten minutes.

I touched his arm. 'I'm sorry you found out like this. It would have been lovely if you'd been able to come to our wedding.'

He studied me. 'Is there a baby?'

I gulped. 'Signor Vitale, your son pursued me, not the other way round. It was his idea we got married. And no, there is no baby.'

He regarded me more kindly. 'Please forgive me. I was rude. It is a shock. My wife is distressed. She and Tommaso are close. She is upset that he has deceived her, our family.'

He'd deceived all of us.

'Tommaso will be home at seven. But you could phone him at the office, I suppose. Do you have his number?'

Signor Vitale shook his head. 'I am not ready to talk to him. I leave now.'

'Don't go. Please. Not without seeing him. I've wanted to meet you for such a long time. I'm sorry you had to find out like this, but there's no reason why–'

'Why we should not be friends?'

Embarrassed by my outburst, I turned away.

As I poured coffee for my father-in-law, his expression

relaxed and his shoulders dropped, but he sipped the coffee in silence.

'I must go now,' he said when he'd finished.

I recalled my fantasies of being met by a host of Tommaso's relatives at Palermo airport; of a celebratory dinner at his parents' restaurant, plied with wine and food, an aged uncle making an emotional speech; of cosy conversations with his mother who would confess to being glad he'd married a Scottish girl, who'd show me his favourite recipes, explain his vulnerabilities and what he needed from a wife. Of less intimate but equally sincere conversations with his father.

So often I had visualised Tommaso driving me to his favourite childhood ports, pointing out where he'd watched the fishing boats unloading their catch, perhaps scrambling to catch an escaping fish, struggling with its grey slipperiness; showing me his school and his boltholes. Stereotypical things, but, nevertheless, ones I'd wanted to know about. Thereafter, we'd be urged to join his family for Christmas and Easter celebrations, first communions and other significant occasions.

'Please don't go without seeing Tommaso,' I repeated. 'I know this is a lot to take in. We did get engaged quickly, but we love each other.'

Signor Vitale scrutinised me before saying, 'He has told you much about his life in Sicily?'

'Is there something I should know?'

My heart thudded. Tommaso knew more about my past life than I did about his. Now I remembered the watch from Elisa. The passbook.

The silence between us made me uncomfortable. 'Please stay for dinner, or at least return for dinner.'

I watched Signor Vitale's changing expressions while he

considered my request. Just as I resigned myself to him refusing, he smiled.

Encouraged, I continued, 'We could go for a walk now, if you like.'

He nodded. Bar the excited call to his wife, he displayed a quiet dignity, and already I trusted him. Perhaps more so than my husband. In addition to intelligence and kindness, his eyes conveyed an openness. Furthermore, an attractive light and interest. As I led him down the narrow stone staircase to the beach, I hoped the sound of the sea would soothe us both. Afterwards we could walk back to the apartment via the harbour.

'This is the Fornillo beach,' I said. 'And there's a lovely walkway to the harbour area. How long are you in Positano for, Signor Vitale?'

'Please call me Fabrizio. And I will call you Rachel. You are my *nuora*, my...I cannot remember the word in English.'

'Daughter-in-law.'

'Of course. In French it is *"belle fille"*. And you are beautiful.'

Like a bud opening to the sun, I sensed him coming round, accepting the situation. And despite having known him for barely half an hour, I needed his approval. To be regarded as a daughter-in-law. But I had to be honest with him.

'Signor Vitale, Fabrizio, there's something you should know – I'm not Catholic. In fact, I'm not religious – if I were, it would be Church of Scotland.'

A minute elapsed before he replied. 'This explains perhaps why Tommaso did not want his mother to know of your marriage. My wife is religious, although perhaps less so than she used to be. For me it is not a problem. But, of course, at some time she must know. I love my son but sometimes he will avoid things that are difficult to face. It is his weakness.'

I couldn't think how to respond.

'I had a business meeting in Roma,' Fabrizio continued. 'I have not visited Tommaso in Positano before. When we take a holiday, my wife prefers to visit other countries. Normally we see him in Sicily. What is your profession, Rachel?'

'Nursing…. Well, it was. But I am studying for a degree in photography, a distance learning course. And I am setting up a photography business.'

'You are creative, I like that. Italy is a beautiful country to photograph,' he said, then fell silent for a moment before continuing, 'Tommaso told me there are many walks in the area. He loves to walk.'

When Fabrizio stopped to gaze over the sea, I studied him: his suit, his handmade shoes, his watch. Sometimes I'd wondered if Tommaso's periodic money worries were due to supporting his parents in Sicily. Owning two restaurants, in fact, didn't necessarily equate to financial security. However, his father's appearance and demeanour suggested the opposite of someone struggling.

When we reached the church of Santa Maria Assunta, the heart of Positano, we stopped to watch a wedding party emerge from the church. The guests were a small group, followed by the priest – Pasha. He noticed me, and after speaking to a few guests, came over. I introduced him to Tommaso's father and they exchanged a few words. Pasha then turned to me, 'Is it working out with the studio?'

'I haven't moved in yet. But I'm sure it was the right decision.'

He smiled and said he must go now to the wedding reception. By the way he gazed at the sea, I sensed he'd rather be swimming than indoors on such a beautiful afternoon.

Tommaso returned in the evening to find Fabrizio and me sipping Camparis on the balcony, watching the setting sun, the gradually changing light on the cliffs. It could have been barely five seconds, but it seemed longer as my husband stared at his father, then at me. He deserved the shock his expression registered. Fabrizio and I had already been through this.

For the first time, I perceived Tommaso as a son rather than a husband, watching his eyebrows draw together as if trying to comprehend the situation. Fabrizio, on the other hand, managed a neutral expression when they greeted each other. Admirable. In his position, would I have been so charitable? As he pulled away from their embrace, Tommaso's eyes narrowed. Then, like a cat spat, they launched into a conversation in rapid Italian, so I retreated to the kitchen to give them privacy.

Several minutes later, Tommaso appeared and grabbed my arm. 'Why didn't you tell me my father is here?'

'Why didn't *you* tell *me* your parents didn't know we were married?'

'There is a reason–'

'There's always a reason.'

'Rachel–'

'Come on, Tommaso. We've been married long enough for you to talk to me about it. Are you ashamed of us? Of me?'

His face collapsed. '*Amore*, it is not possible to be ashamed of you. I love you.'

I swerved to avoid his embrace.

'Open this,' I said, passing him a bottle of *Lacrima Christi*.

He stared at the bottle, prompting me to add, 'Your father's had a greater shock than you. The least we can do is give him a decent meal. Then you must talk to him. You owe him an explanation. And me.'

During dinner, Tommaso hardly spoke, breaking off mid-sentence, wary. I didn't say much, either. Both hurt and angry. Fabrizio, fortunately, seemed at ease.

'This is delicious,' he said. 'My granddaughter is studying to be a chef. She makes bruschetta, but it is not so tasty. There is not too much olive oil, and there is enough fresh basil.'

When Tommaso reached for the balsamic vinegar glaze, he dropped the bottle. '*Sanguinosa inferno*, bloody hell,' he muttered, gathering the broken glass.

I fetched the mop and bucket and did what I could, but the sharp smell of vinegar lingered throughout our meal.

'Your English is excellent,' I said to Fabrizio.

'I read history for two years in Oxford.'

I refilled his wine glass. 'Didn't you want to complete your degree?'

'My father had a stroke. It was necessary to return to Sicily to help with the restaurants.'

What a sacrifice. Given similar circumstances, would Tommaso have behaved so unselfishly? While pondering this, I glanced up from my plate to find him staring at me, as if guessing my thoughts. This comforted me. Brought us closer.

As for Fabrizio, his behaviour was exemplary: considerate of me, affectionate towards his son. Plugging gaps in the conversation, without being overbearing. Throughout the meal, I warmed to him increasingly.

After we finished, I went through to the kitchen to clear up. A moment later Fabrizio appeared, sorting out crockery, putting leftovers in containers.

'You should enjoy a break,' I said.

The men went into Tommaso's study and closed the door. Stomach churning, I abandoned the dishes and retreated to the room I now regarded as my office as well as the spare bedroom, intending to finish the essay I'd been working on when Fabrizio arrived. While reading what I'd written so far, the sound of raised voices drifted through the walls. It was impossible to concentrate. Quietly, I left the apartment, counting my way down the 350 steps to the Spiaggia di Fornillo.

Walking along the empty beach, I waited for its peacefulness to alleviate my anxiety. Maybe the row concerned Tommaso's secrecy in general, not anything which implicated me. There were many subjects father and son could argue about.

Deep in thought, I jumped on hearing a voice, '*Buona sera,* Rachel'.

Natalie and Louis were waving to me from Pupetto's restaurant.

'*Buona sera,*' I returned, and continued walking.

'Drink limoncello with us,' Natalie called out, and I relented, reluctant to appear rude.

The restaurant buzzed with customers, its long terrace arched with heavily perfumed lemon trees, and traversed by waiters with trays of fish, vegetables, wine. I'd have one drink and leave.

I sipped my limoncello and choked. 'I always forget how strong this is.'

'Where is Tommaso?' Louis asked.

'His father arrived today.'

Fortunately, they didn't ask any more questions.

The apartment was dark when I returned. On the bathroom chair lay a green sponge bag, and an unfamiliar scent from a shaving cream canister filled the room. Inexplicable relief enveloped me. Fabrizio was staying overnight, using the sofa bed in Tommaso's study. The fact that my husband hadn't suggest his father use the spare room where much of my possessions were currently stored, suggested an apology of sorts. As for Tommaso, he was fast asleep when I slipped into bed, and I lay silently, hoping he wouldn't waken. Aware it was strange to take comfort from my father-in-law's presence.

What did this say about the state of my marriage?

Omera was shovelling compost into large clay pots on her balcony when I let myself into her apartment for my Italian lesson.

'Few things are more satisfying than working with my plants,' she said, straightening up.

On the sitting room table lay her exercise books and voice recorder. She wiped her hands on a cloth and sat down, re-securing a strand of hair escaped from its clasp.

'Irregular verbs,' she said gleefully. 'Such a challenge!'

I struggled to pay attention and she ignored this for about ten minutes before removing her spectacles and leaning forward. 'What's wrong?'

'I slept badly.'

In fact, I'd hardly slept a wink.

She rose from the table. 'You need one of my herbal brews.'

In the tiny kitchen, I watched her browse through a basket of brightly coloured sachets of tea. The terracotta floor tiles gleamed in the sunlight and the eggshell blue walls felt particularly restful today.

And out it burst, 'Tommaso's father arrived unexpectedly yesterday. He didn't know we were married.... At the time, Tommaso told me his mother had hurt her hip and that was why they couldn't attend our wedding.'

Claustrophobic, I returned to the sitting room and stepped onto the balcony. Omera reappeared with my tea and listened while I relayed what had happened with Fabrizio, her expression cynical.

'Perhaps you need a break from each other,' she said when I finished.

'We haven't been married long.'

Furthermore, I'd only been back from Florence for several months before wanting to escape again. Where would I go? I couldn't keep landing on Diana's doorstep. And I didn't want to be on my own.

'If you need a break, you need a break,' she said, thrusting a postcard of Srinagar into my hands. 'I'm returning to Kashmir next month – my mother's health is poor. Why don't you come? You said you wanted to visit it. It's an amazing region.'

'Aren't foreigners advised to keep away from there at the moment?'

She tutted. 'You'd be with me,' she said, her tone suggesting I should know better than to voice such concerns. 'I know which parts are safe, and what is safe to do. Think about it.'

'My parents often said they'd take me back to Shimla

and to Kashmir. Then they were killed in a car accident. I was meant to be going there last year – before I came to Italy – but the tour company went bust.... I don't know how Tommaso would feel about me going now.'

'Think about it.'

A long silence followed. Omera removed the raspberry tea bag from her mug of water and placed it on a saucer. While waiting for the tea to cool, her right hand tapped out a rhythm on the table, her left supported her chin. In the background the parrots squawked, 'Think about it.' One of them imitated Omera's laugh.

Tentatively, she sipped her tea, winced and replaced the cup. 'He could come, too, I suppose. But this would defeat the object of the trip.'

To my dismay, I realised I wouldn't want to be with Tommaso in India. Not in a country so significant to me. Besides, I couldn't imagine him there, coping with the heat and flies, the relentless attention tourists always attract.

'What's wrong with your mother, Omera?'

'Weak heart. My cousin will look after her until we can find a permanent nurse. My mother's already fired three temporary ones.' Omera went over to the fireplace and lifted the photo of Pasha. 'Pasha will be in London just before I leave. Then he has a convention in Delhi. We will travel together to Delhi, and then to Srinagar.'

'The timing *would* be good. I've had my last Skype with my tutor, so that's it for University for the summer. And there would be loads of photography opportunities: different culture, different light.'

'Exactly. Let me know.... Time to return to work.'

After my lesson finished, I went to the beach, where I sat for hours, watching as daylight turned to dusk, as buildings gradually lit up and smells of cooking meat and wood smoke wafted over. I ignored the flurry of texts from Tommaso. An elderly couple hirpled along the sand, arms round each other and I wondered how long they'd been together. What issues they'd faced in their relationship.

When music blasted from a small restaurant, a group of people came into view, laughing, shimmying, running up the steps, one of them bursting into song. I envied their carefree behaviour. How much did Tommaso's love mean if I couldn't trust him?

## 13

Whe I arrived home, Tommaso rushed to the door and pulled me into his arms. 'Where were you, *amore*? I missed you. My father wanted to say goodbye to you.'

I pulled away. Had I missed Tommaso? My scrambled thoughts prevented me from knowing how I'd felt. Apart from deceived.

'We need to talk,' I said.

'Later,' he whispered, moving closer, kissing my neck.

I disentangled myself from him again and went into the sitting room. 'Now. Come on, Tommaso, you owe me this at least.'

At one time, we would have sat on the balcony on such a lovely, clear night. Having no idea where our conversation might lead, however, I didn't want to be in a place associated with peace.

'Why were you and your father arguing?' I asked when Tommaso handed me a glass of wine.

He sat down on the sofa, but not next to me. For a few seconds, he shifted position and fidgeted with his watch.

My heart raced as I asked, 'Are you already married?'

'*You* are my wife.'

'Were you already married? Why was your father so angry? He told me he didn't mind me not being Catholic but–'

Tommaso turned away. 'I can't talk to you about this now. I tell you – I have no other wife. You must trust me.'

'Trust you?'

'I explain you. There is nothing for you to worry about.'

'The more you won't tell me, the more I worry. Can't you understand that?'

'I don't want to talk about this.'

'I'm your wife. I am entitled to know what the problem is.' I was tired of saying this.

'I did not say there is a problem. There is no problem.'

'You were arguing with your father. I need to know why.'

Perhaps it *was* something unconnected with me. Perhaps it *was* none of my business. Although it was obvious I wouldn't get anywhere with him this evening, I knew my niggle would remain until he opened up. Furthermore, I knew it would fester.

Several weeks passed. Then Costanzo phoned to tell me that Anya had moved out of the studio early and I could take on the rental now. The timing suited. Tommaso was particularly busy at work, and, relieved to have something to focus on in addition to my studies and Italian classes, I spent a week sorting out my studio.

The issue around his father wouldn't leave me alone, nevertheless, and one evening when Tommaso was being tetchy for no apparent reason, I'd had enough. We embarked on the same question and non-answer conversation.

'You ask me too many questions,' he eventually said.

Something in me snapped. 'Omera's asked me to go to India with her. To Kashmir.'

Silence, then, 'You will go without me?'

'Why not?'

'You will go to India to punish me?'

'You make it sound like a game. It's not. I hate that you have secrets: not telling your parents about our wedding; pretending you were happy about living in Edinburgh.'

'I am going to bed,' he said, rising from the sofa.

I remained there. How could I get through to him? What else could I do?

For the second time, I slept in the spare room. Before falling asleep, I phoned Omera. 'I'm coming to Kashmir with you.'

When I told Tommaso about my decision the next morning, he left the apartment without a word. Throughout the following weeks, we argued incessantly about my departure. Replaying the same points, each of us waiting for the other to respond differently. As I prepared for my trip, I continued to ponder how I could persuade him to tell me what was going on with his father. After a particularly acrimonious row, he stopped working from home, and from then on, we avoided each other when he returned from Napoli. The spare bed became familiar.

'You will go to India?' he said, a week before I was due to leave.

'Everything is booked. Besides, I don't want to cancel.'

'When will you return?'

'I have an open ticket.'

His eyes narrowed. 'Open ticket? What is this open ticket?'

'It means I haven't booked a date for my return flight.'

'You tell me you don't know when you will return?'

He stormed off to our bedroom. Through the open door, I watched him retrieve a suitcase from the top of the wardrobe. Shove shirts and trousers into it. He added items from various drawers, lastly going into the bathroom, where I heard the clink of bottles and other noises. When he'd finished packing, he returned to where I remained at the table.

'I will stay in Napoli until you will cancel your flight.'

'Then you'd better find a good hotel because I won't be cancelling my flight.'

The evening before my departure, I became wracked with doubts. Once I clicked on Omera's number, then changed my mind. Twice, I tried to reach Tommaso to see if anything he said could help me decide what to do. The apartment was too quiet, the whirring noise of torrential rain all I could hear, apart from an occasional barking dog. Eventually I fell asleep around three, to wake several hours later when my cell phone rang.

'Please don't go,' Tommaso said. 'I love you.'

'I love you, too, but please tell me what's going on with your family.'

Silence. I waited for ten seconds, then hung up.

As I finished last minute packing, my phone went again.

Natalie sounded miserable. 'I know I should not inter-fere but–'

'Let me guess – Louis asked you to persuade me to stay.'

'Tommaso is very upset.'

'Not upset enough to reassure me. Natalie, I'm sorry

you've been dragged into this.... I must go. The taxi'll be here any minute.'

Heavy traffic delayed our journey to the airport, and when we arrived, I had little time between checking in and the flight leaving. Intermittently, I scanned the surrounding area, hoping Tommaso had turned up to tell me what I needed to know. Reassure me there was nothing to worry about. When I walked through passport control, I resolved to put him out of my mind for the moment.

'For those of you sitting on the right,' the pilot said, 'you can see the tip of Mount Everest peeping through the clouds. Shortly we will begin our descent. The temperature in Delhi is thirty-two degrees Celsius and overcast. Heavy rain is forecast for this evening, but tomorrow it will be sunny.'

And as a swirl of cloud lifted from the mountains, so did my doubts, the in transit hours at Heathrow, questioning my judgement, now a distant memory. My stomach fluttered with excitement. I smiled at Omera, sitting across the aisle. I smiled at Pasha, seated beside her, asleep.

Stepping onto the tarmac at Delhi airport felt like entering a sauna. Inside the building it wasn't much better.

'There's a problem with the air conditioning,' Omera muttered.

Large ceiling fans spun ineffectively and even the local people were struggling: heated conversations taking place; elderly women searching for relatives; young siblings bickering. If only we were flying on to Kashmir. To cooler air.

Once through passport control and customs, Pasha took a taxi to his convention south of Delhi. Omera and I took another one into town where we would spend three nights before journeying north to Kashmir.

Whizzing past shanty towns with tin roof shacks, dusty roads and barefooted children playing in the dirt amongst chickens and skinny dogs, I was gripped by such brutal poverty. Occasionally the taxi had to slow right down because of cumbersome vehicles ahead. Then children would arrive at the open window.

'Hallo – rupees, sweets?' they'd ask, their teeth large and white against grubby faces, their beautiful dark liquid eyes optimistic. The driver would shout, '*Bhaag*, go away,' waving his arm futilely. I had no coins. At one point, I grabbed Omera's bag of peppermints, and flung its contents out of the window. Craning my neck to watch the children dash to the sweets as the taxi moved on.

'You'll get used to this,' she said, waving her hand, bangles jangling.

*Would* I? Had my parents?

When we hit the city centre, we were surrounded by bicycles, carrying one or more passengers, many wearing dust masks to protect against the smoggy air. Hyundais and Suzukis wove through the traffic, crossing our path with inches to spare. To my astonishment, three-wheeled tuk-tuks knew their clearance to the last centimetre. At first I clung to the handle above my shoulder. After a while, laughter akin to hysteria surfaced. Having survived the long flight, how ironical it would be to end up mangled in the road chaos. Traffic lights were barely more than a suggestion.

Amazingly, Omera had fallen asleep.

Through the window, I could see cows drinking from dirty puddles. Smell cloves and turmeric from pavement

stalls. Exhaust fumes and dust. Everything conjuring up
childhood memories.

A scene emerged of being in a tuk-tuk with my mother,
when it collided with a man pulling a barrow of vegetables.
I remembered the two men yelling at each other while
vegetables rolled across the street and cars honked at the
delay. I recalled my mother's resonant laugh. Her confusing
remark about the richness of life in India. Even at my tender
age, I could see that neither man was rich.

Our taxi now turned through a gate and drove up to a
large white colonial style building, fringed with palms and
surrounded by a green lawn. I smiled with relief. All I
wanted was a cool bedroom, a comfy bed, to be on my own.
Fatigue was kicking in.

Within minutes of our arrival, a porter showed me to my
room, a space large enough for three double beds. The tiled
floor was refreshingly cool to my bare feet. The air conditioning quiet and effective. Abandoning my unpacking, I lay
down on the king-size bed. Aware of the thrum of torrential
rain before my eyes closed.

Omera waved as I searched for her in the breakfast room.

'I recommend the aloo parathas. I make these in Italy
but they never taste as good. But you can go Western if you
like.'

At the buffet table, other fair-skinned guests were
helping themselves to breakfast cereals and boiled eggs.

Ten minutes later, my aloo paratha was served.

'This is so good,' I told Omera. 'Fresh coriander leaves
are underrated. They make such a difference.'

'We will have a quiet day,' she said as I ate. 'Wander

around the bazaars, have lunch at a *dhaba* – a traditional open-air restaurant. And you mustn't leave Delhi without visiting The Red Fort. I've booked us on a city tour tomorrow.'

After breakfast, we took a cycle rickshaw to the Palika Bazaar, an underground maze of stores.

'This is amazing,' I said, looking around. 'And it's cool.'

'Air conditioning,' she said.

'And full of local people.'

She tutted. 'You didn't think I'd take you to a tourist trap, did you?'

Within minutes, she was bargaining for saffron and emerald green fabric. Deal concluded, she turned to me, reporting gleefully, 'I got him down from 800 rupees to 500. I'll make two saris for Dhakir, my great-niece. Her mother is out at work all day and doesn't have time to sew.'

'Everything's so cheap, Omera.'

Such low prices horrified me. At least I couldn't see many Westerners. The idea of people like me buying huge amounts of fabrics and pottery was sickening. How had my parents coped? Another memory was struggling to the surface. Strolling through the dimly lit bazaars of Shimla at nightfall. My mother laughingly trying on bangles and beads. Asking my father for his opinion. Sometimes letting me try on something.

'Dhakir would love these bangles,' Omera said, sliding two of them onto her wrist, listening to them jangle. 'And Hazrat has told me that Jameela needs new slippers. I will buy Hazrat sweetmeats. He loves the Ros Mali – do you know these? Cheese balls cooked in syrup and then milk. So long as the children don't pinch them from him. They have so much sugar and it is bad for their teeth.'

At lunchtime, we found a *dhaba* where we ate chapatis

and thick, tasty lentil dhal We drank large glasses of mango lassi. I could almost feel my health improving with each sip. Already I'd taken too many photos and was glad of a reason to stop.

'At the risk of sounding wimpish,' I said, when we'd finished, 'I'm exhausted.'

But there was more to it than tiredness. Since arriving in Delhi, I'd seen too much. Too much poverty, too much dirt. Too much squalid living. Perhaps it would be easier once we reached Kashmir.

'We'll return to the hotel for a siesta,' Omera said. 'Then you'll be fresh for this evening. I've got tickets for a *Dances of India* performance.'

I forced a smile. The last thing I wanted was a show for Westerners.

'Trust me,' she said scathingly.

On the ride back to the hotel, my rickshaw narrowly missed colliding with one full of giggling children and a rotund woman urging them to be quiet. The sight of their driver, an elderly man with spindly legs, heaving so many people around the city distressed me more than I would have believed possible. In the rickshaw behind me, Omera was fanning her face with her sunhat. Occasionally during the journey, my driver turned round to check again the name of the hotel we were going to, teeth stained black from the betel nut he was chewing.

As we pulled into our hotel grounds, I noticed a man standing on the lawn. He resembled Tommaso so markedly that for one crazy moment I thought he'd come to reclaim me. On closer inspection, he looked nothing like my husband.

Ignoring Omera's protestations, I paid my driver twice what he asked. In gratitude, he gave me the "*Namaste*" greeting, moving his head and clasped hands up and down repeatedly.

'You need to lose your British guilt,' she told me as we entered the hotel. 'Also, you must remember that giving extra money raises prices for local people, which they can't afford.'

'I hadn't thought of that.'

Now I felt bad.

In the hotel, Omera ordered tea and gulab jamun. As I feigned enthusiasm for the syrupy milk balls – disappointing compared with my mother's – for the moment my thoughts about the day were replaced by those of Tommaso and our geographical and emotional distance from each other. Perhaps I'd phone him when we reached Kashmir. I pictured him on the balcony, facing the rocky headland, listening to Stefano Gervasoni, glass of *Piedirosso* in his hand, the top two buttons of his shirt undone.

I shouldn't have left him.

As darkness fell, the timeless recorded call for Muslims to attend the last prayer of the day blared out. I smelt sandalwood joss sticks, the menthol scent of cumin and the warm fragrance of coriander seeds. Finally, a wave of peace stole through me.

In the evening, a taxi drove us to a suburb in the west of Delhi. To my relief, I could see few Westerners as we entered a nondescript concrete hall. There, an audience was tightly seated on the floor, the women resembling exotic parrots with their saffron, lime green, orange, red and purple saris. Children slept by their parents' feet. Candles lit the room and a strong scent of rose and pine incense filled the air.

Fleetingly, I was catapulted back to a childhood visit to Delhi, being taken to a similar event by friends of my parents, feeling very grown-up compared to the other children there.

Once Omera and I had made ourselves comfortable on the dhurris and cushions, dancers came onto the stage. Women clad in flimsy trousers and choli tops, twisted and turned, wrist and ankle bracelets creating their own music. Bare chested men in harem pants played circular drums while they moved. The grace and expressiveness of the arm movements captivated me. When the performance ended, Omera had to tug my arm, as if recalling me from a faraway place.

The Fajr pre-dawn call to prayer woke me. As I listened to its lone, insistent voice, I watched the sun rise, detecting already a whiff of spices. Now more rested, I felt excited about the day ahead. Then I fell asleep again.

Later, while waiting for Omera to join me in the dining room, I pored over the language section of my guidebook, determined to learn a few more words of Hindi. When she arrived, I was muttering: '*keemat kya hai? – how much does this cost?; mujhe akela chhod do – leave me alone.*'

She smiled approvingly at the open page. 'You're making an effort.'

'I remember some Hindi from my childhood.'

That morning, we visited the Red Fort and the Jama Masjid mosque. Both impressive. Calculating shutter speeds and focusing for my shots, however, was challenging in the dusty light. Furthermore, the humid, smoggy air pushed my tolerance to its limits, especially while waiting for a tuk-tuk, surrounded by young men selling postcards.

'Beautiful mosque,' one of them said, shoving a faded postcard in front of my eyes.

'Erotic sculptures at Khajuraho,' said another, showing me an equally faded picture of a temple carving of copulating couples.

I jumped as a hand touched my bottom.

'*Majhe akela chor do,* go away,' Omera shouted, and they scampered off, giggling.

After lunch, she suggested we visit the Baha'i Temple.

'Actually, I'd rather go back to the hotel.'

'The temple gardens are lovely, Rachel. You must see them.'

I shoved my bangled wrist in her face. 'I paid thirty pence for this and it's silver. The child was so resigned.'

'It happens here. Don't think about it.'

'I'll see you at dinner,' I said, flagging down a tuk-tuk.

Back in my luxurious bedroom, I remembered the children begging for rupees. Their stoical expressions. Their torn clothes and bare feet. In particular, I remembered the beggar seated outside the Jama Masjid mosque, an infant on her lap. The mother drawing my attention to the child's lower leg sticking out at a right angle. I'd heard stories of parents breaking children's limbs at birth in order to make their begging more productive. Nevertheless, these were no preparation for seeing a deformed young boy.

If I lived here, would I eventually become accustomed to such abject poverty and desperation?

Would I want to?

～

On our last day in Delhi, I told Omera I wanted to visit a neighbouring town.

'I have made plans,' she told me. 'You must see the India Gate and the Humayan's Tomb – the architecture is amazing.'

'I'm going to East Delhi.'

She looked startled. 'But it's so poor there. It will horrify you, believe me.'

'That's why I want to go. I don't just want to see touristy things.'

'It could be dangerous. I suppose I should come with you. I'll order a taxi.'

'I'm going by train. I'll get a tuk-tuk to the station.'

'Train! You're mad.... At least promise me you'll travel first class.'

'See you at dinner.'

The New Delhi Railway Station was mobbed and it took a while to find the ticket office, where I purchased a ticket, eventually being persuaded by an agitated clerk to travel first class. The twenty-minute journey took us through built-up areas, as I'd expected, ramshackle houses feet away from the railway line. When the train arrived, both sides of the line were swamped with rubbish. Never had I seen so much litter in the one place and the stench made me gag.

For a moment, I considered getting the return train. Instead, I forced myself to walk around the town, absorbing the slum settlements, one rickety building on top of another, people sleeping on the roadside under makeshift shelters of plastic sheeting supported by sticks. And everywhere, the piles of rubbish, and cows wallowing in muddy puddles. How could people live like this?

A wave of hysterical laughter overcame me as I gawped at chaotic jumbles of power cables and other wiring. Street sellers peddled their wares: coconuts, mangos, plastic bottles of water. Others sold hats, cheap sunspecs and garishly coloured t-shirts. And yet I witnessed lively conversations, children playing with tin cans and scabby dogs. Seemingly content with so little.

At this point, I hated the Western World. Hated every rich person who was trying to become even richer. Hated people who had luxury homes and poncy cars and spent ridiculous amounts on designer clothes and jewellery.

Most of all, I hated myself for being here.

# 14

'Pasha says we should fly to Srinagar,' Omera said at dinner that evening. 'There have been bandit attacks recently. I told him to go ahead and book flights. An early start tomorrow, but unavoidable.'

I glanced round the half-empty dining room, at the cluster of waiters in their maroon jackets and white shirts, staring at us. Every time I looked up from eating, I'd see at least two of them watching me in fascination. As if I'd hailed from another planet.

My stomach was churning. 'Perhaps I should go back to Italy.'

'We'll be fine once we get to Kashmir, provided we're sensible. Pity about having to fly, however. It's such a scenic road. I'll arrange for an alarm call for six. Don't worry, once we reach Srinagar, we'll slow down a bit.'

I suppressed a smile. Omera slowing down stretched my imagination a tad too far.

~

We couldn't see Pasha when we arrived at Delhi airport. Omera checked her watch and sighed. 'My brother has a dysfunctional relationship with time. I never wear a watch and I'm never late. He wears one and he is always late.'

Five minutes later, he arrived. 'Sorry, sorry.'

As his smile lingered on me, I noticed again those unusual green eyes. Pistachio coloured. Beguiling.

Despite today's functioning air conditioning, sweat coursed down my back as we walked along the gangway to our plane. The sky was the pale blue of sweltering heat, the surrounding green landscape parched. However, our ninety-minute flight quickly transported us over different vegetation and soon I was gazing through the window at snow-covered mountains and green shadowed valleys.

Omera's older brother, Hazrat, met us at Srinagar. After greeting his brother and sister with folded hands, followed by a hug, he turned to me. I folded my hands and bowed.

He smiled. '*Namaste*. Welcome to Kashmir. We will go now to our home. Amani has prepared lunch for us.'

As we left the airport, reality kicked in when I noticed a heavy presence of armed guards.

I clutched Omera's arm. 'Look.'

'It's better this way,' she said. 'You'll be safe with us. Stop worrying.'

I did worry. Using this travel experience as distraction therapy, swapping the pain of marriage difficulties with the edge of entering a war zone, now struck me as idiotic, (and childish, an inner voice whispered). Furthermore, Marion and Geoffrey would be horrified if they knew where I was. Hopefully neither Debs nor Anna would tell them.

During the short drive to Hazrat's home, I searched for signs of unrest. All I could see, though, were poplar trees

and the distant snow-capped Himalayas, and in the foreground, rows of modest bungalows and gardens with faded
grass. At their house, two children of about eight and ten,
rushed to greet us.

'This is Rachel from UK,' Hazrat said. 'Rachel, my
granddaughter, Dhakir, and my grandson, Jameela.' As a
woman emerged from the back of the house, he added,
'This is my wife, Amani.'

She smiled shyly and clasped her hands. '*Namaste*.
Welcome to our home.'

Neither Hazrat nor Amani seemed old enough to be
grandparents, with their attractive brown, unlined skin.
Only a hint of grey in Amani's hair indicated she was no
longer a young woman.

The smell of onions and garlic from the kitchen made
me hungry. Then I jumped on hearing a noise like gunshot.

'It is a car backfiring,' Hazrat said.

Omera unpacked her suitcase, dispensing the presents
she'd bought for her great-niece and great-nephew. They
tore off the brown paper bags, Jameela exclaiming with
pleasure at the red slippers with gold embossing. Dhakir's
face lighting up when she saw the rolls of purple cotton and
lime green satin.

'I will make your saris tomorrow,' Omera told her,
earning another hug.

'How is Mamma-ji?' Omera asked Hazrat.

His expression was glum. 'In one of her moods. Her
asthma is bad and she has headaches. Already we feel sorry
for Anjana.'

'My mother is a difficult woman,' Hazrat eventually told
me, and Amani nodded vigorously. As her daughter-in-law, I
wondered how she'd escaped caring for Suhayma.

'I will visit her this evening,' Omera said.

After lunch, swathed in multicoloured embroidered shawls, Omera and I set off into the misty, purple light for the centre of Srinagar.

'You probably think it strange that my mother lives on her own,' she said. 'It isn't the Indian custom. But she prefers not to be with her family full-time.'

'What's wrong with her? Personality, I mean?'

'If you meet her, you'll realise what a trial Hazrat and Amani have been spared. I suspect Amani often worries about Suhayma changing her mind. They'd have to move in with her as she wouldn't contemplate living in their smaller house. It would be ghastly for Amani. My mother is a control freak.'

Omera was now in full stride. 'I'll take you to the river market. You'll love it.'

When we reached the centre of the old town, I saw what she meant. Yes, it was colourful and picturesque, the slim, wooden gondola shikaras that sold brilliantly coloured yarns, and lotus leaves. The stalls selling walnut ornaments and papier-mâché ring boxes. But, add the context of dilapidated wooden or stone houses fronting the muddy water of the Jhelum River and the picture changed. Were the interiors of such homes as squalid as their façades suggested? How many people lived at subsistence level?

Easier on the eye, certainly on the conscience, was the view of mountains and goat herders driving their flocks against a backdrop of cypress trees. Provoking a fluttering in me. An ache, although for what, I had no idea.

There were more tourists here than I'd been aware of in Delhi. It must be sickening for the locals observing these people parachuted in: gawping at signs of brutal hardship; searching for restaurants serving recognisable food; taking the obligatory shikara ride on Dal lake; shopping for bargains. Then, with enormous relief, returning home to central heating and a myriad domestic comforts. Rationalising about the poverty they'd witnessed, before forgetting.

This was even worse than Delhi. Perhaps because the Punjab heat made deprivation appear more tolerable. Although it was still warm here, every time I saw a pair of thin legs supported by a stick, I wondered about the homes its owners were returning to. If they'd be warm during the winter. If they'd have enough to eat, somewhere comfortable to sleep.

'You are quiet,' Omera remarked.

'How do people keep warm?'

She pointed to a cluster of women sitting outside a building. 'What can you see under their cloaks?'

I peered at an object resembling a wickerwork basket. 'Their shopping keeps them warm, does it?'

She laughed. 'These baskets are called *kangris* – they contain burning coal. Very effective…. Let's go across the Jhelum bridge.'

As we walked over it, people sitting cross-legged were selling watermelons, sliced open to reveal succulent red flesh and dark pips, against the variegated thick green skin.

'You want to try?' a woman asked, thrusting a slice at me.

Omera handed her some rupees and I bit into a delicious chunk of melon.

The bridge railings were covered with colourful floral-designed woollen mats hanging there to dry. I lifted my camera, then changed my mind.

'Why aren't you taking photos?' Omera asked.

'It feels intrusive.'

She scoffed. 'You need to get over this if you want to be a professional photographer.'

We walked and walked, speaking little. Perhaps she was similarly beguiled by our surroundings. Before dusk, the setting sun transformed the wooden and brick buildings of Srinagar's old town into a golden brown. And for a moment, I could see the romance of the place. For a moment, I could stop feeling bad. Besides, my main reason for being here was about reconnecting with my parents.

Around me, vendors packed away their wares for the night. Tired no doubt, dispirited perhaps.

I heard a scuffle and noticed a boy of around ten hitting a younger girl with a stick.

'Omera, stop this.'

'This happens. They'll sort it out themselves.'

The hitting continued as people strolled past and shopkeepers carried on with their packing. Eventually, I grabbed the stick from the boy and immediately the little girl darted down an alley.

'Why wouldn't you do anything?' I asked Omera.

She shrugged, as if having been asked this question many times before. 'The culture here is different. Parents don't talk properly with their children. They don't provide good role models. A husband beats his wife in front of their children. So they learn this behaviour. A brother hits his sister. It's not ideal but what can we do?'

'What does Pasha think about it?'

She shook her head affectionately. 'When he's teaching in schools, he talks about respect for others. About not being violent. But one priest can't make so much difference.'

The following day, I walked out of Srinagar to the Dal Lake, hoping to find accommodation. Much as I liked Omera's family, it was obvious they didn't have room for me and I yearned for time on my own. And yet, it would be more sensible to stay with them, a local family who knew what was safe to do.

When I reached the lake and saw the floating market, for the first time since arriving in Kashmir, I put my camera to use. Photographing the wooden shikaras overflowing with vegetables, flowers and cattle fodder. Zooming in on head-scarved women passing watermelons and bundles of flowers from boat to boat. Low cloud obscured the Himalayas, but the mauve light lent atmosphere to the foreground.

As I photographed the large red chinar trees and sentinel-like poplars fringing the lake, the smell of spicy Kashmiri tea and biscuits drifted across the water. In the distance, I could glimpse the Moghul bridges I'd read about in my guidebook. The scene defined romance. How many couples had fallen in love here? Delivered or received a proposal?

It was so peaceful that temporarily I forgot about the situation.

About to leave, a "For rent" sign on a houseboat caught my eye. Stepping on deck, I peered through the windows where I could see a bedroom, cooking area and living space with armchairs and table. Scatter rugs on the wooden floor and the customary ornate carved woodwork gave it a cosy look. Already I visualised myself here, preparing a vegetable curry, reading on deck.

A notice on the front door provided contact details and

directions to the administration office. Having calculated the rental in sterling, however, I reconsidered. For a while, I wandered round, checking rates for other rented house-boats. All much the same. Perhaps I should retrace my steps and search for a hotel. Then I noticed a smaller houseboat, set apart from the others. Moments later, a figure emerged from within, stepped into the shikara roped to the boat, and rowed ashore. It was Pasha.

'Aren't you staying with Hazrat?' I asked.

'The houseboat belongs to a friend. He's out of the country at the moment, so I'm keeping an eye on it.'

'Do you think he'd rent it to me? How long is he away for?'

Pasha regarded me curiously. 'Another few months.' He checked his watch. 'I might be able to reach him now.'

An hour later, everything was sorted. For the equivalent of £400 a month, I could rent the houseboat. Probably a reduced rate due to knowing Pasha. I'd also been introduced to Deeba who'd been employed to clean the property in its owner's absence.

'Deeba will stay during the night with you,' Pasha had explained. 'You see, it's not appropriate here for a woman to be on a houseboat on her own. And don't worry, she won't get in your way.'

Two hours later, I'd collected my luggage from Hazrat's, taken a taxi to the lake and was ensconced in my temporary home.

Kashmir had bewitched me. Without thinking things through, I'd committed myself to staying here for at least a month. I knew nothing about living on houseboats. What if there was a storm? Or a leak in the shikara which took me ashore? Sitting on the deck, I dredged up all the things that could go wrong. Deeba seemed kind, but she looked about fourteen.

As darkness gradually replaced daylight, my worries evaporated. My mind now switching to what I could do to justify being here.

## 15

'We were devastated when we heard about your parents,' Gillian Stewart said. 'We did write, but it would have been after you moved to your aunt and uncle's home.'

We were on the verandah of the home of my parents' closest friends from Shimla, a British couple who'd subsequently moved to Srinagar. John was a professor of English at the University of Kashmir, Gillian, a translator.

'You're welcome to stay with us while you're here,' John said. 'The house feels empty now our children have moved back to the UK.'

I explained about the houseboat.

Gillian exchanged a smile with her husband. 'So independent, like Ros.'

It sounded strange hearing my mother referred to by her name. Strange and sad. Marion and Geoffrey always talked about "your mother" or "your father".

'Actually, I was thinking about working while I'm here,' I said. 'But I'm not sure how. I have a smattering of Hindi, but no Kashmiri or Urdu.'

Gillian smiled. 'English is quite widely spoken in Kashmir.'

'You said you were a nurse?' John said. 'The paediatric hospital in Srinagar is struggling. Many of its staff have gardiasis and will be off work for a while. Perhaps they could use you.'

A surge of happiness flooded me. Now I'd have a purpose here. Provided the hospital took me on.

He was speaking again. 'As it happens, I know the medical superintendent. I could take you there this afternoon – or do you need time to think about it?'

~

'We will be glad of your help,' the medical superintendent of the hospital told me, turning up the fan when we arrived at his office. He was a tall, slim man with receding hairline and gold-rimmed specs that flashed constantly from the sunshine streaming through his large window. Originally from Shimla, he'd explained, which endeared him to me.

'I don't speak Kashmiri. Or much Hindi.'

He smiled, displaying even white teeth against a pock-marked skin, and repeated what Ros had said about English being commonly used here, adding, 'And there are things you can do that don't require words. A hug or even a smile is particularly important to a child. Perhaps you can help also in the kitchen. We have malnourished children who need supplements.'

Already I visualised myself making high protein drinks. Modifying dishes to add extra calories.

Fortunately, the superintendent didn't ask if my visa was valid for employment. A pragmatist. Once the hospital received a reference from my recent employer in Edinburgh, I could start.

When I surfaced on my first day at work, the mist was slowly rising from the lake, an ascending sun highlighting the burnished gold and yellows of poplar trees. After five minutes of photography, I dressed quickly and walked into Srinagar.

During my shift, I learned about real hardship.

'Poor nutrition in rural areas here is a major problem,' a nurse told me. 'Many children under three are underweight. And many have not been fully immunised. We have a ward of children with measles.'

'There's been a rise in measles in the UK. But not so many fatalities,' I volunteered.

She continued as if I hadn't spoken, and I felt silently reprimanded for comparing the situation in the UK with that of Kashmir.

'Children who live in houseboats that get their drinking water from hand pumps and wells, often develop diarrhoea. So many health problems. And so few resources....'

I remembered the well-nourished kids I'd nursed in the Infectious Disease ward of the children's hospital in Edinburgh.

If I found my first shift emotionally gruelling, it was a cinch compared to the following days. When I heard a nurse singing to these prematurely aged, swollen bellied children, I needed time out to compose myself. Overhearing discussions about who should be given drugs and who might survive without them, I was thankful not to be involved in such monumentally difficult decisions. How those staff managed to work with such inadequate resources and poorly maintained equipment constantly amazed me. By the end of the week, I was fiercely practising what we'd been taught in nursing school: the art of detachment.

Occasionally I glimpsed Pasha in his black cassock, speaking to the staff, comforting distressed parents. Once he noticed me and smiled, but we never had a moment to talk.

~

On my first day off, I arranged to visit the Shalimar Gardens with Gillian. But despite setting my alarm clock, I didn't wake until eleven when she knocked on the houseboat door.

'I've hired a shakira to row us to the Gardens,' she said. 'If you're not too tired?'

I stared down at the waiting wooden shikara, painted in primary colours, with thick brightly patterned cushions and flowing curtains.

'Give me ten minutes,' I said, watching her gingerly lower herself onto the boat again.

As I sat back in the shikara, curtains pulled aside, enjoying the sun's warmth, Gillian talked of Kashmir's history of trading, of the countless caravans traversing the Vale for more than a thousand years. I lay even further back, trailing my hand in the water as she described the journey, mentioning exotically named places such as Khotan, Yarkand and Kashgar. Picturing it all while she spoke: exchanges of saffron, shawls woven from pashmina and ibex, silks and blankets, for silver and gold and precious stones, for spices, tea and cotton, for tobacco and ponies.

'The regal entourage of the Emperor Aurgangzeb made its way over the Salt Route – the high Pir Panjal pass, to Kashmir three hundred years before,' she told me, eyes distant as if she'd been one of the party. 'There were thousands of foot soldiers and cavalry. Hundreds of heavy guns, thousands of porters, and women riding elephants. Imagine.'

I did. I also envisaged sleepy children on grandmothers' laps in primitive Kashmiri homes. Begging again and again for this story. Enthralled by the idea of elephants making hazardous journeys. Picturing all those soldiers, those guns. It was so visual, it would make a wonderful film. Add a touch of romance to broaden its reach.... Perhaps such a film already existed.

After a pause, Gillian's voice softened. 'It must have been dreadful for you, losing both parents at the same time.'

I gazed over the lake, aware of my eyes filling. 'It didn't sink in properly for a while. I missed my father in particular. I was always closer to him.... With Mum it was... different.'

Gillian's expression changed.

The pulse on my neck throbbed. 'What is it? Is there something I should know?'

At this moment, it felt as if I was forever on the cusp of being knocked off balance.

Silence while she considered, a range of expressions inhabiting her face. Then she spoke, her voice gentle and slow, as if to soften her words.

'I don't know if you know this. Your mother had a difficult pregnancy and... and an even more difficult birth.'

I shook my head.

'Before you were born, she'd had two miscarriages, quite late on. In fact, they were so bad that the doctors told her she was unlikely to carry a full-term baby.' Gillian paused, giving me time to absorb. Searching my face to gauge my reaction. 'I think it was a relief for her to know she wouldn't have to go through the same experience again.

But your father was so keen to have a child, especially a girl.'

She stopped, turning her attention to a flock of coots on the lake. A heavenly scent drifted over from a nearby shikara filled with vivid purple, orange and red flowers.

Ironically, having longed to know the truth about important issues, now knee-deep in discovering one, I wanted only to enjoy my surroundings. Later on – in the relative privacy of the houseboat – when I relived the conversation, I realised that what I feared was a surge of grief too overwhelming to deal with. Like my adolescent nightmares of feeling unloved and knowing there was nothing I could do about it. Causing me to wake to a face streaked with tears and a heart so savaged it would take a while to fully emerge from the dream.

My voice was now slow and calm, concealing the inner turmoil from what I inferred: Dad had really wanted me, Mum hadn't, at least, not to the same degree. 'So they kept trying.... Mum never mentioned the miscarriages, or the difficult birth.'

'In many ways Ros was reserved. But she was very possessive when it came to your father.'

'They seemed so close.' Again, memories flooded me of times when I felt supernumerary.

'After you were born, they returned to Edinburgh for six months to give your mother time to recover.'

Gillian stopped now. Did she regret having told me this? Consider it disloyal? I suspected she'd have thought carefully before deciding to share this information with me.

'I always believed there was an ongoing dilemma for your father,' she continued, her words equally measured but emerging more quickly, as if she felt duty-bound to finish what she'd started. 'He adored you, but Ros...your mother,

could be jealous if he lavished too much attention on you....
I know this is difficult to hear. But... well, I wanted you to
know that no father could have loved a child more. And if
he sometimes concealed it, it was because... because of her.
This was a long time ago, of course, but as you'll know,
childhood experiences often linger into adulthood.'

'My aunt and uncle never mentioned this.' But why
would they? I couldn't imagine Marion even implying criti-
cism of her beloved sister. Besides, perhaps my mother
hadn't told her everything.

It made sense now, memories surfacing about Dad being
the one I turned to with a problem; his caring for me when I
was ill; helping me with difficult decisions.

'Your aunt wouldn't want to be critical of your mother,'
Gillian said, echoing my thoughts. 'I know they were close –
we never met Marion.'

'She and my uncle were so good to me. Still are.'

For the remainder of the journey we were silent. When
we arrived at the Shalimar Gardens, I produced my camera,
relieved to focus on photography. Distract myself from
Gillian's revelation about my parents. I'd return to the information again, of course. Sift through the facts. Decide how
this knowledge had affected me.

As I gazed at the chinar trees, aflame with colour against
a misty purply grey sky, elation swept through me. My
father *had* wanted me. So much so that he'd encouraged my
mother to risk her health. Many would consider this selfish,
heartless. And they might be right. For me, though, so
needy of external validation, the important thing was
knowing the extent of his love. Something I'd wear for the
rest of my life, like an invisible locket. Something that nothing, no one, could wrest from me.

'There's a reason for bringing you here,' Gillian said, her

voice now cheerful, as if sensing my thoughts and where these had led me. 'This is where your parents met. Ros was on a cultural holiday with the university. Bill was studying here. "Love at first sight," your mother told me – she'd laughed at the cliché. For the first few years of their marriage, they'd come back here to celebrate their anniversary.'

'I'm glad to see all this,' I said. 'It makes me feel closer to them. This was why I was so keen to return to this part of India.'

I gazed at the famous black marble pavilion. Nearby, Kashmiris picnicked with wicker hampers, the smoke from their samovars mingling with floral scents. Perhaps my parents had shared picnics here.

A faded black and white photo I'd stumbled across when clearing out our family home, now came to mind. It featured my parents standing beside a tree, my mother in a sarong and cotton blouse, my father in tunic and loose trousers. His arm was round her shoulder, their passion for each other flying off the celluloid. Memories of this photo had often filled me with a sense of exclusion. This wouldn't happen again. What I realised now was how life must have been for my father, torn between wife and daughter, knowing that if my mother had shared his devotion to me, how much easier, how much happier his life would have been. No one should have to choose.

On subsequent days off work, I cycled round the countryside. Sometimes Omera joined me, in her baggy trousers, jangling bracelets and oversized sunglasses.

Photography relaxed me, particularly after a stressful

shift. In the countryside, with its constantly changing light, its mix of vivid and muted colours, it was so easy to perceive everything "through the lens". Nevertheless, I observed my self-imposed code. When wanting to capture farmers tending their paddy fields or plucking pears and peaches, I asked their permission. When I photographed children, I gave them rupees, occasionally sweets. Sometimes they'd chase my bike, and I'd slow down and pretend I couldn't keep up with them. It made them happy. It made me happy.

Already I had an idea of themes for next year's study. I was also thinking ahead about doing calendars featuring pictures of children in third world countries. If they sold, I'd donate the money to local charities.

Contrasting emotions swirled in my head. I missed Tommaso, if not so acutely now. It hit me most when I woke during the night and reached for him. However, while sitting on the deck at dusk, conscious of the distant mountains, a peacefulness would flow through me. Despite the fighting. Despite the awful conditions I witnessed each day at work. It felt like being two people: the wife who missed her husband, and the independent woman, glad to be revisiting the place where her parents had met, relieved to be giving something to a struggling community.

Furthermore, receiving such satisfaction from my temporary job made me even keener to do something beneficial with my photography when I finished my degree in two years' time.

## 16

Three weeks into my time in Kashmir, I developed a temperature halfway through my shift and left early, suspecting I'd succumbed to a bug. As I approached the lake, wincing at my aching head, I noticed Pasha sitting on the deck of my houseboat. Immediately he lowered himself into the spare attached shikara and rowed to shore.

'Are you ill?' he asked.

'A bug, I reckon.'

He helped me onto the shikara and had us back in minutes. There, I lurched into the bedroom and collapsed onto my bed. He removed my shoes and covered me with a rug. Shortly after, bringing me a mug of tea.

Noticing me shiver, he lit the gas stove and closed the window shutters. But despite the thick cover and extra heating, I couldn't stop shivering.

'You know, I think I should I call a doctor,' he said.

'It isn't necessary. I'll sleep it off.'

During the following hours I tossed and turned. Vaguely

aware of Pasha cooling my brow with a tepid cloth. Placing mugs of water to my lips.

As darkness fell, I heard him talking to Deeba. Moments later he appeared. 'Deeba will look after you tonight. And I would stay, but it isn't the custom here for a man to be with a woman, if they aren't married.'

'Thanks for arranging this,' I managed to say before drifting back to sleep. Throughout the night, I was conscious of Deeba sponging my damp body, urging me to drink.

For several days I remained like this, hot yet cold, often disorientated. Confused about everything as dreams and nightmares collided. Dad was bathing my child's febrile brow with a lukewarm cloth, Deeba urging me to sip water, helping me to change my damp clothes. I'd fallen into a disused well and no one heard my shouts for help. Dad was kissing my forehead, but it could have been Pasha.

On the fourth day, when I woke, the fever had abated. I wrapped a shawl round my kaftan and padded onto the deck. Pasha was there, watching children sail past in a shikara.

'The hospital – I didn't let them know,' I said, remembering.

'Omera has been in touch with them. She dropped by yesterday, but you were asleep. You look much better – tea?'

Minutes later, Deeba appeared with mugs of pink tea that tasted sweet and not too spicy.

That day I rested on deck in a makeshift bed Pasha constructed from blankets and large cushions. Having ensured I was adequately covered – the air had turned much cooler – he announced he was going to the market. Midafternoon, I awoke from a restful sleep to see him rowing back to the houseboat, a large paper bag beside him.

'Have you any gram flour?' he asked, producing mangos, apricots, apples and walnuts and a large container of lassi. 'I could make a walnut pie. And Dum Aloo.'

'Dum Aloo might be a bit spicy for me.... Is it okay for you to be spending so much time here?'

He nodded. 'Things are relatively quiet, although I visit the hospitals quite often. And of course, I must leave before the night curfew.'

Shortly afterwards, I threw off the blankets and moved inside the houseboat. There, a delicious smell of lentils greeted me. Pasha had set the tiny table in the sitting area, and lit four candle stubs, adding to the cosiness.

When he brought over two plates of lentil dhal and rice, I gasped. 'I can't eat all this.'

'For sure you can. You're getting thin, you know,' he said, eyes lingering on my body.

In fact, I was pleased to have lost weight. It was the sort of thing Tommaso noticed, and although he never remarked on it, I sensed he'd like me to be slimmer.

From outside I could hear the piercing teeree-teeree call of a Himalayan Swiftlet. Then, from a neighbouring house-boat came the rhythmic thud of drums and an oboe's mournful sound.

I took a spoonful of curry. 'This is delicious.'

'Fresh ginger is key.'

Remembering my confusion of dreams with reality, for the first time, I felt self-conscious in his presence.

'I should get back to bed,' I said, finishing what I could manage of the walnut pie. 'Thanks for cooking...and for taking care of me.'

'And I must leave. Curfew time.'

When I woke at lunchtime the next day, Deeba was cleaning up the galley. I attempted to help, but she insisted I rest, so I returned to my makeshift bed on the deck. There I read for several hours, before watching the sun set, transforming the houseboat to a golden brown and tingeing the clouds with mauve. Several shikaras passed, bearing turbaned men with long sticks combing the water for loam.

'Why did you become a priest?' I asked Pasha while we sat on deck the following day.

He turned to gaze over the lake, the ever-changing light. It was a moment before he replied, 'When I was fifteen, God asked me to devote my life to Him. It wasn't a dramatic moment, or anything like that, more like a voice whispering to me.... I was lucky, for me it was an easy decision. With many people, such a decision takes years. But I studied geography at university first. In case things didn't work out.'

'Do you ever have regrets?'

He laughed. 'Do I have regrets? For sure. Whenever I see a beautiful woman, I struggle. And occasionally I yearn for material things. And there's my frustration with the Pope. Although he's been responsible for positive changes, he could be doing more.... He's talked about improving relationships with other religions – Judaism, for example. Yet at the same time, he's shown insensitivity towards them.' Pasha stopped, sipped his tea for a few moments before continuing. 'It's the same with Islam, he hasn't handled things well.'

'At least he's taken a courageous stand against paedophile priests.'

'For sure, I admire him for risking unpopularity with this. But then his view on homosexuality isn't tolerant.'

Pasha continued talking, as if having an internal debate.

I wondered how he'd react if he knew of my termination.

Half wanting to tell him, half not wanting to, in case he'd despise me.

'Being a priest here, in Kashmir, what's it like?'

He hesitated before replying. 'Many things here make me angry.'

'Such as?'

'When tourists purchase Kashmir rugs, I doubt they think of the health risks the children face. Most carpet makers are children, often as young as six. They can work up to ten hours a day, you know.'

His tone became more exasperated. 'If they work on the old type of loom they have to squat. Which causes deformities of the skeleton. And constant knot tying gives them swollen finger joints, and arthritis.' He was peering at his fingers. 'Also, they develop eyestrain from poor lighting. And don't get me started on the mental health risks.'

'Being in a war zone must make life unbearably hard at times.'

'When there's fighting, I see terrible things, the injuries.'

Pasha paused, closed his eyes and I wondered if he was silently praying. 'The excruciating grief of parents losing a child.... That's one of the most dreadful parts of my job. Talking to them, knowing there's nothing, nothing I can say that will truly help them..... Many believe the Kashmir insurgents are responsible for this war. I think Pakistani paramilitary forces have also been involved. And there are anti-Christian skirmishes from time to time. I try to remain positive – I have to – but it's a real test of faith.' Now he was walking around the houseboat, examining the woodwork, stroking pieces of furniture with his slender hands.

He came to sit beside me again. 'I love cedar wood – I do a bit of carpentry.'

'You do? What sort of things?'

'Tables, cabinets, bookcases. My father taught me. I love creating something. And it's a foil for when I've had a bad day.'

'Do you sell them?'

'I give them away. To parishioners who need furniture. Sometimes to my family.'

During those late afternoons, when we sat or lay on deck talking, a sense of peace suffused me. It was partly the ease of communicating with a native English speaker. Although Tommaso's English was good, we used words differently. But there was more than easy conversation delighting me in Pasha's company. His aura, both relaxing and reassuring, was therapeutic. Some would have ascribed such a presence to his Christian beliefs. To me, it was more about spirituality and love. Tolerance and open-mindedness. Qualities I imagined an interfaith minister would possess.

In wilder moments, I wanted our tranquil times together to last forever.

Pasha was waiting for me outside the hospital at the end of my first shift back. 'There's a restaurant I want to take you to. Okay, not exactly a restaurant, but the food is great.'

He led me to a houseboat on one of the many canals winding its way through Srinagar. There, we stepped through the wooden Moorish style arch entrance to rug covered walls and floors, and gentle side lighting. Several times, I glanced up from eating to see him watching me, expression inscrutable. When we stood to leave, he offered a steadying arm and I clutched the rough material of his tunic.

Torrential rain greeted us as we left the restaurant, and we huddled together under shelter for a few moments, arms and hips touching.

'It won't last long,' he said. 'Tail end of the Monsoons.'

When he dropped me off at the shikara, I turned to face him and he stroked my cheek. Then his head moved fractionally closer and I thought he was going to kiss me. My heart thundered.

'I should go,' he said.

Back at the houseboat, the oboe player was in full flow, accompanied by a flautist and a haunting female voice. I wrapped my shawl around me and went onto the deck where music continued to float over the air. Then the mood changed. Now I could hear the low frequency of the barrel-shaped drum. As the smell of spicy tea drifted in the wind, I kept replaying the seconds when Pasha moved his face towards mine.

The flute and the woman's voice faded into the fragrant night air. The oboe now fast and repetitively rhythmic. Drums steady and insistent. A mouse scuttled across the deck, stopped, then disappeared.

Later, I fantasised about how Pasha's full lips might feel on mine. About him touching me. This was due to missing Tommaso, I convinced myself, as I threw back the warm cover, only to replace it minutes later.

The road to the Bhand village of Wathor was unsealed in parts, congested in others, but arriving felt satisfying. Pasha, in his cassock, immediately attracted interest, children running up to him, clamouring for his attention. While he chatted, I absorbed my surroundings.

Several moments later, he came over to me, saying, 'I've been asked to go and pray with a housebound woman. I won't be long.'

A young girl led him into a mud walled, thatched roof hut, surrounded by garlands of red chillies drying on trees. I wandered around, staring at the emerald green shoots of rice emerging from the water, thinking of the processes they'd go through before emerging on a plate of curry.

Harsh music blared and when Pasha emerged from the hut, we turned a corner, to stumble upon a festival, and the source of the screechy music: a wooden loudspeaker hanging on a tree.

On an earthen embankment stood a small shrine, surrounded by stalls selling an assortment of goods. There, I bought cakes and bread for Omera's family and two clay pots for Gillian and John. My attention was then drawn to a group of men clustering around a stall.

'What is it selling?' I asked Pasha.

He laughed before replying, 'Aphrodisiacs, amongst other things.'

Everywhere, an atmosphere of celebration prevailed, children dancing, adults chatting animatedly, but not once could I belittle this magical event by taking photos. And yet, I could hear Omera saying, "If you want to be a professional photographer, you'll have to get over such sensitivity."

'Father, Father,' more people cried out, rushing over to Pasha, beaming. I observed him conversing unhurriedly with them. A headscarf protecting me from unwelcome attention. From feeling so painfully like an outsider.

We didn't talk much while wandering around. Occasionally our eyes met, his serious, mine, unaccountably emotional.

'As I've mentioned before, when I see terrible things

happen, it's so hard to retain my faith,' he told me on the return drive. 'Not only here, of course. In Italy I'm aware of shameful practices in the Catholic Church.... I feel power-less.... But I stay on.'

I yearned to tell him that everyone here seemed to love him, that he must be doing good. Nevertheless, something stopped me. Now I wondered what, if anything, Omera had told him about my marriage, my difficulties with Tommaso. Pasha had shared so much with me, but I'd never discussed my relationship.

'Why Catholicism?' I asked.

He took so long to answer I feared having blundered into a sensitive area.

Then he replied, splaying his hand on the steering wheel, the gold ring on his second finger gleaming in the light. 'At the time, I believed that being a Catholic priest was more of a vocation. More of a commitment, having to give up so much. Wife, children.... I wanted to make this commitment. As if it proved something. And I was very young...unworldly, in many ways. My father spent hours trying to talk me out of it, advising me to choose the Anglican Church.... Perhaps if I'd been older, I would have listened to him.'

As darkness fell, I felt we'd shared a special occasion. I wanted to thank him for taking me to Wathor. For allowing me to experience something I wouldn't otherwise have discovered. Words would have reduced the feeling experi-ence, however. Pasha understood what the day had meant to me.

At the houseboat, as had become a daily routine, I fetched my shawl and settled on deck. The wind changed direction, bringing with it an intoxicating scent of saffron crocuses. I wondered how such a trip would have been with

Tommaso. Despite my best efforts, however, any images conjured up featured solely him. No background. No context. He didn't belong here. But this didn't reduce my ongoing guilt about having left him.

Inside the houseboat, I could hear Deeba brushing the floor. Despite her respecting my privacy, her sensing when I wanted not just tea but green tea or cardamom tea, the tidying and cleaning the galley, her frequent sweet smiles, I would have preferred to be on my own.

Later, I wished I had a photo of Pasha. But what would I do with it? Display it in our sitting room beside the photos of Tommaso's family and mine? Stare at it furtively on iPhoto?

The sound of crying reached my ears as I walked along the corridor to the ward. Not one child's sobs but many. I quickened my pace, noticing the empty medical superintendent's room and ward kitchen as I passed.

In the ward, the first thing I observed was an acrid odour, then muddy footprints. Four nurses were sitting by children's beds, trying to stem the tears. A ward orderly was cleaning the floor, turning frequently to check behind her.

'What's happened?' I asked Aloka.

She stood upright, defiant, all five foot four of her, but the clutching of her cross belied her attempt at composure. 'The security forces were here.'

'Here? In the ward? Oh my God!'

'Thankfully, they didn't hurt anyone but of course the children were terrified.... They...the soldiers burst in. No warning. The sight of their guns...'

'Is that gunpowder I can smell?'

'They fired into the air. Why, I don't know.... Can you check on Darshan? He doesn't cry but this doesn't mean he isn't frightened.'

Trembling, I made my way to Darshan's bed. Despite the military presence around Srinagar – especially in the modern town – and the occasional gunshot, I'd felt safe here. As if hospitals, like temples, were sacred. Despite history having repeatedly disregarded such sanctity. Knowing the security forces might return, rocked me.

That evening, I took stock. Most of the sick staff were now back at work and there was nothing to gain by staying in Kashmir any longer – not if I wanted to give Tommaso and me another chance. I should return to Italy, to my marriage. Decision taken, at the end of my next shift, I announced my intention to leave.

During my final week, the security forces didn't reappear at the hospital, but I never stopped worrying they might. Whenever I heard a loud noise, I jumped and a rush of bile rose in my throat.

My evenings were more relaxing. During some of these, I'd noticed Deeba hovering as I uploaded photos onto my laptop. One night, I asked her if she wanted to sit beside me and look through them. Her face lit up. While I scrolled through ones of the UK she nodded, occasionally saying, 'Buckin Place' and 'Tower London'.

On my remaining nights, after Pasha had left, she sat with me while I edited my photos, her eyes wide with amazement as I sharpened images or adjusted colour. One time she asked to see my camera and I explained how it worked. She understood English better than she spoke it.

Late one afternoon, Omera arrived at my houseboat, shortly after I'd returned from a knackering shift. Stumbling onto the deck, she cursed as she bumped her ankle. Her eyes looked puffy.

'Are you okay?' I asked, aware this was the first time I'd seen her ruffled.

'My mother – nothing is ever good enough for her.'

Something else was bothering Omera. Like a crime scene investigator, she scoured the living area, eyes homing in on a scarf Pasha had left behind.

'This is Pasha's,' she said, lifting it.

'I meant to bring it round.'

To my horror, I remembered wrapping it round my shoulders the evening before, after he'd left. What if she found a strand of my red hair on it and misunderstood?

She shoved the scarf into her bag and stared at me. 'It's time to return to that husband of yours.'

On my last day, a group of staff took me to Nagin Lake, a small expanse of water leading off Dal Lake. We arrived in the late afternoon to water so calm that willow and poplar trees were reflected in it. Herons and kingfishers hovered nearby before taking off in graceful flight. Above towered the Sabarwan Mountain.

We hired shikaras, placed scented tea candles around them, and paddled on the lake. Later, gusts of wind carried the fragrance of saffron crocuses, and at times I could barely speak from a lump in my throat.

Pasha wasn't with us.

When I left the houseboat for the final time, I put my spare camera on the table with a note for Deeba saying I hoped she would use it.

## 17

T ommaso met me at the airport in Napoli. Being a Saturday, we sat on the balcony until dawn, holding hands and talking about my six-week trip: the abject poverty, the sick children with bloated bellies whom I nursed; the horror at being in a country which produced so much food yet couldn't feed its people; the fear and unpredictability of war.

What I didn't mention was being ill and Pasha looking after me on the houseboat. Our conversations on the deck. Our trip to the Bhand village.

'I did not know you will return,' Tommaso said, squeezing my hand. 'You stayed away for many weeks.'

'We're married, of course I'd return.'

He pulled away at my inadequate answer. But at this point, I could honestly say nothing more. Part of me was still in Kashmir: feeding a malnourished child; wandering through the Shalimar Gardens inhaling the scent of frangipani; talking to Pasha on the houseboat deck.

Later, as streaks of daylight emerged through the flimsy curtains in our bedroom, Tommaso and I lay silently beside each other. Then, as I reached the dreamy state between wakefulness and sleep, he cupped my face and we made love with a new tenderness. Afterwards, in the minutes before sleep claimed me, I knew that returning had been the right thing to do. That despite our problems, my love for this man mattered.

I had enough energy to sort out my marriage.

Tommaso, too, must have felt more optimistic about our relationship because the following evening he suggested I apply for Italian citizenship.

Early March I received an email from Diana: *It's finito with Doug. He's coming back in three weeks to pack up his stuff. I don't want to be there and I need to get away from Florence. Can I stay with you?*

The tourist season began the week before Diana's arrival, the environment changing. Strolling to the harbour now invariably meant squeezing past meandering couples, jumping aside at regular intervals to avoid a humming Vespa. Restaurants required reservations and the boutiques and galleries displayed notices restricting numbers of patrons at the one time. Constantly, the unwelcome sound of English voices interrupted my daydreams, and when out and about, I spoke Italian whenever possible, reluctant to be easily identified as British. I missed the late autumn and winter months, when I shared the town only with its locals.

On the plus side, it was lovely wearing sleeveless clothes again, observing the ever-changing colour of the sea. Spending more time on our balcony, watching boats come and go, overhearing the earnest undulating Italian voices. I loved inhaling the fragrance from early budding flowers.

Watching chiffon clouds above the Lattari mountains chase playfully through the sky.

Diana had been back in the UK for several months visiting family and friends, and we were out of touch. To my dismay, she'd lost at least a stone, markedly noticeable on a slim build, and her normally lustrous dark hair was dull. Even the way she moved had altered, the brisk speed and swinging arms as if embracing the world, replaced by a slower, more closed gait. I wondered about depression. Nevertheless, her trousers were smart, if loose on her, and she'd ironed the red and white striped blouse. Her make-up had changed, however, the natural look, (thin layer of mascara and pale lipstick) replaced by heavily pencilled eyebrows and brighter lipstick. The effect aged her.

Tommaso was attending a course that weekend so she and I had time to ourselves. As we made our way to the harbour, she opened up. 'Doug came home unexpectedly one night – fed up with hospital quarters. Anyway, he promised to move his stuff out and told me he was looking for an apartment.' She rolled her eyes. 'But after two weeks he hadn't begun to pack.... Eventually, he admitted he wasn't doing much to find accommodation. I went into meltdown and told him to go.'

I stopped walking. 'You've had no second thoughts?'

'After what he's done?'

'It must have been difficult for him too,' I said, conscious of being on shaky ground. 'Knowing how badly you wanted kids.'

Diana walked on, turning to throw back a comment. 'Christ, Rachel, whose side are you on?'

I rushed after her. 'But he's not a bad man. Besides, how will separating help? Surely you could consider adopting?'

'Christ, you are slow. Have you considered I might actually meet somebody else? Someone who *is* able to have children.'

Her sarcastic tone stung. Discouraging further conversation. When we reached my favourite spot at the far end of the beach, I wanted to tell her I came here when something troubled me. That when I felt truly happy, I also came here. But I couldn't share this with her. Not right now.

Then she put her arms round me. 'Sorry, I'm being a cow. But I'm glad I'm here. It's so beautiful. I understand why you decided to give it a chance. Not that Edinburgh isn't a great place to live.'

In Amalfi, we meandered through the narrow backstreets of whitewashed houses.

'You seem more like yourself today,' I remarked, as we sat on the beach eating ice cream. Furthermore, it was midday and Diana hadn't mentioned Doug, or her indecision about what to do now.

'I'm adjusting. Trying to, anyway.... No photos of me Rachel – I hate how I look at the moment.'

I put away my camera.

For lunch, we ate seafood pasta in a delicious cream and wine sauce and drank two bottles of wine in the square. High above where we sat, washing flapped in the breeze and we could hear the lapping and glugging of waves on the shore below.

'How's the studying going?' Diana asked.

'Almost two thirds through.... The essays are a challenge – as you know, I'm not academic – but I love the practical assignments.'

'Do you get lonely, I mean, doing it on your own, without other students being around?'

'I might have been but I've got friendly with some of the guys studying at the Photography Institute in Napoli. We keep in touch on Facebook and sometimes I go on their field trips. Or out for meals with them.'

We finished our second bottle of wine, and half-cut and giggling stumbled up thousands of steps to Ravello, where we followed the same route Tommaso and I had taken on our honeymoon nineteen months ago. The trip reminded me of holidays during our student days. Sleeping on the beach on Crete and Rhodes. Excursions into the Troodos mountains in Cyprus. Even then, while I knocked back cheap retsina, Diana never drank too much. Determined to do nothing that might adversely affect her health. Decrease her chances of conceiving and having healthy children.

'You haven't talked much about India,' Diana said. 'Was it amazing?'

I described Delhi, Srinagar and the hospital work. She asked what it was like living on a houseboat, and I told her, omitting anything about Pasha. It felt as if I'd locked away these memories of our time together.

'In a way it was hard returning,' I admitted. 'You should have seen the hospital where I was working. The problems with equipment, the lack of drugs, so many things. Now I'm back living my luxurious lifestyle, I need...I *want* to do something for the hospital. Perhaps donate the money I get from Domenico's assignments. Even a small amount could help them buy more supplies, employ more nurses. Maybe in time, updated equipment. It would make me feel better about...about being so privileged.'

Diana slipped an arm round me. 'What a wonderful idea. I'm sure you could do a lot with your photography.'

'I've been thinking about making calendars or holding an exhibition, donating the funds to the hospital.'

She was silent for a while, before asking, 'How are things with Tommaso, anyway?'

'He's suggested I apply for Italian citizenship.'

'But are you any further on finding out what's going on with him, what he might be...hiding from you?'

I shook my head and for once she didn't push me to say more. On this matter, I was biding my time. Waiting until he and I had spent a settled period together. Besides, perhaps he simply needed longer to trust me enough before opening up. Perhaps.

When returning, I noticed Tommaso talking to a familiar-looking man outside our apartment. I was curious to know who it was, but Diana stopped at Giuseppe's to buy flowers, and by the time we reached home, the man had left.

'Who was that?' I asked Tommaso.

'Who?' he asked distractedly, flicking through the pile of paperwork on his desk.

'I saw you talking to someone outside the apartment.'

His eyes narrowed. 'He is a man I know at the church.'

'I'm sure I've seen him before. But not in Positano.'

A pause followed before Tommaso replied. 'It was Maurizio. You meet him at Diana's exhibition.'

I remembered now: the unpleasant man who'd been talking to Tommaso.

The next day, inspired by Diana's encouragement, I phoned the superintendent of the hospital in Srinagar to discuss how to make intermittent donations, then set up an account. Having done this, I felt better. More purposeful. A busy month followed with assignments for my course and ones for Domenico, at the end of which I made my first payment to the hospital. I didn't mention this to Tommaso.

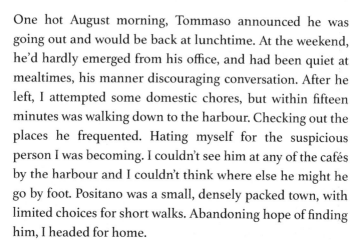

One hot August morning, Tommaso announced he was going out and would be back at lunchtime. At the weekend, he'd hardly emerged from his office, and had been quiet at mealtimes, his manner discouraging conversation. After he left, I attempted some domestic chores, but within fifteen minutes was walking down to the harbour. Checking out the places he frequented. Hating myself for the suspicious person I was becoming. I couldn't see him at any of the cafés by the harbour and I couldn't think where else he might he go by foot. Positano was a small, densely packed town, with limited choices for short walks. Abandoning hope of finding him, I headed for home.

As I passed the park, I spotted him seated on a bench shaded by pine trees, watching children play, his expression wistful. His attention focused on two girls aged around nine or ten who were playing with a tennis ball, their light brown wavy hair bobbing about while they jumped to catch the ball or scrabbled around for it on the rubber tiled ground. I remembered telling him I couldn't have children. His reassurance that it didn't matter. Had he been truthful? Reconsidered? Should I raise the subject again? For the rest of the day, I struggled to erase from memory the expression I'd seen on his face.

'You're quiet. Anything wrong?' I asked at dinner.

Tommaso glared at me. 'You should be a policeman.'

Face to face with him now, I couldn't bring myself to ask if not having children made him sad. If this was true, what then? Discussions about surrogate mothers, adoption? I thought of Diana and what she'd been through, the possible conversations she'd had with Doug about alternatives to conceiving a child themselves.

However, I would have to shelve my worries for the moment. In three weeks' time, I was sitting the A2 level for a Certificate of Italian as a foreign language, which involved extra work. Omera was tutoring me more frequently during the run-up and giving me lots of homework for which I was grateful, despite it being time-consuming. In addition, I was watching as many Italian DVDs as I could find.

To my frustration, despite working hard on conversing in the language, my ear had yet to tune in properly. When Tommaso spoke Italian to me, he made an effort to slow down his speech. Likewise, Omera and Natalie. But with many Italians, when I produced a reasonably grammatical sentence, I'd be subjected to a rapid and often incomprehensible response.

After dinner, I put on *La Dolce Vita*, with English subtitles, and attempted to focus on the film. Tommaso sat through twenty minutes of it before going to his study.

Two days before my CILS, I planned to visit Minori, keen to see it before autumn arrived. Tommaso had left for a dental appointment in Positano before I surfaced, so I dressed and breakfasted at a leisurely pace before heading for the bus stop. While passing the park, I looked in. He was seated on the same bench, watching the children.

Perhaps he valued something about this particular space. Perhaps the kids were incidental. Several minutes later, he reached into his bag, produced a wad of papers and started making notes. Thank God. Here he could work, the cooler air and trees helping him think.

As I was about to leave, a fair-haired girl of about 10 or 11 appeared. Tommaso watched as she sat down on the grass and bit into a peach. Moments later came a woman's voice, 'Valentina, Valentina.' The girl stood, brushed some leaves from her dress, deposited the peach remains in a bin and left. Shortly after, Tommaso packed away his notes. I slipped off before he could notice me.

On the day of my language test, I was relieved to be distracted from my increasing concern that my husband might have an unhealthy interest in pre-pubescent girls. During the bus journey to Salerno, I switched off.

The test was easier than anticipated and despite being exhausted afterwards, I was confident I'd pass.

In Positano, again, I rang Omera's buzzer to tell her about the test.

She answered the door, brandishing a pillow. 'Help yourself to a drink and make me a coffee, please. Pasha's arriving tomorrow.'

My heart skipped a beat. Pasha back in Positano....

She laid sheets on the sofa and rummaged in a drawer for a pillowcase. 'You'll have heard about the Muslim outbursts against the Catholic church in Srinagar. It's horrible there at the moment.' She peered at the pillowcase she was holding and tutted. 'I should have bought more of these at the sale in Salerno. However, he'll only stay with me until they have space in the church accommodation.'

'What will he do in Positano?' I called from the kitchen.

'Work in the diocese,' she said. 'As he's done before. Probably at the Santa Maria Assunta. He might find a part-time post teaching geography.'

I made Omera coffee, helped myself to orange juice and went through to the sitting room. 'Do you think it's working out for him? Being a priest.'

She shrugged. 'Hard to say. Pasha's deep. It can be diffi-cult to know what's going on behind those eyes.'

Emotion must have registered in my expression because she said, 'Go home to that husband of yours.'

I finished my juice. 'The test went well, by the way.'

'I knew it would.'

At the apartment, a delicious smell wafted from the kitchen where Tommaso was stirring dreamily at the cooker, singing to Wagner's *Tristan und Isolde*. The balcony table was set, with long stemmed roses as a centrepiece, and large candles were placed around the railings. My heart contracted.

He poured me a glass of Marsala. 'I have a surprise, *amore*.'

I stared at him. A special dessert? Tickets for a concert? A weekend away?

'Tell me then,' I said, feigning enthusiasm. All I wanted was a normal married life. Not one full of revelations and worrying.

'I bought flight tickets to Sicily.'

'Not another trip?'

'You are not pleased?'

'Tickets? Two tickets?'

'*Amore*, you and I will go to Sicily – you will meet my family.... Are you happy?'

## 18

The tiredness from today's events, from worrying about Tommaso, lifted. Finally, I would meet the rest of his family.

'When are we going?'

'The 1ˢᵗ September.'

'Our wedding anniversary! Oh my God, that's only a few weeks away... Do I have the right clothes? Will I need smart clothes? Do...?'

He smiled. 'We will shop in Rome before we will leave. We'll stay with my parents, of course. They live in a villa overlooking Taormina. There is much to show you.'

When the plane landed in Catania, my hands were trembling. The lead-up to our departure had been so hectic I'd had little time to worry about meeting Tommaso's family. About what they'd think of me. Wanting to get a head start on my course, I'd been reading books on the forthcoming year's recommended list; Domenico had given me filming assignments and I'd been fine-tuning my studio. And, once more, receiving extra lessons from Omera, determined to speak reasonable Italian with my in-laws.

Additionally, Tommaso and I had spent a weekend in Rome where I chose two dresses, a blouse and shoes, he bought yet another suit, and we shopped for presents for his extended family, each item thoughtfully selected. We travelled with one suitcase entirely of gifts.

As we stepped out onto the tarmac, Tommaso took my hand. 'It might be an unusual visit.'

The situation *was* unusual: most people met their in laws before getting married. Before I could ask him if this was what he meant, however, we became separated in the jostle of passengers.

In the arrivals hall, he looked around. 'She should be here.'

Moments later, a woman appeared and embraced him, speaking rapidly. I hadn't know one of his sisters was meeting us.

'*Madre,* Mother, this is Rachel,' Tommaso said.

*Madre!*

He turned to me. 'Rachel, my mother, Irma Vitale.'

Ignoring my extended hand, she kissed me on both cheeks and stood back. Smilingly, we scrutinised each other.

In a tailored cream dress, a green and salmon silk scarf draped round her shoulders, she could have graced the front cover of any respected fashion magazine. Her brown hair was loosely pinned back in a French roll, her almond eyes subtly highlighted, her lipstick toning with the salmon of the shawl. Furthermore, she smelt divine.

'*Bella, bella,*' she said in delight. 'Fabrizio was correct.... Come, we have arranged a celebration lunch.'

Tommaso smiled at me as he pushed the luggage trolley to the car park.

Despite being hungry, I was thankful for the drive to the Vitale family home. While the car spun along the coast road, past houses with red pantile houses, past rocky landscapes, with palm trees dotted here and there, I was still reeling from meeting my stunning but warm mother-in-law. Yet, she and the well-groomed Fabrizio were an obvious couple.

As Irma pulled into the grounds, Fabrizio appeared on the drive, helped me out of the passenger seat.

'Welcome to Villa Bellucci,' he said, kissing me. 'Your flight was smooth?'

'Very smooth and clear, thanks. We saw some lovely views from the air.'

I stared at the imposing two-storey building, its ancient pink walls supporting a widespread purple and red bougainvillea. Tommaso had told me they achieved the paint colour by mixing volcanic earth with plaster and ground shells. His photos, nevertheless, had failed to convey its intensity. He'd done equal injustice to the grandeur of the house, I realised, when the elderly housekeeper Antonia led me across a marble floor and up the wide, curving staircase to a large bedroom with en suite bathroom.

As she quietly closed the door behind me, I studied the wrought iron bedhead and ornately carved wardrobe; the dusky pink floor tiles and matching curtains. French windows overlooked a small courtyard and the familiar sweet fragrance of a frangipani tree floating into our room whisked me back to the Shalimar Gardens of Kashmir, and further back to my early childhood. We'd had a frangipani tree in our garden, and I remembered picking the white, yellow stained petals, holding them to my face, inhaling their glorious smell.

In the bathroom, I washed my face and inspected myself in the full-length mirror. My jacket and trousers had travelled well, also my new blouse. After refreshing my make-up and scooshing myself with my Jo-Malone-special-occasions perfume, I left the bedroom, feeling like I'd stumbled onto a glamorous film set, while navigating the stairs in my new high heels.

A babble of voices emerged from a room to the right and when I hovered at the entrance, Tommaso strode over, grabbed my hand and swept me off to a group of adults and children. Ten minutes later, I'd met his sisters – Abri and Beatrice – their respective husbands, six children aged between two and nineteen, three aunts and two uncles. Furthermore, I'd conversed adequately enough to connect with them. To my gratitude, no one had rejected my efforts by switching to English (which I suspected most of them could easily have done) or intervened too quickly to supply a forgotten word.

Shortly afterwards, we were invited through to the dining room and the younger children escorted to the kitchen where they'd eat. A long walnut marquetry table gleamed in the early afternoon light. Each place setting sporting bundles of green porcelain crockery and red linen napkins. Again, the formality surprised me. Briefly I longed for home and a simple salad on our balcony.

Once we were seated, Fabrizio stood and silence fell.

'*Mio amata famiglia*, my beloved family, we are here today to welcome Rachel to our family.' He turned to me. 'Rachel, we hope you will enjoy your visit and that you will love our beloved Sicily as we love it. Now, please enjoy your meal.'

The guests on either side leaned over in turn to kiss me on both cheeks. A clinking of glasses and a collective '*Buon appetito*' followed as Antonia presented us with bowls of fish soup. Being served by staff didn't detract from the friendly and unpretentious atmosphere, however, and I observed Irma patting the woman's arm. Smiling at her in the way she might with a friend.

After lunch, we sat under lofty palms in the garden, drinking Maraschino liqueurs and corretto, coffee with added grappa. Irma and Fabrizio, working later, opted for caffe latte. At the far end of the lawn, Tommaso's nieces and nephews were running around and I could hear the distant sound of sawing. The combination of a full lunch, alcohol and an early start from Positano made me sleepy and I nodded off on my comfortable chair. The sound of high voices fading. The scent of roses intensifying

Later, once Fabrizio and Irma had left for the restaurant, Tommaso and I strolled along the beach, watching the waves, swathed in a pearly pink hazy light.

He was relaxed then, but by evening seemed unsettled, sitting down for a while, then leaving the room. Preoccupied when I talked to him.

'Is something wrong?' I eventually asked.

'No, no. Everything is fine, *amore*.'

His phone went, he answered and moved away. The expansive movements of his free arm and his tone as he left the room, suggested a difficult conversation, but when he returned, I said nothing.

That night, Tommaso lay silently beside me in bed. Normally he held me even if we didn't make love and, yearning for physical connection, I tentatively touched his arm. He didn't respond. Moments later came the sound of his regular breathing. What could be the problem? Tension with his parents? A rerun of the row with Fabrizio in Positano? The reason for which I had yet to discover.

In Palermo, Tommaso showed me round the Ziza Palace. Despite reading up about it before our visit, I was both surprised and delighted by it.

'These frescos are amazing, Tommaso. And look at the mosaics. The Arabs certainly knew how to build.'

'It is now a UNESCO World Heritage Site. Come, I want to show you the fountain which has fish. People can choose the fish they want to eat,' he told me.

'I couldn't do that,' I said, shaking my head. 'Watch a fish swimming around and then eat it.'

In the ancient Arab quarter, we wandered the streets, stopping at the Piazza Marina. It was hot so we sat in the small Garibaldi Garden for a while, under the shade of an ancient fig tree, gazing at the beautiful old buildings surrounding us.

'I'm hungry,' I said, checking my watch. It was leaving one-thirty and Italian restaurants often finished serving lunch shortly after two.

'I want to show you one more thing, then we will go to a restaurant.'

Tommaso took my hand and we walked through the magnificent medieval Porta Felice, finding ourselves by the sea.

'The gates are a mixture of Baroque and Renaissance architecture,' he told me, launching into a description of other buildings in the port area. He was talking quickly as if running late while delivering a lecture. When I took his hand, his palm was damp.

'Hey, slow down a bit,' I said.

He turned to stare at me but didn't say anything.

We strolled around the port area until we found a restaurant that he deemed good enough for us.

At our table, he scrutinised the menu, saying, 'You must try the sardine pasta.'

'Sardines aren't really my thing,' I said, looking for some other fish dish.

'*Amore,* you must try such a famous dish of Sicily. They cook the sardines with saffron and sultanas, and fennel that is only found in the mountains here. If you don't like it, never will I ask you again to eat something you do not want to eat.'

Although he'd promised this before, he was so keen for me to try the *pasta con le sarde*, that I acquiesced. He was right, though. It was delicious

'Sicily is such a wonderful island, how could you bear to leave it?' I asked after the waiter had brought our dessert.

'Some parts are ugly,' Tommaso said. 'Some parts were badly damaged during the Second World War.'

He talked more about this for a while.

That evening I went to bed immediately after dinner. Tired, and, once again, concerned about Tommaso.

The next day, we borrowed Irma's car and drove through the Sicanian mountains to the large old fishing port of Sciacca on the south coast. There we wandered the cobbled back-streets of the old town. For lunch we ate red prawns, cooked in coconut milk and served with fresh passionfruit.

'Nothing is as good as Sicilian food,' Tommaso told me, as he wiped his mouth.

'Everything seems so wonderful here – why *did* you move to Positano?'

He said nothing.

'Not running away from something? Someone?' I suggested, half-jokingly.

The waiter removed our plates and asked if we wanted dessert.

'You must try the Rum Baba,' Tommaso said, ordering two lots.

Normally I'd be irritated if he chose for me, but today I felt so carefree and happy to be here with him, that I let it ride.

After lunch, we wandered by the Marina, the combination of sun and sea breeze on my shoulders intoxicating.

'I love this place,' I said, for once wishing I could paint the ochre, brown and coral colours of the buildings, the vivid pink and red and orange bougainvillea hanging over wrought iron balconies. I don't suppose we could stay the night here?'

'Not today, *amore*. Perhaps on our next visit.'

Of course there'd be other visits. We didn't have to see everything during this trip.

Tommaso took my hand. 'We must go now.'

'It's only four, and the drive back won't take long.'

'We are driving a different route,' he said. 'By the west coast. There is something I want you to see.'

'Tell me more.'

'You will see when we will arrive.'

An hour or so later, we arrived in the coastal town of Cornino. It didn't look much but before I could ask Tommaso why we'd come here, I realised we weren't stopping. Fifteen minutes later, having driven along poorly signposted minor roads, we reached some caves.

'Here is the Mangiapane Cave,' he said. 'Once there was a village. Poor people lived here.'

At the entrance I could see a cluster of houses carved out of the rock, both inside and outside the cave.

'This is perhaps as old as the Age of Stones, the Stone Age. It is now a museum,' he told me. 'Until the middle of last century, poor people lived here. Come, we will visit the museum.'

The museum was open-air, goats and chickens roaming freely as we studied artefacts and photos of how people lived in those times. And as the caves were so hard to find, the area was thankfully free of tourist buses and tacky paraphernalia.

'This reminds me of the Troglodyte homes in Tunisia,' I said. 'Except that they are underground. Oh Tommaso, there's so much travelling we could do. Once I've finished my course, let's buy a van and travel for a year. It'd be great.... I could take loads of photos and do creative things with them.... What do you think?'

'There is my job,' he said stiffly.

'But you could take a break, surely? While we're away, you could study leather products in other countries. Come back with loads of ideas.'

'I have responsibilities in Italy.'

'Your parents are still young, and fit, as far as I can see – apart from your mother's hip. And we'd be together. Properly together. It would be wonderful.'

Silence.

'We talked about travelling, before we got married. Remember?'

'We've been to Rome and we're in Sicily and–'

'But there's a whole world to see. Not just Italy... or India.'

He shrugged. 'Perhaps.'

His lack of enthusiasm disappointed me hugely, but, more worryingly, I experienced a similar niggle to the one I had at the concert in Ravello, shortly before he announced he wanted us to live in Italy. I was glad when I became drowsy, eventually falling asleep during the journey back to Palermo.

On the Saturday, my husband accompanied his parents to early Mass. When he returned, I waited for him to suggest we visit other parts of Palermo. I wanted to see the Norman Cathedral and the Palace. Visit more markets. To my surprise, however, he claimed a headache. The desire to sleep before lunch. I'd expected his usual enthusiasm.

'Do you wish to visit Taormina?' Irma suggested to me over coffee. 'I have errands to do.'

During the short drive there, she said, 'I am sorry we weren't at your wedding. Fabrizio explained to you that we knew nothing about it.'

I didn't know how to respond, reluctant to criticise Tommaso. 'I was shocked when I found out you didn't know. I thought it was because of your operation.... It would have been lovely if you'd been there – all of you.'

'Yes,' she said, and the subject was dropped.

In Taormina, I wandered the streets, looking at churches, climbing steps to gaze down through bougainvillea-covered alleys to the sea. Constantly thinking how romantic it would be to return here with Tommaso.

On our return journey, I sensed anxiety behind Irma's warmth. And during our late lunch, Tommaso spoke little, frequently exchanging glances with her. Irritation replaced anxiety. We had another four days in Sicily and I wanted to enjoy them, not worry.

After we'd eaten, Tommaso suggested a walk along another beach, a short drive away. It was cooler and windier today with bobbing boats and swaying palm trees.

'My family like you,' he said, squeezing my hand before starting the car engine.

'Tommaso, why have you been so quiet today?'

His face closed down, causing my stomach to churn.

'I want you to meet someone.'

'Intriguing,' I said heartily, my relief overwhelming.

Tommaso and his surprises.... 'Who?'

'You will discover this soon.'

When we reached the beach, I scanned it for people, but all I could see was a huge expanse of sand and a choppy sea merging seamlessly with the grey sky. Tommaso was checking his watch.

'This *is* something nice, I assume?' I asked, but he didn't reply.

He slowed down.

In the distance, two figures were approaching, one of them significantly smaller than the other. When they drew nearer, I could make out a child playing with a ball. The adult was wearing a long skirt that billowed in the wind.

Tommaso stopped.

'Do you know them?' I asked.

He grabbed my hand, pulling me along the beach. Before we reached the couple, a gust of wind blew the ball away and the child scampered off to retrieve it. Tommaso's gaze followed her, then returned to the woman.

When we reached her, they kissed on both cheeks.

He said to her, 'Elisa, this is Rachel.'

'His wife,' I added.

'I know who you are,' she said warmly.

I was facing a woman with long brown hair, a light olive skin and large dark eyes. A stunning woman.... Elisa! The watch....

Sensing my confusion, she turned to Tommaso and a heated exchange in Italian followed, accompanied by flying arms and reprimanding fingers. Then the child rushed up, dropping the wet, sandy ball before reaching him. Tommaso and she embraced.

Tommaso clutched my hand. 'This is Ysabelle...my daughter.'

## 19

The sound of waves roared in my ears. The figures in front of me blurred. From a distance, I heard a child's voice, a deeper woman's voice reply.

Tommaso took my arm. 'Rachel?'

I managed to focus on the little girl. About nine or ten, she was staring at me with a disconcerting blend of childlike innocence and adult knowing. She had long light brown hair, an upturned nose and wide mouth. An elfin look. My stomach felt like a band of steel. Desperately, I searched her face for a feature to convince me she wasn't my husband's daughter. That, somehow, I'd misunderstood. The eyes gave it away. The same walnut brown, marginally too wide apart. Yet she was beautiful.

'*Ciao,*' I said.

Without replying, she turned, her attention once more on the ball that had rolled away, heading for the sea. Like the ball, I longed to take off along the beach but my feet wouldn't move.

From a distance, I heard Tommaso speak. 'I know this is a surprise.'

I stared at Elisa. 'You're her mother?'

She nodded. My mind reeled. From deep within, I found the courage to ask, 'Are you and Tommaso married?'

She reached for my arm. 'We have never been married. We were childhood sweethearts.'

She turned to Tommaso, once again speaking in rapid Italian, chin thrust out, eyes blazing. I observed her sculpted shoulders, toned arms. A gymnast? Dancer? A wave of nausea washed over me. Ignoring Tommaso's entreaties, I stumbled off.

He followed me and grabbed me by the shoulder. 'Rachel–'

'You *bastard*,' I shouted, moving away, my legs strengthening as his deception registered more fully.

Several moments of running along dry sand passed, then I became conscious that the surface underfoot had changed and my face and clothes were damp. As the rain intensified, I squeezed under an overhanging rock, leaning back for support. How dare Tommaso conceal something so important. Marry me under such false pretences.

While sitting there, dampness seeping through my trousers, an inner voice insisted I must play a role. Like a reluctant understudy, shoved onto the stage. But I didn't want to be a stepmother. I didn't want to share my husband.

Eventually, too wet, too cold, to remain any longer on the sand, I wriggled out from under the rock, swaying as I stood. I remembered Irma's tension at lunch. She and Fabrizio would have known Tommaso's plans for this afternoon. Elisa had known.

Everyone had known except me.

While gazing at the dark clouds overhead, a gust of wind knocked me over. My trousers were now soaked and I didn't know whether the water coursing down my face was from rain or emotion.

Something prompted me to return to the others. When I reached them, Tommaso, jacket draped over his head, was watching Elisa chase Ysabelle along the beach. Automatically, I lifted the abandoned ball, Ysabelle noticed and bounded over to me. Fleetingly we studied each other. Then she took the ball and threw it to her mother, before launching into a series of cartwheels, spraying wet sand everywhere.

What did Ysabelle know about me? Anything? More questions appeared and blended into hurtful answers. When Tommaso visited Sicily, he'd have seen her, in addition to working. Perhaps the only purpose for visiting had been to see his daughter. No wonder he'd wanted us to live in Italy.

Elisa came over to me and again I registered her slim, toned body, the alluring eyes. Bedroom eyes. Why weren't she and Tommaso still together?

'I am sorry you have discovered like this,' she said. 'I thought you knew about Ysabelle. You must understand...I was the one who wanted a child. Tommaso agreed, only to please me. Our relationship ended soon after Ysabelle was born.'

'I knew nothing about this,' I said, as if confiding in a friend.

Ironically, despite resenting and feeling threatened by Elisa, I suspected if she and I had met under other circumstances, a friendship would have developed, her warmth and openness appealing. A weird thought to have so soon after meeting her. So soon after learning of Ysabelle's existence.

She pointed to an apartment block at the end of the

beach. 'We live there. The beach is our garden. I teach physical education at Ysabelle's school.'

I remembered the park, the wistful expression on Tommaso's face. Perhaps he'd felt closer to Ysabelle while watching the girls play, as they were of similar age and appearance to her. At least I could dismiss the idea of sinister behaviour.

But if Ysabelle hadn't been born, would he now be with Elisa?

Elisa called to Ysabelle who ran to her father and hugged him. Then, hand in hand, mother and daughter half walked, half ran to the sea where they skipped along the shallow water, stopping to splash each other.

As the figures diminished, I jumped when Tommaso slipped his jacket round me.

I pulled away, and the jacket slid onto the wet sand. 'Didn't you think I had a right to know?'

'I could never find the right time–'

'For God's sake, spare me the clichés.'

He pointed at the sky. 'We must return now.'

In silence, we trudged to the car. He owed me an apology, he owed me more, and my earlier need to scream at him lingered.

'Why now?' I said.

'What?'

'Why choose now to introduce me? What's changed?'

He didn't reply. His head was bowed, his hands clutched the steering wheel.

'Have you *any* idea how it felt to be introduced to your daughter? Especially as you hadn't actually told me you had one?' I couldn't control the anguish in my voice. Anguish mixed with rage and mortification.

I wanted to tear him apart, limb by beautiful limb.

Someone once told me the urge to destroy is creative. But I didn't feel creative.

'You obviously haven't. I was shocked.... I am shocked. And yes, humiliated, too.'

Tommaso raised his head, swallowing hard. I'd got through to him.

'I wanted to tell you many times, but I never can find right words,' he said.

'Come on, Tommaso, there must have been loads of occasions. You could have tried. Before we left Positano. Even before we left your parents' home this afternoon.'

He said nothing. Tears stung my eyes and I willed them to disappear. Noticing me struggle, he put out his arm and leaned towards me. I shoved him away.

'We are invited to eat with Ysabelle and Elisa this evening,' he said.

My laugh sounded hysterical. 'You must be joking.'

'You will go back to the villa?'

His quick acceptance of my refusal hurt, but I felt too unsure of myself, too proud, to change my mind. I needed to be on my own, and with his parents at the restaurant, I would be.

'What does Ysabelle know about me?'

He stared through the misted windscreen.

'Does she know we're married?'

Silence.

'Did she know I existed before today?'

Silence.

I watched our individual puffs of breath reach the windscreen, wondering if they'd merge. They didn't.

Ignoring his distress, I left the car and returned to the beach.

The bar was gloomy and smoky, filled entirely by men, but I didn't care. Having observed me, the barman produced a towel for my hair and brought me a ciabatta to accompany the beer. And when I acknowledged his kindness, he simply pointed to my ciabatta. 'You eat, please.'

What was registering now was that never again would I feel the same way about life in Positano. Ysabelle might be miles away physically, but she'd be between Tommaso and me. Even if he saw her only in Sicily, her existence would limit our love.... I had become my mother.

When I finished my ciabatta, the barman appeared with a cappuccino.

'Is wrong time to drink this but....' He shrugged.

'*Molto grazie*, thank you so much,' I said when paying the bill.

He glanced at my wedding ring. 'You go home now, signora, *si*?'

A rumble of thunder startled me as I entered the Vitale home. Except for a hall light, the house was dark and my footsteps on the marble staircase sounded eerie. Reminding me of Hitchcock black and white movies.

Diana was slow to answer the phone. '*Buona sera*? Hallo?'

'I'm so glad you're there.'

'Rachel! What's wrong?'

'I've just found out Tommaso has a daughter.'

'What?!'

'I met her today...on the beach. She's about nine.'

Naively, I'd hoped that uttering these words would help. But telling Diana made it real. Prevented me from hiding behind the crumbly walls of denial.

I heard my friend's intake of breath. 'I don't understand.'

'I met her mother too. Elisa. He didn't want a child but she did, so he went along with it but—'

'But didn't want to be a father to her. Christ, men are such bastards.'

'Who would have thought that Tommaso and Doug have common traits?' I said. 'Both deceiving the women they love.'

'So much for truth in a relationship.... At least you can be a stepmother, anyway.'

'For God's sake, you know I'm not maternal. And the last thing I want is to be a stepmother. You of all people should understand. You wouldn't even consider—'

From the end of the phone came a laugh.

'Di, have you been drinking?'

'Not a lot else to do round here in the evenings.... My divorce came through today. Nobody to celebrate with. Doug's gone back to England, so I couldn't celebrate with him.... My best hope is to become happily divorced. What a joke!'

'I wish I was with you,' I said. 'We could be miserable together. Drink ourselves into oblivion.'

'Accept Tommaso's child, Rachel. It's not as if she'll be living with you.'

After ringing off, I crawled into bed fully dressed. Shoving aside Tommaso's pillow. Unable to bear the strong scent of his skin that lingered on the soft cotton cover.

Several hours later, I awoke, bathed in sweat. Where was Tommaso? Ysabelle would be in bed by now, I supposed, so what was he doing? Images of him with Elisa flooded my mind: her lithe limbs entwined with his. I visualised them lying in her bed, talking quietly, in postcoital bliss. Him trying not to fall asleep. Her telling him he should go home.

My heart raced. The notion of phoning him came and left in one fluid thought. If only I'd gone to her home with them. There, I might have sensed how close they were.

Further questions reared their treacherous necks: where did he stay during his business trips in Sicily? With his parents? With her? Again, I wondered if there *was* any business conducted here apart from matters connected with Ysabelle.

A sense of helplessness gripped me. I could do nothing about this situation. Tommaso would continue to visit his daughter – how could he not? But, like a sea creature's suckers, the most dominant question wouldn't let go: did he and Elisa sleep with each other? Were they making love right now?

In the bathroom, I undressed and slipped into my nightdress, automatically cleansing and moisturising my face, dry from the salt spray of the sea and from my tears. I brushed my teeth, then my hair.

Several minutes later, the door opened and Tommaso stood there in his wet jacket.

'I am sorry to be late,' he said, dumping the jacket on a chair. I could smell its dampness. 'Elisa and I have to make decisions about Ysabelle.'

Before I could reply, he went into the bathroom. I heard his electric toothbrush buzzing, the bath slowly filling.

I got out of bed and went to the bathroom. 'You slept with Elisa, didn't you?'

He switched off his toothbrush, wiped his mouth. 'No.'

'Have you slept with her since we got married?'

'*Amore*–'

'*Have* you?'

'No.'

Reason prevailed. If he'd slept with Elisa, he would have

showered at hers. Today's revelation had knocked my thinking off kilter. I lay down again, waiting for him, needing his embrace, his love. Despite struggling to stay awake, though, my eyelids became heavy. When I surfaced again at three o'clock, the other side of the bed was empty.

Tommaso wasn't in the bathroom, nor on the balcony, so I slipped on my dressing gown and left the bedroom. A grandfather clock ticked solemnly as I padded along the dark corridor, past closed doors, past large ornamental pots, and down the stairs.

Thinking he might have been thirsty, I headed for the kitchen. The large empty room smelled of real coffee and fresh basil, its exquisite order mocking my chaotic thoughts. I then searched other rooms, eventually finding him in the small sitting room off the drawing room, slumped in an armchair, half obscured by a mature parlour palm. With his back to me, in his silk dressing gown, head bowed, he resembled an elderly` man. All I could hear was the ticking clock on the mantelpiece. And his weeping.

Tommaso was sitting by the bed watching me, when I woke the following morning. Elbow on my pillow, I smiled sleepily at him. Then I remembered. My head ached, my nose was blocked and my eyes felt puffy from so much crying.

'I must talk to you about Ysabelle,' he said.

'I need coffee.'

'It is important to me that you understand. Please.' He took a deep breath. 'Elisa wanted so much to be a mother. She promised she would care for the baby herself. Perhaps she hoped that afterwards... that when Ysabelle was born, I would want to be a father.' He shook his head.

He went to the table, poured a coffee and brought it over to me. It tasted bitter but I was too weary to ask him to add sugar, let alone get out of bed and add it myself. From downstairs wafted a smell of cooking meat and I remembered his cousin and her mother were invited for lunch.

'We parted when Ysabelle was three months old. I did not see her for five years. Then Elisa asked me to visit. She wanted Ysabelle to know her father. She needed to have this...this identity.'

Had I brought any paracetamol? Had Tommaso? He was staring at me, awaiting my response.

'And Irma and Fabrizio?' I said, without being clear what I was asking.

'They are her grandparents. Elisa's father is dead and her mother is living in New York. My parents care for Ysabelle if Elisa is away.'

I got out of bed and wandered into the bathroom to rummage in my sponge bag for painkillers. Avoiding the mirror. Tommaso had never seen me after a lengthy cry and I dared not confront how awful I must look. Elisa, I reckoned, would remain beautiful if she cried for a week: her eyes might be moist and her nose red at the tip, but nothing worse. I found paracetamol, filled a glass with water and swallowed two tablets. Back in the bedroom, I added sugar to my coffee, dropping in an extra cube, as if additional energy might help.

Tommaso was still sitting there when I returned to bed.

'Is this why you and your father were arguing in Positano?'

'Italians are family people. They love children. The men too. Uncles love the children of their brothers and sisters.

My parents...they are confused because I am not a proper father to Ysabelle.'

He turned and stretched out an arm, a plea for under-standing and sympathy. 'It was difficult to live there. She cried a lot and did not sleep. Everything was untidy. Elisa became different. Now she was a mother and things were... changed... different between us. I was unhappy with my work, then I was offered a good job in Napoli so I moved to Positano. Then Eliza wrote to tell me that Ysabelle was upset at school.'

His expression changed to one of pain, and despite my turmoil, I reached for his hand. Head bowed, he continued talking, his voice so quiet I strained to hear him. 'It was the *Festa del Papà*. The teachers were helping children to make cards for their *papà*. She did not have a *papà*.... Elisa asked me to come to Sicily. Ysabelle was almost six at this time.... We did not tell her immediately that I am her father. After I left, Elisa told her the truth. Since then, I have seen them each year, perhaps three or four times. Now, of course, I love my daughter.'

I took my last sip of coffee and lay back against the pillows, thinking about Ysabelle. How it must have been for her then, and how it was now, having a father in her life. Wondering if it was difficult for her to see him so infre-quently. From losing my father, albeit at an older age, I understood such deprivation. But then, Ysabelle was too young to remember Tommaso when he lived with her. Even so, I must try to accept her place in Tommaso's life.

If only he'd told me about her when we became close – I'd have had a choice then. What would I have done? I wondered.

A more generous person would immediately plan visits, harness energy into nurturing the father-daughter relationship. But less than twenty-four hours since discovering the truth, I'd yet to reach this stage. Had Tommaso already considered asking Ysabelle to stay with us? Had she stayed when I returned to Edinburgh to rent out my flat? It seemed odd knowing she might have been there in my absence. As if he'd invited another woman to our home.

Of more urgency, no longer could I postpone asking the question badgering me. 'Are you in love with Elisa?'

He took my hand. 'She is a sister to me now. It is you I love. You must believe this.'

'She is so beautiful,' I muttered.

'She is,' he agreed. 'But there is not the chemicals between us.'

Despite myself, I smiled. 'The chemistry, you mean.'

I did believe he loved me, but as he showered and dressed – immaculate, as always, in a light brown suit and red silk tie – I wondered if, for him, this love might be the sort people are grateful for in later years. Or unlikely couples would thankfully grab. A comfortable love, based on friendship and pragmatism, rather than passion. Second best.

'You should have told me,' I said as Tommaso left the room to join his parents. Feeling old and heavy, I got out of bed, opened the wardrobe door and sifted through my outfits. Wistfully remembering our carefree shopping spree in Rome. I lifted out a shimmery green dress with cross-over bodice which Tommaso had declared sexy, and held it against me. It wasn't right. Too incompatible with my mood. The paracetamol had now kicked in, but my eyes were puffy and dull so I bathed them in cold water.

'What a beautiful dress,' Fabrizio told me, after introducing me to his cousin and her daughter who'd been unable to attend my welcome lunch.

'I agree,' Irma said, kissing me.

I managed a smile. What I wished for most, though, was Tommaso's approval. Fear of comparison with Elisa gnawed at me – did he really simply love her as a sister?

Somehow, I survived lunch, contributing to the conversation when possible, smiling until my jaw ached. Despite my empty stomach, eating was difficult. Tommaso, seated opposite me, could have been a stranger.

'What will you do this afternoon?' Irma asked after our guests had left.

'I must shop with Ysabelle,' Tommaso said. 'She needs things for school.'

I waited for him to suggest I accompany them. Throughout lunch we'd only infrequently caught each other's eye, and it occurred to me that he regretted revealing so much about Elisa and Ysabelle. He wasn't looking at me now, either.

Fabrizio turned to me. 'We invite you to dinner this evening at the restaurant.'

'Thank you,' I said, on automatic pilot.

Tommaso shook his head. 'I will be with Ysabelle. Elisa has a meeting at the school.'

I clenched my fists. But, in a few days we'd be returning to Positano and I'd have him to myself again. With Ysabelle in the background, of course. She'd always be in the background now.

'I might go into Palermo this afternoon,' I said breezily.

Irma stared at me. 'You will go on your own? It is different to Taormina.'

Gently I said, 'You lived on your own in Paris as a student.'

Tommaso laughed. 'British women are independent, *madre*.'

British women are independent. He *was* learning fast.

Ironically, now he'd grasped this fact, I would have willingly sacrificed my last vestiges of self-reliance to feel secure with him. To return to the relaxed companionship of our early days together, when whether to eat in or out was our most onerous decision.

From a distant place, I heard myself thank my hosts again for a meal to which I'd barely done justice. Announce my intention to catch the bus to Palermo. I lingered in the bedroom, hoping Tommaso would seek me out before I left. Eventually I went downstairs. From the library I could hear him in conversation with his father.

That evening, I took extra care when changing for dinner. Despite sensing Irma and Fabrizio weren't the sort who'd compare me with Elisa, I was aware of spending longer on my hair and make-up. Selecting jewellery which best complimented my outfit. How well did my parents-in-law know Elisa? Did she spend time with them when Ysabelle was visiting? Did they regard her as a daughter-in-law? An awkward position for them to deal with, I realised, admiring them even more for their warmth, their dignity, their welcoming me into their family.

During dinner at their restaurant, without other relatives to dilute the focus on me, I threw myself into a sterling performance. Conversing as if all was right in my world. We talked about Palermo; Fabrizio's time at Oxford; Irma's years in Paris, before returning to Sicily and meeting him. They were interested in my photography course.

Eventually I summoned the courage to ask them how

they felt about my religion, or lack of religion, to be more precise.

Irma replied immediately. 'This is not so important to me now. There was a time when it might have been, but, the truth is that I have felt failed by God in the past. Now, my attitude to Him is more...more indifferent. Of course I abide by the Catholic code of behaviour, but no longer do I live in fear of disappointing the priests, or God, Himself.'

The following silence was broken by the waiter appearing with our main courses. A timely intervention.

'Tommaso told us that you have met Ysabelle,' Fabrizio said as we ate, his expression conveying sympathy.

I struggled for control, knowing it wouldn't take much kindness for my veneer to crack.

Irma placed her hand on my arm. 'It is a difficult situation for you.'

Fleetingly, I wished we lived closer to them. Sunny afternoons in their garden, and leisurely visits to Sicilian villages appealed. As did family celebrations. Forgetting her two daughters, I pictured myself shopping with Irma. Helping her select an outfit for a wedding or significant birthday party. Despite her being more elegant and poised than I could ever be. Reduced to rubble by yesterday's revelation, having an affectionate mother and father-in-law, made the going less hard. Only later did I realise that being nearer to them would inevitably mean being nearer to Ysabelle and Elisa.

It was after eleven when we returned to the villa.

'Thank you for a lovely evening,' I said.

Fabrizio pointed to the drinks cabinet. 'Would you like a drink?'

I shook my head.

'*Buona notte, figlia*, good night, daughter,' Irma said before kissing me.

It was the first time she'd addressed me as "daughter" and she would have been surprised to know how much this meant.

Walking along the dimly lit corridor to our bedroom, I resigned myself to waiting for Tommaso to return. Elisa wouldn't be late back from a school meeting, but they'd talk before he left. Perhaps have a nightcap.

When I opened the bedroom door, a red box lay on the bed. I removed the lid, parted the tissue paper and fingered the peach satin nightdress.

'*Buon anniversario di matrimonio*, happy wedding anniversary. I am sorry it is late,' my husband said, appearing from the bathroom.

'It's gorgeous.'

Putting his arms round me, he whispered, 'I love you so much, Rachel. I am sorry I have hurt you. I did not want to do this.'

I leaned against him, for the moment reassured.

## 20

Back in Positano again, a new energy bolstered our relationship. As inexplicable as it was unexpected. At weekends, Tommaso showed me different parts of Napoli, describing the city's complex history. We drank iced tea on pavement cafés, accompanied by buskers – guitarists, flautists and demons on the mandolin. Attended concerts in towns along the Amalfi coast. We took the boat to Ischia and Prochida. Went for drives and walks.

Each morning we awoke to deep blue skies and warm sunshine, more indicative of spring than early autumn. The fiery red of pin oaks made my heart sing. As did lingering morning mist over the headland. Late flowering honey-suckle, planted the year before, had rooted, and infused the balcony with fragrance while we watched the sun set sipping Negronis, the sound of Maria Callas wafting out from the living room.

We didn't talk about Ysabelle.

I threw myself into studying, even more than before. Adhering to my routine of working during the morning and doing some practical photography in the afternoons, having

Italian lessons or going to the Institute of Photography in Napoli. Domenico still gave me assignments, which I welcomed, as they took me all over the Amalfi coast. Occasionally Tommaso attempted to lure me away on a drive. I resisted. Lovely as these trips were, I confined them to weekends. Discovering he had a daughter had been so traumatising that I clung to things connected with my identity. Allowing me to remain grounded.

As for Ysabelle's existence, on a day-to-day basis this was usually possible for me to block out: our weekly shop still only for two people; the spare bedroom, still containing my stuff; our free time mainly spent together.

What differed was that when Tommaso seemed preoccupied or out of sorts in any way, I now pondered whether or not this could be connected to Ysabelle. He hadn't mentioned going to Sicily again. Moreover, he hardly mentioned her. Reluctant to upset me? Worried about her reaction to our marriage? Despite frequently reminding myself of her needs (and his), and pleas to a higher authority for compassion, my resentment persisted. I despised my selfish attitude, my need to be everything to him as he was to me. And when he gazed out to sea, expression unfathomable, I hated myself for not suggesting she visit. For not making it easier for him.

About two months after returning from Sicily, Tommaso announced: 'I want to invite Ysabelle to visit for a weekend.'

I poured myself another Negroni. The sun had cast a pink glow over the sea and I wanted to enjoy the view, not have a ten-year-old girl intrude.

'Okay,' I said eventually, hoping he'd do nothing about it.

Then he rose from his chair and went inside. Shawl now draped round my shoulders, I remained on the balcony, berating myself for my lukewarm response. My coldness and absence of empathy. Geoffrey and Marion had generously taken me in when my parents died. Did they argue about it beforehand? I now wondered. Had Geoffrey resisted? This was hard to imagine. He'd never shown me anything but a low-key kindness and affection.

When the cooler air drove me inside, I went into the spare room. Piles of books rested against one wall, awaiting the bookshelves Tommaso had promised to build. A suitcase half filled with winter clothes stood in one corner.

The weeks passed but Tommaso didn't raise the subject of Ysabelle's visit again. Once or twice, when my kinder side surfaced, I got close to taking the initiative.

'We have to decide where to spend Christmas,' I said at dinner one evening in late November.

I'd just had my second tutorial Skype of third year and was in high spirits, filled with enthusiasm for the course, brimming with ideas for photography assignments.

Tommaso nodded, and the realisation things had changed struck me with renewed force. Last year I hadn't known about Ysabelle. The obvious place for the festive period would be Sicily, but he said nothing. His eyes were dark. The sky was dark, too.

'Let's watch something on Netflix,' I suggested, welcoming the prospect of a cosy evening with him.

'I must work.'

'Can't it wait?'

He shook his head. Half an hour later, I knocked on his study door with a cup of coffee.

'*Si*?' he called out, like a harassed headmaster.

I expected to find him at his desk. Instead, he was on the sofa bed, holding a photo album I hadn't seen. As I was about to suggest Ysabelle stay with us at New Year, his phone went. I left the room. Ten minutes later, he emerged. He stood in front of me, expression haunted.

'Tommaso? What is it?'

'There was a climbing accident.... Elisa... Elisa is dead.'

My hand flew to my mouth. 'Where is she now?'

'She is at the hospital - in *obitorio*. I do not know the English word, where dead bodies are–'

'I mean Ysabelle.'

'She is with my parents, at their house. I must buy a flight.'

I listened while he phoned an airline company and booked a flight for the following morning. Hovered when he sat on our bed, an empty suitcase next to him. Wanting to help but not sure if he preferred to be on his own.

'Elisa was a good mother,' he said. 'She is too young to die. Perhaps this is my fault. If I remained with her, this would not happen.'

'Tommaso, it's not your fault. You mustn't blame yourself.'

'I make so many mistakes.'

Taking his hand, I led him through to the sitting room. Thinking he needed to talk, wanting him to talk. To share his pain. He was slow to begin, like a disused tap, trickling then continuing to a steady stream. Justifying – again – why he had left Elisa. Wondering what impact this had had on Ysabelle. From outside came the patter of rain on the balcony tiles. Inside, the ticking of the kitchen clock intruded more than usual.

'Elisa changed so much after Ysabelle is born.... She became more of a mother. Less of a...lover. I understand that this happens, but I did not love her anymore. I liked her, of course.... And the house – it is so untidy, it is so noisy. Ysabelle cried much. I was too young. Not ready for such responsibility.'

I listened in silence, unable to come up with anything to make Tommaso feel better. As for my own inner turmoil, I'd face this once he left for Sicily.

When he finished packing, we went to bed. There we clung to each other until falling asleep.

Tommaso left for Sicily the following morning. Too unsettled to work, I spent much of the day on the balcony, wondering what might be happening in Palermo. At the moment, Ysabelle was staying with Irma and Fabrizio, but when her father arrived, what then? Would he want her to move to Positano? Deep down, I knew this would be best for her. To my shame, though, I hoped she'd live with her grandparents. Or an aunt and uncle. In Sicily she'd have the continuity of school and friends, in addition to her extended family.

Natalie phoned in the afternoon and immediately sensed I was upset. She listened while I explained about Elisa's death.

'Actually, it would have been so much easier if Ysabelle was really little. It would be hard not to immediately love an infant, I suppose.'

'Ten is still young, Rachel. In a year's time you may love her as if she is yours. This has happened with several of our friends. They have adopted an older child and soon they have forgotten there is no biological connection.'

I hesitated, then the longing to offload overcame my customary reticence about revealing too much family stuff.

'I'm not the motherly type,' I said, explaining about my parents' close relationship and how this had become my role model. Temporarily forgetting how precious I'd been to my father.

'You are not your parents,' Natalie said, when we ended the call.

She was right, of course. But for over a decade, I'd accepted children wouldn't be part of my life.

When I was eleven, my parents enrolled me on a summer school camp for two weeks. All the other kids my age were booked for a week but my mother persuaded me it would be fun to stay longer. Going through the brochure with me, pointing out the adventure park, canoeing and other activities I'd never tried. She and my father had arranged a holiday in Vanuatu where he'd conducted the fieldwork for his PhD on Melanesian culture.

Four days before camp started, we received a phone call informing us of its cancellation due to staff illness. I was at a friend's house when the news came, and by the time I returned home, my mother had already unsuccessfully contacted three families plus Geoffrey and Marion, to see if I could stay with them. I remember my thudding heart when asking why I couldn't go to Vanuatu. The silence. Then my mother replying that it wasn't the sort of place for a child.

It's strange how the mind occasionally needs a key to unlock memories. Intentionally or otherwise, in Kashmir, Gillian had handed me such a key because now I recalled another fact: at the time of booking their holiday, my father remonstrating with my mother that I *would* enjoy Vanuatu. Reminding her that adventure parks weren't my thing. That not being a strong swimmer might rule out watersports. In the end, there being no other option, I did go to Vanuatu. My bedroom was next door to theirs: my mother's expression on learning there were no available family rooms would have been comical to an older and less needy child.

Diana phoned two days later. 'The thing is, I don't feel the same about living in Florence anymore. I hadn't realised how much of my social life was tied up with Doug's. Or how much my pleasure from the city was about sharing it with him.... Anyway, I fancy moving to Positano. What do you think?'

'You don't want to rush such a decision.'

'I'm not. So, what do you think?'

'It would be great to have you closer.'

'So, would you be able to look for an apartment for me? Out of the centre of town. Or even Amalfi. I liked Amalfi.... Hang on a sec, doorbell's going.'

While she was answering the door, I visualised how it could be having my closest friend so near. Lunching together, girlie shopping sprees in Napoli.

Diana returned. 'Anyway, I've put our house on the market and there's been a lot of interest. The asking price is higher than I'd expected and Doug doesn't want any of it. Guilt, I suppose. Compensation for not giving me a clutch of cute kids. So, what say you?'

'I'll check out what's available, it's probably easier for me to do this than you, as I know which parts are nice.... Tommaso's away at the moment.'

'Sicily?'

'Elisa was killed in a climbing accident. He's in Palermo

with his daughter.'

Diana was silent for a moment. 'Why didn't you tell me before? And here's me wittering on.... Goodness, poor child! So, she'll move to Positano?'

I attempted to sound neutral. 'I don't know.'

'You'll adjust, Rachel, you'll have to.'

While mooching around the apartment, pondering over what Diana had said, something drove me into Tommaso's study, despite having promised not to look around it – his word had been "disturb". Today, the desk was clear apart from his computer and printer. The drawers were locked. I sat down at the desk and as I spun round on his office chair, my foot caught on something.

Bending down, I discovered a small fusty-smelling daypack. It appeared to be empty, then I felt a mobile phone in an inner pocket. With trembling fingers, I removed it and stared at it for a few moments, as if it might explode. What could Tommaso's passcode be? I tried his birthday and other passwords he sometimes used. None worked. Then I remembered the name of his childhood dog and keyed that in, experimenting with different numbers.

Eventually one worked. Pulse racing, I studied the contacts. There were three: Maurizio, but no messages from him; Elisa, many texts, to my relief, all platonic in tone. The third contact, listed only as X, had left several indecipherable messages.

Relieved Tommaso wasn't using the phone for secret assignations, his having a separate one for contacting three people didn't greatly concern me. I did wonder about the unknown caller, however.

I was updating my photography course log that evening, when he phoned.

'*Amore*, I miss you,' he said over a crackly line.

'How's Ysabelle?'

'She misses her mother. But my parents are close with her.'

'When are you coming back?'

'I will stay here for the Christmas holidays. Will you come to Sicily?'

'Okay,' I said.

Later, I half regretted the kneejerk reaction which made me agree to Christmas in Sicily. The prospect of being with my in-laws, whom I liked, and my husband's daughter, whom I didn't know and vaguely feared, triggered a hotch-potch of emotions.

On December 23, I flew to Catania. Tommaso collected me at the airport and we broke our journey in order to eat at an old country restaurant. There, he described Elisa's funeral, how Ysabelle was coping, and the tense conversations he'd become embroiled in with Elisa's mother who'd never forgiven him for not marrying her daughter. We both knew we were skirting round the main issue: what would happen to Ysabelle now.

On Christmas Eve, we drove to Collesano in the Madonie mountains to see the *Luminari*: the lighting of large bonfires, traditionally built to keep the baby Jesus warm. Driving up the mountain road past somnolent villages with twinkling lights and wisps of wood smoke was magical.

Troubled by a sore throat, Ysabelle had stayed at home, Beatrice looking after her. For one evening, I had my husband to myself.

In Collesano, we greeted the local people who had built and were tending to the bonfires. After a while, I slipped my arm through Tommaso's. 'Did you come here every Christmas while you were growing up...? Tommaso?'

His voice sounded distant. 'What did you say?'

'I wondered if you – it doesn't matter.'

'It's cold,' he said, shivering. 'We must go home now. How can you be warm in your jacket?'

We returned home to the traditional Festival of the Seven Fishes, *La Vigilia di Natale*. In the elegant Vitale dining room, Antonia served the fish dishes, all accompanied by homemade breads. She and Irma must have spent hours preparing the food, yet when I passed the kitchen there was no indication that a mammoth cooking session had taken place.

When we'd eaten, I waited for soporific feelings to grip everyone. Instead the atmosphere became enlivened.

Once we'd opened our presents, we visited several local churches to see the nativity scenes, another tradition. This time, Tommaso stayed at home with Ysabelle.

At the Vitale house again, Abri handed out nougat and gingerbread. Fabrizio produced more wine. When the midnight bells tolled and fireworks crackled, the younger children woke from their sleep on the sofas, and scampered into the garden, followed by the adults. More '*Buon Natale*'s rang out. Irma had decorated the palm trees with Christmas lights, the effect strangely atmospheric.

On Christmas Day, I woke early and automatically reached over for Tommaso. He wasn't there. Then I remembered Ysabelle appearing during the night because she couldn't sleep, him slipping out of the room with her.

At lunchtime, Ysabelle scowled at her food, even though Antonia had made something soothing for her throat. After unsuccessfully remonstrating with his daughter, Tommaso gave up and attended to his own meal. A moment later,

Ysabelle banged a spoon on her plate, spattering sauce everywhere, and ran out of the room in tears.

'Poor child,' Irma said.

After five minutes, I lifted Tommaso's plate and took it to him in the small sitting room, where he was holding a sobbing Ysabelle. At my entrance, he glanced up and signalled to me to leave his food on the table.

Over the following days, I hardly saw my husband on his own. He took Ysabelle to mass and to visit Elisa's grave. And with Abri and Bea's help, he cleared out Elisa's small apartment. In bed at night, he immediately fell into a deep sleep. As if I wasn't there. Nevertheless, in under a week we'd be back in Positano, I comforted myself. Smothering the voice warning me that Ysabelle might return with us.

'Would you like to drive to Cefalu?' Tommaso suggested.

I nodded, wondering if Ysabelle was also coming.

'My mother will take Ysabelle to visit Abri,' he said, and I tried to conceal my relief.

In Cefalu, we strolled around the old town, then found a café near the cathedral. While waiting for our order, I gazed at the massive crag towering above the cathedral.

'Let's climb the Rocca,' I suggested. The view from the top would be amazing and my camera needed exercise.

Tommaso shook his head. 'Another time.'

Despite being aware of pushing him when he was struggling, I persisted. 'But it would be easier in the winter, less busy and not so hot. Besides, there's a path. It wouldn't–'

'Not today, *amore.*'

Watching his shifting expressions – determination, anxiety, sadness and possibly anger – I wondered what my face registered.

'What is it?' I asked.

'I want Ysabelle to live with us. In Positano.'

Immediately the words were out, his shoulders relaxed although his eyes remained troubled. A man wracked by remorse.

## 21

S trong winds delayed our flight to Napoli for several hours and I grew impatient to begin this unexpected chapter of my life.

As the implications of my situation continued to register, my apprehension increased. Now I'd be sharing my home with Tommaso, always having to consider a child. Ysabelle might be Tommaso's daughter, but her upbringing would involve me.

For most of the turbulent flight, Ysabelle gripped Tommaso's arm and I couldn't relax enough to read. Even the stewards remained buckled in throughout the sixty-minute journey.

After we landed, my stepdaughter stared at me, as if having forgotten my presence.

'I'm glad that's over,' I said to her, to be rewarded with a faint smile.

At the apartment, Tommaso took Ysabelle's hand and showed her around.

'This is your bedroom, *angelo*,' he said, opening the door to the spare room, which I still regarded as my room, despite having a studio. 'You can choose new bedding and we will decorate the room for you. You can choose the colours.'

'Can't I sleep in the same room as you, *Papà*?'

He picked up his daughter and swung her around. 'You are too old to share a bedroom with *Papà*. I share a room with Rachel.'

'I'll clear my stuff out of the room as soon as possible,' I told Ysabelle when we sat down to dinner. 'And we have to make plans for school.'

'She can go to the Asilo Luigi Rossi school,' Tommaso said.

'It's very short notice.'

He stared past me as he spoke. 'I talk to school before Christmas. They have a place.'

He'd planned this before announcing that Ysabelle would live with us. *Che sorpresa*! What a surprise!

'We'll go shopping for uniform tomorrow,' I said to her.

Tommaso took another slice of pizza and added parmesan cheese to it. 'All she'll need is a *grembiule*, an apron.'

'I want to go shopping with *you, Papà*.'

I forced myself to smile at her. '*Papà* is working tomorrow. I'd like to take you.'

To my relief, Tommaso agreed. 'Rachel will buy your apron, and anything else you need for the school, *principessa*.'

After Ysabelle left the table to watch television, Tommaso took my hand. 'I want to move your possessions into the sitting room. It is important to make her feel it is her bedroom soon.'

'I've already said I'll move my stuff out. It can go to the studio. And before you ask, I'll do it tomorrow.'

More than ever, I felt thankful for my bolthole.

Waiting for sleep that night, I listened to familiar noises: the gurgling pipe; a dog barking; a Vespa whining its way along the upper road out of Positano. I imagined I heard a child's regular breathing.

~

After buying Ysabelle's smock, I suggested choosing paint and new bedding for her room. However, she insisted on doing this with her father.

And so our family life began. Despite always wanting to be with *Papà* or have him do things for her, Ysabelle had to tolerate a modicum of care from me. On the days Tommaso worked in Napoli, I collected her from school. Sometimes when I arrived, she'd be chatting animatedly to a friend's mother and when the mother or friend pointed out my presence, she'd glance at me. Turn away again. Eventually trudging over to me, face impassive.

'It's so hard,' I told Natalie. 'I ask Ysabelle about her school day and she gives me monosyllabic answers. Even though her English is quite good. Now I've stopped asking her.'

I broke off, wondering if I should persist. In time, Ysabelle would have to accept me. But how long would this take?

Natalie was waiting for me to continue. 'Then as soon as Tommaso arrives home she rushes to him and chats away. What she's been doing at school. Who's asked her to be their gym partner. A project she's involved in.'

Natalie leant over the café table to pat my arm, her sympathy encouraging me to continue my list of woes.

'She demands his full attention at dinner. She chats to him as if I'm not there.'

'How does Tommaso react to this?'

'He accepts it.... Well, sometimes he catches my eye. Gives me an apologetic look. But if I reach to touch his arm or kiss his cheek when Ysabelle's around, he pulls away. As if our relationship is illicit. Oh, and he doesn't want me to cook Indian food because he thinks Ysabelle won't like it. How can she know until she's tried it?'

'It is difficult for him, too,' Natalie said, and despite her tone, I felt mildly rebuked.

'I *am* trying to have a good relationship with her,' I added.

After talking to my friend, I resolved to establish a relationship with Ysabelle. Devising ploys to achieve this.

'Let's go to the beach,' I'd suggest, to which she'd shrug her thin shoulders.

'There's a wedding in Amalfi this afternoon, we could take the boat there,' I said one day, thinking the excessively romanticised style of such weddings might appeal to a girl her age.

'I must do my homework.'

On the way home from school a week later, we noticed a woman photographing the sea. Experimenting with lenses, adjusting her tripod. Ysabelle stopped to watch.

'Are you interested in photography?' I asked, hoping this was an activity we could share.

'In geography class they show us photographs.'

'What sort of photographs?'

'Different things,' she said, walking on.

That evening, her jacket slipped off the hook in the hall. I retrieved it and put it on another hook. Immediately she rushed over, wrenched the jacket from the hook and replaced it on the one it had fallen off, saying, 'I share this hook with *Papà*.'

Two days later, when Tommaso was delayed at work, I called Ysabelle to the table. '*Papà* is working late, he wants us to eat now.'

She shook her head, lower lip jutting out. 'I want to wait until he is home.'

'Okay, here's the deal. We'll have the main course just now and when *Papà* gets home, we can have the cake.'

To my relief, she agreed. Eating too late affected her sleep. And when hungry, she occasionally experienced low blood sugar. Besides, sooner or later, Tommaso would be away on business and she'd have to eat with me.

The first time the three of us ate out, while Tommaso studied the menu, I turned to Ysabelle. 'What would you like? Spaghetti bolognaise? Pizza?'

'I'll share *Papà*'s meal.'

Keeping my tone light, I replied, 'I don't think he'll like that. Why don't I help you choose?'

Her eyes darkened and she banged down her spoon. 'This is what *Mamma* and I did. She chose something I like and we shared it.'

Tommaso and I exchanged glances. 'I will help you to decide,' he said to Ysabelle.

Feeling my anger rise, I went to the loo. Lingering there, I reminded myself that Ysabelle was struggling with her loss. With a new home and school. With a change of everything, in fact. Hopefully in time she'd settle and be less clingy with her father. When I returned to the table, they'd agreed what to order. Tommaso looked strained, though, and none of us spoke much while eating.

As for afternoons in our apartment, I found myself yearning for more connection with Ysabelle on the days Tommaso worked in Napoli. While she did her homework at the kitchen table, I'd normally cook or tidy, hoping she'd need help – a difficult sum, a word she didn't understand. It never happened. Solemnly, she'd retrieve books from her schoolbag, place them in orderly piles on the table and immediately start working. Rarely did I notice her fidget or gaze out of the window.

In different circumstances, it could have been cosy, especially during a dreary February day when fog blighted the town and lights were on from lunchtime. Occasionally, when I was working on something theoretical for my course, I considered bringing my laptop into the kitchen, but didn't want to crowd her.

One afternoon, I noticed Ysabelle frowning at a blank sheet of paper, flicking her ponytail.

'Do you need help?'

'*Papà* will help me later,' she replied, without raising her head.

'He's tired when he gets home. Why don't you let *me* help?'

She hesitated before saying, 'We have to draw our favourite animal and write about why it is our favourite.'

'What is yours?'

'I love all animals. But I think I like tigers most.'

I waited a moment before suggesting, 'Do you need a picture of a tiger?'

I fetched one of my photography books and skimmed through it. Illustrating techniques for photographing animals, was a striking shot of a tigress holding a cub. Face brightening, Ysabelle reached for the book.

'Can I copy this?'

'Of course. And while you're doing this, think about why you like tigers so much.'

Immediately the atmosphere in the kitchen changed. Later, when I offered her some leftover tiramisu, she smilingly accepted.

Since Ysabelle's arrival, we hadn't entertained, Tommaso keen that we do nothing to exclude her. One evening, I suggested we invite Natalie and Louis for dinner.

'What do you think, Ysabelle?' Tommaso asked.

She shrugged. 'I could sleep over with Daniella.'

I glanced at him. Aware of my face smiling at her suggestion. Welcoming the prospect of an adult evening.

'But you will like Natalie and Louis, *principessa*,' Tommaso said. 'You can help Rachel prepare the food.'

'I don't want to do that,' she said, flouncing off to her bedroom.

He followed her, ignoring my plea to leave her for the moment.

By the time he returned ten minutes later, I'd whipped myself into a frenzy. 'Tommaso, you mustn't spoil her. She must learn that she can't always get her own way. You're overcompensating for...for what's happened.'

I now disliked the way Ysabelle talked to him; how she used her eyes to manipulate him or tilted her head to one side to get her own way.

'She and Elisa were very close.'

'I know, I know. I'm sorry, I *am* trying...'

Did I have the energy to host a dinner party? I wondered, while studying in my studio, which was increasingly becoming a refuge from my changed home life.

The following weekend, Daniella invited Ysabelle for a Saturday sleepover. I'd done nothing about asking our friends for dinner but hoped Tommaso and I would go out for a meal. Both he and Ysabelle closeted themselves in her room for ages before she left and when the apartment buzzer went at five, announcing Daniella's mother, I expected him to go down with Ysabelle to say goodbye. Instead she left on her own. At the sound of her feet tripping down the stairs, I noticed his wistful expression. Regretting the lost years? Worrying that something might happen to her while she was away?

When he looked at me, though, his expression was resentful. Perhaps he'd picked up on the fact I was glad to have an evening with him on our own, when I'd had him to myself for most of our marriage.

Nevertheless, I was confident we'd go out for dinner. I'd wear the coral dress he considered sexy and we'd gaze at each other over a candlelit table and feel romantic again. And later, we'd make love without worrying about being overheard.

I waited half an hour before saying, 'How about going to the restaurant in Atrani? The one we went to on our honeymoon.'

He turned his palms upwards. Ignoring his indifference, I reserved a table. Once we got there, he'd enjoy our evening. When I went into the bedroom an hour later to decide what shoes to wear, however, he was lying on the bed.

'Are you feeling rough?'

'Do you mind if we cancelled our dinner, *amore*?'

'For God's sake, can't you put me first? Put us first? For once?'

He glared at me. 'If it is so important to you, we will go.'

'I'll cancel. Heaven forfend that you should do something for me.'

Once I'd calmed down from my disappointment, I realised the extent to which Tommaso had changed. The man I'd married would have planned a wonderful evening for us: a concert and dinner afterwards, perhaps.

We ended up eating a simple meal on the balcony and afterwards, I went to my studio. When I arrived, Costanzo was sitting outside his workshop, cigarette in hand, a bottle of grappa and plate of olives on his homemade wooden table. In a striped cheesecloth shirt rolled up to the elbows and his dark hair tied back in a ponytail, he epitomised the lightness I craved at that moment.

'Have a drink,' he offered.

I could smell the sea, hear a woman singing, accompanied by the piano. Silently I drank my grappa, watching the fishing boats set off for their night catch. Then we both went inside our respective studios. I didn't do much work, though, instead mulling over the situation with Tommaso and Ysabelle, trying to view things from his perspective, relieved as always to have my own space to retreat to.

When she returned the next afternoon, Ysabelle chatted away about her sleepover: feeding Daniella's hamsters and going to a new beach. Then she and Tommaso snuggled up on the sofa to watch television, she falling asleep, her head on his lap. I studied them, from my familiar position of outsider.

One day, I spotted Ysabelle and a friend dancing in the school play area. Face turned to the sunlight, expression rapturous, she seemed immersed in her movement. In her own world. Unnoticed, I observed her slim, wiry body twisting and turning, and despite knowing little about dancing, could see she had talent.

'I saw you dancing,' I said during our walk home. 'You're very good.'

'I went to a dance class in Sicily.'

'Would you like to go to a class here, in Positano?'

She thought for a moment then nodded.

Later, I relayed the conversation to Tommaso. Next day he checked out local dancing facilities, and by the time he collected her from school, had enrolled her in a class. Subject to an informal audition.

Ysabelle started her twice weekly dancing class the following week. After the first one, she dashed out, whirling her kit bag, searching for Tommaso, before noticing me. She hesitated then ran over.

'We did warm up exercises then the Signora taught us some steps. She told me that I had a good teacher at home.'

Ysabelle's mood improved significantly after her second class. 'There's a girl called Margarita,' she told us at dinner. 'I think she will become my friend.'

'Would you like to invite her here at the weekend?' I suggested.

Ysabelle turned to Tommaso. 'What do you think?'

'I think Rachel's idea is great, *angelo*.'

Her face lit up. 'Will you ask her parents, *Papà*?'

'I could do it,' I offered.

As she nodded, my spirits rose. She needed time with me, this was all. I remembered Natalie saying that in a year I'd probably love Ysabelle like my own child. An exaggeration, perhaps, but when she was in song, my heart opened to her.

Furthermore, I'd now decided on a present for her birthday, fewer than six weeks away. I didn't tell Tommaso about my trip to Napoli. About scouring the city until finding what I wanted.

With excitement comparable to Ysabelle's, I waited for her special day to arrive.

Ysabelle turned eleven on a spring Saturday of sunshine and almond blossom. I rose first to prepare breakfast. The evening before, I'd baked nut bread – her favourite – and now added it to plates of cold meat, tomatoes and goat's cheese, which we'd eat on the balcony. Tommaso had worked late over the last few days so there'd been little opportunity to discuss presents for her. I didn't mind. Mine was ready, painstakingly wrapped in paper from a specialist card shop in Napoli.

Waiting for them on the balcony, I watched fishing boats return with their night catch of red squid. This was the first time I'd been involved with a child's birthday. Would Ysabelle like her present? Should I have checked with Tommaso beforehand?

I heard laughter and the two of them appeared, Ysabelle pulling Tommaso after her, urging him, '*Sbrigati, Papà,* hurry up.'

I'd laid out the presents from Sicily – from Irma and Fabrizio, from Ysabelle's aunts and uncles. Mine was half hidden. At Tommaso's suggestion, we agreed to eat first then open the gifts. A wise decision. Like any other child celebrating a birthday, Ysabelle's face was wreathed in smiles, her eyes sparkling. To an onlooker, we would have passed for a normal family.

Never a big breakfast eater, she accepted a slice of nut loaf to which she added cheese and tomato, but that was it. Tommaso, on the other hand, tackled the food with relish.

If only my butterflies would settle.

When Tommaso finished his second latte, Ysabelle tugged his arm. 'Can I open my presents now, *Papà*? Can I?'

'*Si, si, angelo.* You have been patient.'

As she ripped off paper, Tommaso and I exchanged glances, and he swallowed hard.

How many birthdays had he spent with her?

'Look *Papà*,' she said, holding a blue and green floral patterned tunic from her Aunt Abri. 'Isn't this pretty?'

Books on animals and several novels also received appreciative comments.

'Where is Granny and Grandpa's present?' she asked.

'This is it, I think,' I said, handing her a large, flat object.

She unwrapped the gift to reveal a photograph album.

She opened the pages. 'It has photographs in it already. Look *Papà*, these are pictures of our family.... There are pictures of *Mamma*, too.'

'These are beautiful,' he said.

I watched them together, heads bent over the album. When the right moment presented itself, I'd suggest to Ysabelle that she and I go through it. She now went to her bedroom to put away her presents. As Tommaso slumped at the table, I wondered what was going through his mind.

When she reappeared, he straightened up, forced a smile.

'What about your present, *Papà*?'

'Today you and I will shop for it. But now, there's one more present.'

'Is it from *Mamma*? Sometimes she bought my present early.'

As Tommaso peered at the card and shook his head,

Ysabelle burst into tears. He swept her onto his lap and held her until her sobs subsided. I tried to feel compassion, not cheated of the moment I'd anticipated for weeks.

Eventually he drew her attention to the present again. 'It's from Rachel.'

As she opened it, my pulse raced. A relatively small thing, yet it mattered. She glanced at the flame red flouncy tutu and matching pumps.

'Thank you for my present,' she said, kissing my cheek, then turning to Tommaso, 'Can we go shopping now?'

He whispered to me, 'Thank you. They are lovely,' before allowing her to lead him off.

After they left, I remained on the balcony. My fantasies of her pirouetting round the apartment in her new tutu and pumps remaining just that. Fantasies. All those hours navigating the chaotic streets of Napoli. Traipsing from one ballet clothing shop to another.

Perhaps I'd been trying too hard with Ysabelle. Compensating for the resentful thoughts that would surface from nowhere.

A text from Tommaso, "*Ti amo,* I love you," only partly mollified me.

By the time they returned from shopping, I'd cleared away the breakfast things, done my Italian homework, put on a wash, and was ready to leave for the harbour to catch the afternoon boat to Amalfi. I admired the iPod Tommaso had bought Ysabelle, wished them a happy afternoon and told them I'd be back by six o'clock.

Tommaso grabbed me by the apartment door. 'Why will you not come to the beach with us this afternoon?'

'It's you Ysabelle wants to spend her birthday with.'

To my surprise, I experienced no bitterness.

'Wait, please,' he said, and went into her room. Moments

later, she emerged in the tutu and pumps, and, at his prompting, twirled round several times.

'You are beautiful,' he and I said simultaneously, and laughed.

'It's very pretty, thank you,' Ysabelle said to me.

Leaving them together was the right thing to do. While waiting for the boat, an intoxicating blend of sunshine and sea breezes on my bare arms, I felt more at peace. Even more so during the trip to Amalfi – the foaming waves and patterns of colour as the boat skimmed the water; far above the shore, a backdrop of almond and peach blossom.

At the sound of Tommaso returning from work, Ysabelle rushed to greet him. As usual, I hung back. After hugging her, he reached into his bag, producing an envelope. 'Look what I have, *principessa*.'

'Let me see.'

'Ask politely, *angelo*.'

'May I see please, *Papà*?'

He handed her the envelope and she opened it. 'I've never been to a circus.'

I managed a smile, then Tommaso said, 'The three of us must do more things together.'

Relief at being included made me smile for most of the evening. Even when Ysabelle chatted to her father at dinner as if I wasn't there.

Our tickets to the Belluci circus were for the Saturday afternoon show, eight days away. On the morning, however, Tommaso woke with a sore throat and hoarse voice.

'You *will* come to the circus, *Papà*, won't you?' Ysabelle asked him repeatedly.

By lunchtime, he was feverish and could barely speak. We tried several of her friends, but no one was free to join us.

'It's the two of us,' I said to Ysabelle.

She shrugged. Displeasure? Resignation?

Regardless, I was grateful for the chance to do something on our own.

As I fussed over Tommaso with throat lozenges and *Vicks*, he whispered, 'Thank you for doing this. I know you try to be Ysabelle's friend.'

'Don't whisper,' I said. 'It's more harmful than trying to talk normally.'

Nevertheless, his comments pleased me. Often, I thought he took my efforts for granted.

At the circus, Ysabelle and I bought large cartons of popcorn, and soft drinks then made ourselves comfortable.

The first act was the lions. To my concern, her lips puckered as the lion appeared, but before I could reassure her she needn't be frightened, she muttered, 'I hope they don't use a whip for him.'

I felt equally proud and surprised by her comment, responding, 'If they do, it's to mark out the separate space. Actually, it's not as cruel as it used to be.'

A trapeze act followed, then an impressive display of breakdancing. Then juggling and motorcycle stunts. And, of course, the circus clowns. Ysabelle laughed and clapped, the happiest I'd seen her. Noticing her pleasure, several people smiled at me, and again I experienced pride, as if she were my daughter.

Later, at home, she accepted Tommaso was asleep, and didn't insist on saying goodnight to him. Instead, she made herself hot chocolate and ate some reheated leftover stew.

Before going to bed, she kissed me, saying, 'Thank you for taking me to the circus. It was wonderful.'

A glow of warmth spread through me, followed by a burst of creativity, my head filling with ideas for my next course assignment.

## 22

W hen the estate agents phoned about an apartment for sale on the road to Montepertuso, a hamlet six kilometers above Positano, I had a positive vibe about it. Immediately I saw the old converted building, I could visualise Diana there. It was the right size, having a second bedroom she could convert to a studio. Furthermore, the view from the terrace over the old town and the sea was amazing.

I took loads of photos to supplement the agent's mediocre ones. Texting them to Diana immediately. Two days later she flew to Napoli and loved the apartment even more than I did. As the owners wanted a quick sale and there'd been no other offers, the deal was concluded within a week.

Diana moved down to Positano a month later and after ten days had unpacked her stuff, the apartment already looking homely. I'd forgotten how energetically she launched herself into new projects. She roped me into helping her paint, tidy the terrace area and plant bushes.

Keen that she wouldn't feel isolated here, I introduced her to my friends as quickly as possible. I needn't have worried. Within a month, she'd found a couple of days teaching art at the University of Salerno. It was maternity leave cover and being bilingual made her a strong applicant.

When I introduced her to Omera, they clicked and Omera immediately invited herself to Diana's apartment to see her sculptures.

'She doesn't take any prisoners,' Diana told me later when we were eating ice cream on the beach.

'At least you know where you stand with her.'

Diana chewed on her lip. 'A quality I appreciate more and more.'

She looked so sad and I knew she was thinking about Doug's deception.

I slid my arm round her shoulder. 'Di, you're only thirty-one. Many women don't even start thinking about kids until they're in their mid-thirties or older. As long as it doesn't consume you.'

'My mother had an early menopause. I'm worried I might, too.'

'What about your aunts?'

'Don't have any.'

'There are other factors,' I said, and to my relief, she didn't ask me to elaborate.

After Ysabelle's first five months with us, Tommaso had a business trip to Florence.

'I want to come too?' she said.

'*Angelo*, you will miss school.'

She tilted her head and put on her sad face. 'A few days only. Does it matter?'

He lifted her and swung her round. 'Of course it does.'

When I met her from school the day Tommaso left, she was quiet, claiming a sore tummy. At home, she flopped on the sofa for a while, obviously feeling rough, so I suggested she lie down. Later, at bedtime, she let me read her an Italian children's book, and with an impressive balance of gravity and gentleness, corrected my accent. It seemed unfamiliar but snug, sitting next to her on the sofa, she in her mint green pyjamas, wavy hair brushed and smelling of apricot scented shampoo. Me, in a kaftan I'd bought in Kashmir.

When I went to bed, the tiredness I felt resembled the weariness I reckoned a parent might experience at the end of the day, rather than a drained sensation from too much negative emotion.

During the night, amidst busy dreams, the noise of shouting dragged me into consciousness. Roused from sleep, and being childless, my brain reacted sluggishly to out-of-hours demands and it took a minute to realise it was Ysabelle. When I rushed through to her room, she was sitting up in bed, head darting from side to side.

'Is it your tummy?' I asked.

She shook her head, gabbling in Italian.

'In English, please.'

'I want *Papà*.'

'He's in Florence.'

'I want *Papà*.'

I sat at the end of her bed. 'It's the middle of the night. He can't come back just now. Did you have a bad dream?'

She nodded and lay back again, eyelids droopy. I lingered until certain she was asleep.

The same thing happened the following night. Around two o'clock, Ysabelle woke up shouting.

'It's a bear. It's chasing me,' she told me.

Tentatively, I clasped her hand, and after a while she lay down again. Like the previous evening, I hovered. Nevertheless, when I crept out of her room, she murmured, 'Don't go.'

'Would you like to sleep in our bed?'

Grabbing her doll, she followed me through. In bed again, she fell asleep quickly, not waking when I slipped in the other side.

When Tommaso had to extend his trip, I was glad. More time to consolidate my closer relationship with Ysabelle.

'What about going to a film this weekend?' I said. 'We could see *Harry Potter and the Goblet of Fire* in Sorrento. Have pizza afterwards.'

She nodded, and that evening I heard her singing in the shower for the first time.

Saturday dawned as such a sunny May day, I contemplated saving the film for a rainy afternoon. Ysabelle had talked about it so much, however, that I couldn't change our plans. Several times throughout the screening, she turned to gauge my reaction to an event. This made me happy.

At the pizza restaurant, without prompting, she chatted about school: gym class activities to help her dancing; the chemistry teacher who encouraged them to ask questions.

'Geography is my favourite subject,' she said. 'Father Cowan tells us stories about India, about elephants and how poor people are. He will prepare me for Confirmation.'

Father Cowan – Pasha! I should have realised, but I didn't know he was teaching at Ysabelle's school. That he was connected to my family in this way. On the one hand, I was pleased Ysabelle liked him as a teacher. On the other, our days on the houseboat had been special, making me unreasonably possessive of him.

'Did you and your mother eat out much?' I asked after the waiter brought our bill.

'Sometimes.'

'You must miss her terribly.'

She stared at her plate and said nothing.

I cursed my clumsiness as the earlier happy mood evaporated, rendering her silent on the journey back except for asking when *Papà* would be home.

Tommaso was away during Ysabelle's second sleepover in Positano. Late Sunday morning, about to leave for my studio, I was surprised when she arrived back from Brigitta's earlier than agreed.

'Did you enjoy it?' I asked.

'It was okay,' she said, avoiding eye contact.

'What did you do?'

'We watched movies.'

I didn't pursue it. Had seeing Brigitta with a mother, father and brother upset her? Yet Lavinia, Daniella and Margarita belonged to similar family groups and Ysabelle always returned in high spirits from visiting them. Tired but happy.

That evening, when I went into her room, she was wearing the red tutu, studying herself in the mirror. Although she often wore the tutu to her dance class, I'd only seen it on her twice.

'You look lovely.'

She tilted her head and looked sad. 'I like the colour.'

'What's the problem, then?'

She twisted her hands. 'It's Brigitta. She said–'

'Said what?'

Silence stretched between us.

Eventually, Ysabelle told me that Brigitta didn't think it was much of a birthday present from a stepmother.

Gobsmacked, I replied, 'I'm sorry Brigitta was so unkind. We'll talk about this when *Papà* is back.'

Another silence.

When Tommaso returned from Florence, once Ysabelle was in bed, I relayed what had happened.

He grimaced. 'Brigitta told her that stepmothers are horrible people.'

'Tommaso, for God's sake. Why didn't you mention this before?'

He shrugged.

'Did she say in what ways specifically?'

He yawned. 'She has told Ysabelle that stepmothers hate their stepchildren. They want them to grow quickly and leave home. Or they will wish to send them to boarding school.'

I poured the remainder of my wine down the sink. 'God, where does Brigitta get these ideas? Did you try to reassure Ysabelle?'

Tommaso yawned again. 'Of course I did.'

'Obviously not enough. Will you speak to Brigitta's parents?'

He rose to lock the balcony door. 'No. It could make things worse.'

'Then I'll speak to them. We must stop this. Ysabelle has enough to cope with.'

He glared at me. 'Don't speak to them.' His expression softened. 'You can invite Brigitta here. You might hear her say something horrible and then you can tell her not to be horrible.'

Why was he refusing to talk to Brigitta's parents? More

than anything, he wanted Ysabelle to be happy. I waited for his drink to relax him, but when he finished it, he announced he was going to bed. The opportunity for further discussion had gone.

~

In the school playground, I searched for Brigitta's mother.

'Brigitta had to go to the dentist,' Ysabelle told me. 'She left after lunch.'

So she'd probably be home again.

'I want to speak to her mother.'

'Brigitta is allowed to walk home from school next term,' Ysabelle informed me on the way there. 'I could walk home, too. Then you wouldn't have to collect me.'

'I like collecting you.'

When we reached Brigitta's home, my stomach was in knots. Some conversations were rehearsable. Not this one. Especially in Italian.

Fillippa answered the door, apron clad and with a smudge of flour on her cheek. 'Did Ysabelle leave something here at the weekend?'

'No, but I wondered if I could talk to you about the girls.'

Fortunately, Brigitta appeared and whisked Ysabelle off to her room. In the kitchen I explained my concerns in ropy Italian.

'It is possible that I said something about stepmothers,' Fillippa told me. 'But not that they are horrible people. I am sorry this has happened. I'll speak to Brigitta this evening.'

'Thank you. It's difficult for Ysabelle, having lost her mother so recently. Her father and I are doing all we can to make her feel secure.'

On my way home with Ysabelle, to my amazement I saw

Maurizio enter the house we'd recently left. So *he* was Brigitta's father.

Tommaso was at the apartment when we arrived. 'Why are you late?'

'Ysabelle, go and do your homework in your room,' I said, and for once she didn't argue.

When she'd closed her bedroom door, I turned to him. 'I spoke to Fillippa at their home.'

He whipped his head back. 'What! *Sanguinosa inferno*, bloody hell!'

'She promised she'd speak to Brigitta. Then, the strangest thing – when we were leaving, I saw Maurizio. I didn't know he was Brigitta's father.... Why wouldn't you speak to him? You are friends, after all.'

Tommaso gripped the worktop, knuckles white. 'You have no right to speak to Brigitta's mother. Why do you disobey me?'

I laughed. Such arrogance.

'Actually, Tommaso, I neither obey nor disobey you. And I've no idea why you're so upset about me doing what any normal parent would do.'

The "normal parent" comment got to him, his wounded expression revealed. Then his eyes blazed. 'You have no right to do this thing.'

'Why are you so upset? If you'd agreed to talk to Brigitta's parents, then I wouldn't have had to. Besides, I'm sure it will help, and if it doesn't, we should discourage Ysabelle's friendship with Brigitta.'

Tommaso shook his head. 'That is impossible.'

'What do you mean "impossible"?'

'You don't understand what you have done, Rachel,' he said, then he strode out of the apartment.

I ran after him. 'Tell me what I've done.'

He kept walking.

Five months passed. To my surprise, we became more of a family unit, though I could never hope to be as close to Ysabelle as she was to her father. In time, I learned not to be jealous. Tommaso had enough love for both of us. Or perhaps I learned to do with less. Certainly, with less attention.

Diana and I spent time together, often on our own, sometimes with other friends. She and Omera met to share ideas about painting and sculpting. Omera was also advising her on the best plants to grow on her terrace. In many ways, they had more in common than Omera had with me. Again, this didn't bother me.

As for introducing Diana to Ysabelle, I'd had a feeling this wouldn't go well. My instinct proved correct. Even before she told me, I sensed Diana wasn't taken with my stepdaughter. And although she never criticised him to me again, I knew her reservations about Tommaso remained as strong as ever. After the lunch where I'd got the four of us together, I didn't attempt anything else. Sometimes it was more pragmatic to compartmentalise.

In addition to teaching and her own work, Diana had taken to online dating. Regaling me with descriptions of what she described as "no-hopers". Usually too needy, often clearly unhinged, occasionally disconcertingly gorgeous but married and only looking for fun. Sometimes when we were out, she'd drink too much and I'd end up making sure she got to bed safely. Sitting with her, while she muttered, 'Anyway, there's still time. I'm still young'.

I didn't need to ask what she meant by these comments.

During these months, we were all busy in our different ways. Tommaso with his job, Ysabelle with school and her dancing classes. I was working hard on my final year of studying, involving a major project, for which I was using the photos taken in Kashmir. Two months of hard graft passed and it was May and I'd completed my degree. Tommaso took me out to dinner to celebrate, during which I talked about my plans to focus on work for charities.

The following day, I set to work completing my website. Writing the text was easy enough. More taxing was selecting photos to showcase my work. Tommaso helped me and I was impressed with the effort he put into it. Reminding me of his initial reactions to my photos, his positive comments.

After we finished, we had a glass of limoncello on the balcony. It was the closest I'd felt to him since Ysabelle had come to live with us.

The next task was to finish my website and advertise my services locally. Nothing happened initially. But within three weeks, I'd received two commissions. By now, I was considering returning to Kashmir to take photos for a calendar. When I mentioned this to Omera, though, she advised me it was too dangerous to go, but suggested other places in India. It was then I thought about Shimla, perhaps also other hill stations. Darjeeling greatly appealed. I would go during October and November, the coolest and driest times. Being termtime for Ysabelle, Tommaso could manage without me.

Excitement building, I researched hill stations of India. Planning what aspects of such locations to focus on. One evening, mid May, before Tommaso returned from work, I was shortlisting the places I wanted to visit, when Pasha came to our apartment. I was pleased to see him, but despite his smile, I sensed it wasn't a social visit.

## 23

'It's lovely to see you again,' I said. 'Would you like a drink?'

He shook his head and sat on the sofa. I chose a chair facing him.

'How are you?' he asked, scanning the room.

I remembered the man who'd been so attentive while I was ill in Kashmir. Who'd cooked us meals and talked for hours on the houseboat deck. The man who'd come close to kissing me. Never before had I seen him ill at ease. Had I inadvertently upset or annoyed him? Was Ysabelle causing problems at her Confirmation classes?

'Is Ysabelle around, or Tommaso?' he asked.

'She's with a friend, Tommaso is in Napoli – work.'

Pasha shifted position on the sofa, his shoulders relaxed, but his expression remained serious. 'Good. I need to talk to you on your own.'

'Intriguing.' In my light reply, I recognised a technique I automatically used when anxiously awaiting news, such as blood test results. As if joking with the doctor, or whoever it was, could protect me from hearing something unpleasant.

Pasha didn't smile, and as he searched for the right words, my concern grew. 'It's about your husband, about Tommaso.'

My pulse thudded. I stared at Pasha then at the floor.

'I'm sorry to have to bring this up,' he continued. 'However, I believe you should know what might be going on.'

It felt like being at the theatre, waiting to see how a scene unfolded. 'For God's sake, Pasha, what is it?'

His expression was wretched. 'Rachel, how well do you know Tommaso?'

Mouth dry, I stared at him. I pressed my twitching cheek. This must be about Elisa or Ysabelle, or both of them.

'He wasn't married to Elisa,' I blurted out. 'He isn't a bigamist.'

'Elisa? Oh, Ysabelle's mother.... This has nothing to do with her, or with Ysabelle.'

What a relief....

Pasha continued, his words slow and measured. 'You know, of course, that priests must respect any confessions. However, I want you to be prepared.... And, what I *can* do, without breaching confidences, is suggest that if you've noticed anything strange about Tommaso's behaviour, his lifestyle, you should try to find out more. I'm sorry I can't tell you anything else.'

My mind sped into overdrive. What other secrets could my husband have? Apart from the mobile phone I'd found in his study.

While considering how to reply, the entryphone buzzed and when I answered it, I heard an adult female voice and Ysabelle's young one.

When Ysabelle saw Pasha, she ran over to him. 'Father Cowan, why are you here?'

He stood and patted her head. 'I wanted to tell your

father and Rachel how well you are doing in geography. And with your preparation for Confirmation.'

'I will tell *Papà*.'

'And make sure you do, when he comes home,' Pasha said, before leaving.

I didn't mention Pasha's visit when Tommaso returned home late. Within ten minutes, he'd knocked back two neat Camparis and gone to bed.

The following day, he worked from home, during which time I noticed nothing strange about his behaviour. On the Thursday, when he was back in his Napoli office, however, I couldn't settle, anxiety eventually driving me into his study. Today strong sunshine bestowed a warmth on the cream tiles and the abstract prints. Shone on the yucca. Could there be something in here revealing a sinister side to him?

With no idea what I was searching for, I rummaged through his books and files. Through the desk drawers, today unlocked. I looked through the savings account pass-book, surprised to see the continuing monthly credit and debit entries. Since learning of Ysabelle's existence, I'd assumed this money was for child maintenance. But now Elisa was dead, this couldn't be the case. Had Pasha been alluding to a financial irregularity? Bile gathered in my throat.

Natalie suggested we visit Nocelle, a tiny village built into a cliff above Montepertuso. When we arrived, I was deter-mined to switch off from my worries about Tommaso, and initially this was easy enough to do, surrounded as we were by mountains, even more dramatic close-up, vineyards and lemon orchards.

After walking around the village, stopping frequently, to gaze down at the rooftops of Positano in the hazy distance below, we went to one of Nocelle's two restaurants.

'You must try the onion omelette,' Natalie said. 'It's a local specialty. They fry the onions in homemade lard.'

'A cardiologist's nightmare, in fact.'

'Did Tommaso tell you about the scandal with the church?' she asked as we ate our omelettes. 'When the auditors visited the diocese without warning, they found inconsistencies between the church books and the bank account. Louis mentioned it to Tommaso.'

Appetite gone, I replaced my fork and knife, in my mind seeing the savings account passbook. The regular debits and credits. Inwardly I laughed – how ridiculous to suspect Tommaso of mishandling church money. Nevertheless, I was unsure.

'Have they any idea who's involved?' I asked.

'Not yet. But they will certainly find out.'

Our return trip to Positano involved walking down thousands of steps, which revealed striking views of sky and sea, the cameos of life: bougainvillea straddling stone walls; sleepy cats stretched out in the sun; tile paintings of the Virgin Mary beside front doors. Normally, such things would have triggered flutterings of joy. Now, all I felt was anxiety.

'Are you okay?' Natalie asked, when we rested on a bench with an unobstructed view over the town. 'You've hardly spoken since lunch.'

'Still acclimatising to the heat.'

Shortly after I returned home, she phoned me. 'Apparently the church accountant's wife has confessed to one of the priests about her husband taking money from the account.'

Relief engulfed me. It couldn't have been Tommaso. Natalie was speaking again. 'There's more. He was being blackmailed into giving a third party a bribe to keep quiet.'

'What's the name of the accountant?'

'Marcio? No, Maurizio.... I'll let you know if I hear anything else.'

My stomach lurched. The man Tommaso contacted on his private cell phone? Brigitta's father? But Maurizio wasn't an uncommon name. This was surely a coincidence.

That evening, I hoped to talk to Tommaso, but Ysabelle was desperate to watch a children's film with *Papà*. After it finished, she went to bed and he announced he was going, too. When I tried to delay him, he held up his hand. This conversation would have to wait.

The following morning, Tommaso emerged from the bedroom in smart trousers and a tailored shirt. Ysabelle had been collected early by Margarita's father, and I'd hoped to spend some time with my husband.

'Tommaso! Why are you going to Napoli on a Sunday? I need to talk to you while Ysabelle isn't here.'

He checked his appearance in the hall mirror, saying, 'This evening we talk, *amore*.'

Before I could reply, a car drew up and a man emerged.

I sighed. 'It's Maurizio.'

'*Sanguinosa inferno!* bloody hell!' Tommaso exclaimed, whipping back his head, running his fingers through his hair. When the buzzer went, he didn't move so I answered the entryphone. Heart thumping, I listened to Maurizio's heavy tread on the stairs.

Before Tommaso could greet Maurizio, I escaped to the

balcony, shutting the door. Within moments, I heard raised voices, and dread filled me as I thought about Tommaso's secret bank account with its regular deposits and withdrawals; the mobile phone for communicating with Maurizio and the nameless man.

Ten minutes later, the conversation had stopped. Cautiously, I stepped back into the apartment, and, like a sleuth searching for intruders, checked each room. The sitting room and bedrooms were empty, as were the kitchen and Tommaso's study. Which left the bathroom. I knocked on the door. No response. I knocked again and went in. Tommaso was lying in the bath, clutching a glass of whisky.

For one disengaged moment, I wanted to have sex. Lust triggered by anxiety. The need to escape.

'I must talk to you,' he said, handing me the glass.

I gulped down the remains of his whisky. 'Finally.'

'You will find out soon and I wish to tell you myself.... A few years ago I borrowed money and couldn't pay it back. One evening, I go to a café with a friend. With Maurizio. He was the accountant for the church. He told me he'd...he'd been taking money from the church account.' Tommaso reached forward to turn on the hot tap, waited for the bath to reheat. 'He take the money to invest.... I do not know the words in English... *investimento a breve termine–*'

'Short-term investments.'

'Yes, this is what I mean.... Later, he always returned the money to the account. We both had drunk much wine now...I... I see this is a chance to finish my debt.... I am longing to do this.... Never before have I done such a bad thing but I tell him I will say nothing if...'

Tommaso hung his head.

In horror, I stared at him. Wondering if I'd understood correctly what he was implying.

'Why couldn't you explain the situation to the bank? Tell them you were having trouble repaying the loan?' I was playing for time here, not ready to hear more sickening facts.

'I didn't borrow from the bank.'

I picked up his discarded shirt and socks and put them in the laundry basket. 'Okay, your friend or whoever it was.'

Tommaso said nothing.

My heart sank. 'Was it a loan shark? This isn't connected with the Mafia, is it?'

'Not the Mafia. But bad people.'

'Oh God.'

'I agree with Maurizio he will give me share of his profits.'

My ears were pounding as I replied, 'In return for your silence. You blackmailed him?'

'I needed the money. You must understand...I am not a good salesman. I don't design so many things now. Most of my pay is from commissions.'

Part of me wanted to hug him. Another part recoiled from him and what he'd done.

'Tommaso–'

'Maurizio always returned the money he borrowed from the church.'

'Stole from the church. He didn't borrow it, he stole it.... Do the police know?'

'The diocese does not want a row...a scandal.'

'Why has it been discovered now? Oh, the audits.'

He stared at me. 'You know about this thing?'

'Natalie told me,' I said, handing him a towel as he stepped out of the bath.

'Maurizio's wife confessed to the priest. She is sick in the mind. The priest can't tell anybody what she say to him.'

Fillippa.... Tommaso was talking about Brigitta's mother. It took a moment to collect my thoughts. 'Tommaso, just admit it. Tell the diocese you owed money. It might help.'

He shrugged and concentrated on drying himself.

'Why didn't you borrow from the bank?'

'There was a recession.... Banks charged too much to lend money. Many people borrowed from loan sharks. You must understand how things happen in my country.'

The "my country" stung, another of his reminders that I wasn't Italian.

I returned to the balcony, to the sultry air, the bank of clouds building to the east. Half an hour later, needing to talk more, I went back inside, only to find an empty apartment.

Silence surrounded me as I sat next to the pomegranate tree on Diana's terrace, wistfully thinking of my uncomplicated single days. The sea's glorious blueness mocked me, the pastel buildings, more striking in sunshine, constricted my throat. How would the Diocese respond to Tommaso's behaviour? Blackmailing a church accountant. Taking his cut. Small fry, perhaps, in terms of church improprieties, but even so....

Furthermore, the lending business involvement was only registering now. I hadn't asked Tommaso if he'd been threatened. Or even how much money was involved. Could he be in danger? And Ysabelle and me? Might they use us to get at him?

When I returned home, an official car was parked outside our building, its driver on his phone. In the apartment, Tommaso was changing his clothes.

'The Bishop wishes to talk to Maurizio and me,' he said.

'Here?'

'At his office. The Church does not want people to know what has happened.'

When Tommaso left, I slumped on the sofa, burying my head in a cushion. What upset me most was knowing I'd never love my husband again in the same way.

Despite my financial independence, I now felt more unanchored than I'd been since my parents died. Shame prevented me from confiding in my aunt and uncle. In time I'd tell Diana but preferred to do so face to face. And I was uncomfortable talking to Natalie, because of her husband's friendship with Tommaso. Even confiding in Pasha seemed disloyal, though this was obviously what he'd been referring to when he visited.

It was facing me. On page four of our local newspaper, a photo of Maurizio, one of Tommaso, and one of the Bishop of the diocese, under which the caption read: "*L'abuso della fiducia e il male dell'avidità*", Abuse of trust and the evil of greed."

A small paragraph of text followed, but before I could read it, Ysabelle emerged from her room. I shoved the newspaper into a drawer and went into the kitchen. It was seven-fifty and Tommaso had already left for work. Since meeting with the Bishop, he'd been a shadowy presence at home. Keeping to himself, talking little. All he'd revealed was that the Diocese would handle the matter privately to avoid a scandal. But somehow the papers had got hold of the story.

I prepared toast and cappuccino for Ysabelle. Preoccupied by a test that day, fortunately she didn't notice my demeanour. Nor question my silence while walking to school. Back at the apartment once more, I studied the newspaper article again. The photo of Tommaso showed him with his eyes half closed and his jaw too prominent. When or where it had been taken, I had no idea.

Pleading a migraine, I cancelled my Italian lesson. If Omera knew the real reason for this, she didn't mention it and I felt grateful for her uncharacteristic tact. On automatic pilot, I drove to Sorrento to do a large food shop. As if we might be holed up in the apartment for a while. Melodramatic, I knew, but I wasn't thinking rationally. Besides, I needed to keep busy with something that didn't involve much thinking.

At lunchtime, a taxi halted outside our apartment, and shortly after, Tommaso appeared, raincoat crumpled, hair straggly. Wordlessly, I poured two glasses of wine. Wordlessly we sat down in the sitting room, on opposite chairs.

After a moment, he put down his wine, covered his face with his hands, and wept. I knelt beside him, enfolding him in my arms.

'*Ho perso il mio lavoro*, I have lost my job,' he muttered eventually.

Before I could reply, the phone went, Lavinia's mother asking if Ysabelle could stay overnight. Even though it was midweek, I agreed.

When I finished the call, Tommaso continued, 'Today Viatro told me he can't employ me now.... You must understand that I did this thing for Ysabelle, so that Elisa can give her extra things. I am not a bad person.'

He continued justifying his behaviour: wanting to be a good father, a good son, a good husband. Worrying about how devastated his parents would be. Wanting to deliver the news to them himself. Too scared to do so.

We ate dinner in silence. Tommaso was waiting to hear from the Bishop.

At nine-twenty, he announced he was going for a walk.

'What if the Bishop phones our landline?'

'He won't phone so late.'

'I'll come, too,' I said.

Retrieving his waterproof jacket from the hall cupboard, he slipped it on, for once not checking his appearance in the mirror. 'I want to be alone.'

Despite my escalating worry, all I said was, 'Don't be long, you're exhausted.'

After he left, from the balcony I watched for him on the steps to the Fornillo Beach where I assumed he'd go. I saw cats emerging from shadows then disappearing again. I heard raised voices, then silence. I didn't see him. The strong scent of jasmine after heavy rain gave me a headache and I stepped into the apartment again.

At eleven o'clock, I went to bed.

At three o'clock, I woke and reached for him. His side of the bed was empty. I considered going to find him but fell asleep again.

When I surfaced properly shortly before eight o'clock, Tommaso wasn't lying beside me. I rushed round the apartment, searching for indications he'd returned during the night. The shower floor and bath were dry, no damp towels. No new additions to the laundry basket. No dirty coffee cups or crumbs in the kitchen.

His cell phone took me to voicemail. I tried again every ten minutes for an hour. I sent texts. I phoned his office, knowing it was unlikely he'd be there, having been sacked.

Unless, of course, he had possessions to bring home. But no one had seen him at work. I went to the beach, following routes he might have taken.

After lunch, I asked Lavinia's mother if Ysabelle could stay another night. She agreed promptly, assuring me she'd devise a reason to give to the girls.

I then wondered if Tommaso had gone to the Arienzo beach, east of Positano. He'd taken me there once, a short drive followed by 300 steps to the beach. But his car was parked outside our apartment and there weren't buses during the evening. He could have walked, I supposed, imagining him navigating all those steps, tired, despairing. Fleetingly, I considered driving there but there were other places he might have gone. Besides, I wanted to be here when he returned. If he returned.

During the never-ending afternoon, I defrosted the freezer and decluttered cupboards. Cleaned windows and dusted doorframes. All the time wondering what had happened. Frequently rushing to the balcony for any sign of his return. I phoned the hospitals in Sorrento and Salerno to see if he'd been admitted.

In the evening, reluctantly I contacted Fabrizio and Irma, to see if Tommaso had been in touch. They'd heard nothing from him.

In fanciful state, I now wondered if he'd been kidnapped. Exhausted and anxious, anything seemed possible. However improbable. However dramatic.

Just before ten-thirty, in desperation, I phoned Pasha. He came round immediately.

'It's been twenty-four hours now,' he said. 'We should contact the police.'

I couldn't understand what he said on the phone, but the call was short.

'They suggested we hand in a photo of Tommaso. And they also explained that as it's been only a day and he is an adult, they can't do much yet. If you wish, I'll take them a photo of him.'

I found an unframed photo and gave it to Pasha.

He studied it, then searched my face. 'Will you be okay here, on your own with Ysabelle?'

'Actually, she's with a friend, but yes, I'll be alright.'

That night, unable to sleep, I searched every drawer and cupboard in Tommaso's study. Hoping to find something to indicate if he'd been threatened by the moneylender. An unfamiliar envelope, scraps of paper with obscure messages. Anything. The most likely form of contact would be by his secret phone: the unidentifiable caller, I supposed. But his phone wasn't there. Nor was the passbook.

I then noticed a concertina file box but was too tired to look through it.

Perhaps I was making too much of his debts. Perhaps he had exaggerated the situation so I wouldn't view his behaviour so harshly. If only I knew how much he owed. If he'd defaulted on payments. Our financial position without his share of Maurizio's "investments". I felt guilty about having such thoughts when Tommaso was missing.

In a calmer moment, shortly before sunrise, I realised this situation could explain Tommaso's fickle attitude to money – extravagances one moment, meanness the next. Scant comfort.

Shortly after nine o'clock, I phoned the police who agreed to launch a search. But still I waited for the key in the door. For Tommaso to return. Exhausted, but otherwise okay. This time I'd insist on more information. Answers to my unarticulated questions.

At two-fifteen, the buzzer rang. Finally.... I rushed to

answer it, praying it would be him. That he'd forgotten his key. But it was Pasha's voice I heard when I pressed the entryphone button.

When I opened the door, he said, 'The police are outside. I asked them to let me talk to you first.'

'I spoke to them this morning. They're going to start searching.'

He gripped my shoulders. 'You'll have to be strong, Rachel.'

Moments later, the buzzer sounded again and as I hesitated, Pasha answered.

One glance at the male and female officer, now in our sitting room, and a cold band gripped my stomach. They suggested I sit.

In hesitant English, the policewoman informed me that a body had been found on a beach, east of Positano. They believed it could be Tommaso.

## 24

---

Images of the policemen telling me of my parents' fatal car crash crowded my mind. Of my father when I'd said goodbye to him that dreadful morning, him in his old tweed jacket which my mother kept threatening to take to a charity shop. I stumbled to the sofa and sank down. I saw my mother in her parka jacket and new woollen hat. Smiling, looking so young.

'Both of them?' I asked, and noticed the policeman raise his eyebrows at his female colleague. Pasha said something to them and they backed away, as if responsible for my confusion.

I stared at Pasha then back at the policewoman.

Pasha came over to sit beside me, taking my hands in his. 'Rachel, this is about Tommaso.' He waited until I'd understood. 'They think they've found his body.' He waited for further signs of comprehension. All I could do was nod.

An exchange between him and the policeman followed. I understood the word 'identify' but other than that, nothing. They could have been speaking Mandarin.

Pasha turned to me, now resting his hand on my arm.

'And they want you to go with them to the hospital in Sorrento to identify the body.'

I recoiled. A further incomprehensible exchange with the policeman followed. Then Pasha spoke to me again. 'I'll drive you.'

'Ysabelle! She'll be home soon.' Then I remembered. 'No, she has a dance class after school. She won't be back until five.'

During the drive to Sorrento, I fantasised about this being a mistake. It wasn't Tommaso's body they'd found. Tommaso was at the hotel he sometimes used in Napoli. Soon the police would be apologising for having frightened me unnecessarily. Providing a rationale for their assumptions. The windscreen wipers scraped from side to side, and in their movement, I detected agreement. Yes, mistakes happened.

Fifty minutes later, we reached the hospital. As we were escorted to a waiting room, I realised I'd no idea how the man died. Shoving away imagines of him falling off a cliff, I clutched Pasha's arm. 'Do they know how...how the person died?'

He studied me before replying. 'A head injury. There were steps leading down to the beach. They think he slipped going down and hit his head on a rock.'

As thunder cracked through the sky, I knew the body was Tommaso's.

A woman in a blue lab coat approached me. 'Signora Vitale? Please follow me.'

I turned to Pasha. 'Come with me.'

In the morgue, a mild looking man conferred with her then opened a stainless steel fridge and slid out a shelf containing a body covered in white cloth. Having checked a label, he slowly withdrew the cover.

Tommaso's ghostly white face stared at me. As I gasped, the technician closed Tommaso's eyes and apologised to me.

Feeling numb, I studied my husband's face: the bruises on his forehead and cheek. What horrified me most, was how cold his skin was. Then, while bending to kiss his cheek for the last time, my legs gave way. Pasha caught me, said something to the technician, who led us to an unoccupied relatives' room. Pasha helped me onto a chair, I leant back and closed my eyes.

When I recovered, he was on his knees, praying.

'There'll be a post-mortem, I suppose,' I said as he drove me back to Positano.

'Sometime this week.'

'So soon.'

Too soon.

The sea was grey and rough, the only boat a cruiser. I remembered our mountain drives, and impromptu picnics in coves. Already it felt like a different life.

'I can't bear to think of him being cut open.'

Pasha replied softly. 'They'll have to confirm the cause of death. But they will be gentle and respectful, of course. Would you like me to inform the registry office of Tommaso's death? We have to do this within a week.'

I could only nod.

He swerved to avoid a car approaching in the middle of the narrow road.

'How will I tell Ysabelle? She's been through so much already. And his parents – oh God...'

Ysabelle reacted to the news of her father's death with unnerving calm.

'Have you seen his body?'

'Yes.'

'Are you sure it's him? Completely sure?'

In response, I reached to hold her, but she pulled away. I couldn't interpret her expression and didn't know what to do, no suggestions seeming appropriate. Eventually, she went to her room. When I checked on her, she was sleeping on top of her bed. As I covered her with a rug, she opened her eyes.

'Is *Papà* really dead?'

'Yes, Ysabelle. I am so, so sorry.'

The Vitale phone rang for a while before Abri answered. I broke the news to her, heard her murmur, 'Tommaso's dead?' and a cry in the background. Irma. Fabrizio came to the phone and I repeated what I'd told Abri, mentioning the post-mortem and the coroner's report that would follow.

Later, I sat on the sofa with Ysabelle, wishing she would talk or at least cry. Not knowing what else to do, I switched on a programme about animal rescue, one of her favourites. After twenty minutes she was asleep. This time she didn't waken when I covered her with a rug. In bed myself, I was unable to sleep, despite my exhaustion.

Remembering the concertina box file in Tommaso's study, I retrieved it and brought it through to the bedroom. In bed, I shoved another pillow behind my back and made my way through various documents relating to the apartment; Tommaso's birth certificate, health documents, certificates from university, even a few of his old school reports.

At the back of the container was a brown envelope with nothing written on the front of it. Inside it were credit card statements in the name of Signorina E Di Mauro. In my weary state, it took a moment to work out they were Elisa's. But why did Tommaso have them? Some had *"pagato"*, "paid", date-stamped on them, the more recent ones, shortly before her death, didn't. Others had items circled in green and scribbled notes, which although unreadable, were certainly written by Tommaso. Some entries were debits for flights – two to New York – others for jewellery, bracelets and earrings, mainly. One item, circled in red was for a music system costing €4,000, beside it written, "*Col cavolo*! no way!"

Now I understood. Tommaso had been paying off Elisa's credit card bills or attempting to. Compensating, perhaps, for having left her and Ysabelle. This would account for his borrowing, his taking a cut of the money Maurizio had stolen from the church. I whisked through more of the statements, stumbling across other items circled in red: a large flatscreen television two years earlier, a painting from an auction house.

In disgust, I chucked the statements back into the container, inwardly raging at Elisa and the impact of her reckless spending on Tommaso. At the same time, realising how loyal he'd been to her in not having told me he was paying her credit card bills. I wondered now if he'd wanted to share this burden with me. And if he had confided in me, what might have happened. My mind flooded with questions. And the knowledge I'd never have answers.

When the buzzer went, I stumbled out of bed, drowsy from the sleeping pill I'd taken at five am. It was Diana. I showed her into the sitting room and checked on Ysabelle who was in bed, listening to her iPod.

'They did the post-mortem yesterday,' I told my friend. 'Just to confirm Tommaso died from a head injury.... He was so stressed about the fraud, losing his job. He was worried about telling his parents. About what people would think of him.'

Shortly after Diana left, Tommaso's family doctor phoned to tell me the Coroner's verdict was a subarachnoid haemorrhage caused by a blow to his head. There'd been a little alcohol in his blood, but no drugs. Furthermore, fortunately, no indications of foul play. I wasn't brave enough to ask the doctor if Tommaso would have died immediately.

I didn't feel bereft yet.

'Do you want me to come over, dear?' Marion asked when I Skyped her.

The sight of her sympathetic, loving face was almost too much, and it was a moment before I could speak again.

'It would be lovely to see you,' I said. 'I'm still in shock, I think.... Perhaps once the funeral is over, it will sink in. And Ysabelle – it's hard to know how she is.'

'Geoffrey's going into hospital at the end of the week. Hernia repair,' Marion told me. 'But I could come once he's back home–'

'He'll need looking after for at least a week,' I interjected. 'And Ysabelle and I will be flying down to Sicily for the funeral. Don't come over, Marion. I'll bring Ysabelle to Edinburgh sometime. Perhaps during the summer holidays, if that's okay.'

'Phone me before you leave for Sicily,' Marion instructed.

After ending the call, I could hardly believe I was talking about summer holidays. Tommaso had been dead for less than a week and here I was, thinking ahead. Further evidence the situation hadn't fully registered.

A few days after her father's death, Ysabelle started following me round the apartment. Offering, for the first time, to help with dishes or laundry or preparing meals. One afternoon, she found me sobbing over Tommaso's favourite leather jacket. She said nothing, instead going onto the balcony. Perhaps it helped her to know she wasn't the only one missing *Papà*.

At night, now, I'd hear her crying in bed which reassured me. Despite the fact she wouldn't let me comfort her as Tommaso had done after Elisa's death. Sometimes, I found excuses to go into her room. Hoping she'd let me hold her while she cried. But she'd always stop when she heard me come in.

In the middle of June, eight days after Tommaso's death, Ysabelle and I flew to Sicily with his body. When the plane landed, I bustled her off before the coffin was unloaded. In arrivals, I immediately spotted Fabrizio. But not Irma.

He spoke quietly. 'Irma was not able to come with me.'

'Is she okay?' I asked, realising immediately the stupidity of such a question.

Fabrizio and I didn't speak much on the drive back from the airport. At the Vitale home, there was no sign of my mother-in-law.

'Is Irma avoiding me?' I asked him in the drawing room later when Ysabelle was sleeping. A grey sky heralded rain and it felt cold for June. I remembered seeing this room for the first time, less than two years ago. The weekend when I learned of Ysabelle's existence. Then the sun had streamed in, lending richness to the mint green walls, casting darts of light on oil paintings, the cherrywood bureaux and writing desk.

He hesitated, before saying, 'My wife has reacted badly

to Tommaso's death. It will be difficult when you will see her.'

It took a moment to understand what Fabrizio was implying. 'Does she blame me? For...for what's happened?'

I waited for reassurance this wasn't the case. Racking my brains to understand why Irma might consider me responsible.

Fabrizio wandered over to the window. 'She cannot believe this story about blackmail. She is making excuses for him.'

Dismayed that Tommaso's family knew the details of what had happened, a moment passed before I could ask, 'I know it must be difficult for you to talk about Irma, but... well, why does she think I'm responsible?'

Fabrizio was gazing at the dark clouds rolling in from the west. 'She can't understand why he must need extra money so much that he will blackmail someone.'

'She thinks Tommaso did this for me? Because I am extravagant?'

The idea appalled me so much that fleetingly I was tempted to tell my father-in-law about Elisa's lavish spending. Tommaso's attempts to pay off her debts.

'I've always been financially independent of Tommaso. And this... this money business started before he met me.'

Fabrizio turned round, his expression earnest, affectionate. 'Rachel, I believe you. Irma's mind is...confused, perhaps this is the word. I wanted to warn you.'

My mother-in-law joined us at breakfast the following day. In a black dress, her sallow skin devoid of make-up, she was barely recognisable. Her hair was scraped back in a chignon and her jawline sagged. She wore no jewellery except her wedding ring. When she walked past me, I detected a smell of mothballs. Of all the changes to her – the obvious lack of skin care, an absence of jewellery – the dark dress upset me most. Such a change to the woman who artfully devised colourful outfits without ever looking garish or tasteless.

I rose to greet her, she nodded at me, sat down and poured herself coffee. When I passed her the bread basket, she waved it away.

'Is Ysabelle still asleep?' she asked Fabrizio, her voice deeper than usual, less articulate. Medication, perhaps.

'She's slept a lot since Tommaso died,' I said.

Irma stared at me, her expression a disconcerting blend of vacancy and coldness. My spirits dropped further.

When she'd left the room, Fabrizio explained that normally family and friends would visit to view the body. Irma, however, had forbidden this. I understood. To witness her beloved son's damaged body – albeit embalmed – would be too painful.

In true Catholic tradition, people called at the villa with casseroles and other food. Flowers were delivered which Antonia arranged and displayed in the public rooms. Tommaso's sisters visited regularly. On my third day, Abri suggested she and I walk along the beach. The elder of the sisters, she was the one I felt closer to. Despite being only twelve years my senior, her manner was maternal. She was a tall woman, plain looking by Italian standards, and frustrated by her large tummy, as she swam every day.

It was sunny and windy, clouds racing through the sky. The tide was far out, transforming the landscape to a huge expanse of beach. We set off at a brisk pace, then slowed down.

'You must not let *Mamma* upset you,' Abri said. 'The rest

of us don't blame you for anything. She has always had a blindness with Tommaso. *Papà* has tried to explain this to her but...you see how she is. He was her favourite. The son she waited so long to bear.'

Abri paused to control her voice before continuing, 'After I was born, *Mamma* hoped to have a son. After Beatrice was born, she wanted this even more. She then had two miscarriages, both times, a boy. When Tommaso eventually arrived many years later, she was so happy.'

Touched by Abri's sharing of such a personal thing, I hugged her. 'Thank you for telling me this. I didn't know your mother had been through so much.'

We then talked about Ysabelle and the effect of Tommaso's death on her.

On the day of the funeral, I woke early with a headache and a sense of dread. Perhaps now my grief would kick in properly. The requiem mass was being held at twelve o'clock, and at ten-thirty the extended family gathered in the dining room. Irma, clad in a black dress and jacket, and wearing too much eyeliner, had visibly aged. Fabrizio seemed remarkably calm, but as head of the family, he'd feel duty-bound to be strong.

Ysabelle, in a grey skirt and white blouse, its arms already too short despite its relative newness, looked pale and lethargic. Tomorrow I'd make sure she got out for a decent walk.

Antonia produced coffee, and for the first time I noticed how elderly she was. Well into her seventies.

'She loved Tommaso,' Bea whispered to me. 'When he

was a child, she let him bake in the kitchen. He played with her son.'

The funeral cars arrived at eleven-forty. I travelled with Beatrice, her husband and daughter. Antonia didn't want to come.

'You did not wish to travel with *Mamma* and *Papà*?' Bea asked as we turned out of the grounds.

'Be quiet, Beatrice,' her husband Adriano said, then, turning to me, asked, 'How is Ysabelle?'

'Hard to say. She's cried a lot, but it's early days.'

'Poor child,' he said. 'It is difficult to lose both parents so quickly. Especially when she is only twelve.'

For the remainder of the journey, no one spoke. Natalie had warned me that in Italy posters of the deceased are sometimes hung throughout the town, to alert people to the death and to provide funeral details. I prayed not to be confronted by a large photo of Tommaso.

We took a collective sharp intake of breath when the hearse solemnly drove into the chapel grounds. Having expected a large turnout, I was surprised to see so few people. Forty at most. Perhaps the family hadn't publicised the service.

The pallbearers carried Tommaso's coffin towards the Altar where the priest greeted the body and sprinkled it with Holy Water, speaking slowly in Italian.

A series of readings and singing followed. Being able to understand much of the service, brought me little comfort, however. Beside me, Ysabelle was silent, expression distant. Irma, seated on Ysabelle's other side, trembled. I wasn't brave enough to glance at Fabrizio.

A woody, floral fragrance of incense filled the church.

After Communion, as the pallbearers carried Tommaso's body out of the church, my grief surfaced. Now, I wasn't thinking about the father Ysabelle had lost, the son and brother my in-laws would never see again. My thoughts dwelled solely on my loss. It was too easy to focus on the early months of our marriage, before suspicion and anxiety replaced the excitement and challenge of newness. Easy to deceive myself that the good times had dominated our relationship.

To the sound of bells tolling, one for every year of Tommaso's life, the pallbearers delivered his coffin to the burial site in the Chapel grounds. More mourners arrived. The Priest spoke briefly. I then laid a rose on the coffin, Ysabelle doing likewise. In turn, Tommaso's sisters approached the casket to sprinkle dirt on it or lay a rose. Irma exclaimed and staggered off, Fabrizio supporting her waist as they returned to the waiting funeral car. Tommaso's coffin would be placed in a concrete mausoleum along with those of his forebears.

Ysabelle clasped my hand, triggering an epiphany: I loved her as my own daughter. It had taken two years, but now I could have given life to her, nurtured her from birth, such raging love did I feel for this child who'd already experienced too much loss.

At the Vitale home, guests arrived with food. People ate, drank, prayed. Once again, I was detached. As if observing a stranger's family wake.

Irma was absent.

'*Mamma* is resting,' Bea told me.

'I wish I could help.'

Bea took my hand. 'She will change her attitude towards you in time. *Papà* loves you. He will persuade her she is wrong to blame you for what has happened.'

For the first time, it struck me that I'd lost a mother-in-law in addition to a husband.

Antonia dispensed more canapés and wine. More mourners arrived. Needing to keep busy, I helped her store perishable items in the large freezer. Ysabelle helped, too. Later, after checking with Fabrizio, I suggested a walk to her and two cousins, and we left behind the sadness of the Vitale home.

Within minutes of arriving, the children were chasing each other along the beach. The landscape soothed me. Allowing temporary escape. Guiltily, I wished I'd brought my camera to capture the strange furled patterns left on the sand by the outgoing tide.

I recalled meeting Ysabelle for the first time on a similar beach.

It was only now I remembered my plan to go to Shimla to take photos for a calendar. Of course I'd have to cancel. Once again, my life had changed drastically. I was single parent to my stepdaughter.

On our last night in Sicily, Ysabelle spent several hours closeted in her grandmother's room. What if Irma persuaded her to stay in Sicily? Might this be the best place for her, with her extended family? Did Fabrizio have the same thoughts?

We were in the small cosy sitting room when he raised the subject. 'Tommaso told me that Ysabelle has settled in Positano.'

'I think she has. She's working hard at school.'

He poured me another cup of coffee. 'She's mentioned several friends. They sound close.'

'She does have close friends. She has her dancing. And

she likes the town... The restaurant and café owners give her free ice cream. They're like uncles to her.'

'I've talked to my daughters about it. It is sensible for her to return with you. You have bonded with her.'

My heart swelled at my father-in-law's comment. 'It would give her more continuity. Besides, I love her as if she was my own child.'

'She will always be welcome here for holidays. You both will, Rachel. Please remember this.'

But what about Irma?

Later, in bed, I worried about Fabrizio. He cared so much for others, it was easy to forget his pain. I couldn't bear to think of him being immobilised by grief. Furthermore, I admired his emotional generosity in supporting Ysabelle's return to Positano. A less selfless man might have encouraged her to stay in Sicily, with the strong link to Tommaso her presence would provide.

On the morning of our departure, Ysabelle wandered off after breakfast. I panicked. Was she telling us she wanted to stay in Sicily? The irony didn't escape me. During my last visit here, I'd desperately hoped she would remain here. Now I desperately hoped she'd return to Positano.

------

## 25

For ten minutes or so, we stood around. Then Ysabelle emerged from the back door, Fabrizio admonished her mildly, and we bundled her into the car.

She spoke little during the flight, but immediately the taxi stopped outside our apartment, she leaped out and retrieved her luggage from the boot. At dinner she asked to invite a friend for a sleepover the following weekend.

'Can I have a pet?' she asked a week later while I was ironing. 'Lavinia has a hamster. And another girl has a ferret.'

Having an animal to love would be therapeutic for Ysabelle.

'If I agreed, what would you like?' I asked, praying she wouldn't opt for a ferret.

Her eyes lit up. 'A micropig. They're so cute. Can we buy one? Or a guinea pig if they don't have micropigs.'

I studied her face. So young and hopeful, despite all she'd lost. At this moment, I'd have bought an elephant if it made her happy.

The following day, we drove to the pet shop in Sorrento.

'I've never had a pet before,' Ysabelle said. '*Mamma* had allergies so we couldn't have one. I asked *Papà* to buy me a dog but he wouldn't.'

This was the first time she'd even indirectly criticised Tommaso.

At the pet shop, we gazed at mice and kittens and gold-fish. When we passed the rabbit cages, I saw one white baby on its side. It looked shrunken, its eyes dull. Ysabelle noticed.

'Is it dead? We must tell someone.'

Guessing she wouldn't leave it, I spoke to one of the staff who mumbled something about knowing there was a problem.

When I returned to the cage, Ysabelle hadn't moved.

'They know about the rabbit,' I told her.

'When will they do something about him?'

'Soon, I'm sure.'

There weren't any micropigs, (nor ferrets, fortunately), but when she found the guinea pigs, her face brightened. She liked four in particular, and quickly chose two males, both beige with white patches around their ears.

'We need a cage for them,' she said, 'and bedding and food. We have to buy two lots of hay – one for them to eat, and the other as bedding. And we need sawdust. Everything must be environmentally friendly. Especially their toys.'

By the time we'd left the pet shop car park, Ysabelle had chosen names: Nari and Suri. She insisted on sitting in the back of the car beside their travel box. Checking frequently they were alive. Laughing at their chirrupy noises.

At home, in her bedroom, we set up the cage and spread sawdust on its floor, adding hay. We attached a water bottle it to the cage. Then we set up the "pen" in the sitting room, agreeing that Nari and Suri would use it during daylight hours. Ysabelle spent the remainder of the day arranging and rearranging the toys; reading and rereading information on food for them; going online to see if we had the right equipment. She made me take loads of photos of the piggies for her cousins in Sicily. While I cooked dinner, she chopped up carrots and cucumber and lettuce for them.

When I said goodnight to her later, she'd changed the layout of the cage again. I fervently hoped nothing would happen to the guinea pigs. Already her anxiety about them bothered me.

Pasha called round the following day. It was an unusually cold afternoon for July and I'd been bracing myself for sorting through Tommaso's clothes, so his visit was welcome. Ysabelle had gone to a friend's birthday party, despite my concerns that it might be too early to be surrounded by other girls lucky enough to have both parents still alive.

'I wondered how you were getting on,' Pasha said, when I'd made him coffee. 'And Ysabelle, of course.'

I explained about the party and my reservations.

He lifted Nari and stroked his back. 'Perhaps it is a good thing. And I think at her age she is young enough to be able to escape from her unhappiness temporarily. As long as she is grieving.... And you, how are you?'

'Oh, you know...'

He waited, expression sympathetic.

'I don't know. At one level, I miss Tommaso terribly. We...our relationship, our marriage, began so well. But we had our issues.... even before the money business.... Everyone does, I suppose. Perhaps it's impossible for such intensity, such closeness to stay, but...'

I broke off, feeling disloyal talking about him like this.

During our times together in Kashmir, I'd never discussed my marriage with Pasha, and he'd never asked. Omera might have told him about the issues Tommaso and I had. But she might not. A complex woman, it was hard to predict what would offend her moral code.

'If you want to talk at all, or meet for coffee, get in touch,' Pasha said when he left.

There were almost two months of school holidays still to run. I suggested a holiday to Ysabelle, mentioning the possibility of Edinburgh, but she didn't want to leave the guinea pigs so soon. When I heard of a summer ballet school, though, this fired her up. Fortunately for us, someone had cancelled, freeing a place for her. It would run on weekday afternoons for six weeks, providing her with a grounding structure.

We established a temporary routine. I managed to arrange most my work assignments while she was at summer school. At the weekends, we'd sleep in, then go to a beach, on our own, or with Daniella, Lavinia or Margarita. I'd bought a rubber dinghy that the girls loved. If the weather was poor, we went to a film or the swimming pool. Occasionally clothes shopping, Ysabelle going through a growth spurt. To my pleasure, she showed as much interest in possible choices for me, as I did in what she might buy.

Often, I'd hear crying from her room, and find her curled up on her bed, holding Suri or Nari. I was relieved she could grieve more openly for her father. That I, too, could now cry more easily for Tommaso. Part of my grief was about the way I'd judged him before he died. I knew he'd been aware of my disappointment in him. At the same time, I knew that were he still alive, my feelings for him would have changed. Despite his taking care of Elisa's debts.

He'd irrevocably destroyed my belief that he'd ever be upfront with me.

∼

One Saturday, late August, Ysabelle woke me. Something had happened to the guinea pigs, I thought, heart sinking.

'I want to do the Walk of the Gods,' she said.

Bleary-eyed, I peered at my alarm clock. It was nine o'clock. 'Today?'

'I heard the weather forecast and it's sunny. Can we?'

'It's too late to go today. We'd need to start early to avoid the worst of the heat.... But we could try tomorrow, if the forecast is okay.'

She tilted her head and put on a sad face, leaving my room when she accepted I wouldn't change my mind.

'I'm very strong,' she insisted, during breakfast. '*Mamma* and I went walking in Sicily often. She said it would help me with my ballet.'

The following morning, we left the apartment early, dressed in lightweight trousers and walking boots, and equipped with water, packed lunch and sun cream. We drove, rather than walked, up to Nocelle, Ysabelle's compromise. Only after we arrived, did I remember that August was the busiest time for walking in this area, many Italians escaping to the coast during such a hot month.

'Why were you so keen to do this walk?' I asked Ysabelle as we set off between the white and red guiding lines

'The teachers have talked about it. They told us the path is still used by farmers and woodsmen. And shepherds.

They said we can see lots of birds and butterflies and animals. Margarita did the walk last weekend.'

The walk was enchanting, with its caves and terraces dropping from the cliffs to the sea and deep valleys. Kestrel falcons circled the air, geckos scuttled through cracks in drystone walls, butterflies drifted by. The path took us past lemon groves and vineyards and grazing goats and sheep. Already there were signs of autumn in the foliage. My senses were on fire and for the first time in my life, I wished I could write poetry. Ysabelle scribbled observations in a notebook, perhaps to share at school. To my profound relief, no snakes were visible.

Ysabelle didn't complain about my frequent photography stops, sometimes asking to see the images. I wondered if the mountains brought her closer to Elisa. If her mother and Tommaso could see us now.

By the time we reached the halfway point and sat down to eat our sandwiches, I could smell the salt on my skin from sweating so much.

Afterwards, when passing a vineyard clinging to a mountainside, Ysabelle stopped.

'Ysabelle, what is it?'

'Can I use your camera?'

As I hesitated, she added, 'I'll be careful with it.'

This trip seemed significant. Forecasting the success or otherwise of our life together. Besides, the worst that could happen was her dropping the camera. A minor consideration in the grand scheme of things.

I explained the rudiments of composition. And as she listened, tongue pressed against the corner of her mouth, I experienced such love for her. A fierce determination to do my best for her.

That evening, Ysabelle fell asleep on the sofa. Later, I

half carried her to bed, removed her sweatshirt and laid the duvet over her.

As she turned over on the pillow, she murmured, '*Mummia buonanotte*, good night, Mummy.'

She didn't often call me this and I loved hearing it.

When the autumn term commenced, life resumed a degree of normality. It had to. Ysabelle's five-day school week, dance classes and Confirmation sessions provided a welcome routine for us both. Whenever possible, I fitted photography commitments – assignments for Domenico and work for charities – around her school hours, allowing me to usually be home by the time she returned, at worst, an hour later. I knew she appreciated this because occasionally she referred sympathetically to some of the children in her class as *bambini latchkey*, latchkey kids.

The first thing she'd do was remove Nari and Suri from their cage and tell them about her school day, imitating voices of schoolteachers, some strident, others soft. She insisted on being in charge of the guinea pigs' care: feeding, changing their water and hay; cleaning out their cage and their pen. She loved chopping vegetables for them before she went to school. I'd never seen animals eat so much and would find myself observing them as they chewed their way through carrots, red peppers or celery. Her closest friends had already met the guinea pigs, and one by one, she invited her other friends to meet them. To my delight, the piggies' antics provoked squeals of girlish laughter.

In practical terms, I was now quite well off. Tommaso's pension was larger than expected, the apartment wasn't mortgaged and I still received rent from my flat in Edinburgh. Nevertheless, I worried about whether or not Tommaso owed anything to the moneylenders. I also felt duty-bound to offer compensation to the Church for what he'd done. For several nights I lay, unable to sleep, wondering what to do. In the end I phoned Pasha and explained my dilemma.

'Would you like me to speak to the Bishop?' he offered.

'If you wouldn't mind.... Pasha, how can I find out if Tommaso owed the moneylenders? I haven't been able to find any documents.'

'I expect you would have heard from them by now,' he said. 'It's been nearly two months since Tommaso's death.'

Two days later, Pasha phoned to tell me that the Bishop was grateful for my offer of compensation but considered that Tommaso's untimely death closed the matter.

Ysabelle was now making her own way home from school. After a hair appointment one day, in a salon near the school, I had time to meet her and was glad. I missed conversations with other parents in the playground. Despite the inevitable awkwardness over Tommaso's death. While waiting for her, I spotted Brigitta's mother, on her own, distant from any groups of mothers. I remembered Brigitta had a younger brother. Should I go over to Fillippa? But what would I say? Besides, would *she* want to speak to me? She would surely feel bad about Maurizio being indirectly responsible for Tommaso's death.

'Fillippa? We met a few months ago. Do you remember?'

At first she seemed relieved at being rescued from her isolation. Then her eyes darkened.

I laid my hand on her arm. 'How is Brigitta? I haven't heard Ysabelle talk much about her this term.'

On reflection, I hadn't even heard Ysabelle mention her.

'She has gone to another school, in Rome,' Fillippa said.

And then, perhaps assuming everyone would find out eventually, added, 'It's a school, for children with special needs.'

An uncomfortable silence followed.

'It was for the school fees,' she said.

It took a moment to understand what she meant, her anguished expression painful to witness.

'You mean this is why Maurizio borrowed money from the church?'

She looked appreciative at the word "borrowed". How often must she have attempted to reframe her husband's actions?

Another awkward silence. I wished Ysabelle would appear. I wondered what had happened to Maurizio regarding his behaviour.

Reading my mind, Fillipa grimaced. 'The Bishop didn't want Maurizio to go to prison. But he had to leave the Church.'

Fleetingly, my situation felt preferable. Life couldn't be easy for Fillippa or Maurizio in a small town like Positano, its Catholic church so pivotal in parishioners' lives: people shunning them or whispering when they passed. Furthermore, both parents would have ongoing worries about Brigitta.

Fillippa clutched my arm. 'Does Ysabelle understand what happened?'

'I don't know. She is grieving for her father. When she's older, I'll talk to her about it.'

The children now spilt out of the school, a boy of about seven running over to us. As she turned to walk away, eyes brimming with tears, Fillippa said, 'Please tell Ysabelle that Brigitta misses her.'

That evening I had a migraine. I explained this to Ysabelle and went to lie down. Ten minutes later, she came into my darkened room with a cup of peppermint tea, and the gesture touched me. Before she went to bed, she returned to see how I was.

Very soon, the guinea pigs became a barometer of her mood. Often, I'd find her sitting on the sofa watching them munch their vegetables. If she looked charmed, I knew she was okay. If she was frowning, then something troubled her. It seemed to me that her one concern at the moment was to make sure nothing happened to them. This, I could understand. Having lost both her parents without experiencing their illness – as indeed I had – she must fear suddenly losing more people or animals that she loved.

Autumn arrived. Trees blazed red and gold, the pin oaks particularly glorious. Tourist numbers dwindled. Boat services between Sorrento and Positano stopped for the winter. And boutiques closed on Sundays, earlier during the week. With relief, I reclaimed Positano, this autumn feeling no different, despite my altered circumstances. Despite remembering the first autumn Tommaso and I had shared here. I loved the unblemished blue skies, and crispness in the air. The softness of a lightweight garment on my arms during the evening. The beguiling smell of wood smoke replacing that of jasmine.

One afternoon in the middle of October, I was sitting outside my studio with Costanzo. Autumn leaves drifted past, the sea a deep blue. And yet I felt a sadness unconnected to Tommaso's death.

'It must be hard. Being without your husband,' Costanzo remarked.

'It is. I find working from home isolating.... I'd love to be part of an organisation.' It had taken me a while to realise what was missing from my working life. When nursing, I'd always been part of a team, constantly surrounded by colleagues.

He thought for a moment. 'My friend told me about a project working with refugees. It is in Napoli – *Sorgente*.'

'*Sorgente*? My friend works there as a physio.'

'They wish to hire a photographer for sessional work. Perhaps they have advertised. Wait for a minute, please.'

He disappeared into his studio, returning with the newspaper. He scanned the job advertisements. 'Yes, here it is.'

That evening I deliberated over the job: if I could actually do it; the impact of working with traumatised children. Fast forward to an interview and offer of two sessions a week, subject to references, police check and attending training on understanding trauma. The best thing was that I could fit the sessions around Ysabelle's school hours. I'd been lucky. Another candidate, a strong one, I sensed, had withdrawn his application at the last minute.

The manager, a tiny blonde woman called Lucia, showed me round *Sorgente*. 'It used to be a hotel. Quite a grand one. When the owner died, he left instructions. If ever it must be converted, there must be a good purpose. The Trust agreed that *Sorgente* met the requirements.'

I was impressed by all the facilities: the woodwork building, the music room, the art facilities, and by the room I'd be using for my photography sessions.

At the end of October, after a two-day induction programme, I started my sessional work at *Sorgente*. Natalie was delighted when I told her, and we agreed to travel together on the two mornings I worked there.

∼

Ysabelle was achieving high marks in school, so when the headteacher contacted me to arrange a meeting, I was baffled. She'd moved into *scuola secondaria di secondo grado* that autumn.

'We're concerned about her,' he told me.

'I thought she was doing well.'

'Academically, she is. But she has behavioural issues. She is sullen in class. On occasion she becomes angry with her classmates. Also, she seems often to be anxious.'

'She lost both her parents within two years, her father, only four months ago,' I reminded him.

He removed his spectacles and his expression softened. 'Naturally, we are sympathetic to the circumstances. But it is difficult for the teachers to have a disruptive pupil.'

'Disruptive?'

'With your permission, I wish to refer her to the school counsellor.'

I stared at him. Obviously, I had experienced Ysabelle's volatility but attributed this to age and what she'd been through. I couldn't believe she was disruptive. At home that evening, I attempted to talk to her about school, but she wouldn't open up. The next day I tried again, with no success.

Over the following months, Ysabelle met with the school counsellor on eight occasions, each time returning home red-eyed but more at peace. My interpretation – progress. Occasionally, she now let me hold her while she wept. Once she stumbled upon me crying while sorting through Tommaso's clothes and she comforted me.

Gradually, she became calmer, stopped checking the guinea pigs so frequently, was less anxious if Suri, prone to respiratory infections, had been wheezy for a few days. No longer insisting that I, or even worse, she, sat up throughout the night to check if he'd deteriorated. She laughed more often and sometimes I heard her singing in the bath. And when I next spoke to the headteacher, he told me her behaviour in class had improved. The School would continue monitoring the situation, but at the moment, he was confident about her future there. At home we had our spats, but nothing unmanageable.

I saw Diana often. When I'd been in my studio too long, if Costanzo wasn't around to chat to over coffee or a drink, I'd drive up to Montepertuso and have lunch with her. If it was a teaching day or she had a deadline, for a commission, I'd lounge on her balcony, staring out to sea.

As December grew closer, I broached the subject of Christmas with Ysabelle. 'Would you like to go to Edinburgh and stay with my aunt and uncle? They are keen to meet you.'

'Will there be snow?'

'Not in Edinburgh itself, but perhaps in the country.'

Her face lit up. 'I've never seen snow, except on the mountains in Sicily.'

## 26

Christmas in Edinburgh passed in a blur of cosy family days and excursions. Anna was home from London. Debs, Andy and Julie, now four, had flown back from Brisbane. Ysabelle settled quickly, only once phoning Omera to check on the guinea pigs. Laughingly reporting that the parrots were now imitating Nari and Suri's chirruping noises.

Predictably, it didn't snow in Edinburgh, but on Boxing Day we drove out to Midlothian where there'd been a heavy fall the day before. Julie was fascinated by this strange white stuff.

'Am I too old to build a snowman?' Ysabelle had asked as soon as we arrived at my aunt and uncle's home.

'Never!' we'd chorused.

It was magical, timeless: trees transformed into strange white shapes, red wintry light, distant farm buildings. The silence. I remembered bringing Tommaso here during our first Christmas together. Nestling against the cosy tartan cashmere scarf Marion had given him.

We'd been happy then.

Debs, Ysabelle and I now built a snowman, while Andy and Julie threw snowballs at each other.

I took many photos of Julie.

'Remember the snowman we made, not long after you came to live with us?' Debs said.

'It was a lovely afternoon.'

Her expression was compassionate. 'It must have been so hard for you, your parents gone.'

A memory surfaced of Dad helping me build a polar bear in our garden. A voice summoning him inside, before we'd finished. His exasperation. My disappointment.

'Debs, was it very difficult for you and Anna, when I arrived on your doorstep?' A question I'd never planned to ask.

My cousin hesitated. 'When Mum and Dad told us, I did feel resentment at first. But also fear. As if they'd love us less. How silly.... But I never wished you hadn't moved in. Probably because I loved you. Anna and I both did. You became our sister.'

This was all I needed to go into meltdown and I sank onto a snow-covered bench. Debs enfolded Ysabelle, saying something inaudible. Andy lifted Julie. Kissed her red nose. Placed the child on my lap.

Julie glanced up at me, asking, 'Why are you crying?'

'Sometimes grown-ups get sad,' Debs said.

Julie leant into me as if to provide comfort. It worked.

At Harvey Nichols, Ysabelle gaped at Tag Heuer and Longines watches, luxurious chocolates costing £20 a box, and Fendi monogrammed coated canvas backpacks. I could barely drag her away from anything, her eyes glittering with excitement. Perhaps hoping one day she could afford designer clothes and obscenely expensive delicacies.

Of the main tourist sites, Edinburgh Castle didn't overly impress her, but she loved Princes Street Gardens, the Scott Monument and Calton Hill. She also enjoyed walking in the New Town.

In George Street, she turned to me. 'Maybe I'll live here one day.'

'Perhaps you could study here,' I suggested, already dreading her leaving Positano. Leaving me.

'Or Paris. *Papà* promised to take me to Paris for my eighteenth birthday,' she said in a choked voice.

I hesitated before replying. 'My parents were killed in a car accident when I was sixteen.'

My instinct to share this with her was right, because she slipped her hand into mine.

'You understand what it's like. To have no parents.'

'I do.'

'Do you still miss them? People tell me that soon I will feel better.'

'I think that people who haven't had experience of losing anyone close to them can't really understand. I don't believe you get over such a loss. What I *do* believe, is that you learn to live with the loss. And I hope you will, *cara*.'

To my disappointment, Ysabelle stiffened at the endearment. I avoided using Tommaso's ones – "*principessa*" and "*angelo*" – and thought she'd accept "*cara*".

'Do you still miss *Papà*?'

'Of course.'

'Do you think he can see us?'

'I don't know. Perhaps he knows what we are doing.'

She glanced at me, twisting her hands. 'Sometimes I talk

to him when I play with Suri and Nari. I also talk to *Mamma*. Do you think it's wrong?'

'No, Ysabelle, I don't. As long as you don't pretend your parents *are* here.'

~

For Ysabelle's thirteenth birthday, we agreed to visit the zoo in Napoli. In addition, I planned a surprise for her: staying the night in an upmarket hotel in the city. She often remarked on elegant old buildings and I remembered her appreciation of Edinburgh's architecture.

Natalie had recommended the Grand Hotel Parker, near the coast, featuring a rooftop garden restaurant and spectacular views of the Bay of Napoli and distant Capri. My kind of place. And Ysabelle's, I was sure. All bedrooms had balconies, and I requested one with a sea view. The forecast predicted sunshine for most of the weekend.

I didn't mention my plan until the morning of her birthday.

'Cool,' she said. 'Will I take a dress?'

I nodded. 'We'll have dinner in the hotel dining room. You'll love it.'

'Can I see it on the computer?'

'Why not wait until you get there?'

We arrived at the zoo early afternoon. An hour later, when we reached the tiger enclosure, she flinched.

'Ysabelle, it's all right. They can't hurt you.'

She said nothing. I moved closer to her. 'What's wrong?'

'There's not enough space for them. It's terrible. I want to leave now,' and she flounced off in the direction of the main entrance.

When I reached her, I suggested we eat. Remembering

her tendency to low blood sugar. After we'd had a snack, she announced she wanted to go to the hotel now.

It was four-fifteen, three hours to sunset. Due to Saturday traffic, the drive to our hotel took forty minutes, and we had to keep the windows closed much of the time because of pollution. Driving into the luscious grounds was like entering a different world.

At reception, the clerk inclined his head to Ysabelle, delighting her. She was so like her father with her fluctuating moods.

When she saw our room, immediately she stepped out onto the balcony. 'Come and look at the view.'

In the sunny, clear afternoon, we could see the islands of Ischia, Procida and Capri. The views were even more impressive from the rooftop restaurant. After we'd had ice cream there, we returned to our room, where Ysabelle inspected every cupboard and drawer.

'Do you have anything to put in the safe?' she asked me.

'You're my most precious thing,' I said. 'And you won't fit.'

'Look at all this,' she called from the bathroom.

The hotel hadn't stinted on their complementary toiletries. How Tommaso would have appreciated this, I thought, examining the moisturisers and hair conditioners for men.

'I'm glad you like the hotel,' I said.

'It's a palace. I want to live somewhere like this when I'm older.'

Ysabelle took ages getting ready for dinner, bathing first, despite having showered in the morning. When I emerged from my shower, she was applying eyeliner.

'Where did you get that?'

'Birthday present from Daniella.'

Then she put on mascara, another present, I supposed. I said nothing. At thirteen, I couldn't reasonably object. Nevertheless, I experienced a pang of sadness at how much older it made her look. She was no longer a child. I wondered how Tommaso would have felt, seeing her like this.

When we entered the dining room, a waiter escorted us to our table, pulling out a chair for a beaming Ysabelle. Her pleasure was infectious.

Immediately we sat down, I noticed her staring across the room. My gut twisted. Not another thing upsetting her.

'Are you okay?'

She smiled. 'A girl in my class is here with her parents.'

'Do you want to say hallo?'

'No. Her family has lots of money and she's always boasting. They have horses and a boat. And they go on expensive holidays. I'm glad she's seen me here.... Look at the frescos and the chandeliers.... I love this hotel.'

What would Tommaso have made of this? I wondered, saddened by his absence, then experiencing guilt about not feeling like this more often.

After dinner we sat on the balcony, Ysabelle listening to new songs on her iPod, me chilling out. Relieved the hotel part of her birthday celebration was going well. Pleased our relationship was developing. Wondering if I should take her to India, show her some of the famous buildings there. She'd love the architecture. We could also visit tea planta-tions. Now that she was older and less thin, I wouldn't worry so much about her contracting a bug. In fact, perhaps I could combine a holiday with working on my calendar in Shimla.

～

One hot May afternoon, Diana arrived at my apartment. 'Guess what, Omera and I have bought a shop together. She can sell her paintings and I can sell my sculptures.' Diana paused to embrace me, before continuing, 'And...it's got a room for exhibitions. We got it quite cheaply because it'll need some work done inside – painting, and repairs to floors.... I didn't tell you before because I wanted to surprise you.'

'You certainly have.... Where is it?'

'Fancy seeing it now?'

Ysabelle would be home shortly, but recently I'd given her a key. I scribbled a note for her. Grabbed my bag.

At the shop, Omera, clad in bright red overalls, was painting the walls an unusual sand colour. Perfect for displaying paintings, Diana told me. From another room came the sound of a loud hairdryer, and when I opened the door, I saw Pasha, on a ladder, wielding a heat gun.

In Kashmir, he'd dressed conservatively. And my contact with him in Positano had been for more professional reasons when he'd worn his cassock. Seeing him in shorts and t-shirt, those muscular limbs glinting with sweat, was too much. Rendering me incoherent. Sensing someone there, he twisted round and smiled. His green eyes were bright, his lips even more sensual than I'd remembered. Not trusting myself to speak, I left the room.

He came into the main room a minute later. 'Are you here to help? We could do with it.... Ysabelle seems more settled, by the way. And she told me about Christmas in Edinburgh and how much she enjoyed it.'

Happy memories returned. 'I think it was easier for her than being in Sicily. She behaved beautifully.'

'Any child will enjoy being smothered with attention,' Omera remarked.

Pasha shook his head at his sister. 'Oh Ori, what a cynic you are.'

'Let me show you the other rooms,' Diana said. 'We wondered if you'd fancy selling your photographs. Perhaps as calendars, birthday cards. We're not thinking of a partnership, just an opportunity for you to sell your work. It could help for the hospital.'

I smiled, delighted by her enthusiasm. 'I'm not so prolific.'

She rolled her eyes, then flung her arms round me. 'Now Rachel, you could be. Just think.... You could visit other areas of Italy – photograph the Cinque Terre, the lakes. Anyway, the possibilities are endless.'

'There's Ysabelle. I couldn't leave her.'

'She could stay with me,' Omera offered.

'She's had too much change in her life already. The last thing she needs is to be foisted on another person.'

'Nearer places, then,' Diana said, when I left. 'Have a think.'

That evening I did think about it. It might be possible. On the other hand, perhaps I should wait until Ysabelle was older.

Furthermore, would a business connection with Omera be wise? I suspected she was aware of my developing feelings for Pasha, unleashing her protectiveness of his career. Since Tommaso's death, my Italian lessons had stopped, neither of us having mentioned resuming them.

That night, I dreamed I was in India, teaching at a children's camp. When I woke, the idea came to me: I'd set up a charity called...*Children of India*, no, *Children of Bhārata*. I liked the idea of using the name that had replaced "India". The fact that *Bhārata* meant "The cherished". I'd sell calendars and greetings cards, give the proceeds to the hospital in

Srinagar. Ideas flooded my head. If my charity did well, in time, I'd donate to other children's hospitals in India. I'd keep working for *Sorgente* and Domenico, of course, appreciating having colleagues.

My elation grew, as did my amazement at not having had this idea before. The more I thought about it, the more it made sense, bringing everything together: my love of photography, my connections with India, my desire to do something purposeful with my life.

Then I thought of Ysabelle. If I were to set up such a charity, I'd need to visit India from time to time. Perhaps I could arrange such visits during school holidays and she could come too. Or stay with her relatives in Sicily, if India didn't appeal. Something could be worked out.

Head still buzzing with possibilities, I retrieved my laptop from the sitting room and returned to bed where, propped up against two pillows, a mug of raspberry tea on the bedside table, I googled Italian charities, looking for one which worked or supported work in third world countries. Half an hour later, feverish with excitement, I found the *Centro Italiano Aiuti all'Infanzia* – Italian Centre for Aid to Children (CIAI)) – which provided humanitarian assistance to children in developing countries. I read everything on their website, and before falling asleep again, decided I would contact their base in Milan and request an online meeting to discuss how they'd set themselves up and their general experience of the work they did.

The following day, tired but happy, I returned to Omera and Diana's shop, intending to share my ideas with Diana. Neither of them was there when I let myself into the building and I realised I was actually glad, like a child hugging a delicious secret from the grown-ups. However, I found Pasha where he'd been the day before, tackling the old paint on the windowsill. He glanced at my faded jeans and t-shirt, and handed me the heat gun, saying, 'If you can take over, I'll go and buy some paint.'

I took the heat gun and within minutes heard his motorbike leave. Having found some music on my phone and put on my headphones, I set to stripping paint. It was strangely satisfying watching the old paint melt and blister, scraping off the treacly mass.

A while later, I sensed, rather than heard, Pasha's return. Turning round, I found him staring at me and inwardly blushed. His eyes were particularly bright today, his skin tanned. I knew he often opted to walk to parishioners' homes, that he swam regularly, and it was hard to imagine someone fitter or healthier looking.

'Do you like seafood?' he asked, laying down the tins of paint and a roller brush. 'There's a café several miles along the coast. Basic but good.'

Outside the building, Pasha pointed to the motorbike.

'You okay on this?'

Despite never been on a motorbike before, I nodded, hoping to look chilled out. He produced a helmet, adjusted the strap and handed it to me. Riding pillion was more exhilarating than I could have imagined. Despite my passive role, I experienced a sense of power as the orange and grey Honda surged along the road above Positano, ten minutes later turning off onto a dusty unsealed road leading down to the sea.

He parked, removed his helmet, then mine, and led me along to a building positioned under the overlying rockface. There we had the best calamari linguine I'd ever tasted.

'How about a swim?' Pasha suggested afterwards.

'No swimming things.'

'Substantial underwear?'

I shook my head.

He nodded and walked off. I followed. Near the water, he whipped off his t-shirt and shorts, handed them to me and waded into the sea in his boxers. I stared after him as he broke into an elegant crawl. Wishing I had his confidence, his naturalness. Nothing in his behaviour resembled showing off.

Back at the shop, we found Omera and Diana discussing a floor plan. They looked up as we entered. 'You should try the Casa Blanca. Great calamari,' Pasha told them.

I avoided eye contact with Omera. Diana's expression was hard to interpret.

A Skype with staff from the *Centro Italiano Aiuti all'Infanzia* proved useful. They listened attentively to my ideas and encouraged me to go ahead. They told me about the origins of their foundation and advised me to keep mine as simple, and to choose directors carefully. I'd already considered who to ask. Natalie's husband, Louis, was an obvious choice, with his legal background. Diana, too, with her experience of promoting her work.

To my delight, both Diana and Louis agreed. Natalie was so enthusiastic about my project that it was tempting to invite her to become a director, but not at the moment. Within a fortnight, Louis, Diana and I had written the oblig-atory document declaring our main purpose, assets and how these would be distributed. Following which, a legal colleague of Louis attested to the document. Then we registered *Children of Bhārata* in Napoli, after which the three of us went for a celebratory lunch.

As I sorted through my photos of Kashmir, deciding which ones to use, I often found myself thinking about Pasha: him looking after me when I was ill; the experiences we'd shared. And now another memory: our visit to Casa Blanca. As he'd been back in the UK visiting his father, I hadn't seen him since then.

Longing to talk about him, one afternoon I drove up to Montepertuso. To my dismay, his car was parked outside Diana's apartment.

## 27

I couldn't fathom out any reasonable explanation for Pasha visiting Diana. She wouldn't have decided to become Catholic. And as she had found someone to do small repairs in her apartment, she wouldn't ask him for such help. Yet, I remembered the strange expression on her face when I returned from having lunch with him at Casa Blanca.

Despite feeling stupid and childish, for a week I avoided Omera and Diana, unable to face hearing anything about Pasha. Then Diana phoned. 'Why haven't you answered my texts?'

My heart raced. Should I simply ask her straight out about Pasha? She was my oldest friend, after all. 'I've been busy.'

'Me too. Teaching, of course. Also, much still to do to get the shop ready for business. The only problem is my work/life balance...imbalance. The thing is, where does one find a hot Italian and a fertile one?'

Relief flowed through me and I berated myself for having jumped to conclusions about Pasha and her.

'Big question! How's the business going? How's Omera?'

'Complaining about her car. It broke down a month ago, and the garage is useless, quote. Anyway, she's using Pasha's car, which she detests. She visited me last week and swore she'd never drive here again in it.'

Double confirmation my worries were unfounded. We arranged to meet soon, and after the call, I danced round the apartment to Gipsy Kings until my euphoria wore off.

Ironically, the following day Pasha got in touch to see if I wanted to go for a drive.

After that, we met up every few weeks or so. It felt right to spend time with him. Albeit, difficult to restrict my feelings to those of friendship.

∾

Our lives jogged along. Ysabelle was attending two dancing classes a week and her teacher had suggested that when she was older she apply for a scholarship to the *Teatro alla Scala* Academy in Milan. Tommaso would have been so proud.

Ysabelle spent much of her free time with her small group of female friends, either at our apartment, listening to music or playing with the guinea pigs, or hanging out at a beach café. To my relief, the girls were content to stay in Positano, with the occasional trip to the cinema in Sorrento. They often did sleepovers.

Gradually, she confided more in me about incidents at school, homework worries or a dip in confidence regarding her dancing. At an emotional level, our relationship remained consistent. She wasn't particularly demonstrative but I sensed we'd grown closer since that day in Edinburgh when we'd talked about losing our parents. Occasionally, she'd slip her arm round my waist during a walk, and she always kissed me goodnight. Seldom, though, did she embrace me like she'd done with her father.

Over the summer months, when Ysabelle was with friends, I was busy sorting through the photos I took in Kashmir, editing them. Making arrangements with the Photography Institute in Napoli for them to print my calendars and cards. The buzz remained, so convinced was I that this was where my creative energies would go. So relieved to feel more purpose to my life. Being Ysabelle's stepmother fulfilled me, but at some stage she'd move away.

By the third week in October, my first calendar was ready for distribution. It had been a rush. So many decisions to make: did I want the photos to "bleed" off the edge of the calendar or have white space around them? Did I want to add a decorative border, and if so, the same one for unity or vary it according to the month? It was important to be ready by November in order to promote the calendars in time for Christmas. In addition, I needed to have the images scanned by professional graphics designers whose equipment could handle high optical resolutions. Once I'd approved the proofs, there was a nail-biting time while I waited for the finished product.

While waiting for the proofs, to my delight, three distribution companies whom I'd approached earlier, got back to me with very reasonable estimates, both for the UK and Italy. Several bookshop franchises in the UK had agreed to stock the calendar, initially requesting small numbers, but those increasing towards the end of November.

When the calendars arrived, I sat for ages looking at them, thrilled to have reached this stage, at the same time fearful they wouldn't sell. The following day, I took bundles of them to venues where there'd be craft fairs, community events and school nativity plays. *Sorgente* was particularly pleased to add them to the goods they were selling at their annual Christmas fair.

'What promoting are you doing on Facebook?' Diana asked me one evening when we were seated at my kitchen table, checking through order forms and receipts.

'I've mentioned it but–'

'You need a separate page for the calendars. Like authors do, for example. There's a Shopify app – about £6 a month subscription, and you can take orders with it. And it'll drive traffic to your website. And you could also sell it on community groups' pages, if you have the Admin's permission. And you could–'

I blocked my ears. 'Enough. I'm overwhelmed as it is. Besides, I'm selling them through my website.'

'Just one more suggestion, please,' Diana said, ignoring my sigh. 'Open an eBay charity shop – allow your calendars to reach a much larger audience. It–'

I flicked the remote control at her to indicate she stop talking. 'Next year, perhaps.'

To my shame, it was Ysabelle who mentioned we hadn't planned anything for Christmas. She was leaving for school at the time, so I promised her we'd discuss it that evening. While tidying up, I wondered about Sicily, but nothing had changed with Irma: no apologetic phone call from her, no suggestion from Fabrizio that she knew I wasn't to blame for Tommaso's death. Perhaps I could invite Marion, Geoffrey and Anna to Positano. I lifted the phone to dial their number.

'I'm glad you called,' Marion said. 'I was going to phone you this evening. About Christmas.'

'Snap,' I said. 'Would you like to come to Italy?'

She hesitated. 'Actually, dear, we're going to Queensland.'

Australia! What a treat for Ysabelle.

As I was about to ask if we could join them, Marion spoke again. 'Debs has been blighted by post-natal depression since Charlie was born – Andy's quite worried about her.'

'Ysabelle and I will do something here,' I reassured her. 'Perhaps you could come over in the Easter holidays.... I'm sorry to hear about Debs. I wondered why she hadn't been posting lots of photos of Charlie on Facebook.... Should I phone her, do you think? I haven't spoken to her since the birth.'

'Perhaps leave it for the moment.... Anna's between jobs just now, so she'll stay on in Cains for a while after Christmas. Help Andy with the children. Just until Debs is feeling better.'

'Give them all my love when you next speak to them,' I said, wishing I was closer geographically to my cousin and her family.

'I want to spend Christmas with Granny and Grandpa,' Ysabelle said that evening, returning Nari to his pen.

When I didn't respond, she continued, 'Don't you like going to Sicily? Is it because of Granny?'

'You could go down on your own, I suppose. My friends will be here. I won't be lonely.'

∼

On December 17, the festive celebrations began with a special Novena of prayers and church services. Ysabelle had flown to Sicily the previous day so I went along with Diana. Outside the church of *Santa Maria Assunta* was the nativity, with exquisitely hand carved figures and amazing detail of clothing. Glossy paper, gilt pine cones and miniature coloured pennants decorated the triangular wooden frame, small candles fastened to the sides.

'Isn't this beautiful? It's giving me ideas for my sculpting,' Diana said.

'Ysabelle would have loved this.'

Diana squeezed my arm. 'Take lots of photos to send her.'

The church's yellow, green and blue tiled dome gleamed in the morning light, beyond it a dark blue sea glittered and danced. I would have loved to skip the service, instead watch the sea splashing over the harbour. But Diana was keen to attend.

After the service, she suggested we walk along the beach. About five minutes later, she took my arm. 'So, when were you planning to tell me?'

'Tell you what?'

'About Pasha.... You're in love with him, aren't you?'

'Why would you think this?'

'We used to tell each other everything, Rach.'

'I'm fond of him. He took care of me when I was ill in Kashmir.'

'Fond? It's more than fondness, methinks.'

I gazed at the white crested waves. 'It's hopeless, he's wedded to the Church. How can I compete?' I hated the bitter tone in my voice. 'Do you think it's awful having these feelings?'

Diana wrapped her scarf more tightly round her neck.

'Before what happened with Doug, I'd have been more judgemental. Now, well...it's not as if you're acting on them, is it? And even if you did, Christ...life is so short. The thing is, we never know what's ahead of us. The Church shouldn't make those poor priests live such sexually unfulfilled lives.'

She flung her arms round me. 'Oh Rachel....' Then she pulled back and was silent for a while. 'I'm thinking of applying to a sperm bank,' she told me. 'Do you think this is a good idea?'

We discussed this for a while, then the conversation ended with Diana saying, 'But I did so much want it to be homemade.'

I'd planned to invite Natalie, Louis and Diana for a meal on Christmas Day, but before I got organised, Omera asked me to join her with Pasha. She'd also invited Diana, several neighbours and other friends.

That day, twelve of us gathered at her apartment. When I arrived, marginally late from Skyping my family in Australia, Omera was pacing the kitchen.

'What's wrong?'

'Pasha,' she said, uncharacteristically flapping her arms.

My heart sank. He'd cancelled.

'Is he ill?'

'Not ill. Late, and the food will be ruined. I'll give him another ten minutes then we'll start. He is always late.'

Her buzzer went and a moment later, Pasha opened the door.

'Sorry Ori, to be late, it is my fate,' he said, his face flushed, hair unruly. Had it been anyone else, I'd have suspected he'd come straight from a lover's bed.

Omera had tidied her sitting room so much it was barely recognisable. The table we'd used for our Italian lessons was covered with a white lace cloth, red candles and home-made characters from the nativity. A festive arrangement of dried lilies, holly and roses formed the focal point.

Knowing we'd all be hungry from the customary twenty-four fast, to my relief she immediately served a traditional dinner: spaghetti and anchovies and other fish, broccoli, tossed salad, fruits, and sweets. Then, over a burning Yule log, we toasted each other with wine. I'd experienced these customs before. New to me, however, was The Urn of Fate, a large ornamental bowl containing wrapped gifts. We all helped ourselves to a present. Mine was a burgundy Cloisonné bracelet, with a green and cream pattern. Everyone received something of quality. Omera wasn't a wealthy woman and her generosity touched me.

'I've seen your calendar in several parishioners' homes,' Pasha told me.

'I bought one at a Christmas fair,' one of Omera's friends mentioned. 'The photos are stunning. How do you manage to capture such expressions on those children's faces?'

This was the first face-to-face compliment I'd had, apart from those of friends, and a warm glow spread through me.

A strong wind was whipping up the sea and when conversation halted, we could hear waves crashing to the shore. Exhilarating. Despite enjoying myself, briefly I longed to be on the beach, absorbed by the whishing of water retreating from the shore.

Throughout the celebration, I felt acutely aware of Pasha's presence, occasionally sensing him watching me. I was also conscious of Omera's observant eye. Had they discussed me recently? I wondered. And in what capacity?

Diana knowing and understanding my feelings, comforted me, however.

To my surprise, I didn't miss Ysabelle as much as anticipated.

When the guests left Omera's home, I walked down to the beach and sat on a rock, watching the sea. Despite having enjoyed the celebrations, it was wonderful being on my own now. So close to the elements: the angry sky and salt spray; the thundering pewter waves; the sound of pebbles as the sea was sucked back.

Something made me turn round, to notice a man approaching. Pasha. He sat down beside me, slipped an arm round my shoulder. 'Missing Ysabelle?'

'A bit now. But I expect I'll miss her more on the Feast of the Epiphany. She used to get so excited when she hung up her stocking. Wondering if she'd been good enough to deserve a present. Dreading finding a block of charcoal instead.... Next year, I'll make sure we spend Christmas together.'

At the beginning of the New Year, I received reports that my calendar had sold well in various bookshops in the UK, and – to my surprise and delight – from my Facebook page. Already I had ideas about the next calendar and was negotiating with outlets about greetings cards. I was also greatly enjoying my sessional work at *Sorgente*. Despite my only working there two half days per week, the staff included me in any developmental decisions, and I often joined them for lunch before heading back to Positano. Seeing Natalie so regularly was lovely, too.

∿

Over the following months, Pasha and I continued to meet. We'd sit on my balcony, or he'd drive me into the mountains or to another coastal town.

'How I envy people who make the right decisions,' he said one murky February afternoon. We were at a café in Minori, watching the restless sea. Speculating whether the gathering dark clouds heralded a storm.

In a denim shirt, khaki trousers, and leather jacket, he looked remarkably unpriestlike. Especially the way he sat – slightly leant back, head to one side, relaxed, open. I loved his poised walk, suggesting a readiness to dance, which might have seemed acquired on other men, but with him, looked natural. And all the more attractive. It was the eyes which did it. The green irises, their bluey white sclera.

'Doubts about the church?'

'For sure. At times it feels like there's too much to sacrifice. Then I doubt whether my love of God is strong enough.... And whether I can continue to tolerate all the things I dislike about the Catholic Church.'

'Have you always had doubts?'

'Not at first. Initially it was my only choice. And a vocation then. I enjoyed the sacrifices, the things I had to do without. It made my love stronger. But now....' He broke off, seemingly lost in thought.

As I studied those clear green eyes, I remembered seeing him in his boxers that afternoon at Casa Blanca. Hoped my expression didn't betray such ungodly thoughts.

Pasha continued, his forehead caught in a frown as if unsure of the truth in his words. 'Perhaps it will be better with the next Pope. Someone more liberal. I hope they appoint Bergoglio.' His speed increased with his enthusiasm. 'Bergoglio is so committed to ecumenism with other Christians. He wants to build bridges with Muslims and other religions. And his appointment would be well-received.' Pasha stopped, stretched his arms over his head. 'But even if they did appoint Bergoglio, it might not be enough.... I don't know.'

'And other things – like not being able to marry and have children?' I couldn't help it. I needed to know, I supposed. Theoretically, at least.

He looked haunted.

Committed to this line of conversation, I continued, 'Have you ever broken your vows?'

'Made love? Yes, several times,' he said easily, as if talking about a country he'd visited. 'And the awful thing is that afterwards, initially anyway, I had no regret. Eventually I needed to confess. Accept my penance.'

Jealousy seared me.

'What happens if a priest...falls in love?'

Pasha leant forward, prompting me to look away, worried about revealing my emotions. Embarrassing us both. 'Well, we have three choices. We can keep our "sexual urges" under control and pray for them to subside. Easier, of course, if you don't see the woman.'

He paused and my heart thudded. Had he actually been in love? Forced to break off contact?

'Or we can marry the woman, which would mean leaving the "priestly ministry". In other words, be disqualified as a priest. And such a frightening prospect for sure – for any priest.'

He shuddered.

I waited a minute before asking about the third option.

'Option three is to continue the relationship... but be celibate: impossible, I'd think, wouldn't you?' and as he awaited my response, his expression might have registered desire. How I wanted it to. 'Also, of course, you could have a sexual relationship secretly and continue to be a priest. As long as it didn't become *openly* scandalous... but this wouldn't be very satisfactory, for either party.'

What a waste of love. Romantic and physical.

He was shaking his head. 'I've known a couple of priests who've left the Church. And they went through torment beforehand. And for a long time afterwards...'

I wondered how many people knew or guessed about Pasha's doubts over his vocation.

On our return drive, I felt weak with longing for him. Determined to throw myself into my work even more in order to cope. Fortunately, I was busy with the logistics of producing greetings cards. From now on, though, every time I thought about Pasha, I would force myself to switch off. It was the only way to survive. The alternative was not to see him at all, but this would seem ungrateful after all he'd done for me. Or so I convinced myself.

On an uncharacteristically hot May afternoon, Pasha called by after lunch. I'd just signed a contract to provide blank greetings cards to three bookshops in the UK and was delighted to share my news with him. I offered him a drink and for once he accepted. After congratulating me and asking how Ysabelle was, he sat back, sipping his beer, staring out to sea.

'And you?' I asked. 'How are things with you?'

A moment elapsed before he replied, 'Plagued by doubts. I'm going on a retreat to a Benedictine Monastery at Glastonbury.'

'A programme?'

Pasha lifted a copy of *Il Matino* from the coffee table,

then replaced it. 'Nothing like that. Nothing structured. Simply an opportunity to reflect, and far away from Italy, of course. And even the long flight will be helpful, for sure.... The Bishop has given his permission.'

Glastonbury in Massachusetts, not the UK. Too far away.

'How long will you be away?'

'Four weeks.'

Four weeks.... What if he decided to stay on?

'You *are* coming back?'

We stared at each other and I had to move away. For something safe to do, I retreated to the kitchen to make coffee. Leant against the worktops, clutching the percolator. Two wasps buzzed round the room, their high-pitched hum intensified by the silence. A stench of fish and rotting vegetables came from the bin under the sink. Today the sky was a hazy pale blue, the sea barely rippling as if it, too, had no energy. Woozy from the beer and lack of food, I filled a glass with water and sat at the table, coffee forgotten.

Pasha appeared, pulled me to my feet and kissed me, gently at first, then more insistently.

Leading him to my bedroom, all thoughts dissolved except my need for fulfillment. I pulled the curtains to exclude the harsh light, the bleached colours of outside. Then, fleetingly, we stared at each other, tacitly confirming this was okay. Nevertheless, I feared he might yet change his mind. Adhere to his vows of chastity. Despite having broken them before. Not until we lay together on cool sheets and touched foreheads, did I feel calm.

It was different to being with Tommaso. Slower but equally passionate. Our bodies were mysterious to each other, yet we knew instinctively how to please and I drifted into a wonderful place. A forgotten place. Nothing pulling me back. Afterwards, lying facing him, I experienced no guilt. Nor did the consequences fill my consciousness.

My bedside clock showed three-fifteen – an hour before Ysabelle returned home. Sixty precious minutes. But, as Pasha pulled me towards him again, a voice called out, '*Mamma*?'

Mind in overdrive, I fumbled into my dressing gown and made for the bedroom door. Too late. The door opened, and Ysabelle stared past me at Pasha.

## 28

Before I could stop her, Ysabelle rushed out of the apartment.

I pulled on my clothes and ran after her, stumbling down the steps to the beach. As she turned a corner, I glimpsed her long hair.

'Ysabelle, wait.'

Eventually she stopped, and in a contemptuous tone said, 'How could you do this? How could you do this to *Papà*?'

My mind flooded with possible responses. In some ways she was a mature fourteen-year-old. In other ways, not.

'How could you have sex...with Father Cowan?'

I said nothing. I had no defence.

'Sister Maria sent me home because I have a sore head. I wish I'd stayed at school.'

'I'm sorry you saw me with Pasha... Father Cowan. But you have to understand–'

'Understand what?'

'Look, I don't need to justify myself to you.'

It wasn't what I meant to say, and, to my horror, she

frowned fiercely then her eyes filled. Anger was one thing, contempt even. Distress was different.

'It's only been two years since Papa died–'

'Three years, actually.' I stopped, neither wanting to nor feeling justified in defending myself.

'I knew you were in love with Father Cowan. I noticed your expression when you saw him at Pompeii.'

I needed no reminding of the occasion. During a visit to the Roman ruins with Daniella, we'd bumped into Pasha. Host to clerical colleagues from Kashmir, he'd been wearing a gold embossed cassock, and when the sun emerged from behind the clouds, lighting his face, I could barely breathe.

'Teachers talk to us about having self-control,' Ysabelle said. 'They should talk to parents. What you've done is disgusting.'

I felt winded.

She continued scampering down the steps, but as I followed, my right sandal caught on something sharp, splitting the sole. I abandoned my chase: she needed time on her own to calm down. One foot bare, I limped back up the steps to the apartment where Pasha, now dressed, was pacing the sitting room. He searched my face. I shook my head.

'Should I go after her?' he offered.

'Better to leave it for the moment, I think.'

For a while he hung around, in case she returned. We drank coffee but didn't talk.

That evening, Ysabelle stayed in her bedroom, refusing dinner. I hoped Nari and Suri were comforting her.

Two days later, Pasha came round to speak to her, but she told him she had too much homework. The following day he returned, but again she wouldn't talk to him. Perhaps he was relieved. How would he defend what had happened?

Despite keeping busy, time dragged while Pasha was in Boston. As well as missing him, the situation with Ysabelle was upsetting me more than I could have imagined. Naively, I'd hoped she would recover relatively quickly from what she'd seen, and we could be friends again. In fact, she avoided me where possible, and when we were together, she was either frosty or downright rude.

The week Pasha was due back, I waited for him to contact me. When he didn't get in touch, I assumed this meant he was remaining with the Church. During his absence, I'd tried to prepare myself for this. Occasionally felt close to accepting it. Despite my increased love for him since sleeping together. Nevertheless, whatever his decision, I needed to hear it from him. Once or twice, I hovered near the Santa Maria Assunta church. He never emerged.

A week after his return, I received a letter from Pasha, telling me he'd decided to stay with the Church. The retreat had helped greatly and he felt much better for having reached his decision. He'd like us to remain friends but would understand if I found this too difficult. I waited a few days before replying, wondering if I could accept only friendship with him. Although I wanted so much more from him, nevertheless any contact was better than none. We met up for lunch soon after and agreed to see each other from time to time.

Several times over the following months, I attempted to talk to Ysabelle about what had happened. On each occasion, however, she walked away. Regardless of where we were.

She was now spending more time with Lavinia and Daniella, often doing weekend sleepovers. In many ways, I didn't mind. I liked both girls and trusted their parents to keep an eye on them. But when Ysabelle and I were on our own, she continued to be surly or cold.

If I hadn't had my burgeoning sense of self, due to my charity, I might have crumbled. I never knew when to tackle her for her rudeness, and when to view her compassionately, remembering all she'd lost. Trying to imagine how I'd feel if I stumbled on a parent – step-parent – in bed with someone who should be out of bounds, was impossible. Visualising either of my parents even flirting with another person, equally impossible.

When the school informed me Ysabelle had stopped attending Confirmation classes, I was at a loss as to how to respond. She and I knew why she'd dropped out. And Pasha wouldn't try to persuade her to change her mind. Furthermore, recommending she transfer to another priest's class, would lead to unwelcome speculation. Eventually, I wrote to the school stating it was her decision and requesting they didn't pressurise her to rejoin the classes.

As the end of the school year approached, I spoke to Ysabelle about holidays. 'You remember the hotel in Napoli? How you loved the architecture? We could go to India and stay in some of the grand old palace hotels. You'd love it. There's such a–'

'I want to go to Sicily to see Granny and Grandpa.'

'We could do that, I suppose.' But it would be awkward with Irma. If it were Christmas, Tommaso's sisters and their families would be around much of the time. In the summer, it would only be Fabrizio and Irma as Bea and Abri tended to visit other parts of Italy during these months.

'On my own.'

'Your *own*?'

Her eyes challenged me. 'I went myself at Christmas. You didn't mind then. There's also the problem with Granny.'

'I could stay in a hotel.'

'Then what's the point of coming, *Rachel*?'

To be with you, I wanted to say. To get back to where we were before you stumbled in on me with Pasha.'

'We could go to India when you return.'

She didn't reply.

Reluctant to display my hurt, I went into the kitchen to prepare dinner. During our meal she sat with a grim expression. She didn't offer to clear up.

Three days later, I saw Ysabelle off at Napoli airport. She tolerated my hug without reciprocating it and didn't turn around to wave or smile.

On my return to the car park, I spotted a familiar figure. Salvatore. Except for one visit early on in my marriage, I hadn't seen him since my wedding. He strolled over to where I was standing.

'Rachel,' he said, embracing me. 'You look great.'

'Back for a holiday?'

'Longer. I've taken a job at a law firm in Sorrento.'

'Had enough of California?'

'My mother's not so fit these days. I wanted to be closer to her... I'm sorry I couldn't get back for Tommaso's funeral. I had pneumonia. I hope you got my letter.... How are you?'

My effort to keep my tone light failed miserably. 'Ysabelle's gone to Sicily to visit her family. I've just seen her off.'

Salvatore smiled compassionately. Why couldn't I meet a man like him – uncomplicated, available? Then I remembered Steve and why that relationship hadn't worked.

'Can I give you a lift back to Positano?' I asked, hoping Salvatore would accept.

He nodded. 'Wonderful. Jet lag will kick in soon.'

His company provided the perfect antidote for my sadness over Ysabelle's departure. Entertaining me with anecdotes from a flight plagued throughout by stroppy passengers.

The following day, Salvatore invited me to dinner in Maiori, a picturesque town on the Amalfi coast, dominated by the medieval Castle of San Nicola de Thoro-Plano. At a harbour restaurant, he described the pros and cons of life in California: clichéd greetings; frequent invitations never followed up; the surfing and hiking opportunities. We talked about Tommaso's death and the circumstances surrounding it. About my charity.

I was burning to ask one question. 'Did you know about Ysabelle – I mean, right from the start?'

It was the first time I'd seen Salvatore disconcerted.

'Tommaso begged me not to tell anyone. He was my closest friend... I had to agree. This doesn't mean I was comfortable about you not knowing.... I did suggest he tell you.'

I believed him.

After dinner, we strolled along the large expanse of beach, listening to revellers. My spirits lifted. All I needed to regain perspective was a social life not completely involving or reminding me too much of Ysabelle. Besides, she'd be back in three weeks' time. We had the rest of the summer.

Ysabelle's greeting at the airport was chilly. Unsurprising, if depressing. I waited for a while before asking questions, nostalgic for the time when she'd chatter away about what she'd done. Her replies were brief, her tone begrudging: she'd enjoyed being with Fabrizio and her cousins; she'd shopped for clothes with Abri; they'd picnicked on the beach; she'd even spent a long weekend in Malta with Bea and her children. She didn't mention Irma.

'Let me see what you bought,' I said when we arrived home, hoping a girlie session about clothes might bring us closer.

She went into her bedroom to see the guinea pigs. 'I left the clothes there.'

A band of steel gripped my stomach. 'Why?'

'Why not?'

Silence.

'I need to have clothes there for when I visit, *Rachel*.'

I nodded, partially reassured. Despite rationalising, however, the niggle wouldn't shift.

Over the following week or so, Ysabelle and I limped along together. Daytimes she often spent out with her friends, and at dinner, conversation was sporadic and flat. Whenever I suggested doing something with her, she wanted to bring a friend. I understood: at her age girlfriends were particularly important. Yet I longed to spend time on our own. Nevertheless, I didn't reintroduce the subject of going to India, not robust enough to invite rejection. Perhaps next year.

If we'd argued, the situation might have improved, I thought. But her indifference chilled me – the bond between us remaining broken.

One evening in the middle of July, I returned from Diana's to hear scuffling sounds on the balcony. Without thinking, I rushed out, visualising an intruder. Ysabelle was there with a boy. She glared at me; he made his apologies and left.

'What were you doing?' I asked.

'None of your business. You're not my mother,' she said calmly.

Aware of my shaking hands, I replied, 'I'm in charge of you and you're only fourteen.... How long have you known him? What's his name?'

Her expression was contemptuous. 'I'm going to bed.'

Determined to defuse the situation, I went to waken her at nine-thirty the following morning. She wasn't in her room. Or elsewhere in the apartment. I rang round her friends.

Margarita's father sounded surprised to hear from me. 'My wife has taken the girls to Salerno for the day. We assumed you knew.'

When Ysabelle got home at five o'clock, I was waiting for her. 'We need to talk.'

She raised her eyebrows in exaggerated fashion. 'Not *again*.'

'Why didn't you tell me you were going to Salerno today?'

She shrugged. 'You don't need to know everything I do, *Rachel*.'

'When you're living here, I do.'

'Well, you won't have to worry about that for much longer.'

Her eyes glinted and I felt the edge of fear. I hadn't the courage to ask her what she meant.

'About last night...'

She wouldn't look at me. 'He's just a boy I met.'

'Where? Come on, Ysabelle, you can't bring back boys

you don't know. Surely you understand that? What would have happened if I hadn't returned then?'

Her eyes remained lowered. We hadn't discussed sex like this before.

'I wouldn't have let him...do anything,' she muttered eventually.

I allowed myself to smile. 'Good. That's a relief. I'll make cappuccinos. We should talk about what you're going to do after next year. If–'

'I'm tired.'

'Okay. Later then, this evening. After dinner.'

She lifted her shoulder bag and traipsed to her room, closing the door behind her. Shortly after, I heard her talking, but not softly, like she did with the guinea pigs. Was she phoning a friend? The boy?

While preparing our evening meal, I contemplated confiding in Ysabelle that I'd got pregnant at sixteen, how easy it was for this to happen, for it to happen at an even younger age. Perhaps tell her about the complications arising from my termination. I'd have to pick the right time for such a conversation, however, not when she was so challenging. Moreover, I wasn't sure if it was wise to share something so deeply personal with her. Information she could use against me.

At dinner, Ysabelle played with her food, before announcing she had to practise her dancing.

'You've hardly eaten anything.'

'Back off.'

'This is what stepmothers do,' I said, my level tone belying my turmoil. 'Besides, we need to discuss what you'll do after next year. I've got brochures for dance schools. There's a good one in Rome, and the *Accademia Teatro alla*

*Scala* in Milan, that your teacher mentioned. Rome would be nearer–'

'I am going back to Sicily in September. To live with Granny and Grandpa'

I gulped. She couldn't mean it. I waited for a reassuring comment, one indicating uncertainty. Or, better still, that she was testing me.

Nothing. Expression stony, she went through to her bedroom and closed the door.

I slumped on the sofa, vaguely aware of darkness falling, of shivering despite the warm summer evening. Then my brain kicked in. She couldn't insist on leaving: according to Italian law, at fourteen she was a minor. But if she wanted to live with another adult, this changed things. Could I be awarded custody, having already cared for her? In anguish, I remembered Tommaso's suggestion I become her legal parent, my fobbing him off.

The next day, I attempted to act normally at breakfast. After all, Ysabelle might change her mind about Sicily. Our relationship might improve again and we'd rekindle the closeness established since Tommaso's death.

'Have you plans for today?' I asked.

Without lifting her head from *Il Mattino,* she muttered, 'I'm going to see Cristiana.'

'Put the newspaper away, *please.*'

She pouted, laid down the paper, and concentrated on the crusty bread on her plate, periodically sipping her cappuccino.

'We need to talk about last night,' I said eventually.

She scowled at me but I noticed her twisting her hands. Not as confident as she wanted to appear. 'What do you mean?'

'Going to live in Sicily with Irma and Fabrizio.'

'What's the problem? I move to *scuola secondaria superiore* after the summer. I want to go back to Sicily.'

'Ysabelle, have you actually talked to your grandparents about this?'

She looked sheepish. 'I mentioned it. They said it was up to you.... It should be *my* decision.'

'You're fourteen. I would have to give permission.... Isn't Positano your home now?'

Her delayed response was theatrical, a work of art. 'When *Papà* was here.'

Cruel. So deliberately cruel. Any activities we'd shared, any mutual support or closeness, rendered meaningless. In the kitchen, I bowed my head over the sink, briefly fantasising about her wrapping her arms around my waist. Saying she wanted to stay with me. Her mother. When I'd summoned enough composure to return to the sitting room, however, she'd left. At this moment, I missed Tommaso more than I'd done since his death.

I spent the next few days speaking to my lawyer, to friends, to Fabrizio, to Pasha. In different ways, they all said the same thing – kindly but firmly. If Ysabelle wanted to return to Sicily, was it wise to challenge this?

It was Diana's comment that finally resolved my indecision. She understood me best. 'The thing is, Rachel, if you love something, you need to set it free, blah, blah,' she said one afternoon. We were on her balcony, watching the sullen clouds and tossing sea, eating a coffee cake she'd baked the day before. 'If you don't let Ysabelle go now, things will continue to deteriorate. Anyway, once she's left school – well, who knows? It's not that she doesn't love you, anyway. You mustn't think that.'

'You're right, you're right. Everyone is saying the same thing, actually.'

She bit hard on her thumb. Then she flung her arms round me. 'Oh Rachel...'

~

At the end of July, I saw my stepdaughter off on a flight to Catania. School wouldn't resume until the middle of September, but she'd made up her mind about returning to Sicily, therefore asking her to stay until near the time wouldn't make any difference. Besides, I still had some remnants of pride.

What hurt me most was her taking the guinea pigs – a sure sign of her certainty about leaving Positano. Leaving me.

Readying them for travel had involved acquiring an airline approved pet carrier and a Certificate of Veterinary Inspection. Ysabelle and I lined the carrier with a soft blanket for extra comfort, adding two small cloths for Nari and Suri to slip under if necessary. During this preparation, we barely communicated, she in stroppy mode, me so choked I could hardly speak.

'How about going out for pizza tonight?' I suggested on the eve of her departure, hoping this might improve our relationship before she left.

She added more CDs to a plastic box and slipped it into her suitcase. 'Daniella's parents are taking us out for a meal.'

I wanted to ask if I'd been invited. Certain I would have, it being Ysabelle's last evening in Positano. Her defiant expression stopped me, however. Nevertheless, later I hovered. Hoping right until the last minute she would tell me I could join them.

~

For three days after Ysabelle left, I struggled to get up in the mornings. Convincing myself I needed more sleep. When eventually I rose, I wandered aimlessly round the apartment. Drinking too much coffee. Living on bread and tinned soup. Entering her room was so painful that I avoided doing so. All I wanted was for us to live together again. Regardless of how difficult she might be.

Knowing how I was feeling, Pasha had suggested meeting up, but even the prospect of spending time with him meant little. The irony didn't escape me: if he and I hadn't made love and been discovered by Ysabelle, it was unlikely she'd have wanted to return to Sicily. And yet I could never regret my coming together with him.

Every second evening for two weeks, I phoned Ysabelle. Hoping she might be rethinking. Realising how much she'd left behind. Missing me, even. If she harboured any doubts, though, she didn't mention these during our stilted conversations.

Diana was in the UK visiting family, and I missed her, too.

Feeling desperate one day after returning from *Sorgente*, I phoned Pasha and asked if we could meet. Within half an hour, he had arrived and we sat on the balcony, the one area of our apartment that I didn't associate with Ysabelle her as she'd seldom sat there with me.

'I feel bereft,' I told him.

'You love her as a daughter,' Pasha said. 'And deep down, she probably loves you as a mother. Maybe she wishes to punish you for us.'

'Probably, but I don't regret what happened between us.'

Pasha said nothing. Perhaps we were both thinking we'd paid a high price for our commingling.

Not until Ysabelle had been gone a month, did I venture

properly into her room to put away laundry. There, I studied
the animal posters on the walls and ornaments on her chest
of drawers. Straightening one of the posters. Uprighting a
glass tiger. Her walking boots caused an irrational sense of
hope that she might return to live here, before I noticed a
hole in the right one and the frayed laces on both. Stuffed
into the left boot was a crumpled t-shirt. Opening a drawer, I
riffled through matchless socks and a pair of shorts long
outgrown. Hastily, I laid the newly laundered clothes in an
empty drawer. Trying not to register that most of them
seemed too small for her now or were things she'd never
particularly liked.

The table where Nari and Suri's cage had sat seemed
enormous in its emptiness. I heard myself talking to them,
pictured them – food suspended in their paws – sympa-
thising over my situation. If only I'd concocted a reason why
they shouldn't travel with Ysabelle. Then she'd be more
likely to return.

Their cage might be gone, but evidence of their existence lingered in the surrounding area: half chewed alfalfa
pellets and strands of sandy hair. Bits of hay. I fetched a
damp cloth to clean up the debris. And for one crazy half
hour, considered buying another guinea pig.

Occasionally, after those initial weeks, Ysabelle phoned
me. No doubt urged to do so by Fabrizio. She provided me
with snippets about the family, but I could hear her sigh
during the silences. Knew she'd see through my efforts to
sound cheerful. Occasionally, Fabrizio emailed me for
advice, but I recognised his guise to involve me. And it didn't
help. As she was no longer living with me, I couldn't regard
myself as her stepmother. Much as I longed to.

Sometimes, I considered booking a last-minute flight to
India. Anywhere in India. A country unassociated with

Ysabelle. I visualised myself strolling along the beautiful beach at Goa at sunset, or visiting tea plantations further north. But it would be better to wait until October, after the monsoon period.

Moreover, in the meantime, I should be working on my second calendar. Only after deciding to include some information about each photo, had I realised how difficult a task I'd set myself. Repeatedly deleting sentences, mulling over descriptions.

Things changed when Domenico contacted me to see if I could take on additional work, some of it involving travel. Willingly, I agreed, knowing I wouldn't feel better until I focussed more on my photography. The extra assignments would help fill my days as well as distracting me from missing Ysabelle so much. Fortunately, I continued to derive enormous satisfactions from my sessions at *Sorgente,* from witnessing the children's improved physical and emotional health. Furthermore, the frequent praise about the work I was doing, helped at an existential level. I was more than a stepmother grieving for the child now living apart from her. And my charity helped my identity.

When I arrived at my studio one sunny autumnal evening, Costanzo was sitting outside the building. 'Have a drink with me.'

He poured me wine and for a while we chatted, then his phone rang. After the call, he said, 'I am going to Frank's Music Bar in Sorrento with my friends. Do you want to come?'

I pointed to my faded jeans and old t-shirt. 'Like this?'

'You look fine.'

Shortly after, two cars arrived and six men and women jumped out. Costanzo introduced me and within minutes we were navigating the winding road to Sorrento. Situated off the Piazza Tasso, Sorrento's main square, Frank's was an underground bar, with arches, rough walls and chunky solid wooden tables and chairs. The lighting – subtle behind metallic shades – bestowed a warm glow. A Moroccan pianist's hands flew over the keys, producing resonant chords. A drummer accompanied him.

After several hours, Constanzo tapped my arm. 'I need to go now. My aunts and nieces are visiting tomorrow.'

'Ten more minutes?' I pleaded.

Being so absorbed in the music, I'd hardly talked to his friends.

After this, I often spent Saturday evenings with them, at Frank's or another nightclub on the Amalfi coast. Occasionally Diana joined us. Even though she hated dancing. I liked Costanzo's friends.

One night, a bunch of us went to the Africana Famous Club in Priano, an amazing space of natural caves and innovative audio light installations, located a few steps from the sea. There, we ate seafood and imbibed large quantities of wine on the panoramic glass panelled terrace. We didn't dance much but everyone agreed we should return soon and rectify that.

Six weeks after our first visit, eight of us returned to the Africana. Fortified by wine, I took to the floor with unusual confidence. Drawn to the rhythmic beat, the clapping. Aware of the aromas of hash, sweat and alcohol.

After shimmying on my own for a while, a man asked me to dance. He wore vinyl trousers, winkle-pickers, and a tie-dye t-shirt, and in the low light, it took a moment to recognise Pasha.

'Oh my God,' I said.

'Don't look that bad, do I? How are you?'

He didn't hear my reply above the music.

We danced. Together. Separately. I was euphoric. He was euphoric. We could have been teenagers at a nightclub. Fuelled by alcohol or drugs. Giving it all to the music. The beat changed to a jive and now I couldn't stop watching him – the effortless, fluid movements of his hips and knees. At the end of one dance, he pulled me into a bearhug, the mix of sweat and aftershave on him, intoxicating. I wanted to drag him away, imprison him in my apartment.

A smoochy number followed and we glanced at each other, before he mumbled that he needed to get home. As I watched his retreating back, Costanzo asked me to dance.

'Who was that?'

'No one,' I said. 'A friend.'

Costanzo didn't hold me too close as we danced, and I appreciated his sensitivity.

After that, whenever we returned to the Africano, I searched for Pasha but never saw him.

Although we continued to meet as friends, the situation with Ysabelle lingered between us like mist on a damp day. Frequently he mentioned his regret about our being discovered. I hoped he didn't regret the lovemaking.

One Monday afternoon, he appeared unexpectedly at the apartment, minutes after I'd returned from Napoli. Immediately I knew something was wrong. Before I could offer him coffee, he said, 'I've been thinking about us. Perhaps we should stop meeting. I'm being selfish.... I can't offer you more than friendship. And I'm so sorry.'

He waited, giving me time to respond, but I could think of nothing to say. He gripped my shoulder and left.

## 29

Early autumn, I returned to India, spending time in Darjeeling, Manali and lastly, Shimla. It was a strange trip. If I'd had any notions about practising yoga and meditation while there, these disappeared as soon as I arrived in Darjeeling. My itinerary was packed full of appointments with schools and community projects, and estimated times of day to photograph the wonderful scenery surrounding me. Likewise, in Manali.

Only when I reached Shimla did I slow down. By now I had more than enough material for two additional calendars, greeting cards and perhaps diaries. Shimla was more of a spiritual journey or perhaps a homecoming. Wandering along the misty Mall, childhood memories assailed me, in whole or fragments. Passing my first home provoked a strong yet undefinable emotion. The colonial style building remained intact but a side entrance had been added and I reckoned that more than one family would be living there now. And rightly so. The overgrown garden would have horrified my mother, but at least the frangipani tree was still there and I had to restrain myself from wandering into the garden to pick up its waxy white petals on the grass. Choked with a transient longing for the past, I imagined I could smell its sweet scent from the street.

That night, I experienced the strongest urge to return to Srinagar. Even though Pasha was in Positano. I googled websites about the current situation in Kashmir, only to receive the same message: it was too dangerous to contemplate visiting.

In Italy again, I worked hard on my second calendar and first batch of greetings cards, finally sending off the material to the printers during the first week of November. Just in time to promote them before Christmas.

When Fabrizio invited me to Sicily for a long weekend mid-November, I didn't accept immediately. Would Ysabelle freeze me out? And equally important, how would Irma react to my presence? As a compromise, I booked a pensione ten minutes' walk from the Vitale home.

At the airport, Fabrizio embraced me. '*Benvenuto, figlia*, welcome daughter. Your flight was smooth?'

Ysabelle greeted me as if I were a burdensome elderly relative. With sinking heart, I now acknowledged she wouldn't return to Positano.

My apprehension about being with Irma was justified. Virtually a chronic invalid, she hardly spoke during her brief appearance at dinner on my first evening. She was dressed in black, her clothes hanging loosely. Gone were the bright scarves with which I associated her. Gone, too, the antique jewellery, Fabrizio's gifts over the years. After that meal, I hardly saw her. When I did, she was trudging along the marble floors. Gripping the bannisters, while navigating the stairs to the seclusion of her bedroom. An atmosphere of sadness and heaviness hung over the house and my heart bled for Fabrizio. How did he cope? Bereft of a wife in addition to his son.

'My wife has lost interest in the restaurants,' he admitted after that first dinner, when we were on our own.

'It must be difficult for you, managing everything.'

'Abri helps me.'

'I am thinking I will sell the smaller restaurant,' he said, while we drank Agrumello. Something I normally declined but now welcomed for fortification.

'Do you think Irma is depressed?'

He shrugged. 'Depressed, sad.... I'm not sure that I understand the difference.'

'Has she seen a doctor?'

'Beatrice suggested that she visits her family physician again, but she refused. She says there is no medicine that will relieve her pain. She takes sleeping pills.' He reached for the liqueur bottle, refilled my glass. 'My daughters will take her for a drive sometimes, but they can't go near the sea.' Not so easy, living on an island.' Silence descended, then, in an effort to change to a more positive topic, he said, 'Ysabelle is doing well. She is working hard at school, and with her dance classes. At the weekends she is now doing voluntary work for an animal shelter.'

I was surprised, although I shouldn't have been. Given her love for the guinea pigs, her disgust and pain at zoo and circus animals' maltreatment, it would be a logical choice for her.

'She feeds the dogs that are too unwell to eat, and she washes the animals, and is sometimes allowed to give them their medicine,' Fabrizio added. 'Once I asked her if she had considered studying to be a vet, but she told me she would hate having to end an animal's life.'

'She would.... I hope she'll have a future in dancing.'

While soaking in the pensione bath later, I thought about Fabrizio. He still dressed smartly and moved agilely. His hair, however, had markedly whitened, his eyes dulled, and sometimes he'd break off mid-sentence. At least our relationship remained unaltered, which suggested that Ysabelle hadn't told him about Pasha and me. An enormous relief.

I'd wondered how it must be for Ysabelle living in such an unhappy home, but Fabrizio had told me that she often sat with Irma in the evenings, the one thing which seemed to provide his wife with a modicum of peace. Ysabelle also visited her cousins regularly.

On the Saturday, I asked Ysabelle if she'd like to go shopping.

She looked at me sullenly. 'I don't need new clothes.'

'Come on, a fourteen-year-old who doesn't need new clothes? Let me treat you.'

In Palermo, we strolled the main streets, viewing window displays. Nothing interested her. As I was about to give up, though, she stopped at a dance supply shop.

'I like the wrapover cardigan, the green one on the mannequin.'

I smiled with relief. 'Let's see if they have it in your size.'

Half an hour later, we emerged with the cardigan, two pairs of leggings and four leather padded ToeSocks to cushion her feet while practising. I'd hesitated before agreeing to the leggings. Worried she might later accuse me of buying her affection. Her forgiveness.

When she showed Fabrizio her purchases, he looked sadly at me. 'It's a pity you won't be here next weekend. Ysabelle is dancing in a school ballet. The funds will be given to a lifeboat charity.'

'We're rehearsing on Monday,' she said. 'There are parents coming to watch. You could come too...if you want.'

Fabrizio and I exchanged glances. He understood how much this invitation meant. I wanted to hug him.

On Monday evening, Fabrizio and I walked to the school for Ysabelle's rehearsal. He'd tried to persuade Irma to join us but she pleaded tiredness. In the main hall, parents chatted excitedly while the orchestra tuned up – we could have been in London or Moscow with the atmosphere of expectation. The ballet was *Cinderella*, and, to my delight, Ysabelle had been cast in the leading role.

'Did you know?' I asked Fabrizio.

He nodded, eyes brimming with pride, and I fervently hoped Irma would attend a performance the following weekend. For his sake, as much as her granddaughter's.

I'd last watched Ysabelle perform several months before Tommaso's death. Now dancing *en pointe,* she was even more poised and graceful.

Immediately, I escaped into the ballet and its rousing music. Forgetting I knew her while she performed her pirouettes, fouettes and other moves whose names escaped me. Tommaso would have been incoherent with joy.

'If she does decide to go to dance school, the teachers advise her to go next autumn,' Fabrizio told me during the interval. 'Do you think this is too soon?'

'Her teachers will know if she'll be mature enough to

study by then. Did Ysabelle mention which dance school she'd like to go to?'

If she chose Rome, she'd be nearer me. More appealing to her, I reckoned, would be Milan's prestigious *Accademia Teatro alla Scala*.

'She hasn't decided yet..... Rachel, I know that you must have been very hurt when Ysabelle returned to Sicily, but I believe that when she is older, her relationship with you will improve,' my father-in-law said. Intuitive as always.

When Ysabelle joined us after the performance, I embraced her. 'You were wonderful. *Mamma* and *Papà* would have been so proud of you.'

She frowned fiercely, the way she did when trying not to cry.

In Positano, my mood lifted. The visit to Sicily, my time with Ysabelle, had gone better than predicted. Progress indeed. Maybe I'd invite her to Positano for Easter. Present it as an opportunity to see Lavinia, Daniella and Margarita, who, I knew, missed her hugely.

My raised spirits extended to hosting a dinner party and I ruminated for hours over what to cook. Stubbornly refusing Diana's offers of help.

The day of my party dawned sunny and calm, and after cleaning the apartment, I set to cooking, Santana playing in the background. Invited for seven-thirty, in true Italian style, no one arrived before seven-fifty. We had pre-dinner Camparis on the candlelit balcony, before sitting down to eat.

Halfway through the soup, my doorbell buzzed. It was Pasha. He looked flushed, as if he'd been running, and I detected a whiff of sweat. Catapulting me back to the afternoon we made love. My body throbbed with longing.

'I needed to see you,' he said, after embracing me. 'And I wanted to apologise for how we left things when we last met.'

We stared at each other. I read longing in his face and wondered what he saw in mine.

'I'm having a dinner party.... I don't think I can invite you to join us.... It would–'

He rested his hand on my arm. 'For sure, I understand.'

Diana appeared, Pasha greeted her and left.

She raised her eyebrows. 'Is he okay?'

'I'll tell you later.'

For the rest of the evening, I was on automatic pilot. Serving food and refilling wine glasses. All the while, seeing Pasha's disappointed expression. Fortunately, conversation flowed, and I didn't need to contribute much. One positive thing about the dinner party was that Salvatore and Diana got on well, and I hoped they'd see each other again.

The following day I lay on the sofa with an aching head. The day after, I phoned Pasha, only to reach voicemail. I then hung around the church residency and when one of his colleagues emerged, asked if he knew where Pasha was.

The priest's expression was inscrutable. 'He's returned to Kashmir. They need him there.'

I wanted to ask if he knew how long Pasha would be back in Kashmir but decided against.

Several years came and went, during which Pasha and I exchanged intermittent letters. By now I'd produced four calendars, was working yearly on Christmas, birthday and blank cards and negotiating with several UK charities about diaries. *Sorgente* still employed me for two sessions a week and Domenico was giving me assignments, mainly for weddings and celebration parties along the Amalfi coast. Sometimes, further afield. To my delight, I was now included on the *Centro Italiano Aiuti all'Infanzia* – Italian Centre for Aid to Children (CIAI)) charity website, on the related charities' page.

My working life therefore satisfied me, and I had a small but close group of friends with whom I frequently socialised. Communicating about *Children of Bhārata* helped me feel closer to Pasha, nevertheless I missed his presence as much as ever. Occasionally, he mentioned the resurgence of his struggle with the Church and I tried not to take encouragement from this.

Anna and her boyfriend came over for several holidays. Nursing friends dropped in during trips to Napoli. Marion and Geoffrey visited for long weekends. I loved showing everyone round the area, urging them all to return.

Diana had thrown herself into teaching and her own work with such gusto that I worried she might experience burn-out. When we met, we talked about two things – commissions and offers of exhibitions for her sculpting, and her ongoing longing for a child.

'Perhaps I should adopt,' she said one evening. We'd been to see an arty film in Napoli about a woman who, against the odds, was allowed to adopt a six-year-old boy. I said nothing. Diana didn't want a response, certainly not platitudes. She just needed someone to listen to her. Someone who knew her well.

We were both thirty-eight now. Both aware of the implications for her.

The Easter before her nineteenth birthday, Ysabelle invited me to a performance in Milan. She was now halfway through her ballet training there.

'Grandpa can't come because of Granny. And my aunts must manage the restaurants.'

'I'll try to be a worthy substitute.'

She hesitated. 'We could meet for coffee before the show. I'll have free time.'

After hanging up, I danced round the apartment. At least she considered me family. Even if her manner lacked graciousness. The following day, I shopped in Napoli, spending too much on a knee length teal coloured dress with a twisted waist. I'd lost weight. I felt fitter. She couldn't be embarrassed by me, I reckoned.

At a café in central Milan, I gazed in amazement at Ysabelle. Several years had elapsed since we last met, and she'd grown into a graceful beauty, with a dancer's slim, toned body. Her tailored amethyst dress would be elegant enough for the smartest of dinner parties and she wore her fair hair up, secured by an elaborate series of plaits. I couldn't believe she was only nineteen.

Hopefully, anyone who fell for her would be strong enough to break down her barriers.

'How long are you staying in Milan?' she asked.

'Depends.'

She studied my face, then her distant expression returned. 'Has Positano changed much?'

'The summer season is busier, so it's good to be somewhere else at weekends. Particularly during July and August.'

'Are you still a photographer?'

I talked about *Children of Bhārata.*

'*Papà* would have been proud of you,' she said. A comment which surprised as much as it delighted me, encouraging me to talk more about my charity.

'So far, we've donated enough money to the hospital in Srinagar for it to buy a portable x-ray machine. This means that very sick children don't have the extra distress of having to go to the x-ray department. It's also less upsetting for the parents. And we've helped the hospital open three more beds.'

'It makes my job seem superficial,' Ysabelle said.

'Nonsense.... What's the ballet?'

'*Romeo and Juliet.* I have the part of Juliet.... I was the understudy, but Gabriella is ill, so now it is me.'

'You must be doing well.'

She shrugged. 'It's not so difficult, if you work hard.'

I noticed she was twisting her hands. 'Are you nervous?'

'I hope I won't let the company down.'

I resisted making any platitudes. It had been years since she revealed her insecurities to me.

We sipped our coffee.

Our conversation continued, avoiding contentious issues. Grandpa was worried about Granny who rarely left her bedroom those days and took high doses of antidepressants which didn't seem to help. Abruptly, Ysabelle then changed the subject. Perhaps fearing she'd been disloyal to her grandmother.

At that moment a young man approached our table. He was of average height, clad in jeans and a yellow shirt and was pleasant looking rather than classically handsome. He carried a scuffed briefcase which I sensed contained important documents.

'This is Sebastiano,' Ysabelle said.

'You must be Rachel,' he replied, continuing, 'Ysabelle told me you are a photographer.'

I described my recent project to photograph "hidden" churches, a commission from one of Natalie's contacts. We discussed photography, with the odd interjection from Ysabelle.

'Sebastiano's had three books published by Arabi Finici,' she told me.

I'd heard of the family run publishers. 'What genre?'

'Historical fiction.'

'He's only twenty-six,' Ysabelle added, gazing at him proudly.

'How did you meet?' I asked, my question addressed to both of them.

'We were sitting next to each other at a concert,' Sebastiano replied. 'I was with my mother and grandmother. Ysabelle was with her friends. She started coughing, I offered her a bottle of water.... After the performance, my mother and grandmother were tired, but I invited Ysabelle for a drink. She agreed immediately.'

'I did not,' Ysabelle said.

'She did. This was a year ago.'

He reached for her hand and her expression changed to one of devotion.

When we parted company, both of them hugged me. Perhaps Sebastiano would become a much-needed ally.

The new theatre in Milan was decorated in greys, mauves and purples, instead of the more traditional reds and gold. I took my seat in the third row. Stomach stirring with excitement while the orchestra tuned up.

When I was a child, my parents took me to the Christmas pantomime. On my birthday, to a show. On such occasions, I'd sit between them. Relishing the attention. Feeling so important and loved. At the interval, they'd buy me ice cream or chocolate, and one time, my father presented me with a carnation before we left home. Even at this age – nine perhaps ten – I sensed my mother's disapproval. Relieved when the following day he returned from work with roses for her.

This evening, when the curtain rose, I felt once more like Ysabelle's stepmother. So proud was I of her pivotal part. For two hours, the dancing and music absorbed me, transporting me to a magical place. Her body seemed particularly lithe and graceful. Worthy of her leading role. When I'd seen her dance at her school performance in Sicily, she was a girl. Now she'd grown up, her face leaner, more expressive.

Later, backstage, the atmosphere was a mixture of elation and work to be done *pronto*. Staff bustled about, flowers were delivered. Announcements came over the tannoy: a physiotherapist needed, a seamstress, an electrician. Eventually, I found Ysabelle's changing room, knocked on the door.

'*Venire*, come in.'

Sprays of flowers littered the small dressing room, the varied scents intoxicating. Ysabelle was seated by the mirror, in a red kimono, removing her eye shadow with cotton pads. Her face was flushed, her sparkling dark eyes so like Tommaso's.

'What will I do with all these flowers?' she asked, but I recognised her delight. 'I like your outfit,' she continued. 'Did you buy it in Milan?'

'Napoli.'

'Napoli! You've changed your hair this evening. You look younger. People will think you're my sister, not my–'

With exasperating timing, a young man popped his head round the door. 'Yse, *andiamo via*, we're leaving.'

'*Stai calmo*, stay cool,' she told him, slipping into a shirt and jeans.

I cursed her friend's timing. Now I'd never know how she would have described me.

'You were wonderful,' I told her, about to add, "I was so proud of you", but holding back. Reluctant to risk a rejecting comment.

Distractedly, she said. 'There's a party. Come along if you want. Sebastiano will be there.'

'I think I'll go back to the hotel.'

She checked in the mirror, removed some lipstick and kissed me. 'I'll call you tomorrow,' she said, adding awkwardly, 'Thank you for coming to Milan to see me dance.'

By lunchtime the following day, Ysabelle hadn't contacted me. Probably sleeping in. Or preparing for the evening's performance. For several hours, I wandered around Milan in drizzling rain. Frequently making sure I hadn't missed her text or call. Then I brought my flight forward by a day, keen to return to Positano.

---

## 30

Diana and I were disembarking from the hydrofoil to Napoli one Saturday when Natalie emerged with a tall dark-haired man.

'This is my cousin, Marcello,' she said. 'I'm showing him the sights in Napoli. What are you guys doing?'

I explained that Diana was shopping for shoes and I was visiting the Monastery of San Martino.

'We're meeting Louis later for dinner at Piazza Giuseppe Garibaldi. Join us,' Natalie suggested.

Diana was beaming. And I hadn't eaten out for ages.

Natalie took Marcello's arm. 'Seven pm, then, at the Ristorante del Ettore. I'll text you directions because it can be hard to find.'

Once we were out of earshot, Diana grabbed my arm. 'Wow! I do so hope he's single.'

'You're turning into a man-eater.'

'But don't you *see*? Marcello is the Roman God of Fertility. This must be a sign. Anyway, he is *seriously* hot.' She smiled wickedly.

'You've given up on Salvatore, then?'

She shrugged. 'Don't think he's interested. Probably for the best. The thing is, he might return to California and no way could I live there.... So, what do you think about Marcello? Do you have a hunch?'

'You'll find out more about his relationship status at dinner. But don't interrogate him and for God's sake, *don't* get your hopes up.'

A shadow crossed Diana's face, then her expression brightened. 'I had an email from Doug. He's got together with a widow with three children. She's older than him. Anyway, the perfect solution, don't you think? His tone was apologetic, like a confessional. But he wanted me to hear it from him.'

I squeezed her arm. 'I hope things work out for you, I do. But stay cool.'

Natalie, Louis and Marcello were on their second bottle of wine when we arrived at Restaurante Del Etori. Immediately, Louis ordered champagne. Diana, uncharacteristically quiet initially (perhaps worried about making an unfavourable impression on Marcello), soon relaxed and at the same time, I settled into the evening. The food was amazing and the atmosphere of people having fun, infectious. Diana was seated next to Marcello and chatted with him for much of the meal. Afterwards, we caught the last day ferry with seconds to spare. When we reached Positano, she and Marcello exchanged business cards.

She came back to my apartment, too inebriated to drive home.

'What do you think, Rach?' she asked, while I brewed coffee.

'It was a great evening. I've never seen that side of Louis before. He could be a stand-up comedian. The ideal partner for Natalie.'

Diana sat down heavily at the kitchen table. 'I mean about Marcello *et moi*?'

'Seems nice. And obviously single.'

'And so *hot*! Wow…. If only he lived closer…' She yawned. 'As long as he's not hiding any ghastly secrets. Hurry up with that coffee.'

Two months later, Beatrice phoned to tell me Ysabelle was engaged and would be married in Milan in six months' time.

'I liked Sebastiano when I met him,' I said.

'*Papà* is happy. Sebastiano is from a respectable family and *Papà* thinks he is suited to Ysabelle.'

Beatrice told me about Irma's stroke two months earlier, about Fabrizio's forgetfulness and their worry about him being in the early stages of dementia.

'Will they make it to the wedding?'

'*Mamma* cannot take such a journey. She will stay in a residence. Abri and I will travel with *Papà* and the children.'

After the call, my thoughts dwelled on Fabrizio. Saddened by the idea of him having dementia. Nevertheless, this would explain why I'd heard so infrequently from him over the last year. Until then, he'd regularly updated me with family news, especially regarding Ysabelle.

When the wedding invitation arrived, I phoned him. He reiterated what Beatrice had told me: they were delighted about Ysabelle's wedding, they loved Sebastiano and believed they were well-matched.

It was only after speaking to Fabrizio that I realised the wedding date coincided with another trip to India. Since its establishment, *Children of Bhārata* had sent funds to my children's hospital in Kashmir. At a recent Trustees' meeting, however, we'd decided we could now support another children's hospital in India, after research, selecting one in New Delhi. The plan was that I'd visit it.

Nevertheless, I couldn't miss Ysabelle's wedding, so it was agreed that Louis would travel to India in my place. At the same time, we invited Natalie to become a Trustee.

Four weeks before the wedding, Ysabelle contacted me. 'Will you come to Milan? I need help with my wedding shower.... I've had 'flu and I still feel dreadful. Another infection, my doctor says.'

'Where should I stay?' I asked, hoping she'd suggest her apartment.

'There is a hotel near the apartment. I will book you a room. Let me know when your flight arrives.'

I hung up, conscious of my mixed emotions: glad she'd asked me to help; irritated at being spoken to like an employee.

'You're such an easy touch,' Diana said when I told her of my summons to Milan. 'The least she could do is put you up in her apartment. Anyway, doesn't she have a friend who could help her?'

Ysabelle took ages to buzz me into the building, opening the apartment door in her dressing gown.

'You look awful,' I said, kissing her.

'I explained: I've had flu and now I have a sort thoat,' she croaked. 'I'm too tired to sort out the presents for my shower.... It's on Friday.'

Three days away.

'Don't talk. Get back to bed. I'll sort things out.'

She seemed relieved. 'I've left instructions about how to arrange the presents.'

The spacious sitting room was strewn with gifts, discarded wrapping paper and cardboard boxes. A vase of wilting roses sat on the marble mantelpiece, a wastepaper basket overflowed. Everything was coated with dust. Even so, it was a wonderful space with its floor to ceiling double window, tiled floor, wrought iron mirrors and mature palms. I wrenched open a window to admit the June air.

Two hours later, I'd dusted the room, swept and mopped the floor and replaced the flowers. Sorted out presents and arranged them on the table as instructed. Several times, I'd glanced in on Ysabelle, to find her asleep, face flushed, hair limp. As I scribbled a note – planning to slip off – she came into the sitting room and sank onto the chaise longue.

'Do you want me to make us a meal?' I suggested.

'I'm not hungry,' she said, as an afterthought, adding, 'There's food in the fridge, help yourself.' She scanned the room. 'You've done a good job. Thanks.'

The following day, I wandered around Milan, peering into courtyards, browsing in secondhand book and photography shops. Thinking how lovely it would be to bump into Salvatore. Have his company here. While scrutinising the menu of a pavement café, my phone went.

'Come immediately,' Ysabelle said. 'Please.'

'Are you worse?'

'Just come.'

I hailed a taxi and twenty minutes later was ushered into her bedroom.

'It's my wedding dress,' she said. 'There's a problem.'

She slipped off her t-shirt and tracksuit bottoms and donned the gown: an exquisite affair of matte duchess cream satin with a Chantilly lace overlay dotted with pearls.

Strapless, it displayed her toned dancer's shoulders and slender neck to perfection.

'It's wonderful, Ysabelle. I can't see anything wrong.'

To my amazement, she was trembling. 'I wish *Mamma* and *Papà* were here.'

Tentatively, I put my arms round her and she let me hold her for a moment before pulling away. 'I must sort out this problem.'

'Turn round.'

She did. Even in anxious mode, moving gracefully. The back of her dress was equally beautiful.

'I don't see a problem. You sound much better today, by the way.'

'Perhaps,' she said, pouting, then pointing to a side seam. 'Look.'

I examined the slightly puckered material. 'Do you really think anyone will notice?'

'I phoned the shop. But they were too busy at the moment and I don't want to leave it too late. Could you alter it?'

I hesitated, tempted to try. Keen to bask in her gratitude. If I got it wrong, though....

'I can't sew. I think you should leave it. Unless...you *could* take it to another tailor.' I stepped back several paces. 'From here, no one will notice. They'd have to be standing very close and peering at it.'

'Perhaps,' she said, frowning fiercely.

She changed back into her tracksuit bottoms and t-shirt, carefully slipped the dress into its cover.

'You could stay to dinner, if you like,' she suggested.

Refusing my assistance, Ysabelle busied herself with aubergines, parma ham, fresh artichokes, cream and wine, and before long, an appetising aroma wafted through the apartment. In the sitting room, she opened another bottle of wine and poured two enormous glasses.

Halfway through our meal, the doorbell rang.

'Who can it be?' she said irritably. 'Sebastiano is working this evening.'

She answered her buzzer, exclaiming in pleasure. In the hall, she introduced me to her friend, Flavia.

Hopefully she wouldn't stay long.

'Join us for dinner, Flavia,' Ysabelle urged. 'I haven't seen you for ages.'

Over the meal, the friends spoke rapidly. Periodically slowing down, when they remembered my presence.

Afterwards, Ysabelle changed into her wedding dress once more. Beseeching Flavia for an honest opinion. I left them to it.

On the day of Ysabelle's shower party, I woke with a fever and aching joints. Going anywhere was unthinkable.

'You must have caught my bug,' she said when I phoned her. 'Drink plenty of fluids, and sleep.'

'I'm sorry I won't be able to come to your party. Hope it goes okay.'

'It will. Flavia will arrive early to help me. Thanks again for your help.'

I was about to ask about her wedding dress, but Ysabelle had rung off.

On my return journey to Positano, I thought a lot about Ysabelle, combing through memories from my first traumatic meeting with her on the beach in Sicily, to the difficult early months of her living with Tommaso and me. Then to the good years, when we were close after Tommaso's death. And the rapid deterioration after she'd discovered Pasha and me in bed together. Now, I reckoned, we were somewhere between uneasy friends and stepmother/daughter. Of course I longed for the latter without any idea how to achieve it. She'd contacted me because I could help her, but once she was married, what then? I dreaded to think there might be nothing. Especially if she and Sebastiano moved away from Italy.

The need had been building. I had to return to Kashmir. I had to see Pasha. Letters were so inadequate, what there were of them, and some days, I could think of little else but him. Also, I'd loved to visit the hospital again although I knew Louis would do a good job when he was there. Despite the ongoing struggles in that area, the Indian Government weren't actually advising against tourist travel. I would go after Ysabelle's wedding.

Before booking my flight, I emailed Gillian Stewart. Her reply arrived ten minutes later: *John has been ill, so we're returning to the UK next month, probably settling in York where one of our daughters lives. If you are ever in our area, please do visit. It would be lovely to see you again. Of course you may decide to return to Kashmir but the atmosphere here is far from pleasant and I'd advise against doing so at the moment. Hopefully one day peace will be restored. Our years in this beautiful place have been so happy.*

I'd justified going to Kashmir partly because I could visit John and Gillian. But not being able to stay with them tipped the balance in favour of not going. Disappointment swept over me. Followed – surprisingly – by relief. If I went to Srinagar, I might make a fool of myself with Pasha. Besides, I'd despise myself for applying even the slightest pressure on him to leave the Church, regardless of whether or not he agreed to. Nevertheless, I spent time scrolling through my photos. Lingering on special ones. Wishing now I had one of him. Something to convey the precious, intimate time we'd spent there.

Perhaps I would return to Kashmir one day. Perhaps as an elderly lady, using guides and taking tuk-tuks everywhere. Reminiscing about my first visit. Sifting through each detail to make sure I'd fully understood its significance.

## 31

Ysabelle's wedding took place in the beautiful Romanesque church of *Santa Maria del Carmine*. Sunday bells rang out over Milan as I showered and dressed. While studying myself in the mirror, my thoughts returned to my own wedding. I could hear Diana's voice, 'More make-up, Rachel, this is your big day.'

I wished she was with me now. Reassuring me I looked okay.

The room phone went. 'Your taxi is here, Signora.'

I grabbed my bag, glanced once more in the mirror and left the room. On entering the church, I hesitated. At a family dinner the evening before, we hadn't discussed seating arrangements for the service, and I'd no idea where to sit. About to make my way to the middle of the church, I was stopped by Beatrice.

'*Buongiorno*, Rachel,' she said. '*Papà* is waiting for Ysabelle. Abri is with him to make sure he is okay and Adriano is with the children.'

Bea took my arm and we walked to the front row.

My eyes filled when Fabrizio escorted Ysabelle down the aisle. She looked wonderful, as did her three bridesmaids. Tommaso would have been thrilled. Proud to give her away to Sebastiano. Beside me, Bea was in tears.

I understood most of the hour-long service, and when lost, contentedly stared at the crossed vault ceilings and the flowers decorating the altar. The music was exceptional: a mixture of organ and singers accompanied by a harp. Yet, as the rose and spicy fragrance of incense filled the church, it was Pasha I thought of. Not Tommaso.

After the service, a radiant Ysabelle kissed me. Smiling the way she had as a child. I longed to hug her, tell her what she meant to me. But this wasn't the moment. Not with so many people wanting to congratulate her. Nevertheless, Sebastiano seemed pleased by his wife's reaction to me. I had, indeed, found an ally.

Towards the end of the reception, Ysabelle went to change, reappearing in a charcoal grey trouser suit and primrose yellow blouse. At this point, I experienced another surge of emotion. Again, I held back while she said goodbye to relatives.

Sebastiano was by my side. 'Ysabelle wants to say goodbye to you.'

'Thank you for your help with the shower party,' she said, hugging me. Again, I glimpsed the child, sensed a latent vulnerability. She hesitated. 'Now that I am in love with Sebastiano, I understand more about you and...and Pasha. I am sorry I was so horrible to you.'

'Keep in touch. Please,' I said.

Her expression softened before she turned away.

After the couple left, I regained my composure, dancing the mazurka with a relaxed and lucid Fabrizio.

Diana was glowing when I next met up with her. She'd put on weight which suited her, her dark hair, recently cut in a chic layered bob, gleamed and the lilac and green floral dress she wore enhanced her bluey/purple eyes. It was the middle of August and we were at my favourite outdoor café in Positano. Vespas zipped past, discharging petrol fumes, and most patrons chain-smoked, but the coastal view compensated. Today the azure sea was particularly enticing.

'No need to ask if things are going well with Marcello, then,' I said.

She smiled. 'I'd forgotten how wonderful it is falling in love. All this stuff about...I read somewhere that the brain of a person falling in love looks exactly like the brain of someone who's taken cocaine. I can't remember the biochemistry – something to do with dopamine, I think – you'll know more about this stuff.'

'And a weekend relationship is working?'

'Mostly. You know the drawbacks, of course. But yes, although I find it easier when he comes to Positano.'

If she hadn't been my best friend, I would have felt envious that she and Marcello were both free to fall in love. If only it were that simple for Pasha and me. Most of the time, I now managed not to think of him and how much I missed him. And when seated in ancient cathedrals and basilicas, I came closer to accepting his love for God.

'Are you okay, Rachel?'

I dragged myself back to the present, listening as Diana talked about all the things she and Marcello had done.

'I'll miss you if you move down to Catanzaro,' I said without thinking.

'It isn't anywhere near that stage,' Diana said hastily. 'Anyway, I'd hate to leave Positano. I'm simply enjoying what we have. I suppose I felt this way about Doug once.'

Again, I thought of Pasha. We were still exchanging letters. He wrote a lot about his work in Srinagar and I surmised that security was a huge issue. That wearing his cassock, in fact, could endanger him as much as protect him. The tone in which he wrote was friendly, bar the occasional ambiguous comment which I tried not to over-interpret. We could have emailed or texted each other, and occasionally we did, but there was something special, more intimate, about receiving a letter, or so I allowed myself to believe.

In weak moments, I visualised us being together. A normal couple. I wouldn't mind how important the Church remained to him: he could be away from dawn until dusk, provided he returned to me. Such dreaming proved destructive. Setting me back days. I didn't confide this to anyone – there was no point. Occasionally, I'd catch Diana studying me, expression curious, but we didn't discuss him again.

Often I dreamed of Dal Lake. Especially the time when Pasha cared for me while I was ill. I could hear the swish of passing shikaras, feel his lean body as we lay side by side on the deck. Waking to the reality of life in Positano was painful.

When would I see him again? *Would* I see him again?

Three months later, Diana arrived at my apartment one afternoon. I hadn't seen her for several weeks.

'Guess what?'

'You're not....'

'I am. I used four different test kits, just to be sure. All positive.'

'Di, that's wonderful.'

We hugged. Then I made sure she sat on a comfy chair, brewed peppermint tea. Asked her if she was too cold, too warm.

'I'm pregnant, not ill,' she said. 'Apart from throwing up.'

'Of course, sorry, sorry.... How far on are you?'

'Nine weeks, bit more. I wanted to tell you earlier but I was scared it would jeopardise things.'

'I'm so pleased for you. It seems as though everything is coming together now.... New man, plenty of work, and especially this.'

'Would you be my birthing partner?'

As I stared at her, she continued, 'I'm not asking you to deliver the baby. Just keep telling me to breathe deeply, and...and encourage me to push harder. The thing is... I'm terrified about my body splitting in two. There, I've said it. My biggest fear.'

'That's most unlikely to happen! How did Marcello react?'

She looked sheepish. 'He's okay about it. We didn't plan it, you see. I was so... so caught up with the deliciousness of being in love again, so thrilled by the whole process, I hardly even thought about having a baby. Can you imagine me not thinking of this? Anyway, even if Marcello doesn't want to be involved, it'll be okay. You'll be around, and other friends, and I'm earning enough to afford childcare once the baby's older.'

She lapsed into silence, her expression dreamy, and I prayed the pregnancy would go well, that she'd deliver a healthy child.

Later, I bought some blue and sea green wool and began knitting a baby jumper. Hoping not to tempt fate with such premature action. Hoping that the baby would bring Diana and Marcello even closer. Soon I discovered that knitting helped me unwind after a stressful session at *Sorgente*. And for some strange reason, it triggered ideas for my charity, and I'd stop, mid-row, to make notes.

A week later, Diana phoned to say she was feeling terrible, could I visit. Immediately I drove to her apartment and she clicked me in before I'd had time to buzz. I scrutinised her in concern. Normally she looked gorgeous in her lavender kimono. Now the rich colour emphasised her pallor. The shadows under her eyes.

She attempted to smile. 'It's barely ten o'clock and I've been sick three times already.'

'Shall I make coffee?'

She flinched. 'Can't bear the smell. Would you do a smoothie? There's oranges and raspberries in the fridge.'

She rushed to the loo.

'I can't find the raspberries,' I told her when she returned.

She burst into tears. 'I bought them yesterday, I'm sure I did.'

I went into her bedroom, grabbed the grip bag on top of the wardrobe and bundled t-shirts and trousers into it. She followed me in. 'What are you doing?'

'Packing. You're staying with me until you're over the vomiting.'

'I'm not even ten weeks, Rachel. The thing is, it could be ages. Often women have morning sickness for months and–'

I turned to face her. 'Di, I don't want you here on your own... When are you seeing Marcello again?'

'Next weekend, probably.'

'You can return for a few days then, if he's here.... How *are* things with him?'

She managed a smile. 'Good and I do think he's pleased about the baby.'

'Have you told Omera?'

She frowned. 'She's my business partner. And more conventional than she lets on. Not that she wouldn't be happy for me, but she'd expect a wedding announcement.'

Apart from Marcello's visits, Diana stayed with me until the nausea passed. On a *Sorgente* day, if she was able to, she'd prepare a salad for a late lunch– she couldn't tolerate the smell of cooked food. I enjoyed returning to a meal. To her imaginative use of ingredients. I enjoyed her company. And I derived satisfaction in caring for her when the vomiting was at its worst.

When she finally returned to her apartment in Monte-pertuso, loneliness struck. To my surprise, strong enough for me to consider returning to the UK to live. I'd been in Italy for twelve years now. Perhaps being home again would help me forget about Pasha. There were no associations with him, there, and I could continue running *Children of Bhārata* from my flat.

Three weeks later, having reassured myself Diana was okay, I flew to Edinburgh. Fortunately, my flat was between tenants so I could stay there. The first week, I met with friends, went for long beach walks and dealt with small repairs in the kitchen and bathroom. Being home again was okay, so far. Then, one night, unable to sleep, I slipped on an old dressing gown and went through to the sitting room to sit by the window.

Tangled up with a paper hanky, I found a scrap of paper in the pocket, on which, during my last visit here, I'd scribbled down the things I planned to describe in an article about Positano. With increasing emotion, I read through my list: church bells; terracotta and salmon houses huddled under jagged limestone peaks; chattering of twilight starlings, labyrinthine streets of whitewashed boutiques and art galleries.

I stopped reading, an ache in my throat. Across the street, the outline of the church was sharpening as the sky gradually changed from black to inky blue. Apart from some toneless singing from a late-night reveller, the streets were quiet. I returned to my list: terraced lemon orchards beneath an azure sky; purple and red bougainvillea, aroma of pine trees and damp earth; reds, golds and browns of autumnal oak and chestnut trees, waves crashing against the stone jetty, spraying foam over the whitewashed buildings.

I missed all this. I even missed the out of season tourists in damp jackets and soggy sandals. Taking refuge in galleries, gazing at rich oil paintings. Sitting in vine covered outdoor restaurants, sipping one more cappuccino, eating one more mozzarella and pomodoro sandwich. Waiting for the rain to ease, the sun to come out, for life to return to the town.

The following afternoon I booked my return flight.

At eight o'clock one overcast morning, my phone rang. It was Diana. 'I want to go to Sorrento now. My contractions have started.'

'Have your waters broken?'

'No, but I've a hunch that things'll happen soon. I need to be close to the hospital.'

I googled hotels, booking us into one near the maternity hospital. Then I collected her and drove to Sorrento. In the hotel room, I helped her onto the bed. Rearranging the pillows to support her back and remove the pressure from her hips.

'The thing is, I'm terrified,' Diana said, shifting position. 'Now it's about to happen.... Sorry about phoning so early.... Will you take one last photo of me pregnant? After the baby's born, I'm going to make sculptures of them. All the ones you've taken of me since I got pregnant. I didn't tell you this, did I?'

'Three times, at least.'

She grimaced. 'At antenatal classes they warn you about your memory going while you're pregnant.... Nobody said how bad it would be. What if it doesn't come back? Did you notice the receptionist's face when we booked in?'

'She's young. Probably never seen someone close-up in such an advanced stage of pregnancy.'

'Or worried she'd have to deliver the baby in reception,' Diana added. 'Did I bring dental floss?'

I searched her sponge bag. 'Two lots!'

After photographing Diana, I lay on the spare bed. An hour later, she woke me. 'The contractions are getting more frequent.'

'How frequent?'

She chewed her lip. 'About every twenty minutes. Do you think I should go to hospital now? I am an elderly primigravida, after all. Such a horrible term – makes me feel like a gorilla.'

'I think we should wait – until they're closer together.'

She groaned and closed her eyes. 'I'd like to go now.'

She was flushed and trembling. Unnecessary anxiety wouldn't help.

The streets were mobbed, people pushing and chanting. A demonstration by civil servants for increased pay.

'Hey, watch it,' I said to a woman who bumped into me in the car park.

I couldn't drive in this. Thankfully, I spotted a taxi and helped Diana into it.

Two hours after we checked in at the hospital, Marcello arrived with a bunch of roses. '*Tesorina*, sweetheart,' he said, rushing over to Diana who was partly sitting, partly lying on her bed. He hugged her awkwardly, then noticed the monitoring equipment, the drip stand. '*Oh Dio*, Oh God.'

'This is normal,' I reassured him. 'I'll be outside.'

'Rachel....' Diana began.

I left them to it. Being at the birth would bond Marcello to her even more. I wanted things for them to work out, even if it meant her leaving Positano.

Jack Beaumont King arrived at 9.02 pm. Four kilograms exactly, healthy and beautiful. I'd never seen Diana so radiant. Nor had I seen Marcello look at her the way he did now. His expression while holding their baby, gave me further hope they'd stay together.

Feeling intrusive, I went to the door but she called me back. 'Photos, photos.'

I photographed them in various combinations until Diana was satisfied. Then, as I was putting my camera away, I discovered my phone was missing – it must have been stolen during the pushing in the street, I reckoned – so I reported the theft at the police station. Finally, I returned to the hotel and slept for twelve hours.

At home, the following afternoon, I found a note in my mailbox: *Sorry to have missed you. Have been in Napoli for a conference and came to Positano on the chance of seeing you. Tried phoning and texting. Returning to Kashmir tomorrow. Hope you are well. P.*

## 32

I n the sitting room, I sank onto the sofa and buried my face in a cushion. This was so cruel. My only record of Pasha's cell phone number was on my stolen phone. If Omera had been around, I would have risked her disapproval, asked for his number. But she was travelling in remote places.

The following day, I drove to Sorrento. Diana was tired but pleased to see me. 'Hope you got a bit of sleep, Rach.'

'How's Jack?'

'Feeding well. The midwife brought him at four am – her face wreathed in smiles – and he fed for twenty minutes. Then she brought him back at seven. I'm knackered.'

I sat down on her bed and Diana flung her arms around me. 'Oh, Rachel...'

'Where's Marcello?'

She stared with distaste at her distended stomach. 'I'd forgotten it would be a while before this shrinks.... He didn't like our hotel so he's finding another one. He'll be back later.'

'Do you need anything?'

While shopping for her, I bought another phone. However, when I returned to the ward, Natalie and Louis were visiting, so I didn't stay long. I wondered if Natalie was privy to Marcello's plans for Diana and the baby.

The following months felt flat, despite enjoying my work. Until recently, apart from seeing Diana, most of my social life had been with *Sorgente* staff, but some of them had recently moved to other jobs or gone on maternity leave, so the impromptu meals after work, the weekend get togethers, happened less frequently. Costanzo was working flat out to meet a deadline, so there was no Saturday night clubbing for the moment.

I still lunched with Natalie, but socially, the highlight was often visiting Diana and Jack. Marcello had agreed to move to Positano, but because he had his home and business to sell first, his extended weekend visits were fewer than he and Diana would have liked.

Consequently, I helped with domestic chores, allowing Diana to nap while the baby slept. She never complained about the fatigue of twice-nightly breastfeeding, so thrilled was she with motherhood. She laughed when Jack regurgitated milk over her leather jacket. Rolled her eyes when he filled his nappy within minutes of having it changed.

It took a while to reassure her I was happy to be so involved. And I was. For starters, it distracted me from missing Pasha. From wondering when he'd next write. From wondering when, and in what capacity, I'd next see Ysabelle. Equally important, it provided a much-needed sense of local family. Especially when Diana asked me to be godmother. Besides, I relished spending time with Jack:

cuddling him, tickling his feet – which he loved – photographing him. I was present for his first smile. A cherished moment.

To my astonishment, Omera appointed herself as substitute granny. Fussing over Jack. I hadn't encountered this side of her before, gentle and affectionate. Singing to him in Kashmiri as well as Italian.

'He'll be trilingual before long,' Diana said, smiling at Omera who was making sure there were enough nappies.

'I keep waiting to feel intruded on,' Diana told me as we drove down to Positano for pasta. 'But I don't think I will. My mother wasn't specially "hands on" with Richard and me....' Diana broke off to navigate a particularly windy section of road. 'I mean, she loved us to bits. No doubt about that.... Of course I'll take Jack to meet her and Dad. But I can't imagine her fussing over her grandson as Omera does.'

'It's a new side to her,' I said. 'Who would have guessed that such a feisty woman could be so mushy with a child?'

When Jack had colic, I stayed overnight with Diana. She opened a bottle of wine, saying, 'I've been on six websites and they all say as long as I keep to one or two units of alcohol once or twice a week while I'm breastfeeding, it's safe.'

She then produced a lemon cake – 'bought, sorry' – and when not attending to Jack, we talked as we hadn't done for years. Initially we sat on the terrace within easy hearing of him – she was scathing about baby monitors – the sky clear and starry, the scent of honeysuckle evocative. When it grew chilly, we moved into the sitting room. It was then I told her about sleeping with Pasha.

'I wondered,' she said.

'How?'

She clasped her hands, resting her chin on them. 'Something about your demeanour.'

'It won't happen again. But once was better than never.' I nodded several times, trying to convince myself.

Letters from Pasha were sporadic. Two in a month, then nothing for three months. Sometimes, when I couldn't bear being so distanced from him, I reread his letters which I stored in a carved box I'd bought in Delhi. Or I wrote, even if it was his turn to. Updating him on *Children of Bhārata*, *Sorgente*, relaying news of Positano and neighbouring towns. I described Jack's progress. I was always careful not to reveal to Pasha how much I missed him.

Two years after her wedding, Ysabelle phoned me. Having begun married life in Paris, she and Sebastiano had returned to Italy, basing themselves in Milan. We arranged to meet in Terracina, an old seaside town between Rome and Napoli.

When I arrived at the restaurant, I spotted them immediately. Sebastiano looked younger than I'd remembered. As for Ysabelle, she was glowing. And around twenty-four weeks pregnant.

Sebastiano rose to embrace me. She remained seated. 'Emilio,' she said to her bump. 'This is Granny.'

My heart sang. *Granny*!

Throughout lunch, I couldn't stop smiling. Finally, I might become close to Ysabelle again.

For weeks, I carried around this conversation. Repeating the word "Granny". Revelling in the implication of a more significant role in Ysabelle's life. Hoping this would further fill the void in my heart. And at the point when I thought it might, Pasha wrote to me: *I am visiting Italy and would love to see you. I hope this will be okay.*

Heart racing, body trembling, I studied the words now dancing before my eyes. Pasha wanted to see me again. He hoped this would be okay.... Much as I yearned to see him, though, was it a good idea? Despite striving to accept the limitations of our relationship, I knew deep down I would always love him as so much more than a friend. Being face to face with again would rip open the wound I needed to heal.

Furthermore, his visit would coincide with a photography commission in Verona.

For twenty-four hours, I thought of little else. Then I texted him a date and my address.

The intervening days were preoccupied and anxious. And in Verona again, part of me actually wished his visit over. Regardless of outcome. As I traipsed around the city, trying to focus on my assignment, I had a sense of waiting. Of killing time. At the end of each evening, my predominant emotion being relief that another day had passed. I was constantly indecisive: what to wear; what food to buy, what buildings to photograph next.

I'd repeatedly rehearsed Pasha's visit in my mind. Its possible conclusions. As much as I could, resigning myself to the worst. Or so I believed. But when his car pulled into the driveway of my rented house in Verona, my heart thudded. Apart from wearing my favourite amber drop earrings, I'd made no effort with my appearance (how great it would have been to justify a glitzy outfit). And as I went to greet him, I knew I'd done the right thing in dressing casually. In his black cassock, he could have been visiting a parishioner.

'Rachel,' he said, embracing me.

Except for some greying round his temples, he'd barely changed. His skin smelt of the same rose cream. His arms held me gently.

'It's lovely to see you,' I replied, tone subdued. In reality, I'd barely prepared myself for the inevitable bad news – inevitable because he wore his work clothes; he had no luggage.

He was staring at me. 'And I have got the right day?'

'Yes. But you haven't brought a suitcase. And this means.... You must be hungry. Let's eat.'

Below me, the Adige river was grey in the fading light.

I pointed Pasha to the table in the garden and went inside to collect the food. Unsure of when he'd arrive, I'd kept it simple. He ate with relish, while I rambled on about various events. Fearing if I stopped, emotion would take over.

I didn't ask about his work in Srinagar. His life was with the Church. Always with the Church.

'I've been in the UK,' he told me. 'Visiting my father, amongst other things.'

He talked about his father for a while, mentioned other relatives he'd caught up with while in Somerset.

When dusk came, I considered lighting the candles. No, inappropriately romantic. And yet candles had felt so right on the houseboat on Dal Lake.

We should go inside, have coffee and soon he'd leave.

'What is it?' I asked abruptly when Pasha took my hand. I needed him to leave now. It was too painful. Surely he must realise this?

'Come on,' he said, pulling me to my feet.

He led me to his car and opened the boot. 'I'll need help with my luggage.'

'You're staying, then?' I asked, beset by conflicting feelings. I'd wanted, needed, him to leave. Yet now I craved more time with him, regardless of how bad I'd feel when he finally did go.

'For sure. For a few days.... If that's okay.'

My voice sounded brittle. 'And after that? Positano or Srinagar?'

'And then I'm back to the UK – England.'

'To visit your father again?'

'If there's time.'

I was on automatic pilot. At the same time, weary. So *dread*fully weary. I didn't want to hear about his plans. All I wanted was his love. Now was the time to sever ties with him. Somehow, I'd rebuild my life.

As he took my hands, I forced myself not to pull away.

'Listen to me, Rachel. The reason I have been in England and am going back again soon, is to convert to Anglicanism. And in case you're wondering, I've been considering this for months – it isn't a whim. You see, this way, I can continue to serve God but have other things. Other loves. You. If you'll have me...'

He pulled me closer to him. 'What do you think?'

Printed in Great Britain
by Amazon

32464914R00219